LaShonda Bowman

The Complete Langston Family Saga

He Restores My Soul

Then Sings My Soul

My Soul Is Satisfied

PARKER FINE

For Jacqueline Collier & the beautiful ladies
of the Blessed Sistas Book Club

In the words of Ms. Patti LaBelle:
"You are my friends…"

Introduction

I'll keep this short and sweet.

When I wrote and published the first novella in The Langston Family Saga, I never expected more than a few people to find and read it. I certainly never expected the trilogy to be picked up by book clubs.

Thank God it was!

Because of the book club interest, I've put together this omnibus in digital and paperback form, complete with discussion questions. I hope it makes it more convenient for all of you who have contacted me about wanting to share the books with your friends and family.

Before I go, I'd like to send a very special "thank you" to the *Blessed Sistas Book Club* in Pittsburgh, PA. They invited me to my first book club meeting and it was one I'll NEVER forget!

He
Restores
MY
Soul

The Langston Family Saga: Book 1

Chapter 1

ould God strike me down for lying in church?

That was the first thought that came to Pam Langston when the Master of Ceremonies at her mother's homegoing service asked that someone from the family say a few words.

It was an overcast, midwinter morning and the sanctuary of New Life Tabernacle Church was filled to capacity. R&B legends and gospel superstars packed the pews. City officials and dignitaries from at least five different denominations crowded the platform.

Most of the singers and musicians in the building had been trained by Dr. Mahalia Marie Langston. Some during private lessons, others through her work with various choirs around the country. In one way or another, everyone in the building felt they'd been her son, daughter, brother or sister.

But the "family" the MC was referring to was Pam Langston and her two sisters, Kristina and Tamia.

"And would it be too much to trouble Ms. Langston for a song?" He looked directly at Kristina, flashing a toothy grin.

Pam felt her sister stiffen. It wasn't an unusual request. It seemed Kristina couldn't step outside her front door without someone asking her to sing. That wasn't an issue. Singing at their mother's funeral, however, was.

Pam grabbed her sister's hand and squeezed it. Kristina understood what it meant and immediately relaxed.

Pam didn't want to speak at her mother's funeral any more than Kristina wanted to sing. But she was willing to take the bullet if it meant sparing her sisters any more trauma than they were already experiencing just by being there. She stood and approached the podium as the sanctuary broke out into applause.

By the time she got onto the stage and took the microphone, she was shaking. From where she stood, she could see the full length of her mother's polished mahogany casket, covered with yellow roses. She reached out and grabbed the top of the pulpit for support, while she closed her eyes and tried to compose herself. Various members of the congregation showed their support by shouting, "It's all right, baby," "Take your time" and "Help her, Jesus."

Pam knew people thought she was devastated and grieving along with the rest of the mourners. She knew that that's how she was *supposed* to feel.

She'd heard from friends that'd lost their mothers over the years what a tragedy it was. The effect it had on one's life to lose the person that loved you more than anyone else ever could. But that hadn't been her experience.

Pam opened her eyes and looked at her sisters. They sat clinging to each other, stiff and stoic. Like her, they were trying to hide their true feelings. Feelings no person seated in the sanctuary could ever understand.

They were all trying to hide the fact that when they looked at their mother's casket and were overcome with tears, it was not from sadness or loss, but an overwhelming sense of relief.

"You've heard about Joe Jackson, right? Well, this one right here?" Pam motioned toward the casket. "This was *Josephine* Jackson."

The room roared with laughter.

So far, so good. Maybe I won't have to lie after all.

"For most of you, that needs no further explanation because you either came up under her in one of the choirs she directed and recorded with or you took vocal or piano lessons in our childhood home."

At the word "home," she could see Kristina flinch. The house they grew up in was many things, but a *home* wasn't one of them.

"For those of you that don't know, let me break it down for you. My mama must've learned how to use a ruler from a pair of nuns, because she sure didn't rely on it for measuring things. If you hit the wrong key, she'd rap your knuckles. And that was on the piano. God help you if you were hitting the wrong note while singing! I guarantee you were leaving that house with bigger lips than you came in with!"

Again, the crowd exploded with laughter and scattered applause. All over the building people nodded in fond memory. The only ones not laughing were Kristina and Tamia. Then again, Pam hardly expected them to.

Once the laughter died down, Pam continued. "I can say, without a shred of doubt, our mother was the most influential person in our lives. The impact she made will last for years to come."

Amens and more applause came in agreement.

"I would like to thank Pastor Thomas and all the members here at my mother's home church for all you've done for us over these past few days. And all of you." She extended her arm toward the sanctuary. "I thank you on behalf of my sisters for being here and supporting us, as well. So many of you have shown your love and respect for our mother through flowers and cards and kind words." She put her hand over her heart. "Please know that we appreciate it from the bottom of our hearts."

The audience stood and applauded as Pam turned to locate the MC. He rushed to her side to take the microphone. As he helped her down the steps from the podium, he whispered in her ear.

"God really blessed you girls when He gave you your mother. Hopefully, you'll carry on her legacy and find your way back into the fold. The church doors are always open. Don't waste all the godly training your mother spent her life instilling in you."

He flashed his toothy grin for the second time that day, so Pam decided to be polite and smile back.

It was all she could do not to punch him square in the face.

Chapter 2

When the Langston sisters entered the hotel ballroom being used for the repast, the space became hushed. That's what usually happened when Kristina Langston entered a room. She had the looks of a model and the voice of an angel—a combination that made for indescribable star presence.

The minister from New Tabernacle that had accompanied the sisters from the burial escorted them to the table reserved for family. Over the next two hours, the three of them watched the minutes tick by as mourner after mourner came to express their sympathies.

Although it was already well into the afternoon and they were indoors, Kristina kept her sunglasses on, just as she had since they'd left the hotel that morning. Pam could only imagine the looks her sister was giving from behind her shades. But if the comments she made now and then under her breath were any indication, they were all better off with half Kristina's face hidden.

After what seemed an eternity, the line in front of their table dwindled enough for them to see an end in sight. They'd already endured a mountain of memories and tears and even had one woman pass out from grief right in front of them.

Pam tried to remind herself that the mourners were well-meaning, but still, it was hard to sit through. The woman she and her sisters knew was nothing like the woman they'd spent the last few hours hearing stories about. And it wasn't as if they could tell anyone the truth, because no one would even believe them.

A squat man wearing an orange and yellow plaid suit straight out the seventies approached the table and jutted his hand out at Kristina. It was something that had happened repeatedly that afternoon. Although all three were Mahalia's daughters, Kristina, being the most famous, was the one people gave their attention to. Not that either of the other two minded. They were accustomed to it. Tamia, as a background singer for Kristina, was used to being seen in her shadow. And Pam, as her manager, was used to not being seen it all.

"Ms. Langston, I'm Malcom H. Block, head of the music department at New Tabernacle. Let me just say how heartbroken I am over your loss. Your mother was a beautiful, beautiful soul. The international gospel community has lost one of its pioneers with her homegoing." He paused and cleared his throat, then smoothed his jacket lapels with the palms of his hands. "I was wondering…has anyone told you about the citywide musical we're having in honor of your mother? Oh, there's never been anything like it! Multiple denominations and a mass choir made up of nine churches. It's really going to be a sight to behold. The choir's singing all of your mother's songs, including the duet you recorded with her. Perhaps the Spirit will move you to even join in." He started laughing, positively tickled by the possibility. "What a treat that would be! I can just imagine her smiling down from heaven!"

He'd kept his hand extended, although Kristina didn't take it. Out of the corner of her eye, Pam could see Tamia trying to hide her smile. Anyone that knew anything about Kristina Langston, knew that she didn't shake hands with strangers. She was friendly and always genuinely happy to meet with fans, but under no circumstances did she ever encourage the spread of germs.

Instead, Kristina only smiled at him.

That's it. He's going down, Pam thought.

That smile was Kristina's way of "killing them softly". She'd used it to slay more than one man in her lifetime. And by the looks of Mr. Plaid, she'd struck again.

"Unfortunately, our plane heads out tonight. But we're truly touched by the church community honoring our mother. We wish we could attend. But know that we'll be there in spirit."

The man was so mesmerized by her dazzling smile, velvet smooth voice and the fact that she was giving him her undivided attention, Pam wasn't even sure he comprehended a word she'd said. Either way, he walked away nothing but grins.

After he left, Kristina leaned over and whispered to her sisters, "Haven't we served enough time today? I don't know how much more of this talk about Saint Mahalia I can take."

"The line is almost done. Just a few minutes more, then we'll leave. I promise." Pam whispered back.

A young lady came up and offered her sympathies in a rush and then launched into a monologue about what a big fan of Kristina's she was and asked her what in the world could her fans in the Dallas-Fort Worth area could do to get her to come there on her next tour.

Kristina looked over at Pam and now it was Pam's turn to hide her smile. It was like a game between them. Kristina had been asked the question at least a hundred times and each time she gave a different answer. Pam had started looking forward to how creative her sister would get with each one.

Kristina had repeatedly refused to make a stop in the Metroplex since she'd become a big enough name to do so. Never mind that she had a huge fan base there. Never mind that ticket sales would be astronomical. When Kristina Langston made up her mind, wasn't nobody changing it. And she'd decided the day she left Dallas and Mahalia's house, she wasn't coming back.

Pam watched Kristina put on her most sad and apologetic face. The same one she used in the music videos featuring her tragic love songs or the movies where the leading male had done her character wrong. She launched into an incredibly complex explanation about agreements and riders and stadiums and promoters. Things that the young woman had no clue about, but that sounded very important and complicated. Kristina talked about how horrible she felt that her Metroplex fans had to go all the way to Houston or Austin to hear her and that on the next tour, she'd be sure to fight for them adding a date to her schedule.

By the time she finished, the girl was practically in tears over the compassion of her favorite superstar and Pam had nearly bought the whole explanation herself.

Finally, the last two people in line approached the table. Yet another duo of young men hopelessly enamored with Kristina. However, both politely made eye contact with each of the sisters and not just Kristina. They offered their sympathies and explained their family's connection to Mahalia.

"We wanted to tell you how much your mother meant to us. We were going through a rough patch, financially, when she stepped in to help us. I don't know where we would be if it hadn't been for her. In fact, she became a part of our family. Like a grandmother—"

Kristina stood so abruptly, she bumped the table and nearly knocked over the glasses of iced tea. Tamia shot a glance at Pam. They knew what her reaction meant. Kristina had had enough. Yet another comment about what a saintly person their mother had been, put her over the edge. Kristina bent over and snatched up her purse.

"I'm sorry, but if you'll excuse me."

She took off toward the ballroom doors and without saying a word, Tamia jumped up and rushed to catch her.

They were out of the ballroom and halfway down the corridor of the large hotel when Kristina looked back over her shoulder. "I can go to the bathroom by myself, T."

Tamia, the youngest and the shortest of the three, practically had to run to keep up with her sister's long strides. "I know. I'm just coming in case you need some help."

Kristina stopped and twirled around to face her. "What? You gonna come inside the stall and roll up the tissue paper for me?"

Tamia shifted her weight from one leg to the other and looked around to make sure no one is in earshot. "Krissi—"

Kristina put her hand up to stop her. "I'm not gonna do anything. Sometimes a bathroom break is just that. A bathroom break." She kissed her sister on the cheek. "But thanks for looking out for me, okay? Now go sit your behind down. Someone needs to be in there to hear about what a *wonderful* mother we had."

At first, Tamia didn't move. But then, Kristina put one hand on her hip and cocked her head to the side, pulling rank. Reluctantly, Tamia gave in and turned around. Kristina watched and waited to make sure her sister actually went back into the ballroom before she continued down the corridor in search of the ladies restroom.

When she found it, she went inside and looked under the stall doors to make sure it was empty. Satisfied she was alone, she entered the handicap stall at the farthest end of the room.

A quick glance around made her realize she'd have to settle for the top of the tissue holder as her surface. She fished inside her bra for the small baggie filled with the white powder. Her sisters rifled through her handbag on a regular basis, so she'd taken to hiding her stash in more creative places.

Credit card and rolled paper in hand, she got to work.

And not a moment too soon. With all the people that had been buzzing around since earlier that morning, this was only her second hit of the day. And she'd been feeling the effect of going without for so long.

Wiping the white residue off her nose, she took out her compact to check and make sure she'd left behind no evidence. Already, she could feel the drug doing its work, giving her the lift she needed. She tossed the mirror back into her purse and started to rid the stall of any evidence, just in case one of her sisters decided to be cute and come up behind her to check things out.

But then, something went wrong.

At first, Kristina thought it was because the batch wasn't as cut as her previous buy. She felt strange, but wasn't worried or startled. But soon, she realized that the reaction she was having was not due to the coke's purity.

She became lightheaded and reached out to the wall for something to steady herself. Finding nothing, she lost her balance and stumbled backwards, the cold, marble surface breaking her fall. She clawed at her chest as she fought to take a deep breath. She didn't know whether what she was feeling was real or the result of panic, but it was as if her heart were seizing. She blinked and shook her head, trying to normalize her vision and get rid of the spots floating in front of her and the flashes of light that seemed to come from the sides of her eyes.

As Kristina slid to the floor, she realized that this was it—the moment her sisters had spent the last few years in constant fear of. And immediately, Kristina was sorry. Sorry they would have to deal with it, but not sorry it was happening.

Her thoughts were interrupted when she heard the clacking of high-heeled shoes across the marble floor of the bathroom. From where she lay on the floor of the stall, she could see a pair of red shoes and a pair of black. The two women were talking at high volume as they came in the restroom, but it didn't matter. Even if Kristina had wanted to call out for help, she couldn't move, much less speak. But that didn't prevent her from hearing every word of their conversation.

"I mean, I guess she still looks good…for a *crackhead*."

A high-pitch laugh sounded. "Girl, no!"

"Yes! Why do you think she always wearing them sunglasses?"

Kristina watched the pair of red shoes stop in front of the floor to ceiling mirror that ran the length of the wall.

"Naw, girl. You know how celebrities are, they wear sunglasses all the time because they think it hides them. Besides, I grew up with them at Mt. Zion Baptist. Kristina's always been shy."

"You mean stuck up."

Both women giggled. "I'm guessing you're not a fan?"

"Child, please. Okay, so I didn't know them back in the day, but they all seem a hot mess to me. You wouldn't believe some of the stuff I've read about them online. Especially Kristina."

"Some of that is just made up, Kiki. Besides, Ms. Mahalia didn't play. They may have gone secular, but they were raised right. They know better."

"Maybe the other two, but you can't defend Superstar Langston. Not to me. Didn't you see her at the Grammys? She was so hyped up, I thought she was gonna fall right off the stage. Beyoncé was trying to act like she didn't notice when Kristina presented her with that award. I was like, no Bey, even you not that good an actress!"

They laughed again.

"Girl, you are so bad..."

Kristina could hear one of the women toss whatever she'd used to touch up her face back in her makeup bag.

"I can't stand people like that. She got everything. Voice, looks, money, a mother who adored her, and it's still not enough! Just greedy."

"Well, I guess—"

For the first time since the women entered the restroom, both suddenly became silent. Then one whispered, "Do you see that? It looks like— Is that someone's *hand*?"

Kristina watched as the shoes inched in her direction.

"Oh my gosh... Somebody's in there on the floor!"

Through Kristina's blurred vision she could make out one of the women crouching and looking under the door. The look on her face was one of horror.

"Go get help!"

Kristina could hear the panic in the woman's voice. She wished she could tell her not to worry. She wished she could tell her not to bother for help. She wished she could explain that everything was finally as it should be.

Kristina had imagined her death a hundred times. She'd

wondered, would she be alone or performing before thousands? At home or backstage at an event? Where it would happen, she never knew, but it was something she'd been waiting for a long time.

She was grateful for one thing; her sisters wouldn't witness it. She never wanted them to have to live with the memory of frantically trying to save her in her last moments. She'd already put them through enough.

No, she'd rather be gone before they found her, beyond any help, so they wouldn't be stuck replaying the incident over and over in their minds, wondering what more they could've done.

She didn't want anyone else to save her, either. She was tired. Had been for over half her life. She was more than ready to leave this life behind.

Not that she had any delusions she'd open her eyes in heaven. Sure, she'd come to Jesus as a girl. Kristina was born and raised in church and loved Him with all her heart, no matter what others thought.

But she'd failed Him too many times to count. She was such a mess, she could hardly even bring herself to pray anymore. She used to. Every night, she prayed the same prayer for years. Eventually, she came to realize He wasn't listening. Not to her, anyway.

At least, that's what she'd thought. But lying there on the cold floor, hearing the shouts of strangers, she felt herself slipping away and understood that He *had* heard her after all.

Knowing she had only moments left before being swallowed up by eternal darkness, she said the last prayer she expected to ever pray again:

Thank you.

Chapter 3

Robin Jones stood at the window, looking out over the hospital parking lot and silently asked God to give her direction. It was late, the night before last, when she got a call from her old friend and pastor, Avery Thomas. He told her there was a family drowning in the midst of tragedy and that he could use her help. She never thought in a million years that that family would be the family of Kristina Langston.

Robin hadn't slept since she'd gotten the call. Instead, she'd stayed up with the sisters, Pam and Tamia, as they spent the hours in a continual cycle of praying, crying, and waiting.

To the glory of God, their prayers were answered. Kristina was finally moved from intensive care into her own room. Now, it was just a matter of waiting for her to wake.

But Robin knew the trouble was far from over. Pam had confided in her that it wasn't Kristina's first brush with death.

Both of her sisters had spent the last year on pins and needles, waiting for the call. *That* call.

Less than two years ago, Kristina was diagnosed with an underlying heart condition. She was also warned more than once by medical professionals that her continued drug use would lead to the grave a lot sooner for her than it would for a normal, healthy individual. But even that hadn't been enough to slow her. In fact, according to her sisters, it seemed to only make her more bent on destruction. As if she *wanted* to die.

Robin was a certified therapist and had more recently begun life coaching. She'd worked with all kinds—from addicts to sex workers, homemakers to celebrities. But the one thing they all had in common was that they wanted help. Kristina, however, did not.

According to Pam, her sister had refused all attempts to get her into rehab. At one point, she threatened to have Pam replaced as her manager and Tamia replaced as her background singer. And although their sister's life was more important to them than their jobs, they eventually gave in to her just because they knew they were the only two in her inner circle close enough to keep an eye on her.

"She can be a handful." Pam told Robin. "I won't lie to you. But that's the drugs. When she's not using, my sister is one of the funniest, kindest, most gentle people you'll ever meet. I'm afraid that if we don't get through to her now, she'll be six feet under this time next year."

After hours of talking about what could be done, they devised a plan. If Kristina wasn't willing to go to rehab or therapy, they would just bring the therapy to her.

"Krissi?"

Tamia's voice and sudden movement toward her sister's bed pulled Robin's attention from her thoughts. She turned to find Kristina stirring and Tamia leaned over on her chest, hugging her.

"You said you weren't going to do anything! I should've known better. I should have gone with you."

"For the hundredth time, Tamia, this wasn't your fault."

Robin couldn't help but notice the edge in Pam's voice. She knew that she loved Kristina, but right then, she looked as if she wanted to scratch her eyes out.

Kristina opened her mouth to speak, then closed it again, swallowing. "I'm okay, Tamia." Her voice was hoarse and raspy. "It's no big deal."

"No big deal?" If Pam looked angry before, she looked ready to draw blood now. "You almost died! Do you have any idea what you looked like when they rolled you out of that bathroom? Like a corpse!"

Robin put her hand on Pam's shoulder. Pam stopped talking and turned toward the window. They had talked about this the night before. If they had any hope of getting Kristina to agree to this therapy retreat, they'd have to tread carefully.

Kristina finally noticed Robin in the room and squinted her eyes to get a better look at her. Robin approached the bed, put out her hand and introduced herself. Kristina wouldn't take her hand, but she nodded slowly.

"Okay…I thought you looked familiar. I've seen you on TV, right?"

Before Robin could answer, the curious expression on Kristina's face gave over to one of exasperation. "Wait…" She rolled her eyes and stared at the ceiling. "You've got to be kidding me."

Pam turned around.

"Is that what this is? An intervention? I already told you—"

"Yeah, we know. You don't do rehab. You don't do shrinks.

Fine. But you're doing this. It's already been arranged. Three days. All of us in a hotel suite. Together. No interruptions. We need to work through this, Kristina." Pam came to her sister's bed and put her hand on her leg. "And I'm not just talking about the drugs," she added, quietly.

Kristina shook her head and continued staring at the ceiling. She was pretty sure before it was all over, she was gonna wish she'd just gone to rehab.

It took an elaborate escape route through the back ways of the hospital, a look-alike stand-in for Kristina, and a decoy black SUV to get them out of the hospital without alerting the paparazzi camped out in the parking lot to their departure or eventual destination.

Tamia left ahead of them to check in to the hotel so Kristina could bypass the lobby and go straight to the suite from the back entrance.

Once they were there and inside the hotel elevator, Robin took a few moments to study the superstar.

She was wearing a calf length faux fur coat over jeans and a ribbed white tank top. Her short and usually styled haircut was in disarray, pointing in every direction but down, subdued only by the stretchy headband she wore. She had no makeup on, but still somehow radiated what Robin could only describe as star quality.

And she acted like one, too. Even at the hospital, she had a way of getting whatever she wanted, when she wanted it. Both doctors and nurses deferred to her and tended to act like they were in the presence of royalty. She was used to commanding a room and Robin was slowly beginning to realize how much work she had cut out for her.

The high-pitched ringing of a cell phone broke the cold silence that had begun at the hospital when Kristina first learned of their plan and that had continued all the way to the present moment.

Once Pam realized it was her phone making the noise, she dug into her purse and pulled it out. The anxiety that had held her hostage over the last several hours faded the moment she saw the name on caller ID.

It was her husband, Reiland.

"Hey baby, we're just arriving at the hotel."

"How's Kristina doing?"

Pam glanced over at her sister, leaned up against the side of the elevator wall, staring over her sunglasses at the ascending floor numbers and looking more like a thug than any best-selling popstar should.

"You know, the usual."

He chuckled. "Well, I'll tell you one thing. Any other day I might be jealous you're getting a few days off and spending them in a luxury suite. But under the circumstances, I don't envy you at all."

She didn't want to, but even she had to laugh at that. He continued. "But listen, your mom's lawyer wants to talk to one of you girls. Apparently, there's an issue with the will."

That was news to Pam. She didn't even know her mother had a will. She was glad, though. They all sent her money every month and Pam was happy to see Mahalia had taken her advice about putting her affairs in order. But she couldn't imagine what the issue could be. If she knew her mother at all, she was sure whatever she had was left to New Life Tabernacle.

"What's the problem?"

"He didn't say. I told him the three of you would be unreachable for the next few days, but whatever it is, it's something that's got him all in a tizzy."

Pam smiled. Her man worked out like a bodybuilder and had the body to prove it. Why he talked like a little old lady, she did not know.

"Is it something you can handle?"

"I don't know. But don't worry about it. You ladies do whatever you gotta do and I'll hold it down over here until you can take care of it."

Of course, he would. He always did. With all the hell that had gone on in her life, the best thing that ever happened to her was Reiland. To all of them, really. He was the rock in their family. Having been abandoned by their father when they were young, Reiland became not only a brother-in-law to her sisters, but at times, a father, as well. She thanked God for him daily.

"I appreciate it, baby. I love you. I'll talk to you soon."

"I love you too. I'll be praying for you."

෴

Once they were in the hotel room, Kristina gave the suite a quick once over and dropped down on the sofa, wrapping her fur coat around her and putting her feet up on the table.

"How many days is this again? 'Cause you know I got things to do to get ready for this tour."

Pam walked past her and opened the door to one of the bedrooms, motioning toward Robin to let her know that it was hers. "Yes, diva. Being that I'm the one who books these things, I know. The more cooperative you are, the quicker this will be."

One of the bedroom doors opened and Tamia came out, holding something in her hand. She took a glance at Robin and turned whatever it was up into her palm. Robin continued to her bedroom, saying nothing, but made a mental note of it.

"Where's my bags?" Tamia asked Pam.

Pam made her way to the sliding doors and pushed back the drapes to let more light into the room. "The bellboy should be up any minute now. Was there something you needed?"

Tamia shoved whatever she was holding into her jeans pocket and shrugged. "Nothing important. I can wait."

❧

Once the bags had arrived and everyone had settled into their rooms, they came together in the main living area.

"So," Robin said. "What is it that you three want to accomplish over the next few days?"

Nobody answered. Instead, Tamia and Kristina looked at Pam.

"This was your idea," Kristina said.

"I think there are some things we might need to…work through. Things having to do with our past." She hesitated before continuing. "With our mother."

Kristina covered her face with her hands and groaned. "Haven't we talked about her enough the past few days? I mean, if that's what this is going to be about, I can just leave now, because I'm not interested." She stood and started toward her bedroom.

"Kristina."

Kristina turned around to face her sister. "What?"

Pam scooted forward to the edge of her seat. "This isn't gonna be like the funeral. This is gonna be about who *mama* really was. About the things she did."

"I don't live in the past."

Pam tilted her head forward as if to say, *Are you kidding me?* But then she caught the expression on Robin's face and took another approach.

"Okay, fine. But this isn't just about you. What about me? What about Tamia? We need to get over this stuff. And you're our sister. You were there. You're the only person in the whole world that can even understand what it was like. Can't you just do this for us?"

Kristina tapped her toe, her hands shoved into the pockets of the fur coat hanging off one shoulder. She looked over at Tamia. "You want me to stay?"

Tamia nodded. "I don't think we could do this without you."

Kristina sighed as loudly as she could and trudged back to the couch before dropping down in the same spot she had previously occupied. "I'll do it. But this is just…" Her voice trailed off and she groaned again.

"What?" Robin asked.

Kristina halfheartedly punched at the pillow beside her. "I think all this talking about your feelings and stuff is a waste of time. What's done is done. You can't go back and change it."

"No," Robin said. "But we can change how it affects us." Robin uncrossed her legs and leaned forward, her elbows on her lap. "For instance, issues with our parents sometimes spill over into our parenting. How have your experiences with your mother affected your relationships with your own children?"

Robin immediately sensed the change that occurred in the room as a result of her question. Though all three women remained quiet, their silence spoke volumes.

"Anybody?"

The sisters exchanged glances and avoided Robin's gaze. Finally, Pam answered.

"None of us have children."

Although the answer seemed straightforward, there was more to the story. That much, Robin could tell. But because she didn't know exactly what, she proceeded with caution. "Any particular reason why?"

Silence.

Without warning, Kristina jumped up and went to her bedroom. After a few moments, she emerged, tapping the bottom of a cigarette pack, lighter in hand. She headed straight for the balcony doors.

"Kristina. We're in the middle of something." Pam said.

Kristina didn't turn around. She opened the glass sliding door and before stepping out onto the balcony, said "Y'all go ahead."

With that, she closed the sliding door and no sooner than it had begun, session one was over.

Chapter 4

Robin put on a sweater and joined Kristina on the balcony. It had been a rather mild winter, but there was still a bite to the air. Robin wrapped her sweater tight around her body and leaned against the railing.

"I thought cigarettes were a no-no for singers."

Kristina cast her a sidelong glance and blew out a cloud of smoke. "And I thought you were a shrink, not a vocal coach."

Robin noticed a slight tremor in the hand holding the cigarette and wondered how much it had to do with the cold and how much it could be attributed to the beginning of withdrawal.

Seeing Kristina like this made her heart ache.

They were close to the same age, Robin being just a bit older when Kristina hit it big around the age of twenty. She was everywhere. Commercials, award shows, talk shows. You couldn't walk into a gas station or grocery store without hearing Kristina Langston's voice coming from the speakers.

But even then, being that young, it was clear to Robin that Kristina's heart was a broken one. She watched the news footage of the singer being spirited into the back doors of concert halls or flanked by bodyguards shielding her from rabid fans. Everyone screamed her name, reached for her, wanted a piece of her, but few seemed to *really* look at her.

If they had, they would've seen what Robin did. The sadness, the weariness in her eyes. Something like disappointment.

Robin saw more of it in the years since, as a therapist working with other celebrities. They were talented, sometimes fragile people, looking for love and acceptance and the opportunity to show their worth. What many of them didn't understand was that being loved and being famous were two different things. By the time the most desperate of them found out, it was too late.

"I remember... I had to be, what?" Robin said, looking toward the sky. "Twenty-six? That's how old I was when the *Sweet Kisses* music video first hit. I went out the next day and got the same haircut."

Kristina stopped mid-puff and turned to look at Robin, then she laughed so hard, she made herself cough.

"Did you really?"

Robin nodded, a pained expression on her face. "Worst mistake of my life. Fashion-wise, anyway."

"Lawd, yes!" Kristina shook her head, still laughing. "I shouldn't have walked around looking like that, much less anyone else."

She put her hand on Robin's and poked her lip out. "I'm so sorry I led you and countless others astray."

Robin chuckled. "It's okay. It grew back." She let another moment pass, then turned to face Kristina.

"I also remember this one interview. The guy asking the

questions seemed to have it out for you. He was so catty. He said something like, 'Why do you think none of your relationships ever last more than a minute?' I couldn't believe he said it. Turned out he was just getting started."

Kristina's face became hard and she looked away and out at the bustling cityscape below. Flicking the ash from her cigarette over the balcony, she nodded.

"MTV. Yeah, I remember." She took another drag off her cigarette. "His name was Rick or Richard. Something like that." She left the railing and sat in one of the chairs in the outdoor patio set positioned on the balcony.

"For just a second," Robin continued. "I saw this flash of hurt move over your face. It was so quick, I thought I'd imagined it because he just kept right on with the interview, as if nothing had happened. And I remember thinking, he doesn't even think of her as a person. He can't even see that she has feelings. That was the moment I started looking at celebrity differently. And now," she said, releasing a deep sigh. "With Facebook and Twitter and Instagram and YouTube… I don't know how any of you even handle it."

She sat on the chair next to Kristina. She could see the light of the setting sun reflecting off the sunglasses that hid the singer's eyes.

"You're just a commodity." Kristina spoke quietly, her voice barely above a whisper. "And don't ever start to lose your value, because they have ten more lined up to replace you."

She put out her cigarette in the tray on the table and shook her head. "Don't get fat, don't get sick, don't be sad. No one has time for that. Just get on stage and sing like a happy little bird. And that's the important part. You have to be *happy*. Because people with problems aren't sexy or cool or fun."

The words settled into the silence between them. Robin, hoping Kristina would continue, waited.

"You know, I actually went to this therapist once." Kristina tightened the edges of her coat up around her neck. "I had nightmares that wouldn't go away. I didn't want to go to sleep, so I started taking stuff to stay awake and ended up completely exhausted. I knew something had to give. I thought he could help me. I told him everything. Well," she said, cocking one eyebrow, "almost everything. I don't know what I expected him to say or do, but I had hoped..." Kristina closed her eyes. "I'd prayed he'd be able to tell me *something*, but..."

"What happened?"

Kristina drew a deep breath. "His professional advice was basically this: You're rich, you're famous. Stop whining and get over it." She laughed, but it was void of any humor. "I thought he was right. I mean, he was a therapist. That was his job. He had to know what he was talking about, right? People go through stuff every day. A messed up childhood didn't make me special."

She tapped her index finger on the edge of the table. "Then two weeks later my publicist called me about the exclusive a tabloid had gotten with a 'family source.' It was everything I had told him." She shook her head, a grimace on her face. "Every. Single. Detail."

Again, she laughed out loud. But this time there was an edge to it. "Funny thing is, the story was so outrageous, hardly anyone believed it. It didn't even make Entertainment Tonight. I bet he had been hoping for a book deal or at least an on-camera interview."

"I'm sorry you had to go through that."

Kristina shrugged. "The point is, I've tried this before and it didn't work." She looked over her shoulder and through the glass doors at her sisters talking to one another on the couch. "But if they need this, I'll stay here for them."

She looked back at Robin and emphasized her point. "For *them*. Try any of your head shrinking on me, and I'm out."

Kristina stood and stretched her arms out, filling her lungs with the crisp, Texas winter air.

"I'm starving!" She tapped Robin shoulder and opened the sliding glass door. "Let's order room service!"

She went inside but Robin remained in her chair, shoulders slouched. She looked up to heaven. "Now what?"

Apparently, when Kristina said "order room service", what she really meant was, order everything on the menu.

Literally.

Not being able to decide what she wanted, Kristina asked for everything. It took seven hotel staff members, each with a crowded, wheeled cart, to bring up the food.

Prime rib, filet mignon, lobster tails, crab legs, pizza, macaroni and cheese, a platter of nothing but pickles—just about anything Robin could imagine, was somewhere on the long and polished wood dining table. By the time the servers left, the table was completely covered with hot dishes.

Pam came out of her room after taking a shower and, upon seeing enough food to feed an army, stopped in her tracks.

"Kristina! What did you do? There's no way we'll be able to finish all this."

Kristina eyed Pam over her sunglasses before taking them off and tossing them onto the couch, followed by her fur coat. Then she took out the lollipop hanging from her mouth and said, "Watch me."

Kristina's movements were abrupt and Robin could see tiny beads of sweat across her forehead. It was definitely withdrawal. And from what little experience she had with Kristina so far; she expected it was going to be a very interesting evening.

Pam shook her head as she made her way to the dining table and sat down next to Tamia. "I don't know how you're not the size of a house, eating the way you do."

"It's called cocaine. You should try it sometime."

At that, Robin, Pam, and Tamia froze.

Kristina rolled her eyes in an exaggerated way and yanked the lollipop from her mouth. "Ugh. It was a joke. If I'm going to sit through a dinner with you three sad sacs, I'm gonna need some music."

She skipped to the entertainment center and connected her iPod to the dock. Music from the Black Eyed Peas came blaring out the surround sound speakers and Kristina started dancing. She hopped to the mini bar, singing at the top of her lungs on her way there. She then grabbed as many bottles as she could carry and danced back to the dining table, dumping them next to her plate before going back for more.

Pam and Tamia shot glances over at Robin. Pam looked completely exasperated and Tamia offered a weak and apologetic smile.

Kristina came back to the table with her second load of mini bottles and took her seat.

"Kristina…" Pam shook her head, but didn't finish the sentence.

Kristina opened one of the bottles and downed it in a couple of swigs. "Don't start on me, Pam." She turned to Robin. "You know what we used to call her? Pam the Priest."

Kristina started laughing and got up from her chair. She

came around behind Pam and hugged her shoulders. "This is our resident church girl, isn't that right, Tamia?"

Tamia looked up from where she sat next to Pam, her eyes pleading and her voice quiet. "Kristina, please... Let's just eat." She cut a bit of the meat from her plate, put it on the fork and offered it up to her sister. "Taste this prime rib. It's perfect."

Kristina leaned back, refusing the offer and made her way back around to her own chair. "Now, wait a minute. Y'all said you wanted to talk about the past. Work out your mommy issues. I think Pam is a good place to start." Kristina dropped down in her chair and tucked one leg under her, placing the foot of the other on the seat.

Pam reached out for Tamia and Robin's hands. "I'll say grace."

While she did, Kristina kept her eyes open and stared Pam down during the entire prayer. When the others opened their eyes, Kristina used her butter knife to tap the table near Robin's plate.

"See what I mean?"

Robin shook her head. "I'm sorry. I don't."

Kristina waved her butter knife around and pointed in Pam's direction. "That. All of that. Saying grace, quoting Jesus, muttering some mess called 'The Serenity Prayer'. It's just an act. It's what she would do to get on mama's good side. And apparently it worked. Because no matter what, she always had a soft spot for Pam."

"Kristina, please..." Tamia said.

Now, with her sunglasses off, it was a lot easier to see the effects of the withdrawal in Kristina's eyes. Watery and bloodshot, she kept blinking them wildly.

Robin wondered if she should find a way to end the conversation. Yes, Kristina was finally talking about their mother, but in her current state, there was a good chance she'd say or do something she'd regret later.

Kristina picked up the linen napkin next to her plate and dabbed at her forehead before tossing it back on the table. "It's true. If we got ten lashes with the stick, she got five. If we got eight hours in the box, she got four."

Tamia and Pam became still.

Now, instead of avoiding Kristina's gaze, both stared right at her.

This sudden and complete shift of attention caught Kristina off guard. She closed her mouth and looked back at them, confused.

"The box?" Robin looked from sister to sister. "What's that?"

Chapter 5

Kristina realized what she'd let slip and stiffened.

Flushed, she reached for another mini bottle, opened it and chugged it. Then she opened one of the small bottles of whiskey, got up on her chair, leaned over the table and poured it into her sister's iced tea.

Pam nearly jumped out of her chair. "What are you doing?"

"What am I doing? You a favor." Kristina replied. "Mama's dead. You don't have to be Little Miss Perfect anymore. Have a little fun already."

Pam snatched her napkin from her lap and wiped down the table where the extra whiskey had caused the iced tea to splash out. When she was done, she balled up the napkin and threw it on the table, all the while glaring at Kristina.

"First of all, not drinking is a personal choice. Not a religious one. And how dare you have the nerve to comment on me or how I live my life. I've never said anything when either one of you had a cocktail or a glass of wine. I've never cared. I've never judged you. So why do you care so much that I don't? What is wrong with you?"

"What's wrong with *me*?" Kristina snorted. "Oh, I think everybody knows what's wrong with me! I'm the crackhead. I'm the one who can't get through the day without a pill or some powder."

She turned toward Tamia and jabbed her arm in her direction. "Our baby sister can't even—"

Kristina stopped short when she saw the humiliation on Tamia's face, her café au lait colored cheeks turning a deep burgundy. Kristina swallowed hard and sat down. When she spoke again her voice was quieter, but still filled with an undercurrent of rage. "She still deals with stuff, but not you. Nope. Not mama's little angel."

Pam sat back in her chair, looking as if she'd been punched in the gut. When she spoke, the words came out more like a sigh than anything else. "That's not true…" She picked up her knife and fork and proceeded to eat.

But Robin saw something had changed. It was if the perfect calm and confidence that Pam wore as a shield had cracked.

And Robin wasn't the only one to notice.

Kristina, seeing that her verbal hits had finally caused some damage, plowed ahead with a renewed sense of self-assurance.

"Please. It was always, '*You look tired, mama*', '*Let me make you some tea, mama*', '*Let me rub your feet, mama*.'"

Tamia put her knife and fork down. She glared at her sister. But Kristina was too focused on Pam to notice.

"Never mind that you just knocked me or one of my baby sisters six ways to Sunday. Let me make sure *you're* all right!"

Kristina was close to yelling at that point and Robin began silently praying.

Pam continued to show no reaction. Or, at least, she tried. She kept cutting into her prime rib with a knife and fork and eating it along with her mashed potatoes and gravy as if nothing was happening, but her face was a mask of pain.

"Pam?" Tamia said. She put her hand on her sister's back.

Robin touched Kristina's arm and whispered, "Maybe we should all step away for a moment. Let things calm down."

Kristina jerked her arm away. "Why are you two acting like I'm attacking her? It's the truth! Mama was mean as the devil, beat the hell out of us on a regular basis and this one," she said, jabbing her finger in Pam's direction. "This one was over there offering her foot massages and acting like she was some saint. She. Wasn't. No. Christian!" Kristina banged on the tabletop to emphasize each word. "I don't care what all those pastors and evangelists and missionaries that came to the funeral thought. She was a hypocrite and she was a drunk!"

Kristina stood and walked away from the table, then back again. Her face was contorted with anger and she paced like a caged animal.

No one moved a muscle. Robin felt like they were all sitting on a pressure sensitive bomb waiting to go off the second someone took a breath.

"She wasn't a drunk."

It was Pam that finally spoke. Kristina stopped pacing and threw her hands up.

"Oh, here we go again." She stretched her arm toward Pam, as if presenting someone. "Pamela Langston Scott, ladies and gentlemen. The champion of the late great Mahalia Marie Langston!"

Pam sat up straight and glared at Kristina. "She never took a drink. Not one day in her life."

Kristina came back to the table, put her hands on it palms down and leaned in so she was staring Pam dead in the eye. "She. Was. A. Fall. Down. Drunk." She dragged the words out, low and full of venom. "Not that I'm complaining." She smirked. "As long as she was passed out on the couch, we only got beat half the time. But let's call a spade, a spade."

Pam pushed her plate away and stared at Kristina for a few moments before speaking. "She wasn't drunk, Kristina. She was drugged."

The words hung in the air, leaving Kristina in shock and Robin confused.

Kristina shook her head and backed away from the table. "Wait— What? What are you talking about?"

Pam swallowed hard and stared down at the table. She looked over at her baby sister. Robin noticed an almost imperceptible nod from Tamia to her older sister, as if to give permission for her to answer the question.

Pam nodded and then turned to Robin.

"It was during Easter weekend. Our assistant pastor was invited to speak at another church and he wanted the choir to accompany him. It was in Lubbock." She looked at Kristina. "Remember that?"

Kristina's eyes became wide and she reached out for the back of her chair. When she found it, she slouched down into it, all the manic energy of the previous moments, gone.

Pam turned back to Robin. "I'd had a bad feeling about going. About leaving Tamia there alone. Grades came out that weekend and I knew she'd been struggling with her spelling lessons. But I went anyway." Pam paused. "I so wanted a few days away…"

She looked at Tamia, her eyes welled up with tears and

regret. "I left you alone. I never should have left you alone with her."

Tamia remained still, her jaw tight.

"Two days and one afternoon. Sixty-two hours. That's how long we were gone. When we got home, mama was sitting in her chair, reading her Bible. Just as calm. Just as peaceful. As if everything was normal. I asked her where Tamia was at. When she told me, I couldn't even wrap my mind around it."

Pam put her elbows on the table and covered her face with her hands. "And when I saw her... When I saw my baby sister—"

Pam began sobbing, her body shaking uncontrollably. Kristina turned away and leaned over on the back of her chair, her arms wrapped around herself as if to protect her from the onslaught of emotion she was holding back.

Tamia buried her face in Pam's shoulder. "Don't cry, Pam. Please, don't cry."

Pam nodded and took a deep breath. When she looked at Robin again, there was a fire in her eyes and a hardness about her face.

"I wasn't going to stand by anymore and let mama do whatever she wanted. That's how I felt, anyway. But the truth was, she terrified me. I knew I had to come up with something she wouldn't suspect. After a few days, I had a plan."

Pam directed her attention toward Kristina. "Do you remember Crystal?"

Kristina straightened and looked over her shoulder at Pam. "Grade school Crystal? That rich girl you were friends with?"

Pam nodded. "Her mother's nightstand was practically a pharmacy. She told me about how she'd slipped her mother some of her own sleeping pills, so she could sneak out of the house and go to a party. I scraped together the money I had made from babysitting the neighbor's kids and started buying pills from her. I made tea and rubbed mama's feet because I knew it relaxed her, anyway. So, if she ended up falling asleep every time I did it, it wouldn't seem out of the ordinary. She'd assume it was the hot tea, and not what was in it, that made her drowsy."

Pam let out a deep breath. "I couldn't do it every day. I didn't want her to catch on. The entire time, I was terrified I'd get caught. So I would wait until she was especially angry. Of course, there were those times when she'd just go off. Like flipping a switch. I never saw those times coming, but I did my best to stay on her good side, to be close so I could predict her moods and prevent as many beatings as possible."

The atmosphere in the room was heavy. Each woman at the table looked exhausted, more like she'd run a marathon than simply sat down for a meal.

"So, Kristina, I won't argue that she was a hypocrite, but it wasn't because she was a drunk." Pam swallowed and clenched her jaw. "Now me, on the other hand…" She took a deep breath and sank back in her chair.

Tamia didn't look surprised, but Kristina's mouth fell open so wide, it looked like it unhinged at the jaw.

Pam shrugged. "Turns out Little Miss Perfect wasn't so perfect after all." She slid the whiskey filled iced tea back across the table toward her sister.

Kristina kept shaking her head, as if doing so would cause everything she just heard to suddenly make sense.

"If Crystal's mother's nightstand was a pharmacy, her father's office was a liquor store. Those little guys right there?" Pam pointed at the pile of miniature liquor bottles next to Kristina's plate. "They were my best friends back in the day.

By the time I was sixteen, I couldn't get through a day without them."

"How did I not know about any of this?" Kristina shook her head. "Why didn't you tell me?"

Pam tilted her head to the side and gave her sister a sad smile. "Honestly? I didn't think you could handle it. That's why I never told you about it. Or mama, either."

Kristina's shoulders dropped, hurt etched all over her face.

"Krissi, I know you love me. I know that you love both of us, but I can't depend on you. Not when it comes to the heavy stuff."

Pam got up, came around the table and sat next to Kristina.

"When mama had her stroke, you never even asked about it. And I'm going to guess you never wondered what it was like for me, either. To come back here and take care of her. To diaper and wash and feed the woman that made me live in constant terror while I was growing up. Did you?"

Pam stared at her sister, but without judgment or accusation. She waited for an answer, but Kristina didn't have one to give.

"I know you didn't. Because you knew I'd handle it. I always handle it. I clean up the messes. I fix the mistakes. I put it back together when it's fallen apart. But it's a hard job, Kristina," her voice cracked. "It's a really hard job."

The room was so quiet; there was only the sound of their breathing.

"How long have you been sober?" Robin asked.

Pam's face brightened. "Going on five years. I thank God for that husband of mine. We waited for years to go to Bora Bora. It was his dream vacation spot. But he didn't hesitate to take the vacation time and money he'd saved for a second honeymoon to check me into the best rehab center he could find."

Pam patted Kristina on the knee. "It wasn't that I was unaffected. It's just that, before him, I didn't have anyone to help me through it."

While listening to Pam, Robin kept her eyes on Tamia. She'd been quiet, but Robin imagined there was a torrent of emotion under the surface. Although the intense pressure cooker like atmosphere of the previous hour had been released, Tamia's body was just as stiff and tense as it had been when the whole thing started.

Robin didn't want to hurt her or make her uncomfortable, but she didn't want her to be the only one that held on to her secrets, either.

"Tamia?"

Tamia started, as if her mind had been somewhere other than there, in the room. But when she looked at Robin, she smiled.

"When your sisters came home that weekend from Lubbock... What did they find?"

Instantly, the light of Tamia's smile faded. She looked to Pam, this time being the one asking for permission, it seemed. Or, maybe, just help.

Pam looked at Robin and said, "It would be better if we just showed you."

Chapter 6

The next morning, the mood in the hotel suite was solemn as the four women readied themselves to visit the Langston family home.

When Robin went into the living room to wait for the others, she found Tamia sitting on the desk chair, her crossed leg bobbing up and down.

"Did you already have breakfast?"

Tamia started, unaware Robin had entered the room. "Uh, no. I'm not hungry."

They sat in silence for a few more moments. Tamia glanced at her watch several times before jumping up from her chair.

"I'm gonna go downstairs and wait for the car." Without waiting for Robin to respond, she hurried out the front door.

Robin read the display on the entertainment center clock.

The car wasn't scheduled to arrive for another forty-five minutes.

The tension from dinner the night before didn't even come close to that in the car ride over. To Robin, it felt more like a trip to the gallows, than a childhood home.

When they arrived, the Langston sisters got out of the car, but made no move to enter the house.

Tamia, body held tight, stared at the windows as if ready to run should anyone peek through the curtains from the inside.

Kristina stood apart from everyone else and lit a cigarette.

Pam watched the house, adjusting and readjusting her scarf around her neck a few times before saying, "Let's just get this over with."

Kristina took a few steps away. "Y'all go on ahead. I need to make a call real quick."

Pam shot a knowing glance at Robin and Tamia. "Go. I'll deal with Kristina."

Pam waited until they were inside before going to Kristina and snatching the phone out of her hand.

"What the—"

"I know what you're doing."

"Well… me saying I'm making a phone call, then actually dialing the number doesn't make it much of a mystery, does it?"

"Don't try that with me. You said you would support us in this. You're not the only one that went through stuff. Tamia needs us today. *Both* of us. You're not about to play like you're taking care of business just so you can wait the whole thing out."

Kristina sucked on her teeth. "I'm not having some *kumbaya* moment in that hellhole. You acting like this is all about

Tamia. Please. You're trying to get me in there so I can break down and spill all my business to the so-called life coach." Kristina shook her head. "You know how I feel about people like her."

Pam threw her hands up in the air. "Oh my gosh! Everything is not always about you! For once, just once, can you focus on someone else? Sixty-two hours, Kristina! *Sixty-two hours.* She was in there. *Alone.* At nine years old, for sixty-two hours! She needs this. She needs *us.*"

Kristina's face crumpled and she flicked her cigarette to the ground, staring at it.

"Fine." She stepped on the butt, the toe of her shoe grinding it into the concrete.

"Thank you." Pam turned toward the house, but Kristina grabbed her arm.

"But under one condition." Tears pooled along the bottom rim of her eyelids. "If I have to go into that house and relive every horror I've tried to forget since the day I left, I want something in return."

Pam ran her tongue along her upper molars, shaking her head. "What?"

"No more talk of rehab. No more going through my stuff, taking my stash. No more personal escorts to the bathroom. If I use, I use. And if I OD as a result, so be it."

Pam took a step back. Was her sister asking for what she thought she was?

Realization hit her like a freight train. For years she'd done everything she could to protect Kristina. To keep her alive and well, but it wasn't until that moment that she realized why it'd been such an uphill battle. She was trying to save the life of someone that didn't want to live.

Reluctantly, Pam nodded. What else could she do? A person intent on taking their own life always managed to do so, no matter how many people surrounded them. And when Kristina Langston made up her mind…

"I have your word?"

"You have my word."

Kristina gave a slight nod of her own and turned toward the house. Pam watched her walk away, a grief deeper than any she'd ever known, clawing at her chest.

She couldn't help but feel she'd just signed her sister's death certificate.

⌒

"And this was our bedroom."

Tamia opened the door to the room, but remained in the hallway. Robin stepped inside. There was a set of old bunk beds along one wall and a twin without a headboard along another, but not much else.

A tiny, rickety table held a lamp, but other than that, the room was bare. There was nothing to indicate three young girls had grown up there. No posters or pictures on the bland, wood paneled walls. No colorful comforters or pillows. No vibrant rugs to brighten the dull brown carpet that covered the floor.

Robin turned to walk out, but stopped short when she saw Kristina. She stood in the doorway, facing Robin, but staring right through her.

"Kristina?"

When Kristina didn't respond, Pam put her hand on her shoulder. Kristina started and blinked, her face void of all color. She slowly backed away from the open door, her hands pressed to the wall for support.

"I… I don't feel well."

"Kristina—"

Tamia interrupted Pam, her hand on Kristina's back. "You don't have to go with us, Krissi. Go to the front room and lie down on the couch. We won't be long."

Without a word, Kristina walked away. Pam reached for Tamia's hand. "You don't have to go, either. I can take Robin."

Tamia squeezed her sister's hand. "No, I need to go. Now that mama's gone, I want to go down there knowing she can't hurt me anymore."

❦

Robin almost didn't want to go, herself. With the damage she'd seen on the Langston sisters, she'd imagined all sorts of horrible things awaiting them there.

But as she followed the sisters into the basement, she saw that it, much like their bedroom, was nearly empty.

She thought maybe whatever they'd been referring to had been moved. Then she saw the look on Tamia's face.

The young woman's expression was tight and grimaced as she walked to the opposite end of the dimly lit room. She continued until she was at the far wall and in front of a black box. A footlocker.

She stood still for several moments before bending over, unlocking it and opening the lid.

"This is it. This is where she used to send us for punishment. This is the box."

❦

"After a while, you feel like you're going crazy. No sound. No light." Tamia closed her eyes. "You lie in your own waste for so long, you stop smelling it."

Robin recognized the distancing language Tamia used

as she spoke. It was a coping mechanism common among survivors of traumatic experience. Sometimes it was the only way they could talk about what happened and remain intact.

"When your time was up," Tamia walked behind the box and pushed it over and off the wood wedges along its bottom edge. "She pushed it over so you could roll out. And over here…" Tamia walked a couple of feet to two plastic bowls on the floor. She opened her mouth to continue speaking, but all that came out was a weak and childlike whimper.

It took everything Robin had in her not to break down. The woman that had done this to her children was one of the most respected women in the gospel community, both local and international. She had chipped away at her daughters' spirits bit by bit, nearly destroying them and no one even knew it was happening.

"There'd be water and—" Tamia's eyebrows knit together and she bit her upper lip. "Dog food." She looked at Robin, her eyes brimming over with humiliation. "But you'd be so hungry…"

Pam stepped forward to put her arms around Tamia, but Tamia backed away. "She'd watch you eat. And when you were done," Tamia glanced at the mop and bucket in the corner. "She'd stand with the belt in her hand, watching you clean out the box."

Tamia wrapped her arms around herself and Robin finally understood why Kristina had fought so hard not to talk about their mother.

There were things in Robin's own past she never talked about. Things that she tried to pretend never happened. But this?

She couldn't imagine how they held it together as much as they did. Robin at least had her parents to get her through the experience that nearly leveled her. Who could the Langston girls have turned to when the person who was supposed to protect them was the one causing all the pain?

"The longest we ever had to stay in was a night and a day." Pam stared at the box. "But the weekend we came back from Lubbock…" She looked at her sister. "I'm so sorry."

"I know, sissy."

Pam continued, her voice unsteady. "We had to pick her up and carry her to the bathroom to wash her. She was so dehydrated, she couldn't keep anything down. She had sores—" Pam stopped for a moment and covered her mouth. She used her hand to finish the sentence by running it along her left arm, torso and thigh.

When Pam was able, she continued. "She kept Tamia home from school while she healed so no one would ask any questions. Made us tell her teacher she was sick so we could pick up her assignments."

Pam shook her head and lowered her voice. "And this was only one example of the things she would do to us. We spent all our lives trying to recover from it." She stared at the black footlocker as she spoke. "But I'm more afraid now than I was then."

Tamia looked up from the floor and turned to her sister. Pam motioned toward the steps that led up into the house. "I'm afraid that, even though she's dead, what mama did will always stay with us. And I'm afraid we're going to bury our sister soon because of it."

Chapter 7

Robin silently prayed on the car ride from the house back to the hotel. She felt completely out of her depth. Being a therapist or a life coach didn't mean she had all the answers. She knew that from experience. But usually, she could see people's problems from a perspective they couldn't. And that new perspective usually came with a solution, as well.

But at the moment, she saw nothing but heartache and broken spirits. She didn't have months to work with the Langstons, she had days. Days to prevent the slow, but sure suicide that the remaining two sisters wouldn't recover from.

On her own, the situation seemed impossible.

But with God…

All things are possible, she reminded herself.

Once they arrived and made their way to the elevators, Tamia broke away and said she'd meet them later. The elevator chimed and the doors swung open. And as Robin and the other sisters stepped in, she finally put two and two together.

At the hospital, Tamia had left ahead of them. Earlier that morning, she'd done it again. She said she was going to wait for the car, but that wasn't it at all.

"She's claustrophobic." Robin said the words more to herself than anyone in particular.

The elevator doors opened on their floor and Kristina glanced over her shoulder at Robin as she stepped out into the hallway. "Being locked in a box will do that to you."

"She tries to manage it," Pam said once they were inside the suite. "The anxiety issues, I mean. She's been on several different meds, but eventually they stop being as effective and her doctors have to put her on something new."

Kristina took off her coat and tossed it onto the couch, barely missing Pam where she'd sat. "You ladies continue to discuss disorders and doctors. I'm going to lie down."

Pam waited until Kristina's door was closed to speak again. "She's jonesing. Bad. The first chance she gets, she's gonna…" Pam leaned her head back on the couch and covered her face with her forearm. "The very person we did all this for is the only one not making any progress."

Robin sat on the couch across from Pam. "Don't worry about it."

Pam's head jerked up. Her eyes were narrowed and she was looking at Robin like she'd just spoken in tongues.

"Don't worry about it?"

Robin put her hands up. "For now. Look, it's been an intense day. We all need a break. When Tamia gets here, let's make some popcorn, rent a funny movie and just decompress."

Pam sat up. "You know, that actually sounds pretty good.

Ever since we got the call about mama passing away, we've been in crisis mode. Maybe a good laugh is what we need."

And that's exactly what they got.

Robin, Pam and Tamia all changed into their pajamas and piled on the couch with a bowl of popcorn to watch a Kevin Hart movie. They laughed so hard, they ended up getting more popcorn on the floor than into their mouths.

But the much-needed fun and relaxation came to a screeching halt the moment they heard Kristina scream from her bedroom.

Immediately, Pam jumped up and rushed down the hall. She entered Kristina's room, but didn't turn on the light. Robin was right behind her, but before she could push the bedroom door open, Tamia grabbed her wrist and stopped her.

"It's better if Pam handles it."

"But—"

Tamia shook her head. "Kristina's not even awake. The less people in the room, the easier it'll be to calm her down."

Robin stepped back and leaned against the wall next to the door. "Not awake? How do you know?"

Tamia leaned against the wall next to her. "She never fully wakes up when she has these nightmares."

Robin nodded. Yesterday, when she and Kristina were out on the balcony, she'd mentioned having terrible nightmares in the past. Robin didn't realize it was something she still struggled with.

From outside the room, Robin could hear Pam muttering. Her voice was soft and soothing, as if calming a baby. She could also hear Kristina choking back sobs. Robin peeked through the crack of the partially opened door. The light coming from the rest of the suite illuminated the silhouette of Pam on the bed with Kristina gathered in her arms. She rocked her as one would a small child.

"He's not breathing, he's not breathing." Kristina whispered the words repeatedly as Pam continued to rock her.

"I know, honey. I know," Pam said as she wiped away the tears from Kristina's face.

"We have to do something."

"There's nothing we can do, baby. But he's in heaven with Jesus. You know what that means? He's safe. No one can ever hurt him."

The words did little to calm Kristina. In fact, they only served to make her more desperate. The sobs became wails that seemed to come from the core of her being.

Robin closed her eyes and pressed her lips together. It was a sound she'd heard before. The sound of a grief too deep to be comforted.

After a while, the wails became moans, and finally, whimpers. Kristina became still. "I need—I need my makeup bag." She struggled against Pam's arms, but Pam wouldn't let go. She continued to rock her and spoke softly, just as she had before.

"We already cleared it out, Kristina. You don't need any of that, anyway. You're just tired. What you need is sleep."

Pam started humming, then softly singing, as she continued to rock her sister back and forth. Kristina's mumblings came less and less, and pretty soon, they stopped altogether. Pam held her for a few moments longer before taking her time to slide her arms, then her folded legs, from beneath Kristina.

Pam came back out of the room and closed the door. Robin couldn't help but notice that she looked at least five years older than she had when she went in.

"That?" Pam said as she nodded toward Kristina's room. "That's what she's trying to hide from when she's using. And if we can't figure out a way to help her, she's gonna keep going until she's six feet under."

Robin went to the kitchen to put on a pot of coffee. The moment she was out of earshot, Tamia folded her arms and looked at Pam. "If she's going to help Kristina, she needs to know what happened."

Pam exhaled. "I agree. But it's not something Kristina talks about, so how do you propose we make that happen?"

Tamia raised her eyebrows. "Duh. *You* tell her."

"It's Kristina's story to tell." Pam walked away, but Tamia wasn't giving up.

"But she's not telling it. And where has that gotten her? Nearly dead on the floor of a public restroom." Tamia grabbed her sister's arm and forced her to give her attention. "I always follow your lead. I never give you a hard time and I respect you as the head of our family, but if you don't tell her, I will."

Robin returned from the kitchen, a steaming mug in hand. She stopped when she saw the looks Pam and Tamia were giving each other. "I get the feeling I just interrupted something. Do you want me to give you two a minute?"

Tamia stared at Pam. Pam rubbed her face with her hands and dropped back onto the couch. She sighed.

"No. In fact, we'd like to talk to you about Kristina."

Robin sat. "About what just happened?"

Tamia nodded and took a seat beside Robin. "But to really explain it, we have to go back to the beginning." She looked at Pam. "To when we first met Omar."

Pam sat still for a few moments, a grimace on her face. But then, she began to tell the story.

Chapter 8

O ur mother used to give music lessons—voice, organ, piano. She was hard on all her students. Not as hard as she was on us, of course. But still, she was tough. She wasn't the type to give any sort of praise or encouragement.

"She certainly never had any favorites. That is, until she started teaching Omar. I believe his last name was Williams. For some reason, she took to him in a way she never did with any of the others. Maybe it was because he was so talented." Pam smiled at the memory. "My Lord, that boy could play the organ. She loved him so much, she would invite him to stay for dinner after each lesson.

"We could hardly believe it because she never had people over. Ever. No school friends, church members or even family. But *especially* not a handsome, teenage boy.

"We were grateful though, because the nights when Omar

was there, she was on her best behavior. I mean, we actually had conversations. Real conversations about things other than head voice or vibrato or whatever other vocal technique she felt we needed to work on."

Pam looked down at the floor, a grave expression marking her face. "But you know how it is, you get two good-looking teenagers in the same room, laughing and talking, eventually sparks are gonna fly.

"Turned out Omar was a couple of grades ahead of Kristina at the same school. So they started hanging out together between classes. It was an innocent flirtation. At least, that's what me and Tamia thought. Mama watched us like a hawk so I don't even know how it happened, but Kristina ended up pregnant."

Robin straightened up. Her mind went back to their first day at the hotel, when she asked them why none of them had children. It was the question that caused Kristina to abruptly leave the room and end the session.

"If your mother was willing to lock you in a box over something like getting a low grade in school, I can't even imagine how she reacted to that news."

"Kristina could," Pam said. "That's why she hid it for so long. Even from the two of us. Didn't say a word. But we slept in the same room, changed clothes in front of each other, so when she started showing, we noticed.

"We managed to get our hands on a small girdle and would help her into it each morning and help her out of it each night. But she was getting bigger every day. We were all terrified of what would happen when we couldn't hide it anymore.

"Omar, wanting to protect Kristina, suggested they run away. He had it all planned out. But even Kristina knew a pregnant sixteen-year-old and her seventeen-year-old boyfriend weren't going to get very far without any help. And help was the one thing we didn't have. So we all just waited."

Pam laughed. "It was like sitting on death row. Constant fear of the inevitable." Her face darkened. "There were nights…" She closed her eyes and pressed her hands against her cheeks. "I'd beg God. I'd ask Him to let her miscarry. To make it so mama never found out."

The two women waited in silence as Pam tried to regain her composure. After a few moments, she wiped the tears from her eyes and continued. "But, of course, she did. I don't even know how it happened, but I can remember *what* happened as if it were yesterday. I was in the bedroom, studying for some big history test I had the next morning…" She looked over at Tamia.

"Me and Kristina were doing our homework at the kitchen table," Tamia said. "Mama was getting started on dinner. Fried chicken and mashed potatoes. She had just put the cast-iron skillet on the burner when she told Kristina to get down the oil. She was the only one tall enough to reach into that cabinet. Still, she always had to get up on her tiptoes and stretch. But that time, when she reached up, the dress pulled tight over her middle."

Tamia swallowed. "It happened so fast, but at the same time, it was like it happened in slow motion. Kristina's arm was coming down, the oil in her hand, and mama had this look on her face. Like she'd never seen Kristina before. She hissed, 'You nasty little…'

"She reached for the skillet and swung it in Kristina's direction. Kristina covered her head with her arms and turned away, but it landed hard on her forearms and neck, knocking her against the door of the refrigerator and down to the floor.

"Kristina made this sound, like a gasping noise. I guess it was from the wind being knocked out of her when she fell.

She was trying to get air, but couldn't. I kept thinking, *she's dying, my sister is dying.*

"I ran to her, but mama got there before I did. She kicked her, over and over, as hard as she could. In the neck, in the head, in the back." Tamia's voice caught in her throat. "I just knew she was gonna kill her. I couldn't let her do that. So I picked up the knife she'd taken out to cut the potatoes.

"I raised it, but she saw me out the corner of her eye and turned to look at me." Tamia shook her head and raised her shoulders. "I froze. She was beating my sister to death and I froze."

"That's about the time I came in." Pam said, still looking at Tamia. "I heard screaming and all this noise, so I ran down the hall. But when I turned the corner into the kitchen, it was completely silent. The two of them staring at each other. Mama said, 'Put it down'. The second Tamia did, mama backhanded her so hard, she knocked her to the ground. Then she grabbed Kristina by the collar and pulled her along the floor.

"After dragging her down the stairs, mama poured rock salt all across the basement's concrete flooring. She made Kristina kneel on it, arms stretched out like Jesus on the cross. She had to stay like that and beg Him to forgive her. If her arms started to drop, mama caned her across the shoulders and back with her so-called 'rod of correction', the handle she'd taken off the broom.

"After what seemed like forever, I was finally able to convince her to go upstairs. I told her I'd make her some tea and give her a foot massage. But she was too worked up to even wait for the water to boil. From the kitchen, we could all hear Kristina downstairs, moaning and making choking sounds.

"It aggravated mama so much, I thought she'd head back down for round two. But instead, she told the two of us to go get Kristina and take her to our room. She said she couldn't stand to look at any of us any longer, much less, hear us.

"We woke in the middle of the night to Kristina crying out in pain. She was delirious and kept saying she was thirsty, so Tamia sneaked out of the bedroom to get her a glass of water. She was sweating so bad, her pillowcase was soaked through. I dried her face and changed her pillowcase while Tamia tried to get her to drink. She did, then said she didn't feel good and threw up.

"We took off the covers to clean her and change the blankets, but when we pulled them back, we found the sheets and mattress drenched in blood. Kristina, too. Everything. Her nightgown, her underwear, her legs. We panicked. I mean, we were eleven and seventeen. We had no idea what to do.

"The first and only thought that came to my mind was, we needed to hide it. We needed to hide it all before mama found out.

"Every time I think about it, I have to thank God. I know He must've been watching over us. I don't doubt for a minute that Kristina could've died that night.

"As fast as possible, Tamia and I pulled off the sheets and wrapped up the blankets. I helped Kristina out of her clothes, got her a tee-shirt and clean underwear and told her to change while we finished cleaning.

"But when she leaned over to put them on, a pain hit her and she tumbled forward against the dresser. That put us in a cold panic because of all the noise it made. Both the dresser knocking against the wall and the lamp crashing to the floor, not to mention her crying out in pain. We helped her to the bottom bunk, trying to quiet her in the process.

"She kept saying she was hurting, that she needed to push. We were terrified. We kept telling her, 'No, no, Kristina. You can't have it. Not now.'" Pam shook her head. "Can you imagine? We were too young and stupid to even know that you couldn't stop a baby from coming."

"I told Tamia to sneak upstairs and call Omar to see if he could bring his dad's car. We figured we'd sneak around back and he could take her to the emergency room. But before Tamia got out the door, I called her back.

"The baby's head was out, but the face didn't look right. The skin was gray and its little eyes were open, but there was no life in them. She kept pushing and pushing until the baby was completely out and lying on the blood soaked sheets.

"We waited. For what, we weren't even sure, but we at least knew it should've made a noise or moved or something. But he didn't move. Not even his chest. Kristina started sobbing. We tried to cover her mouth to keep her quiet, but it was too late. Just moments later, we heard mama coming down the hallway, slapping the belt against the palm of her hand. She used to do that just before she used it on us.

"She barreled through the door but then stopped cold when she saw the bed. She was just as speechless as we were. The only sound in the room was Kristina's quiet cries and her mumbling the same words over and over. 'He's not breathing. He's not breathing. He's not breathing'.

"Mama gritted her teeth and left the room without saying a word. When she returned, she had a shoebox. A shoebox and a towel." Pam squeezed her eyes shut.

"She picked up the baby and wrapped it in the towel. That's when Kristina completely lost it. She grabbed mama's arm and tried to take it back. Mama smacked her, but it wasn't enough to stop Kristina. She kept pleading to keep it. Asking her not to take it away. Mama told us we needed to shut her up before she really gave us something to cry about.

"We got in the bed with Kristina. One of us on either side. I turned her head into my chest and used my hands to cover her eyes so she didn't see when mama put the small bundle in the shoebox and covered it with the lid. She walked to the door and told us that she wanted the mess cleaned up before she got back.

"And that was that. We never talked about it again after that night."

Tamia sighed. "Not even when the nightmares started."

Pam nodded. "She'd wake up screaming like it just happened. And one of us would rock her until she had calmed down. And then when she woke up, we'd all pretend it never happened. For close to twenty years now. Before concerts, after award shows. On private jets, in the back of tour buses. It got to the point she dreaded going to sleep. It wore her out."

"The only thing that stopped the dreams were the drugs," Tamia said.

"And that's what scares me." Pam's voice broke. "She can't live with this thing eating at her, not if the drugs are the only way she can have any peace"

Robin reached out and put her hands on Pam's knees. "They're not the only way. Jesus is called the Prince of Peace for a reason. And I know from personal experience, He can do what drugs can't."

Chapter 9

Once Tamia and Pam left the hotel suite to pick up takeout from across the street, Robin went outside and sat on the balcony. Although winter was her least favorite season, the chilly breeze was what she needed to clear her troubled mind.

I need Your grace, Father. I need Your direction.

The thought of the stillborn baby kept crowding out all others, no matter what she did. She bit her bottom lip and rubbed her hand over her chest, hoping to massage the ache away. It was always there, something she'd learned to live with. But there were times, times like this, that the heartache refused to be ignored.

But she couldn't give in to it. She'd learned that lesson long ago. It was like quicksand, waiting to pull her under. And once it had her, it was the fight of her life to try to get back on solid ground.

What was done, was done. There was no going back. She

could only trust God now. She could only have faith that He would, indeed, give her beauty for ashes.

Robin was so lost in her own thoughts and memories; she didn't hear Tamia open the sliding door and join her on the balcony.

"Are you okay?"

Robin wiped at her eyes and waved her hand through the air. "Oh, I'm just thinking about all that you girls have been through. Especially your sister, losing her baby…" She let her voice trail off before the emotion in her throat could rise up and betray her.

Tamia sat in the chair opposite her. "Do you have kids?"

Robin stared out across the Dallas cityscape for so long; Tamia assumed she had chosen not to answer. Then, finally, Robin shook her head no.

Tamia saw the tears begin to well up in Robin's eyes again but didn't want to embarrass her, so she looked away. She couldn't help but wonder if Robin had a story of her own. But she didn't ask. They'd had enough heartbreak for one day. So instead, she just sat with her as they watched the sun paint the sky a brilliant, fiery orange and slip beneath the horizon.

Robin went to her bedroom and shut the door behind her. She'd spent at least an hour out on the balcony trying to figure out how to help Kristina and all she managed to do was get weighed down by the regrets in her past. She knew that wasn't going to be any help to anyone, herself included.

But she also knew that what she couldn't do, God could.

There was no way she could understand what was going on in Kristina's heart and mind. There was no way she could figure out on her own what to say or do that would make a difference. Only one Person could.

She sat on her bed and took her Bible off her nightstand and opened it to 1 Corinthians 2:10.

"Father, I know that the Spirit searches all things, even the deep things of God. And if He knows that, He knows the heart of Kristina and how to speak to it. In Proverbs, it's written that You hold the heart of the king in Your hand and turn it any way You will. I'm asking You to turn her heart toward You, Father. I'm asking You to do the very thing You sent Jesus here to do. To heal the brokenhearted and set the captive free."

Robin continued to pray and before long, she was worshiping and thanking God for what she knew in her heart was already done. But then, she heard loud talking coming from the living room. At first, she figured someone had turned the television on.

She looked at her bedside clock. She thought she'd been praying for about fifteen minutes, but the digital display showed it was more like an hour and forty.

The talking became shouting and she immediately recognized the voice as Kristina's. In between the yelling, she heard another, much quieter voice. She figured it was Pam. Though Robin couldn't make out all the words, it was obvious Kristina was upset and Pam was trying to calm her.

Her first instinct was to go and find out what was the problem. But before doing so, she became still and listened. The moment she felt the release to do so, she went to the living room.

❧

"I don't care!" Kristina was agitated and roaming the

space like a feral cat. "You had no right to say anything! I told you I'd stay for you two. But I wanted to be left alone!"

"We've been leaving you alone for years and what good did it do you? You overdosed, Kristina! You could've *died*!" Though she tried to control it, Pam's volume had reached the level of Kristina's.

"And so what if I had died? Maybe I should have!" Kristina clenched her fists at her sides. The desperation in her voice was almost too much for Robin to take.

"Don't say that, Kristina." Until she spoke, Robin hadn't even noticed Tamia, tucked into one corner of the couch, tears streaming down her face.

Kristina wept, as well. "You gave me your word!" Kristina beat her open hand against her own chest. "What I do with my life, live or die, is my choice. And you promised you would leave me alone. And now here you are, going behind my back, telling my business and trying to use my private life to manipulate me into doing what you want me to do!"

"All we want you to do is live! All we want you to do is be happy!" Tamia said as she stood and came closer.

"I. Can't. Be. Happy!" Kristina slammed the fist of one hand into the palm of the other as she emphasized each word. "Everything that could've made me happy is gone. I don't have anything left."

She dropped her hands at her sides. "Y'all don't understand. I'm *tired*. Ever since we was kids, it's been one bad thing after another. And if going to that house today did anything, it convinced me once and for all that I've had enough. Stop trying to save me."

She turned back toward the hallway but stopped short when she saw Robin. Kristina took a few steps back, then spun around, searching the room until she located the phone on the desk. She snatched it up, yanked at the length of the cord and brought it to Robin.

"Go for it." She took the receiver off its cradle and shoved it in Robin's face. "Do it."

Robin had no clue what she was talking about. "Do what, Kristina?"

"Find the highest bidder. You got all the dirt now. Go ahead. Use it."

"I would never do that to you."

Kristina dropped the phone on the side table against the wall and started clapping. She laughed, but it sounded hollow and full pain.

"That was good! No, really. I should start taking you to auditions with me. Except... I wasn't born yesterday."

Her voice turned low and grating. "I know exactly what you're going to do the second you leave here. You're just like all the rest of them. You look at me and all you see is a damn blank check."

She came closer until her face was only inches from Robin's. "At least have the decency not to deny it."

Robin looked into Kristina's eyes and something unexpected happened.

It was as if she had a vision.

In a flash, she could see Kristina as a little girl, cowering in her bed. Praying to God to take her in her sleep. To take her before the sun came up and she had to face another day. Robin felt the fear and hopelessness as if it were her own. She experienced the ache for a mother's affection. The longing for touch that didn't bring pain with it.

And with the vision came an overwhelming sense of love. Robin could only imagine it was the Spirit of God allowing her to feel what He felt for Kristina. The hurting little girl standing before her in the body of a woman.

The love was so deep and profound; there was only one thing Robin could do: she encircled her arms around Kristina and held her.

At first, Kristina, primed for a fight, went stiff. Then she struggled to pull away. But Robin wouldn't let go.

"I know you're afraid, Kristina. You've gotten used to it because you've hardly known much else."

A choked sob escaped Kristina's lips and she struggled harder. "No. No."

But Robin continued to hold on. "Father, let her feel the love You have for her. Show her how much she means to You."

"No," Kristina cried out again. But still, Robin wouldn't let go. Instead, she leaned her head onto Kristina's and caressed her hair.

"You don't have to be afraid of me. I'm not here to hurt you. God sent me for one reason and one reason only. And that's to tell you this…"

Kristina stopped struggling as Robin lifted her chin so she could look her in the eye and know she was speaking the truth. "He *loves* you. More than you love your sisters. More than you loved your baby. He loves you. He always has. You thought He never answered your prayer because He didn't care. Because He wasn't listening. But sweetheart, He didn't answer your prayer *because* He cared. And He's *always* been listening."

Kristina's eyes grew wide and she covered her mouth with her hand. She'd never told anyone about that. Not even her sisters.

She backed away, her hand up to prevent Robin from coming any closer. "I don't know how you know about that, but God doesn't love me. Maybe when I was a little girl, but not now. After everything I've done?" She shook her head. "I can hardly look myself in the mirror." Her voice caught in her throat. "So I know there's no way in the world He wants anything to do with me."

"That's not true."

"No. My mama said—"

Robin took a step closer. "It doesn't matter what your mother said. It doesn't matter what anyone else on this entire planet has ever said. Not if it doesn't agree with what *He* said." Robin pointed upward and took another step toward Kristina. "Do you want to know what He said?"

Kristina didn't answer. A part of her wanted to know, but another part, a much larger part, was too afraid to ask.

"For God so loved the world, He gave His only begotten Son. You know what that means? That God so loved *Kristina Langston*, He gave His only begotten Son."

Kristina stopped backing away and stood completely still. She'd heard that verse a hundred times. No. A thousand, at least. Never once did she think it had to do with her personally. As much as her heart longed to believe it, her mind wouldn't let her. She was just one person and not even a very good one at that.

As if she could hear her thoughts, Robin nodded. "I know. It seems too good to be true, doesn't it? He's perfect and we're just...us. But Kristina, the only reason you even exist is because He wanted you to. So you see, it doesn't matter if your parents didn't want you or some man left you or anybody else threw you away. The Creator of the universe wanted you and if that's not a reason to live, I don't know what is."

Once again, tears streamed down Kristina's face. "But I've messed up. Things you don't even know about."

"But He does. He knows and He *still* wants you. And every day is another opportunity to turn to Him. To accept the love He sacrificed to give you."

"But if He loves me so much, why won't He take this pain

away?" Kristina put her hand over her chest. Robin stepped up to her and put her hand over Kristina's.

"Why won't you let Him?"

"What?"

Robin took Kristina's hand and led her to one of the big, overstuffed chairs in the living area. Kristina sat down and Robin sat on the coffee table in front of her.

"You hold on to hurt and unforgiveness like a shield. You use it to protect your heart from sustaining any more damage. But what about laying it down and letting Him protect it, instead?"

Kristina shook her head and wiped at the tear streaks on her cheeks. "But I don't know any other way. I want Him to help me, but I don't know how."

Kristina buried her face in her hands and began sobbing. Robin pulled at her wrist, bringing Kristina's hands away from her face and blotted her tears with a Kleenex.

"You stop trying. That's how. You stop tending to your own wounds. You stop struggling to be clean and struggling to keep your secrets and struggling to deal with your pain. You stop struggling and you start letting go."

Robin snatched up a few more of the Kleenex from the box on the coffee table and used them to dry Kristina's face. "Can I pray with you?"

Kristina nodded and bowed her head.

"In your heart, repeat this prayer with me. Father, I know Your Word says the only reason You sent your Son was out of love for me. But I'm struggling to believe it. To be honest, I'm struggling with a lot. But I actively choose to stop struggling and start believing You, despite what I see. I've tried taking care of myself. I'm not up to the task. But I know that You are. From this day forward, I let go. I lean on You and Your ability. Teach me daily to rely on Your help more and more.

On my own, I have failed, but through Christ, I can do all things. Help me remember that I'm never alone. I need only depend on You to find Your support. I recommit my life and come to You just as I am…"

When they finished praying, Kristina grabbed more tissue from the coffee table and dried her face. She looked at her sisters, both sitting on the couch, drying their eyes, too.

"Pam, you still have the number to that rehab center you stayed at?"

Pam looked up, her face bright with hope. "I carry the card in my purse."

"Good. I think it's time I pay them a visit."

Chapter 10

The next morning, Pam was having breakfast with the rest of the ladies when her phone rang. After a quick glance at the screen, she excused herself and went to her bedroom.

"Hey, baby!"

"Oooh, girl," he replied. "I've missed that voice!"

As usual, Reiland made a goofy grin spread across her face. "Not as much as I've missed yours. I'm so glad I get to see you tomorrow night."

"Me too. How are things going there?"

"Actually," she said, her smile spreading even further. "We've made some real progress. We've talked about things I didn't think we would ever talk about and this woman the pastor sent to help us has been a literal godsend."

"I'm so glad to hear that." She knew he meant it. She could hear the smile in his voice.

"What's going on with you? I hope my being here hasn't left you swamped with too much work."

"Well, you remember that thing I called you about the other day? The lawyer and Mahalia's will?"

"Yeah," she said. "I've been thinking about that. Were you able to get it cleared up?"

He let out a heavy sigh. "Not really. I mean, we know a bit more than we did before. But I can see why her lawyer was concerned. It's not making sense. I was hoping maybe I could run it by you and see if you knew anything more than we did."

"Okay…" Pam sat on the edge of the bed. She and her sisters had made such strides in the last couple of days, she was reluctant to even hear what her husband had to say.

"Do you know an Xavier Morris?"

Pam's eyes squinted as she contemplated. "Xavier…?"

"Morris."

"Umm…"

A few moments passed as she searched her recollection. Pam shook her head. Xavier was such a unique name, she was sure that if she did know one, she'd remember that right away.

"Is it possible you have a cousin by that name? Or, did your mom have any godchildren?"

She snorted. "Um, yeah. Especially after the stroke. I don't know, maybe she was lonely. But it seemed like she 'adopted' a lot after that. Especially from the church. Why? And what does this Xavier Morris have to do with it?"

"Quite a bit, actually. She left just about everything she owned to him."

It took a few moments for Pam to register what her husband had said.

"Wait. She did what?"

"Yep. Everything. The money, the house, her vehicles.

Her church was endowed with a trust, but everything else went to him."

Pam couldn't make sense of it. That her mother left everything she had to someone else, wasn't what bothered her. Truthfully, she and her sisters didn't need or expect any sort of inheritance. With her working as Kristina's manager and Tamia working as her background singer, they all had more than enough. In fact, most everything her mother had, came from them. But why in the world would she leave it to someone they'd never even heard of?

An uncomfortable thought crossed Pam's mind. Could it be her mother had kept a secret boyfriend? Almost as soon as the thought occurred to her, she dismissed it. The world might be full of spry seniors, but her mother wasn't one of them. She was too old-fashioned. No, this had to be something else.

The more likely story, the one Pam didn't even want to consider, was that someone had taken advantage of her mother. At the thought of it, Pam felt something in her chest she could only describe as a pang of guilt.

While she had come back to Texas to take care of her mother immediately after her stroke, she also left the moment she was assured by her mother's doctors that she was in the clear. She hired a nurse to be with Mahalia on a daily basis for the next six weeks, but after that, she was mostly on her own.

Whenever she talked to her mother on the phone or visited, she never got the impression that she had any sort of diminished capacity. Physically, she wasn't able to do the things she'd done previously, but mentally, she was as sharp as ever. Had something changed? Had her stroke affected her in a way that Pam hadn't noticed?

"So what is the lawyer doing to find out who this is?"

"You know, the usual. Background checks, things like

that. But he's already pretty sure it's someone at her church. According to him, it was all she really talked about. And like I said, besides this Xavier person, the church is the only other benefactor."

The church…

A thought struck Pam. "Hey, baby, Robin has attended New Life for years. Long before mama became a member. Let me go check with her and see if she knows anything. I'll call you right back, okay?"

"Sounds good. Love you."

"Love you, too."

Pam knocked on Robin's door and entered the room to find her packing her suitcase.

"Hey, can I ask you something?"

"Sure." Robin said, folding a sweater.

"Do you know of anyone at New Life named Xavier Morris?"

Robin paused, holding the sweater close. "Well, I know of a family named Morris. They have five boys. All singers. The jewels in the crown of New Life choir, in fact." She chuckled. "Thanks to those boys, we've won plenty a gospel sing-off."

Pam went back to her room and called her husband. "Check with Pastor Thomas. Robin says a Morris family goes there. He might know more."

"More what?"

Pam looked over her shoulder to see Kristina leaning against the doorframe, a lollipop in her mouth. Just behind her was Tamia.

"Call me when you know something." Pam disconnected with her husband and gave her sisters the news.

Kristina took her lollipop out of her mouth and waved it through the air. "Wait, wait, wait. Mama did what?"

Pam nodded. "Nobody even knows who he is."

Tamia came in the room and sat on the bed. "But how does her lawyer not know? Isn't that his job?"

Pam shrugged. "From what I understand, she allowed him to handle most everything but her will. The only time she ever even mentioned it to him was to make him promise that he would enforce it, no matter what."

"Well," Kristina said, popping her lollipop back in her mouth. "She could leave everything she had to Bobo the Clown, for all I care. It's not like any of us need it. Besides, come to Jesus moments or not, I have no desire to step into that house again, much less, live in it."

Tamia was obviously in agreement and with that being the end of the story, the sisters returned to their separate rooms. But Pam couldn't let it go. Mahalia Langston didn't let any of her girls get very close to her, but out of all of them, Pam knew her the best. And based on what she knew, nothing about this situation made sense.

After a round of tight hugs and emotional goodbyes, Robin and the sisters promised each other to stay in touch.

When Robin headed out the front door of the suite, Pam followed. "Do you mind if I walk you to your car so we can talk?"

"Of course not." Robin said, pushing the DOWN button on the elevator panel.

"Can you tell me more about this Morris family?"

The elevator chimed and the doors slid open.

"Well," Robin said, stepping in. "I know a bit more about the parents than I do the boys. The mother, Esther, is a nurse at Presby. Her husband, Deacon, is a sweetheart. A big teddy bear of a man. If I'm not mistaken, he's been a janitor with the Dallas Public School system for most of his life.

"Deacon?" Pam asked. "That's the father's name? His full name?"

Robin grimaced. "I'm sorry, but I don't know. That's all I've ever heard anyone call him. I'm not even sure if it's his given name or just a nickname." Robin studied Pam's worried expression. "Why the sudden interest in the Morrises?"

"Apparently, our mother left all she had to someone with that last name. I'd like to know why. And since there's a family with that name at the church…"

"Gotcha."

Once again, the elevator chimed. This time, to notify them of reaching the first floor. Pam shoved her hands in her pockets and followed Robin out of the elevator and into the lobby. A hundred thoughts raced through her mind, none of them getting her any closer to the answers she needed.

"What do you know about the rest of the family?"

"Like I said earlier, there's five boys. The youngest one was a bit of a surprise, because—."

Pam looked to see why Robin had stopped talking.

"What?"

Robin stood there in the middle of the lobby, her mouth open, but no words coming out. She kept blinking as if she'd seen something she couldn't believe.

"When did you say it was that Kristina miscarried?"

"Uh…almost eighteen years ago. But what does that have to do with—"

Robin grabbed Pam's upper arm. "I started to say that the youngest was a bit of a surprise because Esther hadn't planned on having any more children. Her boys were already preteens. Then late one night, the doorbell rang. But when

Deacon turned on the porch light, no one was there. No adult, anyway. Just an abandoned, premature baby."

Chapter 11

For a moment, Robin's words didn't make sense to Pam.

But when they finally did, the room started spinning. Robin grabbed Pam's arm and led her to a seating area in the middle of the lobby. They sat down and Robin put her hand on her back.

"Breathe. Just breathe."

Pam leaned over on her legs, her eyes closed, her mind racing.

It couldn't be. It was impossible. She was *there*. In the room. The baby wasn't breathing.

He was *dead*.

When she was finally able to catch her breath and think clearly, she asked, "A preemie? You're sure that he was premature?"

Robin nodded. "I remember because the doctors didn't expect him to make it, so the pastor assigned a group of women to pray for him twenty-four hours a day. When he finally came out of the hospital and they could bring him to church, there was a dedication ceremony. Esther had to put him in doll clothes because none of the regular christening outfits were small enough."

Pam could've sworn her heart skipped a beat. As if it literally stopped and then started again at the meaning of Robin's words.

At the hope.

She shook her head. No. She couldn't let herself hope. The chances of it meaning all that she wanted it to mean were slim. Kristina's baby had already died once. To believe this and then find out it wasn't true would be like losing him all over again.

And yet…

"Did your mother ever mention anything about the baby?"

"You mean, like, what she did with him?"

"Yes."

Pam shook her head. "We never spoke about it. It was like it never happened. The beating. The birth. None of it."

"I'm sure all of you must've wondered."

"I can't speak for Kristina or Tamia. I imagine they did. But me? Oh, yeah. Definitely."

Just after it happened, it was *all* she could think about. She was haunted with questions like: Did she bury him? Where? Did she dump him somewhere? Did she just throw him in the trash?

It was what made it so hard for her to love Mahalia. Even when she was sick and incapacitated by the stroke. People would have assumed, had they known their history, it was the beatings and the abuse. But for some reason, for Pam, those would have been easy to forgive. Or, maybe not easy, but possible. But the way their mother had handled the birth? That was something altogether different.

Pam always assumed that her mother had thrown him away. Like garbage. And though she never knew him, though he hadn't lived long enough to take a breath, it was the one thing Pam never forgave.

"It never occurred to me," Pam finally said. "It never even crossed my mind that maybe he wasn't dead. I mean, he was so limp and still."

As much as she would've liked to believe Kristina's son survived and had been alive and well all this time, it just didn't seem likely. And not only because of the way he looked when he was born.

"The thing is, I don't see how my mother could've kept this a secret. I mean, she was furious when she realized Kristina was pregnant. Like we said, she nearly beat her to death. And if you had seen the way she came in there and stuffed him in that shoebox," she shook her head again. "No. Even if he had lived, I can't imagine she would've left all she had to him. I can't imagine she would've acknowledged him, at all."

"Not then. Not the Mahalia you girls knew that night. But what about later? What about after you left? What about after the stroke? You yourself said that she was different."

It was true. After the stroke, her mother *was* different. But a complete personality change? That was almost as hard to believe as the baby surviving. But then again, nothing else was making sense, either.

"Okay, for arguments sake, let's say that he did survive. I still don't know if I could buy my mother having any sort of connection to him, much less leaving him an inheritance."

Robin shrugged. "Maybe she felt guilty."

Guilt. Now *that* was something Pam could imagine. And

after everything her mother had done, the only thing that made sense. She might not have become a whole new person, but she could've changed enough to at least feel sorry over how she'd raised them.

Pam took a deep breath and exhaled. "So what do we do now? Is there any way that I can see him? Talk to his family? His parents, maybe?"

Robin put up her finger. "Just one minute." She pulled out her phone and dialed. "Hey, Deandra! Listen, what time do you all have choir practice today?"

Pam watched and Robin looked at her and nodded. "Okay. And one more thing. Do you know if the Morris boys are going to be there?"

Again, Robin looked at Pam, only this time, she gave her a thumbs up. "Thanks, love. I'll talk to you later, okay? Bye."

"Okay." Robin said, returning her phone to her handbag. "You know that musical in honor of your mother?"

Pam nodded.

"Well, the mass choir is having a complete run through today at New Life. And not only are the boys going to be there, at least two of them are featured soloists. During the day, the sanctuary is always open. You could go in and sit near the back if you wanted to. You're bound to see him."

Again, Pam felt it.

The beat, the pause, and the beat again.

Of course, she wanted to see him. But at the same time, she wanted to drive to Dallas International, get on the first plane out and never look back again.

There were only two outcomes.

One. He was Kristina's son. While it was extraordinarily happy news, Pam could only imagine the emotional land-mine it would be for Kristina's recovery.

Outcome two? He wasn't Kristina's son. And Pam would

have to mourn her nephew all over again. And though she told her heart not to hope, it had already gone that route without her.

But good outcome or bad, Pam *had* to know...

"Could I bother you to stay one more day? Just in case it's him? If it is, I'm going to need your help. Because I don't have any idea what I'm going to do."

"Of course, whatever you need."

Despite how much Pam had tried smother it, hope fluttered around in her chest, fragile as a butterfly.

Chapter 12

When Pam arrived at the parking lot of New Life Tabernacle Church, it was already full of cars, with more still arriving. Some choir members and musicians stood out front, laughing, talking and greeting one another.

She turned off her ignition and waited. No doubt, she was far less recognizable than Kristina was, but after being at their mother's funeral, she didn't want to take any chances and end up having to give a reason for being there.

After the last of the stragglers made their way into the church building, Pam did the same.

Only the lights over the pulpit area were on, casting the huge cavern of a sanctuary into darkness. One look at the platform stopped her in her tracks. She'd never seen a choir so large. They covered the platform and overflowed onto the steps leading down to the altar. She quickly located the tenors and was disheartened to see how many people were in that section alone.

She'd planned on staying in the back of the church, but decided to move in for a better look. She found a seat close enough to watch, but still far enough to be hidden in the shadows from any singers and musicians that could easily look out into the sanctuary.

Her eyes rapidly moved from face to face, looking for any familial resemblance amongst the tenors. Finding none, she encouraged herself to calm down and start again. Slowly, she studied the face of each young man.

Some were laughing and talking to friends. A few were flirting with a nearby soprano or alto. A few others waited quietly for rehearsal to begin. One was reading.

None of them looked like Kristina.

Pam steeled herself against the wave of heartache that crashed up against her.

Not seeing him didn't mean he wasn't there. There were at least a dozen reasons no one looked familiar to her. Maybe he hadn't arrived yet. Maybe he was behind someone taller. Maybe he looked like his father.

But studying the faces of the younger male choir members for the third time in a row made her have to admit another explanation. The only one she wanted to ignore.

Maybe she didn't recognize anyone as her nephew because he'd already died close to twenty years before.

It was a long shot from the beginning.

The idea that an obviously stillborn baby had somehow survived and become the only heir of the grandmother that kept his existence a secret sounded too much like a soap opera. Even to her.

Not just a soap opera, but a fairy tale.

But this was no fairy tale. It was real life and things like that just didn't happen. Her brain told her to get up and walk out the door. But for some reason, her heart wouldn't let her move.

At the direction of the organist, the choir members settled down and took their places. The choir director, after a few words with the organist, came to the front.

"Okay, y'all. We're gonna run through the whole thing, from top to bottom. If there's anything we need to work on, I'll give you some notes after we finish that selection. But for the most part, we want to move straight through so we can get an idea of what we're looking at, time wise."

The organist started playing and the strains of the Hammond B3 organ filled the sanctuary. Pam closed her eyes to take it in.

Someone that hadn't grown up in the church wouldn't understand, but there was something about the sound of a B3 that touched her like nothing else could.

This was where they were from, she and her sisters. The church. Kristina may have teased her, called her the church girl, but the truth was, they were all church girls. Born and raised. Whether it was their home church of Mt Zion or the little white COGIC chapel their mother served as minister of music, the Langstons were the first to arrive when the doors opened and the last to leave.

It was something that couldn't be explained to an outsider. The shut-ins, the all-night prayer sessions, the Easter programs, the first Sunday dinners, the congregational songs, the unmistakable sound of the B3. It filled her with a sense of home unlike anything else.

The choir started singing their first selection. She recognized the music immediately. It was one of the many hymns her mother had rearranged for choirs to sing in parts.

It started with the rich mid-range tone of the altos, joined by the warm and deep sound of the tenors. Rising, then falling, one behind the other. Finally, the crystal-clear voices of the sopranos blended in.

Just as I am—without one plea,
But that Thy blood was shed for me,
And that Thou bidst me come to Thee,
O Lamb of God, I come...

She hadn't realized she was crying until she felt the wetness of her teardrops on her folded arms.

Just as I am—poor, wretched, blind;
Sight, riches, healing of the mind,
Yea, all I need, in Thee to find,
O Lamb of God, I come...

No matter what hell they might have endured at the hands of their mother, somehow, the church itself was never tainted by it. Then, as now, she always felt a peace and comfort in the pews of a church that no amount of alcohol could ever provide.

Just as I am—and waiting not
To rid my soul of one dark blot,
To Thee, whose blood can cleanse each spot,
O Lamb of God, I come...

But along with the comfort, there was something else. Something dark and ugly. Something she never spoke out loud.

She hadn't said anything the day before, but she understood how Kristina felt. She knew what it was like to love God, but not be able to believe He could love her back.

Just as I am—Thy love, I own,
Has broken every barrier down;
Now to be Thine, my joy and crown,
O Lamb of God, I come...

Pam hugged her arms tight around her middle. It made her ache, that uncertainty. She'd give anything to know, to *really* know deep down, that He loved her.

Like back when she was a girl. Then, she knew. It was the only thing that kept her sane. He was the best friend that she told all her troubles to. The One to Whom she whispered her deepest fears and darkest secrets long into the night.

Just as I am—of that free love
The fullness and the depth to prove,
Here for a season, then above—
O Lamb of God, I come!

Her sisters always considered her the strong one. What they didn't know was that she drew every ounce of strength from Him. It was choir rehearsals like this that helped her get through.

While their mother used to make them rehearse for hours and hours, sometimes to the point of hoarseness, it never did anything for Pam. She hated those practice sessions. But choir rehearsal? That was different.

Sometimes, the choir would sing and sing and get so caught up, rehearsal would break out into praise and worship. It would go on for hours and hours, just like her mother's practice sessions. But unlike her mother's practice sessions, Pam never wanted it to end.

After those Saturday afternoons, she felt strong. Like God

Himself was with her. And she knew that she could go back home and face her mother for another week.

Everything that happened—the beatings, the box, the verbal abuse and torture—she only survived it by leaning on the love of God.

But something broke the night Kristina gave birth. Nothing, including her view of God, was ever the same again. And with each year that passed, it became harder and harder for her to believe. And the less she believed, the harder it was to sing. And before she knew it, she didn't sing at all.

Chapter 13

"Sister Pam?"

Pam looked up to see Pastor Thomas smiling down at her.

"I didn't expect to see you here today!"

She motioned at the choir. "I thought I'd listen in."

His grin widened. "Yes, I'm here for the same thing. I can't imagine a better way to honor the legacy of music your mother left to the church community."

She tried to give him a smile that didn't look completely fake. Whether he bought it, she didn't know. He sat in the pew in front of her, but turned so he could face her.

"I've been calling Sister Robin daily. Checking in on you ladies. Sounds like Kristina's had a breakthrough."

Pam nodded. "Still, keep her in your prayers. She has a long way to go."

"Of course." He studied her as she watched the activity on the platform. The choir director was giving notes to the altos.

"And how have you been doing?"

She swallowed hard. Why did it seem the only time she was tempted to lie was when she was in church?

"Oh, you know, there's a lot to deal with. But it's all going to work out." She flashed him her most confident smile. The one she always used when she was trying to convince people there was nothing more to the story.

They watched as the choir prepared for a new selection and the featured soloist took her place at the mic stand.

"You know, we're a lot alike. Me and you." He swung one arm over the back of the pew and interlaced his fingers.

She said nothing, but waited for him to elaborate.

"As a pastor, I tend to get wrapped up in the task of taking care of my members. I sometimes forget I need to let Jesus take care of me."

He let the words sink in before he went on. "You spend so much time carrying your sister's burdens. I can't help but wonder… Don't you ever get tired?"

Pam quickly turned away from him and started digging around in her purse to hide the tears that sprung to her eyes. She didn't know why his question caused such an emotional reaction. She sure didn't know how she'd explain it.

"Others look at people like us and think we've got it all together, but…"

He remained silent for a long while. After Pam felt satisfied that she'd gotten a hold of herself, she looked back at him. He was staring into the distance, his eyes moist, as well. He cleared his throat.

"I've made mistakes." His voice was low and rough. "Mistakes that, to this day, I can't let go of. I know I should give it to God and I know I should lay the burden of it on Him, but sometimes we, even as pastors, find that hard to do."

Pam was surprised that he felt comfortable enough with her, nearly a stranger, to share something that was so obviously personal. Maybe her being a stranger was what allowed him to do it. She let him continue.

"We think, since it was *our* mistake, we should be the ones to fix it." He sighed. "The truth is, we'll never be able to fix it. Not really. We can patch it up. Add a new coat of paint. But when it's all said and done, it's still a mess. A very well-decorated mess, but a mess, nonetheless."

It wasn't that Pam didn't know where he was coming from or what he was trying to say. If she'd heard it once, she'd heard it a thousand times. Let go and let God. It was one of those Christian catchphrases that they loved to use. But what did it really mean? And who did it apply to?

While she considered herself a Christian, having recommitted to her relationship with God when she was in rehab, she definitely wouldn't call herself a good one. If God was going to pick anyone to fix problems for, she was pretty sure she'd be at the end of the line. There had to be a million other people, at least, that lived better and did more.

"How can you be sure He's even willing to fix it, though? I mean, I can understand Him doing that for you. You're a pastor. But for regular people…"

Pastor Thomas' eyebrows shot up. "Regular people?" He let out a hearty laugh. "So…what? You think preachers are superhuman?"

She tilted her head and smiled. "You know what I mean. *Good* Christians."

Pastor Thomas shook his head. "Good Christians, bad Christians. Sunday Saints or twenty-four hour ones. Each and every one belongs to Him. Mistakes and all. And to answer your question, I know He's willing because that's what He said. 1 Peter 5:7 reads, 'Cast all your cares upon Him, for

He cares for you.' In Matthew 11:28, Jesus said,' Come to Me, all ye that labor and are heavy laden, and I will give you rest.'"

She remembered those verses from Sunday school. But she hadn't heard them in so long, it felt like a lifetime ago.

"Many other Bibles translate that phrase as 'weary and burdened'. And I hope I don't offend you by saying this but, if I've ever met a soul that was weary and burdened, it's yours."

It's not like she could deny it. It was true. Nothing was heavier than a secret and she'd been carrying more than just her own for too many years to count.

She looked at the choir as they swayed and clapped their hands to the beat.

"But how do you do it? How do you give it to Him?"

"Well, first, you confess it. God gave us great power when He granted us the privilege to speak over our lives. Every time your heart is troubled, however big or small that trouble is, you say, 'I let not my heart be troubled. I let not my heart fear. I cast all my cares on You, Jesus, because I know You care for me'. It won't be easy. At first, you'll find you have to say it nonstop. But just keep speaking it. And meditate on His love for you. In the face of fear, stress, a bad report—meditate on it until you know it like you know your own name. Because when you know, beyond a shadow of a doubt, that He cares for you, faith is easy."

After saying a word of prayer with her. Pastor Thomas went back to his office. And although she hadn't wanted anyone to see her when she came in, she was glad she hadn't gotten her wish. There was a lightness and sense of freedom in her heart she hadn't felt in years.

Maybe ever.

Somehow, and in some way she couldn't explain, she knew that everything would be okay. No matter what.

If Kristina's *son* had survived, she trusted that God would eventually lead him to them. But if that didn't happen, it only meant that her nephew was safe in the arms of Jesus. And on this side or the other, she knew there was no better place to be.

"Okay, y'all. This is it. This is the last song. I know you're all tired. And tomorrow night, at this point you'll probably be exhausted. But I need you to push it and go all out. Give me everything you've got."

Pam put her coat on and made her way toward the sanctuary doors, fishing for her phone in her handbag.

She dialed and Robin immediately picked up.

"Hi. I'm on my way back now. Turns out you're not gonna need to stay tonight. But could you wait until I get there so I can talk to you before you leave?"

Robin responded, but Pam had no idea what she said.

That was because of what she heard over the church sound system. And what she heard made her spin around and nearly drop her phone in the process.

"Come on up, Xavier. Close this thing out, my brother."

Chapter 14

As Xavier came up to the organ, Pam realized why she couldn't locate him earlier. He hadn't been in the tenor section at all. He was with the other musicians, playing the keyboard.

The second thing she realized was that she'd seen him before. At her mother's funeral. He and his brother were the last two people to come up to their table before Kristina ran off to the restroom.

Pam reached out for the nearest pew and used it to steady herself. Her heart banging against her chest, she sat and watched.

As he took the mic off the stand, some of the choir members shouted, "Sing, X!"

And sing he did.

He may have looked timid and shy when the others shouted out, but his voice was anything but. Rich and smooth, it filled every corner of the sanctuary. Pam had to cover her mouth in an effort to contain herself.

She may not have recognized him by sight, but after hearing him sing, she felt certain he must have Langston blood.

She closed her eyes and let the sound of his voice wash over her. Stylistically, she'd never heard anything like him. He could comfortably navigate his lower register and smoothly modulate all the way up to what her mother used to call the whistle pitch. He had complete vocal control and the confidence to use it correctly. He didn't wildly run up and down the scales just to prove that he could. He took his time and imbued every lyric with meaning and heartfelt conviction.

And she should know. The song he was singing wasn't an easy one. It was a duet Kristina and her mother recorded as the final song on what turned out to be her breakout album. It was the last time they ever sung together. The last time they saw each other, for that matter.

Pam leaned forward and rested her elbows on the back of the pew in front of her own, unable to do much more than watch him.

He was the same beautiful pecan brown as Kristina, but he definitely took more after his father, feature wise. He was medium height and slender, but not skinny. He certainly didn't seem big enough to house the powerful voice he possessed.

Voice...

Pam sat back in the pew. At the repast, he mentioned Mahalia helping his family. Was it just financially? Or, did she actually spend time with him?

The thought of it sent a flash of anger through Pam. That her mother would not only keep him a secret, but also get the privilege of watching him grow up while Kristina continued to mourn him, was too much. And if that's how Pam felt about it, she could only imagine what Kristina's reaction would be.

Kristina…

How in the world was she supposed to tell her about this? Especially now? When she'd finally agreed to go to rehab?

It seemed that every mess Kristina had ever gotten herself into, was somehow connected to the grief she carried over her stillborn son.

At first glance, finding him seemed the miracle they all needed. But Pam knew her sister. She'd feel guilty that he'd grown up without her. She'd be angry with their mother for keeping her from him. She'd hate herself for being the mess that she was, instead of a mother he could look up to.

Stop. You're getting too far ahead of yourself. Remember what Pastor Thomas said.

Quietly, she prayed. "I cast this care over on You, Father. I know You care for me and my sisters and Xavier. I ask that You work this all out for us. Let this be a blessing in all our lives and not a hindrance."

Immediately, she felt a release of the anxiety that had built up in her chest. She took a deep breath.

It wasn't like she should tell Kristina right now, anyway.

While the young man did resemble Omar and one could argue that he sounded like a Langston, all the "evidence" Pam had could be explained away.

It was possible that her mother had taken up time with the boy because his circumstances reminded her of her only grandson. It was possible that what sounded like Langston blood was really just Langston vocal training. And as far as his looks, it was also possible that she was just seeing what she wanted to see.

As much as she would've liked to believe this Xavier was her long-lost nephew, the odds were greater that he wasn't.

Well, she thought, *there's only one way to find out.*

After the singers and musicians were dismissed, Pam waited in the back of the sanctuary so she could catch Xavier on his way out.

But as he came down the aisle toward her, laughing and talking with some of his friends, she got scared and had second thoughts. Maybe it was better to leave well enough alone. He seemed like a happy kid. And if she was wrong about her suspicions, there was no reason to bother him, anyway.

She snatched her purse up off the seat and quickly navigated her way around the pew, down the aisle and toward the door.

"Ms. Langston?"

Pam froze mid step. Slowly, she turned around to find Xavier staring right at her. He said a quick goodbye to his friends and approached her. It was too late now, she'd been caught.

She offered him a weak smile and put out her hand. "Hi. My name is P—"

"I know who you are!" He grinned and took her hand. "You're Pamela Langston."

Pam was too shocked to hide her surprise. "You know who I am?"

Maybe her mother hadn't kept the secret. Maybe she had told him the whole story. Was it possible that he already knew? Pam felt that flutter of hope in her chest again.

"Of course, I do. Your mother talked about you all the time. You probably don't remember, but my brother and I met you a couple of days ago."

"No, I remember." She did her best to hide her

disappointment. Of course, he knew who she was. He was at the funeral and the repast.

"Um…" He shifted his weight from one foot to the other, as if he were hesitating. "I hope it's okay for me to ask… How is your sister doing?"

"She's doing much better. Thank you."

He put his hand over his stomach and exhaled, genuinely relieved. "I'm so glad. My family and I have been praying for her ever since she was taken to the hospital."

His family. Pam wondered what they were like. They had to be good people to have raised such a compassionate young man.

"Thank you. We appreciate it."

They stood an awkward silence until Pam finally spoke up. "Well, all right then. I should probably get going. Thanks again."

Though it felt like it was killing her, Pam turned and walked away. As much as she would have liked to talk to him longer, what was there to say? The truth wasn't an option. And that's what she'd have to tell him in order to learn whether her suspicions were correct.

"Wait a minute." He jogged to catch up to her. "Were you here for rehearsal? Did you hear us?"

Pam was so relieved to have an excuse to keep talking to him, she almost laughed. "Yes!"

"What did you think?"

She smiled. "The choir, the musicians, you… Amazing. All of it was absolutely amazing."

He grinned so hard, it made her laugh. Just before they got to the church doors, he rushed ahead of her and opened them so she could walk out.

Although it was barely 5 o'clock, the sun had already started to go down. Noticing that, he offered to walk her to her car. He didn't have a sweater or a jacket and he shoved his hands in his pockets, teeth chattering.

"Do you think you'll be coming to the musical?"

She frowned. "I doubt it."

He nodded quickly, as if he expected as much, but she could see he was disappointed.

"That's probably for the best. After the funeral and everything, y'all probably really need some rest. And there's gonna be a ton of people at the musical, so…" He sounded more like he was trying to convince himself than her.

As they got closer to Pam's car, she found herself slowing her pace. She didn't want to say goodbye to him. Not yet.

"Are you a fan? Of Kristina's, I mean?"

His eyes lit up. "Am I a fan? I'm the president of the fan club! Well, actually that would have been Mother Langston. But I'm definitely the Vice President!"

Pam couldn't help but chuckle at his enthusiasm. But then his expression darkened.

"We used to listen to your sister's albums together. The day a new one came out, she'd buy it for us. Later, when I got older, I'd buy it. Either way, we'd go to her house and put it on in the living room. We always listened to the entire thing straight through, at least twice." He smiled at the memory. "Then she'd take apart each one, like a mechanic with an engine. She'd explain why the song worked and what vocal techniques were used. After that, we'd make a bet on which would become number one hits." He bit at his bottom lip. "She always got 'em right. Every single time."

Pam didn't know her mother had ever heard Kristina's albums, much less bought them. And she certainly never would've guessed that Mahalia was listening to them with Xavier.

"You two were pretty close, weren't you?"

He nodded and cleared his throat.

They stood next to the car, neither wanting to leave. Finally, he broke the silence. "Well, it was really nice to see you again. And I'm so glad you got to hear the run through."

"Me too. You have a beautiful voice. A real gift."

Even with only the parking lot lights to illuminate his face, she could see him blush.

"Well, tomorrow night, I'll make sure I blow the roof off for all of you since you can't be there." He took his hand out of his pocket and gave her a wave. "Have a good night."

He turned around and walked away. A pang of panic struck her. She still wasn't ready to let him go.

"Actually…"

Xavier stopped and turned to face her. Pam took a few steps in his direction. "Would you mind joining me for dinner? I'd love to hear more about you and my mother."

He stood there for a few moments, blinking.

"I can drive you home after, if that's a problem."

"Really? Seriously?" He produced a grin that looked like he'd just won the Texas State Lottery.

"Seriously." Pam said.

He put his hands up as if to ask her to stay right where she was. "Let me just tell my brothers to go ahead without me. I'll be right back." He took off running across the parking lot, calling over his shoulder, "Just wait a minute and I'll be right back!"

Chapter 15

They ended up at a fifties-themed hamburger joint that looked like a diner. The retro booth they sat at even had a miniature jukebox on the table. But Pam didn't notice any of that. She was too focused on the superhuman feat taking place before her.

She shook her head and blinked as she watched Xavier stuff yet *another* handful of fries in his mouth. Despite his slight build, the boy ate like he was The Rock. She'd kept a straight face for as long as she could, but eventually, she lost the fight and fell over on the booth seat, laughing.

Xavier froze. "What?"

"Where do you put it all?"

Xavier looked down at his plate, then back at Pam. He dropped his chin to his chest in shame.

"My brothers always called me The Little Piggy. They said one day I'd figure out why. I think I just did."

He groaned and covered his face in embarrassment. Pam reached out, grabbed his wrist and tugged on it.

"It's okay, little piggy. No need to be embarrassed."

He groaned even louder and then started laughing.

Pam felt like she was dreaming. This was the kind of moment she'd imagined at least a hundred times over the years. What life would have been like of Kristina's son had lived. What kind of food would he have liked? What kind of music? Would he have a sense of humor? An appetite like his mother's?

Now, by some miraculous twist of fate, she finally had the answers: fries, 80's pop classics, yes, and most *definitely*, yes.

She couldn't stop looking at him. She'd spent the last hour studying every part of his face, every change in his expression.

The dark and long lashes that curled like they should've belonged to a girl. The way he crinkled his eyes when he thought something was funny. The way his smile was completely lopsided.

She just couldn't get enough. She thanked God that he *was* The Little Piggy, because had he not been so enamored with his fries, her staring might have freaked him out.

But that wasn't why she'd invited him to dinner. What she really wanted was any clue that might confirm her suspicions without having to ask him outright.

She folded her arms on the table and leaned in. "At the repast, you mentioned my mother helping your family. Can you tell me more?"

He nodded as he took a sip from his straw. "If it hadn't been for her, my parents would have been ruined. I was a preemie and had all kinds of crazy medical issues. As soon as they got one thing working right, something else would break down. I was like the world's tiniest clunker."

Pam laughed. She'd done a lot of that. From the moment

he got in the car, he was saying crazy stuff and making her think, *Where did this kid come from?*

And if this was the stuff coming out of his mouth at seventeen, she could only imagine the mess he might've come up with when he was four.

The thought made her chest ache. If he was, in fact, her nephew, she'd have to really pray through to find it in her heart to forgive Mahalia. There was no way to replace what they'd missed with him, what had been stolen.

"You okay?" He was looking at her, worry etched across his brows.

"Oh, you know…just thinking about all that's happened in the last few days." She tried to smile, but it was a struggle.

He put his napkin down and sat back.

"Yeah, I miss her, too. She was the closest thing I had to a grandparent."

"Why is that?"

"Well, my mom and dad are older. By the time I came around, both had buried their parents. I always heard all these great stories about my grandparents when my brothers shared memories, but I didn't have any because I never knew them. Of course, mom and dad were always saying stuff like, 'Your grandma Florence sure would've loved you'. Or, 'You would have gotten along well with your grandpa Simon. He liked fishing, too.'"

He shrugged. "It was nice of them to say it, but it didn't make me miss having grandparents any less. So when me and Mother Langston became close, I felt like it was a chance to have all those relationships I missed."

"When did you meet her?"

He put his elbows on the table and rested his chin in the palm of his hand. "You know, I don't remember. I must've been small because I don't remember her *not* being there.

We didn't get really close until I was older, but even when I was little kid, she'd always come to the hospital and visit me. Like when I had a surgery or something like that. She had this notebook she would always bring. We must've played tic-tac-toe a thousand times. And not *once* did she ever let me win."

He made a face and Pam snorted. "Yeah, that sounds like my mother."

"She was just always there. I remember this one time, I was feeling awful. My mom was working crazy hours. And even though my dad was there, it just wasn't the same as having your mom, you know?"

Pam nodded.

"She'd come by at night and sing me to sleep and in the morning she'd sing me awake," he said, smiling.

Pam could hardly believe what she was hearing. Sat by his bedside? Tic-tac-toe? Singing to him in the morning and at night? Mahalia *never* did anything like that when they were growing up. Turning off the light switch was her way of saying good night and banging on the wall just above it was how she said good morning.

"Then we started singing together. She taught me how to harmonize. As I got older, she gave me piano lessons, free of charge. Singing lessons, too. Grandma always—" He stopped, his eyes wide. "I'm sorry."

"You called her that? I mean, she *let* you call her that?"

He nodded. "Really, I'm sorry. I don't mean any offense."

Pam put her hands up. "No. There's nothing for you to be sorry about. I'm not offended."

He reached for his glass and traced his finger on the condensation.

"You really miss her, don't you?"

He scooted his glass a few inches away from him and

nodded. He stuffed more fries into his mouth and wiped his eyes with the back of his hands.

And that's when she saw it.

When he was aching with longing and the grief was written across his face, that was the moment she saw his resemblance to Kristina and it nearly broke her heart.

Chapter 16

When Xavier suggested that Pam meet his parents, she was quick to agree. He called ahead to let them know she was coming and by the time they got to the front door, his mother, Esther, practically tackled her in a bear hug.

The easy show of affection was apparently a family trait that carried over into the home itself. Walking into the house felt like being wrapped in a warm blanket. There was something about the spirit of the place. Not only was it warm and cozy, there was a peace that permeated the whole space.

It was easy for Pam to see why once she got to know the Morris parents a bit more.

Deacon was tall and husky. Quiet, but jovial. The warm and gentle smile on his face seemed a permanent fixture. Esther, on the other hand, was anything but quiet. Pam didn't think she'd ever met anyone so quick to laugh. She was a woman that not only loved life, but wanted to help everyone else love it, too.

The walls and just about every available surface was covered with framed pictures of the family. The boys, the parents, all of them together, each of them separately. And every photograph had one thing in common—expressions of complete joy. It was the kind of thing Pam had only seen on TV. The kind of thing she thought was only meant for stories in books. But here she was, standing in the midst of it. An honest-to-goodness, happy family that loved one another more than anything else.

She found her way to the fireplace mantle that seemed dedicated solely to photographs of Xavier. From pictures of him as a newborn in the hospital, all the way up to recent candids of him with his brothers.

Esther came up beside Pam and pointed to one picture in particular. "That's always been my favorite."

Pam could see why. It was Xavier around two years old. He sat in his highchair with a pickle in each hand and a grin so full of glee, his eyes were nothing but two slits.

"That child is a pickle fool." Esther laughed, loud and vivacious, causing Pam to laugh, too. "My Lord! He would eat absolutely anything we put in front of him. And I mean *anything*. But don't let him see a pickle. The child would lose his mind!"

She looked at Pam, her eyes wide and disbelieving. "Do you know we actually had to hide the jars behind other stuff in the refrigerator when he was growing up? Have you ever heard of anything like that?"

She had. Its name was Kristina.

Esther moved in closer to Pam and lowered her voice. "How's your sister doing, baby?" Her tone was gentle and without judgment. As far as most people knew, Kristina had just collapsed. But Pam was sure at least some congregation members knew the truth. She wondered if Esther was one of them.

"Better. God's working it out."

Esther nodded and put her hand on Pam's back. "The Word says if any two touch and agree, so you can count me in as agreeing with you."

Pam felt a lump rise in her throat. From the moment she realized what her mother might've done, she'd felt so much anger and loss. But if this was the result, if the outcome of her mother's deception was that Xavier grew up with these people and in this house, how could she be angry? Xavier had better parents than she and her sisters ever did.

At that point, Pam was pretty much convinced that Xavier was Kristina's son. But she still needed some sort of solid confirmation before she went to her sisters with the revelation. This was too much of a life-changing event to not be 100% sure.

"I should probably get going. Would you mind walking me out to my car?"

Esther rubbed her back. "I'd be happy to, baby!"

Pam said her goodbyes to Xavier and Deacon, then she and Esther went outside. All the way out to the car, Esther chatted about how much the family loved Mahalia and how big a fan Xavier was of Kristina.

Pam stopped at the driver's side, but made no move to unlock the door. She lingered for a moment, trying to decide how in the world to even ask the question she needed answered. She decided to start small and work her way up.

"Umm, has a man named Taylor Lincoln contacted you?"

Esther squinted her eyes and tilted her head. "Not that I know of. I suppose he could've talked to my husband, but Deacon hasn't mentioned it to me. Who is it?"

"My mother's lawyer. He might be waiting to talk to me and my sisters before contacting you. But since I'm here, I might as well tell you. Mama left everything she had to Xavier."

Esther's mouth dropped open and she shook her head. "That must be a mistake. I mean, they were close, but I don't see why... Everything?"

"Everything."

Esther put her hands up, waving them. "Don't you worry yourself for even one minute about that. I know Xavier. He wouldn't want y'alls inheritance going to him. I don't know what she could have been thinking to do that—"

Pam put her hand on Esther's arm. "No, you misunderstand. There's no hard feelings, whatsoever. She left it to him because she wanted him to have it and we fully support that."

"But it doesn't make sense. I just don't understand why she would do something like that. Why would she leave it to him and not her daughters?"

"I think I know why. But I need you to answer a question for me to confirm it."

"Okay." Esther straightened her back, focusing all her attention on what Pam was about to say.

"The night he came to you... Do you remember what he was in? Could he have been wrapped in a towel? A burgundy one?"

Esther's eyes grew wide and she took a step back. "Yes... He was in a towel and inside a—"

"Shoe box."

Esther's hands flew to her mouth.

"It was for work boots, wasn't it?"

"How could you know that?"

Pam shut her eyes and pressed her lips together in an

effort to hold back the avalanche of emotion that threatened to wipe her out.

There was no denying it now.

She no longer had to defend herself against the hope it could be true.

It *was* true.

Xavier was Kristina's son and he was alive and well.

Tears streamed down Pam's face as she choked out the words.

"I know because I was there the night he was born."

Chapter 17

By the time Pam got back to the hotel suite, most of the lights inside were turned off. As she entered, she saw only a faint glow coming from the direction of the hallway. No sooner than she'd taken her coat off, Robin came rushing around the corner.

"Where have you been? Are you all right? We were on the phone one second and you were gone the next. I tried calling back but didn't get a response."

Pam put her hand on her forehead. "I turned the volume off before I went inside the church and forgot to turn it back on. I'm so sorry."

Robin grabbed a hold of her wrist and led her to the couch. "No, no, no. I'm just glad you're all right. But from the look on your face, I'm guessing our suspicions proved true?"

Pam could only nod, afraid that saying anything more in the moment would cause her to start crying again.

She'd already spent the entire car ride from the Morris

house doing just that. She hadn't felt such an overwhelming jumble of emotions since the night she got the call that her mother had died. It was exhausting. Joy one second, anger the next. Relief, quickly followed by anxious anticipation.

After a moment to collect herself, she relayed the whole story to Robin.

"The best I can figure is that my mother had intended on disposing of him, but then realized he was alive. We didn't attend New Life. Mt. Zion was our church home. But mama worked with the New Life choir a lot back then. In fact, that's how she came across Omar. Esther said that it was around that time that she and mama met and became friends. I guess when mama saw the baby was alive, her first thought was to take him to the only nurse she knew. Now I understand why, after the three of us left Texas, she left Mt. Zion for New Life."

"To be closer to her grandson…" Robin shook her head. "I knew about him being a preemie and about him being abandoned. But I never would've guessed he had blood relatives attending the same church."

"Esther said that initially, somebody would leave envelopes full of cash in their mailbox. The only means of identification was the same sentence scrawled across the front of each one: *this is for the baby*. She never made the connection between the two, but after I talked to her tonight, we figured it was my mother leaving the money. Because after she approached them in church and started taking an active and financial role in Xavier's life, the envelopes stopped coming."

"So, is Esther going to tell Xavier? Did you two even talk about that?"

"We did. But I explained to her Kristina's situation. We're both concerned about how vulnerable she is at the moment. On one hand, I want to tell her this second. On the other, I can't help but wonder if it'd be better to wait until she's gone through rehab. I don't know…" Pam took a deep breath. "I don't know what to do."

"I do," Robin said. She took Pam's hand into her own. "We're going to pray. All night, if we have to. And by the time Kristina wakes up in the morning, we'll have some direction."

Pam's mind went back to the conversation she had with Pastor Thomas. *Cast all your cares on Him, for He cares for you.*

Robin was right. There was only one thing they *could* do. Have a little talk with Jesus.

꩜

Pam was surprised at how good she felt for having stayed up all night. She remembered hearing someone once say that the presence of God was refreshing. She could certainly testify to that. She and Robin had spent most of the night praying, reading the Bible and meditating on the Word. Initially, it was just so they could have some direction on when and how to tell Kristina, but it ended up being much more than that.

While she couldn't say that the night had erased all her negative feelings toward Mahalia, something had certainly changed.

The day before, all she could think about was what she and her sisters had lost: his first words, his first steps, his first solo.

But in the light of morning, she could see all the good that came out of it. He had incredibly loving parents. He grew up in church and loved God. He had older brothers that adored him. She and her sisters might have lost out, but he certainly gained more than he would have, had he stayed with them.

If she were honest about it, keeping Xavier might have

damaged him as much as living with Mahalia had damaged them.

Pam left the house the moment she turned eighteen, taking Kristina and Tamia with her. The three of them were just babies. They'd been so sheltered, they hardly knew enough to function on their own. Until Kristina landed the record deal, they were living well below the poverty line, sometimes going days without food to eat. Pam couldn't even imagine how they would have supported Xavier back then.

But even if they'd somehow managed to make it until the label picked Kristina up, the music industry was no place to bring up a child. She'd seen more celebrities' children struggle than the celebrities did themselves. It wasn't the kind of life they would've wanted for him.

The doorbell rang, pulling Pam from her thoughts.

She opened the door to a hotel staff member with a rolling cart and family-style breakfast. After tipping him, she and Robin started laying out the scrambled eggs, bacon, hash browns and pancakes. And just as they'd expected, in no time at all, Kristina and Tamia were coming out of their bedrooms looking like a couple of hungry bears just out of hibernation.

Tamia smiled upon seeing Robin. Kristina smiled upon seeing the food.

"Now that's what I'm talking about." She dropped down in one of the dining chairs and proceeded to stack her plate.

"Why are you two up so early?" Tamia asked. And then, before they had a chance to answer, she said, "And where were you all day yesterday? When did you get to bed?"

"I didn't." Pam said.

Both sisters looked up from their plates.

"Why not?"

"We were praying," Robin said, grabbing a couple of slices of bacon.

Kristina swallowed, her eyes wide. "All night?"

"Yep."

"Hmph." Kristina piled her fork. "Y'all go head on, then. I, for one, prefer my praying done during daylight hours."

After what was probably the most tension free meal the three sisters had had together in a long time, Kristina stood, stretched and announced she was going to her room to pack.

"What time am I supposed to report to rehab?"

"Any time during the next three days. I explained to them our situation and that I couldn't give them an exact time. But before you do that, we need to talk to you."

Kristina, already halfway to her bedroom, turned around. "Okay. What is it?"

Robin and Pam exchanged glances, then stood and went to where Kristina was, in the living area. Pam motioned at Tamia.

"Come on over here. This is something you need to hear, too."

Kristina narrowed her eyes. "Umm, this is sounding kind of serious. I already said I'd go to rehab. What else do you heifers want?"

She laughed, but nobody else did. Kristina rolled her eyes. "Next time y'all get together and pray, you need to ask God for a sense of humor."

Pam had peace about the decision to tell Kristina about Xavier. But that didn't keep her from feeling nervous. She had no idea how her sister was going to react and that scared her. She just kept repeating silently to herself, *cast your cares upon Him, cast your cares upon Him.*

But Kristina saw the anxiety on Pam's face. "What? What happened?"

Robin sat on the arm of the couch. "It's nothing bad, Kristina. In fact, it's good news."

Kristina put her hand on her hip and tilted her head toward them, obviously not convinced. "Well then, why are you two wearing the same expressions you had when I woke up in the hospital?"

This time it was Pam that spoke. "Because we don't want anything to interfere with your recovery and what we have to tell you… Well, it's life-changing."

Kristina eyed her warily. "If it might interfere with my recovery, then don't tell me."

"We considered that. But after a night of prayer, we're convinced that this is something you should know. In fact, if you let it, it might be the key to finally kicking this addiction once and for all."

Kristina shifted her gaze from Pam to Tamia. "Do you know about this?"

Tamia shook her head. She looked at Pam. "Just tell us."

Pam took a deep breath and decided to take the band aid pulling approach. The words came out in a rush.

"Your son didn't die that night, Kristina. He survived and his name is Xavier."

Chapter 18

Not only was Pam's revelation met with complete silence from Kristina, it got zero reaction. Tamia at least covered her mouth with her hands and looked at Robin, as if for some reassurance that she'd heard correctly.

Kristina, however, didn't do a thing. No tears. No histrionics. Nothing.

She stood there for a few moments, then walked to the couch and sat down. Robin moved to sit beside her and Pam knelt in front of her.

"Kristina?"

"Could you say that again, please?" Her voice was small and weak.

Pam reached up and put her hands on either side of Kristina's face. "Your son is alive. He's alive and doing good."

Ever so slightly, Kristina shook her head. Then she patted her chest, her words coming out small and airy. "I can't—I can't breathe."

Robin rubbed her back and Pam continued to talk to her.

"Look at me, Kris. Hey, look at me." Pam took in a slow, deep breath. "Come on. Do it with me. In. Out. Okay? Again. In. Out."

Kristina did as she was told and when she could inhale normally again, the dam broke. All three women surrounded her and held her as she wept.

"But I don't understand." Kristina pulled down the sleeves of her pajamas and used them to blot away the wetness on her face. "I saw him. He didn't move. And his face…" Kristina shut her eyes against the ugliness of the memory.

Pam shook her head and wiped away the tears on her sister's face. "I don't know the details. Mama took those to her grave. I can only assume that his throat wasn't cleared out or something like that."

"But how did you find this out?" Tamia said. "Did she put him up for adoption? Where is he?"

Pam got off her knees and sat on the coffee table opposite her sisters. "It looks like she left him with a nurse and her family. Longtime members of New Life. Apparently, she gave them financial support for his medical needs throughout the years."

"Medical needs?" Kristina said. "You just told us he was okay."

Robin patted her knee. "He *is* okay. But because he was a preemie, there were some medical problems early on."

Tamia stood and paced the floor off to the side of the couch. "Let me make sure I understand this. You're saying the baby lived and mama knew about it this whole time and never said a word? To any of us?"

Pam had expected there'd be anger. She'd felt it herself. But she thought for sure it would come from Kristina, not

Tamia. She couldn't remember ever seeing Tamia lose her temper. But from the looks of it, that's what was happening.

"What was done wasn't right, Tamia." Robin spoke in a soothing tone. "But we should probably focus on what's good—"

Tamia cut her off before she could finish. "I know! That he's alive. I get that. But it's no thanks to her, is it? He wouldn't have even been a preemie if she hadn't been kicking Kristina like she was something lower than a dog that day. And after she did that, she kept him a *secret*? She paid a few medical bills so we should just smile and say, oh, well, looks like it all worked out?"

Tamia's volume had risen to shouting. Pam could tell she was trying hard not to cry, but her voice kept catching in her throat. Pam stood and approached her, but Tamia backed away, her hands up.

"Not now, Pam. I can't." Tamia stormed to her bedroom and slammed the door behind her.

"He was her baby."

Pam turned back to Kristina. "What did you say?"

"That's what she used to call him. Her baby." Kristina shook her head. "I was so scared about what mama would do when she found out. There were times I actually wished I would just miscarry so she would never have to know. I would lie in bed at night and try to think of some solution, some way to make it okay. I would just end up crying out of frustration because there was no way out. Tamia heard me one night and crawled into my bed with me and hugged me. She told me not to worry and she made up these little stories about how great it would be, having him around."

Kristina smiled, remembering. "She said she would show him how to eat a doughnut and teach him how to walk." Kristina chuckled. "But she didn't want to teach him too soon, because until he learned how to walk, she wanted to carry him everywhere. Just like he was her baby." Kristina pressed the edge of her sleeve to the corner of her eyes. "Out of all of us, I think she might've missed him the most. In her imagination, they'd experienced a lifetime of memories and he hadn't even been born yet."

Pam sat in the chair nearest the couch. "I never knew that."

"Oh, yeah. I don't even know how many nights she spent in my bed, talking about him." Kristina shrugged. "But after he was born, she never mentioned him again. And knowing how much she'd wanted him, I couldn't bring it up."

Kristina exhaled and leaned over, burying her face in her hands.

"Did we do the right thing? Telling you?"

Kristina turned her red-rimmed eyes toward her sister and nodded. "It's just a lot to take in. I feel like I'm dreaming and somebody's gonna wake me any minute now and snatch it away."

Robin put her arm around Kristina's shoulder. "You're definitely not dreaming."

"What do you two know about him? Tell me everything. What's his name?"

"Xavier."

Kristina smiled. "Xavier. I like it."

"And he's such a sweetheart, Kristina. And handsome." Pam sat up. "Oh my goodness, I just remembered! You've seen him!"

"What? When?"

"At the repast. He was the young man that came with his brother. At the end of the line."

Kristina's eyes darted back and forth as she chewed on her lower lip. She shook her head. "I don't remember…"

"It was just before you went to the bathroom."

Kristina made a face and dropped her head back. "No! Please don't tell me it was that boy I cut off so I could go get high?"

Pam grimaced. "Believe me, he didn't see it that way. He's a huge fan."

Kristina leaned forward and buried her face in her hands again. "That's even worse. If what he sees on TV is who he thinks I am, can you imagine what a disappointment it'll be once he gets to know me?"

"Kristina…"

Kristina shook her head. "He doesn't know yet, right? Did mama tell him?"

"No. She didn't even tell him who she was."

"Good. He doesn't need to know. If what you say is true and he has a wonderful family and a good life, then I think we should leave well enough alone."

Pam shot a glance at Robin. "Wait, wait. Kristina, think about this first."

Kristina stood and pulled down on her pajama top. "I have thought about it. And I've made my decision. Him being alive and happy…" She covered her mouth with her hand and tears began streaming from her eyes again. "Him being alive and happy is a miracle in itself. I'm not going to be greedy. This is already more than I deserve."

Pam jumped up. "More than you deserve? You're his mother! Having him in your life is what you deserve."

"I've already decided, Pam. Please. *Please* don't make this harder than it already is."

With that, she retreated to her room and closed the door behind her.

Pam looked at Robin. "This is what we prayed all night long for?" She motioned at both of her sisters closed bedroom doors.

But Robin didn't look the least bit perturbed.

"We walk by faith, not by sight. Leave it alone and let God handle it."

Chapter 19

Despite herself, Pam decided to follow Robin's advice and leave the situation in God's hands.

Not that it was easy. What she really wanted to do was march into Kristina's room and change her mind. But she had to trust that God knew what was best for all of them, Xavier included. Besides, no matter her opinion, she was just his aunt. Ultimately, the final decision belonged to his mother.

Instead, she turned her attention to doing her job as Kristina's manager. She made a call to the jet sharing service that they sometimes used and confirmed their flight out that night. She did the same with the rehab center and returned a few business calls. Then, she packed her clothes and got in the shower.

She hadn't realized how much she needed one. The hot water seemed to wash away all the tension her body had held onto for the past twenty-four hours.

When she'd decided to do the retreat, she'd hoped for change. Of course, she had no idea just how much they'd endure before it was all over. The past few days had been something like an emotional hurricane.

From revealing their secrets to Robin, to going back to the old house, to discovering the biggest tragedy of their lives had been a lie—Pam knew it was only the grace of God that kept each of them from completely spinning out. And they were going to have to continue to lean on that grace in the days to come.

Walking away from Xavier was going to be one of the hardest things she'd ever done. And she was just his aunt. She couldn't imagine what Kristina was going through. But she was proud of her sister for putting him first. She understood that Kristina was only staying away because she thought it was best for him. But that didn't mean it'd be easy.

Still, Pam wasn't willing to give up hope just yet. Maybe rehab would make a difference for Kristina. Maybe getting her life together would give her the courage to know her son. Either way, Pam remained firm in her commitment to leave it in God's hands.

After drying off and getting dressed, Pam came out of the bathroom to find Tamia sitting on her bed.

Her eyes were red and puffy and she avoided looking Pam directly in the eye. "I'm sorry."

"Don't be." Pam went to her sister, sat next to her and took her into her arms. "I felt exactly the same way you did when I found out."

Tamia nodded and tried to blink back the tears. "What's he like? When do we get to meet him?"

Pam hesitated. "We don't." Tamia's face dropped. "At least, not yet."

"Why? Is it his parents? Do they want us to stay away?"

"It's me."

Tamia and Pam swiveled around to see Kristina leaning against the door frame to Pam's bedroom.

"Pam said he's happy. I think we should just let him be."

Tamia looked devastated. "So, that's it? He's the only living relative we have and we just pretend he doesn't exist?"

Pam rubbed Tamia's arm. "That's not what we're doing. It's not like we're abandoning him. And who knows? Maybe one day…" Pam's voice trailed off when Kristina shot her a withering glare.

"But that's not fair. I don't even get to see him? So, the only memory I'll ever have of my nephew is as a stillborn, premature baby?"

Pam glanced at Kristina. When she made a decision it was nearly impossible to talk her out of it. It was a well known and much despised fact among record producers and label executives. Once Kristina Langston laid down a law, it was written in stone. And nobody, not *nobody*, could change her mind.

But that was Kristina Langston, the superstar diva. Pam saw Kristina Langston, the doting big sister, wavering in her resolve. Pam took it as a sign.

She looked back at Tamia. "So, you're saying that you'd be okay with just seeing him? Not approaching him, not talking to him, not telling him who you are, but just *seeing* him?"

Tamia nodded. "That's all I want." She looked at Kristina, pleading in her eyes. "I just want to see him with my own eyes and I promise, after that, I won't bring it up again."

Kristina took a deep breath. "And how is she supposed to do that, Pam? How is she supposed to see him without him knowing something's up?"

"Well, actually," Pam said, a smile spread across her face.

"Tonight is the musical in honor of mama. And he's one of the featured singers."

Kristina straightened up. "He sings?"

"He does. And he's good, Kristina. Really good."

Kristina's eyebrows furrowed as she considered it.

"Please, Kris. Just this once."

Kristina's resolve was no match for her baby sister's puppy dog eyes.

"Okay. Just this once. But if you two go, I'm going with you."

Chapter 20

As they passed through the administrative area of New Life Tabernacle and on toward the sanctuary, the Langston sisters could hear a rousing rendition of one of their mother's songs. And from the response of the congregation, the choir was setting the house on fire.

Pam kept her eye on Kristina, just as she had during the ride over from the hotel. At least twice, Pam thought her sister would change her mind and order them back to the suite. Even now, Pam still wasn't convinced Kristina would go through with it. She reached for her sister's hand.

"How are you doing?"

Kristina looked at her and smiled. It wasn't just any smile, but the one she reserved for award shows and on-screen appearances. The dazzling one that never failed to make people fall in love with her. But Pam knew what it really was—the mask that she wore when it was time to be the superstar.

Kristina squeezed her sister's hand. "How many times you gonna ask that question?"

"How many times you gonna avoid giving me a straight answer?"

"I'm fine. Really. But so we're all clear," she said, reaching for Tamia, who was steps ahead of them, eagerly following the minister ushering them to their seats. "We're not staying long. Ten minutes. Fifteen minutes max and then we go."

Before they knew it, they were standing at the side door of the sanctuary where the pastors and dignitaries usually came in.

"You look beautiful," Pam whispered to Kristina. She smiled at Pam again, but this time it wasn't the smile of a superstar. It was the far less confident half smile of her anxious, younger sister.

"Okay, ladies." Kristina took a deep breath. "Let's do this."

The minister opened the side door for them and they walked through to find the musical in full swing. The place was packed. Like their mother's funeral, it was standing room only, save for a segment of the front pew to the left side sectioned off by a velvet rope and a sign that read *RESERVED*.

The congregation was caught up in the choir's current selection and just about every person there was rocking, clapping and stomping their feet.

The choir finished the song and the crowd broke out into shouts and applause. The sisters settled into their seats, seemingly unnoticed by most, save for the dignitaries on their same pew and maybe a few people in the row behind them.

But that all changed when the Master of Ceremonies, the same man that had presided over the funeral, saw them. He jumped up and snatched the mic out of the hands of the featured soloist.

"Ladies and gentlemen, before we continue on with this fine concert, let's take a moment to acknowledge and welcome the daughters of the very woman we honor here tonight. Kristina Langston, Pam Langston, and Tamika Langston!"

The congregation roared with applause and shouts.

Tamia leaned over to her sisters. "Did he really just call me Tamika?"

"That's it! That's it! Make 'em feel welcome!"

Reluctantly, all three women stood, turned to face the crowd and waved.

Once everyone had settled down, the organist started playing the music for the new song and the concert was back underway.

Tamia leaned in once again. "Which one is he?" Her eyes darted back and forth as she searched the faces in the tenor section.

Pam pulled in Kristina so she could hear what she was saying to Tamia. "He's over with the musicians. The young man in the red tie, on the keyboard."

Pam's eyes welled up with tears as she watched her sisters' expressions. Kristina could only look for a few moments before turning away, blinking back tears. But Tamia, much like Pam, couldn't stop staring.

Tamia reached over Pam's lap and held Kristina's hand. "He's so handsome."

When she was finally able to pull her gaze away from him, she turned her attention to Pam. "When is his song? Is it coming up soon?"

"No. His is the last one."

"The last one of the entire musical?" Tamia's face fell. She looked back up at him and then Kristina. "The concert is at least halfway over. Can't we just stay until the end?"

Kristina sat back in her seat and exhaled. Before she

could say no, Tamia added, "*Please*, Kristina. I never ask for anything. Just let me have this."

That was it. Pam knew it. There was no way Kristina would be able to say no.

"We stay until he sings, but we're out before the benediction. I don't want to be stuck up in some three-hour meet and greet, you hear me?"

If she could have, Pam was sure Tamia would have grabbed Kristina by the head and kissed her face. Grinning ear to ear, she stood and started clapping and swaying along with the rest of the congregation.

Pam nudged Kristina with her elbow. Kristina only acknowledged her with a sidelong glance before saying, "What?"

"You know what. Thank you."

Kristina nodded and tapped her foot to the beat.

After a break for offering and a few more selections, the moment they'd all been waiting for finally arrived. Xavier made his way to the mic, giving Pam a little wave as he did.

Pam didn't know if it was their presence or that he was singing in front of a packed house, but she could tell he was nervous. He kept running his hands down the side of his slacks, as if he were drying them.

The organist played the opening notes of the song and the piano came in shortly after. Kristina grabbed Pam's wrist.

"This is the song me and mama did."

Pam nodded. Kristina put her fingers over her mouth and waited.

Xavier started singing and, unlike the songs performed earlier that evening, the sanctuary became still. And for good reason. What Pam heard in rehearsal was nothing compared to what she experienced at that moment.

She hadn't been in a church service in years, but she'd never forgotten what it felt like when the presence of God blanketed a room. A hush fell over the congregation and hands started going up all over the building in reverent worship.

Pam couldn't help but feel everything had led to that most holy moment.

From Xavier's birth to her mother's secret, from Kristina's overdose and now, to this song. There was a healing taking place in each of their lives. She could see it in her sister's eyes when she looked at them. She could feel it in her own heart, as well. Before long, the three of them were on their feet, hands raised like everyone else.

Pam closed her eyes and just let it wash over her. She let herself completely drown, body, soul and spirit, in the immeasurable love of God. It was like water in the desert. The one thing her soul had longed for and for much too long.

She felt the air stir and opened her eyes to see Kristina on her knees. Her arms wrapped around herself, rocking back and forth and crying out to God. It was something she never imagined she'd see. Just a few days ago, she'd watched paramedics roll out what looked like a corpse on a gurney. Now, she was seeing God bring a complete soul restoration.

The song ended and the music stopped, but the worship didn't. Pam didn't know how long it went on because it seemed as if time stopped. They had all somehow entered into a place between heaven and earth and no one wanted to leave. Even when they all came down from the high that was the presence of God, the space felt so sacred, no one wanted to disturb it.

There was no official benediction. Instead, people spoke

quietly to one another as they gathered their belongings and left the building.

Pam and Tamia helped Kristina up and the three of them embraced. They felt light enough to fly. It was as if every chain and shackle they'd carried since childhood had been broken in one fell swoop.

Pam felt a light tap on her shoulder. She turned around to find Xavier standing next to her.

"Thank you for coming." Then he smiled at Kristina and Tamia. "Thank you to all of you."

He looked directly at Kristina. "I know that was the only song you ever recorded with your mother. I hope I did it justice."

"You did. Trust me. You did."

A blush spread across his cheeks and he dipped his head, a grin on his face. "I'm glad."

Then, just before he walked away, Kristina reached out and pulled him toward her, hugging him. From the expression on his face, Pam could see he was surprised.

And that he had no idea he was actually hugging his birth mother.

Kristina drew back and put her hands on the sides of his face.

"You have been given a gift from God. And you're going to use it to change many lives. You've already changed mine."

Chapter 21

Six weeks later...

Kristina sat on the edge of her bed, legs crossed and holding the phone between her ear and shoulder.

"I know I signed the contract, but that was *before* I decided to go to rehab."

"Well, I don't know what else to tell you," Pam said on the other end of the line. "The production company is not interested in whether or not you've changed your mind. All they care about is the fact that they have your name on the dotted line. So, you either do the show or we get sued. It's as simple as that."

Even though her sister was hundreds of miles away, Kristina could imagine the look of utter frustration on her face. They had been going back and forth about this throughout Kristina's stay in rehab.

A couple of months before her mother passed away,

Kristina had agreed to let The Muse Network cameras follow her for a behind-the-scenes miniseries on this latest tour. At the time, it looked like a great opportunity. The announcement and the publicity surrounding it, had created major buzz and increased ticket sales.

And that was no small thing. She hadn't been on tour for so long, even the record company was concerned it might not do well. The press release promising backstage access had proven them all wrong.

But that was before rehab. Before the retreat. Before she ended up on the bathroom floor of Dallas's finest hotel. Before her mother died.

And before Xavier.

She'd come a long way in only six weeks and she had God to thank for that. But she was still a work-in-progress. She was grateful to have a second chance at life, but she hadn't been prepared for what it'd be like to be clean. There was nothing to hide behind. Nothing to create a wall of protection between herself and the rest of the world. She couldn't remember the last time she'd felt so exposed, so vulnerable. It was a frightening experience, to say the least.

And although she had told her sisters she had every intention of staying out of Xavier's life, with each passing day, she wondered if it were possible to rethink that decision. But if that was the plan, she had to make some changes. Real, lasting changes.

She also had to think long-term. The last thing she wanted was Xavier to think of her as a failure. But with everything that had happened and the fact that she was going to be fresh out of rehab, she wasn't so sure she could keep it a secret. Especially with cameras following her around twenty-four-seven.

"I don't need the added stress of an entire production

crew with me all the time, Pam. Not right now. What I need to focus on is this tour. I'm already behind schedule because of the funeral and having to be in here."

Pam sighed. "Kristina, your fans are the most loyal out there. You know that. Maybe instead of trying to keep it a secret, you should just tell everyone. *Before* the production crew gets here. Because I know that's what you're worried about. Isn't it?"

Kristina rolled her eyes. Pam always thought she knew everything. Unfortunately, she was usually right.

"Get out in front of the story. Tell it yourself so you can control the spin. You might be surprised at the show of support you get."

Kristina snorted.

Support? Yeah, right. She'd be the butt of every late night talk show host's opening joke. She'd be the gossip on the ticker tape running along the bottom of the screen on the E! Network. She was sure to get plenty of attention. Unwanted attention, at that. But support? Not likely.

It hurt to know that there were complete strangers making judgments about her on hundreds of forums, blogs and comments sections online. It was painful to hear daytime talk show hosts using her failures to make their audiences laugh. But it wasn't as if it was her first time. She'd been through all of that and much more.

But things were different now. Now, every time she heard a cutting remark or biting judgment, all she could think about was Xavier and what his reaction might be.

In group, the therapist talked repeatedly about the harm of keeping secrets and the masks that addicts wore. About how each of them needed to confront their true selves.

It sounded good. The idea of coming out and telling her story, of not having to hide anymore, sounded wonderful.

Keeping secrets was exhausting. Always trying to be the person people thought she was, was hard to do. But even though she knew her therapist was right, her thoughts kept returning to Xavier. If she was ever going to be a part of his life, could it really be as the person she was? Not Kristina Langston, the singer. But, Kristina Langston, the drug addict?

It was a decision she'd been teetering on the edge of for the entirety of her stay. It was time she made her choice.

Kristina exhaled and brought her feet up so she could lie down on her bed. "Okay. Tell them the show is back on. And I'll think about issuing a statement like you said."

She could hear Pam breathe a sigh of relief. "Okay, good. Good. I'll work on a rough draft so when you come home, you can look over it and tell me what you think."

"What time are you guys coming tomorrow?"

"I'll be there in the afternoon. But Tamia should be there today. Girl, I had to talk her out of busting you out of rehab more than once." Pam chuckled. "She really missed you. She left early so she could help you pack."

Tears slid down the side of Kristina's face and soaked the fabric of her pillowcase. She didn't know why her sisters loved her so much, but she sure was grateful they did.

"All right, then. I'll see you tomorrow. I love you."

"I love you, too."

Kristina reached over to the nightstand separating her and her roommate's bed and returned the phone to its cradle. She stretched out on her back and stared at the ceiling.

The group therapist was right. So was Pam. She needed to stop living behind a mask. But she couldn't bring herself to do that and still reach out to Xavier.

Up until this point in his life, he'd had a mother and father he could be proud of. A family anyone would want to belong to. She was the absolute opposite of that. She couldn't imagine anyone ever being proud of being related to her. And once she issued the statement and put the truth out there for public consumption, that would be doubly true. Why should she burden him with that?

Kristina exhaled and covered her face with her forearm.

She had to stop hiding and make a commitment to living a life of honesty and integrity. It was the only way she was going to stay clean. And while she was ready and willing to do that, it meant sticking by her original decision to leave Xavier alone.

"Help me do this, God," she whispered.

She had no doubt He would. But it still broke her heart to know that after the press release and the news of her rehab stay broke, she'd never be anything more to Xavier than the popstar he used to admire.

❦

"Kristina!"

Kristina opened her eyes as her roommate, a country singer from Nashville named Savannah, bounced through the door.

"I thought you weren't leaving until tomorrow. I can't believe you weren't going to say goodbye!" Savannah jumped on Kristina's bed. The twentysomething had hair the color of fire and a personality to match. She and Kristina had leaned on each other a lot during their stay. She was one of the two people Kristina would greatly miss.

"I'm not leaving till tomorrow."

Savannah shook her head. "Not according to the front desk. Your family is already here."

Kristina got up and headed toward the door. "It's just my

sister. She's here to help me pack. I'll be right back. I want to introduce you."

Kristina made her way to the front desk and leaned over the counter. Behind it was the other person she dreaded having to say goodbye to, a nurse named Barbara.

"Hey, pretty girl!"

Barbara had called her that from the day she arrived. She wasn't sure why, since she'd spent most of her time there with dark circles under her eyes or her head over a toilet. It could've just been because there were so many patients, Barbara couldn't remember Kristina's name. Either way, it still made her smile.

"Savannah said my sister was here."

The phone rang and Barbara picked it up, whispering as she did, "In the visitor's lounge, baby."

Kristina turned the corner and continued down the hall, giddy over the fact she was going to finally see family. Although she'd only been gone a little over a month, it felt like forever.

She opened the double doors, then stopped dead in her tracks.

It was family, all right. But it wasn't Tamia.

Chapter 22

Xavier was holding a large bouquet of Gerber daisies. And although he was smiling, he approached her slowly and cautiously, as if he were afraid to scare her away.

"I read these were your favorite flowers."

She opened her mouth to speak, but failed. She could only imagine what the look on her face must've been. But if Xavier's own expression was any indication, it had to be something between mortified and furious.

"Please don't be mad." Xavier's voice was almost a whisper. "And please, don't send me away. Again."

Again…

The word brought tears to Kristina's eyes. She never wanted him to feel like she'd abandoned him. Not even once, much less twice.

"How?" It was the best she could do. The most she could

get out, but even then, it was more like a breath than an actual word.

"Your mom. Mother Langston. She left me everything. Did you know that?"

Kristina nodded.

"There was also a letter. She said you were really young and had a hard life. She asked me to forgive her and to not blame you. Not that I ever would have anyway."

Kristina shook her head. *Unbelievable.* Even from her grave, Mahalia Marie Langston had to control things. It wasn't enough that she had kept the secret, she even had to be the one to decide how it was going to come out.

Kristina clenched her fists at her sides and started counting backwards. She'd learned all sorts of techniques to deal with her emotions rather than reach for a powder filled baggie. But at the moment, none of those techniques proved very useful.

"She shouldn't have done that. It wasn't her secret to share. She had no right to tell you. Especially when she hadn't even told me."

"I understand." Xavier reached out to touch her, but pulled his hand back. "She explained that you and your sisters wouldn't know until after she'd died." He stopped and looked at the floor. "I know I probably shouldn't be here. I figured as much when I talked to Pam and—"

"Wait. Pam knew you were coming here?"

Why in the world would she not warn her? Especially since they had just been on the phone not ten minutes ago?

"No, no, no. She has no idea. I was just trying to get a feel for things. To find out what she knew. I tried to ask about you without being specific and she dodged me so much I eventually put two and two together. Your collapse at the hotel and then no one seeing or hearing from you, even a month later.

I have this friend… Well," he said, rubbing the back of his neck. "He likes to call himself an information archaeologist."

Kristina folded her arms and arched an eyebrow. "In other words, a hacker?"

Xavier gave her a lopsided grin. "Yeah, something like that. He helped me track you down."

Kristina stood there a moment, studying his face. She couldn't believe he had come all this way alone. And for her. Even after knowing what she was. *Who* she was.

She reached out and took the flowers from him. She held them close to her face and let the velvety soft pedals caress her cheek. "They're beautiful."

His face lit up like the sun. She took his hand and guided him to the bank of seats along the wall and both sat down.

"This isn't just some one-off incident. It's not like I'm one of those people who had a surgery and then got addicted to pain pills for a couple of months. This is cocaine and alcohol and…" She bit at her lip and looked down, unable to meet his eyes. "I'm not that woman you see on stage. She's just an image. I'm really just the girl that got knocked up at sixteen, then turned to drugs and partying to deal with the aftermath. My voice isn't what it used to be thanks to all that and the smoking. And now, there are more people who *don't* know who I am, than do. I can't fill stadiums like I used to. Lately, I can hardly even keep myself together."

Reluctantly, she looked back up at him, dreading the judgment she was certain she'd find in his face.

"I have an irregular heartbeat. I don't take my shirt off in front of people because I've got scars left over from surgery. I have an inexplicable addiction to pickles. I watch My Little Pony with my baby cousin and I like it. As Aaliyah once said, you got issues, I got issues…"

He stared back at Kristina, solemn and earnest. She kept

a straight face for all of three seconds before she folded over laughing. He joined her.

"Look, you may think I'm just a kid, but I'm old enough to know that nobody's perfect. I don't need perfect. I just need my mom."

Kristina shrugged, nearly too overcome to get the words out.

"Here I am."

Kristina opened her arms and he fell into them. Her laughter was mixed with tears, but for the first time in a long time, they were tears of joy.

Chapter 23

Omar Williams loosened the knot of his tie with one hand while working the tv remote with the other. He pressed the DOWN button repeatedly, flipping through channels, giving each no more than two seconds of his attention. But when he saw a face he recognized, he quickly flipped back to take another look.

"… confirmed Langston's recent stay in rehab when she issued a statement earlier this month."

The voice of the entertainment reporter covering the story was played over video footage of Kristina Langston leaving an apartment building in New York City, surrounded by a couple of bodyguards and a sea of paparazzi.

Omar sat on the couch, unwilling to take his eyes off the screen.

"But that's not what has everyone talking. The mystery currently blowing up Facebook and Twitter is the identity of the hot and decidedly younger "protégé" that she's been seen out and about with."

Omar stood and came close to the tv to get a better look at the guy wearing sunglasses and a hoodie. In the video footage and pictures being shown, he was glued to Kristina's side.

"The young man and Langston have been inseparable since her stay at rehab, according to sources. And although little is known as to how the couple met, it's apparent that Kristina's got her groove back."

Omar pushed the power button and turned off the TV.

Rehab?

That would explain the incident at the hotel last winter. The news footage of her being rushed out of that Dallas hotel was one of the most horrifying things he'd ever watched. People had speculated all sorts of causes, but he figured it was probably an overdose. After all Kristina had told him about life with their mother, he wasn't surprised that she'd turned to substance abuse to deal.

What did surprise him was the twinge he felt at the mention of this new "protégé". It wasn't as if he had any right to be jealous. What he and Kristina shared ended nearly twenty years ago. And it's not like he'd been single all that time, either.

True, he was divorced now, but what difference did that make? He and Kristina Langston were worlds apart. And if this young man was the key to her happiness and getting clean, then more power to her.

He was truly happy for her. Just like he was every other time he heard about some new actor or singer she was seeing.

Omar went to the kitchen, grabbed the bag of takeout from the counter and shoved it into the fridge. Then he turned off all the lights and headed up the stairs to his bedroom.

All the while, he reassured himself that his sudden loss of

appetite and instant exhaustion were due to the long day he'd had at work and not Kristina Langston's love life.

He thought if he kept telling himself it was so, eventually, he'd be able to believe it.

THEN Sings MY Soul

The Langston Family Saga: Book 2

Chapter 1

Kristina Langston sat on the floor of the linen closet and peeked through the slats of the door. When she was sure she hadn't been followed, she took out her phone and tapped the first name listed on her call history.

"Hello?"

Kristina smiled. Even the sound of his voice brought her joy. Having Xavier in her life was better than any drug she'd taken or award she'd won. Every thought of him was a reminder of how incredibly good God was.

"Hey, baby! Sorry I couldn't pick up earlier."

"Um, it's okay... Why are you whispering?"

"I'm hiding in the closet."

Kristina had to cover the phone in an effort to muffle the howling laughter that came through from the other side. Then she had to cover her own mouth for the same reason.

"Hold up," Xavier said, still laughing. "It sounded like you said you were hiding in the closet!"

"I did! And if you don't stop making me laugh, I'm gonna get busted."

"Please explain to me why America's Queen of Pop is hiding in a closet."

"It's that dumb reality show."

"Oh, yeah. The one about the tour."

"Yep."

"Why in the world are they making you hide in a closet?"

"It wasn't their idea. *They're* the ones I'm hiding from. They're like stalkers, X. Worse than the paparazzi. Especially the producer's assistant. This little girl named Amy. I caught her waiting outside the bathroom door last time I went!"

"Maybe she really had to go," Xavier said, now laughing harder than before.

"And that explains why she had her ear to the door? Uh… no. I don't think so."

"Wait. She had her ear to the door? Why?"

Kristina sighed. "You know, the usual. That producer is hoping for a little more than behind-the-scenes footage. I think he's hoping for Dallas."

"Oh."

"Yeah."

Neither she nor Xavier had ever brought up her overdose in Dallas. Knowing that it took place right after the first inter-action she'd ever had with her son made Kristina cringe. Even now, months later, it hurt to think about it. A few moments passed in silence.

"How are you doing? I know you got a lot going on with this show and the tour. You okay?"

"Yeah, I'm good. I've been reading my Bible every day and I talk to Robin on a regular basis. I'm handling it. You don't have to worry. They may want Dallas, but they're not gonna get it."

"I'm really proud of you."

Kristina felt warmth spread across her cheeks. "Thanks. That means a lot, baby."

She heard Xavier take a deep breath. "Hey. I, um, wanted to talk to you about something…"

Kristina's gut clenched. She had a pretty good idea what it was Xavier wanted to talk about. She'd been dreading the conversation since he'd come to see her at rehab.

"I was wondering—"

Before he could finish his sentence, Kristina stopped him. She thought she'd heard the laundry room door open, then close. She ducked her head to peek between the slats again. All she could make out was gray, loose fitting slacks coming straight toward her. Seconds later, the linen closet door opened.

"Scoot over!" Pam nudged Kristina with her foot as she squeezed into the closet with her.

"What are you doing?"

"What does it look like I'm doing? Same as you. Hiding from Amy!" Pam sat on the floor and sucked her teeth. "Has it really come to this? Grown women hiding in a linen closet? I should have killed the contract for the show like you wanted me to. A lawsuit would have been preferable to this mess!"

"Aunt Pam?"

Pam stiffened and shot a glance at Kristina. Kristina held up her phone for Pam to see. Pam grabbed her chest and then the phone.

"Xavier? Boy, you scared me!"

Again, Xavier's laughter filled the small space.

"Oh man, I wish I was there right now. I'd give anything to see the two of you packed in a closet like a couple of sardines."

"Shut up."

Kristina covered her mouth to stifle her laughter. Xavier didn't even try.

"You two are just alike," Pam said into the phone while cutting her eyes at Kristina. "Messy. Both of you."

Just then, the laundry door opened once more. Pam stuffed the phone under her thigh. Kristina lowered her head to look through the slats and saw Amy poking around. A few moments later, the girl walked back out.

"She's gone," Kristina breathed.

Pam picked up the phone, but the call had been disconnected. Kristina cocked her head to the side.

"Did your big ol' thigh hang up on my son?"

"Shut up."

Pam felt for Kristina's hand in the darkness and returned the phone.

"I don't know how much more of this I can take. That little girl is driving me crazy."

While Pam ran through all the possible solutions to their Amy problem, Kristina tried to think through one of her own. She was sure Xavier wanted her to help him find his father. But while Kristina loved her son with all her heart, she couldn't think of anything she wanted to do less.

"Is this more like what you gentlemen had in mind?"

Omar Williams looked around the somewhat dilapidated house and nodded. "It's a definite possibility."

The young real estate agent that had asked the question, blushed. "I'm so glad! Let me show you around."

She reached for Omar's elbow just as his friend and business partner, Brock Collier, spoke up.

"Can you give us a few moments?"

She froze, mid-reach for Omar's arm, a pained expression on her face. But she quickly recovered with a smile and chirped, "Of course! I'll be right outside. Just holler if you need me."

When she'd gone out the front door and closed it behind her, Omar found Brock staring at him.

"What?"

"I was just wondering if I should check your arm for bruises. She's been hanging off it every chance she gets. If we look at any more houses today, you might have to have her surgically removed."

Omar fought a grin and opened the coat closet door to look inside. "Don't start with me, man."

"You *did* notice she's interested, right? I know women usually have to send up flares to get your attention, but she looks like she just stepped off a Victoria's Secret runway. Please tell me you noticed that."

Omar walked through the living room and into the kitchen, Brock close behind. He opened one of the cabinet doors and knocked on it. "Real wood. And in good shape, too. We'd just have to paint them."

"She probably works out. Did you see how tight her a—"

"But these countertops will have to go." Omar said, cutting Brock off before turning down the hall and entering a bedroom. "We should make the windows bigger. Let in more light. It'll open up the smaller rooms."

"What we *should* do," Brock said, standing in the doorway, hands stuffed in his pockets, "is talk about your inability to recognize a beautiful woman making passes at you."

Omar took out a tape measure and anchored the end at a corner of the room. "Sure. Right after we talk about your inability to shadow a church door."

Brock dismissed Omar with a wave of his hand. "Man, I

already told you a million times. If I step foot inside a church, I'll get struck down in two seconds flat."

Omar adjusted the measuring tape to a new position and snorted.

"Besides, those sermons are too long. You know how black folks are. They make church an all day event. Now if you become Catholic at some point, I might reconsider."

Omar clicked a button and the measuring tape snapped back into its casing. "You're wrong, man."

"I know. That's what I'm trying to tell you." Brock followed Omar to the hall and into a small bathroom.

"I'm not asking you to come every Sunday. But you should be there for the house donations. It's once every two months. Six times a year. You could do that. It would give the families a chance to thank you." Omar leaned over and turned on the tub spout. "We'll need new fittings on this."

"Naw, man. I'm good. They thank you enough for the both of us."

Omar straightened up and folded his arms. "You could at least come this Sunday." He held up an index finger. "One time. You're already coming to my house for the party afterwards. You might as well."

Brock's eyes lit up. "Oh, yeah! Miss Chloe's birthday!" He rubbed his hands together and grinned. "I've been looking forward to this. Tell me. Just how many hot and ready single mothers you got coming to this thing?"

Omar shook his head and went back to the hallway. "Besides Marisa?"

Brock dropped his head and groaned. "Why did you even have to bring her up? Especially when I was having such a great day."

"Because," Omar said, stepping into another bedroom. "I'm talking to both of you about this. No beef, you hear me?

There's going to be a lot of children there and I want Chloe to have a good time. Don't make me have to kick you two out of my house. This is not a joke. You act up, that's exactly what I'll do. Understood?"

Brock sighed. "Understood. I won't throw any buckets of water at the wicked witch until the next time I see her."

"See? That right there. Don't. I mean it, Brock. Either of you even looks at the other one sideways and I'll show you the door."

Brock put his hands up in surrender. "Fine. I'll avoid her. I promise."

"Thank you." Omar knelt down and pulled up the carpet in one corner of the bedroom. "Looks like we got hardwood down here." He stood. "If the master is good, I think we should make this our next donation house."

Brock nodded, but remained silent.

Omar stopped in front of him. "What? You gonna pout now?"

"You just told me no fighting with Marisa. What do you expect?"

Omar couldn't help but snicker as he made his way to the master bedroom.

"Hey," Brock called as he followed. "We've got a few buyers on the Centre Street property. I think we should take it to negotiations."

Omar went into the master bedroom and nodded. "Okay. Have it scheduled."

Brock made a note on his iPad. "And we are definitely a go on this one?"

"I say yes. You?"

Brock nodded. "Looks good to me." Then, with a mischievous glint in his eye, he added, "I'll go get your arm candy. Should I give you two some time alone?"

Omar grinned. "I don't know. Should I give you directions to my church?"

Brock pressed his lips together and slowly shook his head. "You really know how to ruin my day, don't you?"

Chapter 2

Kristina brought the warm mug of steaming Earl Grey tea to her nose and inhaled. The morning light came through the huge bay window at the breakfast nook where she sat and outside, birds happily chirped their sweet sounding song.

The golden sunlight that filtered in was the perfect complement to the neutral tones of the French Country style kitchen that surrounded her. She'd had the space completely remodeled years ago, while on the road. But it wasn't until the last few months that she'd come to fully appreciate it. Turned out there was no better place for early morning one-on-one time with her heavenly Father.

Although it had become her daily routine, the peace and calm she felt each daybreak as she read her Bible and meditated on God's Word was something she was still getting used to. For the first time in her life, she understood why it was called *being born again*. She felt like an entirely new person.

The thought brought a smile to her lips. Wasn't that what the Word said? *Old things are passed away, all things are made new...*

She was repeating those words, letting them soak down into her spirit, when Pam came through the archway and into the kitchen.

Kristina reluctantly put down her cup of tea.

"I know that look. It's the one you get right before you tell me something I don't wanna hear."

Pam didn't deny it. She sat across from Kristina and folded one hand over the other. "Okay. You know the promotion I told you about? The one the record company wanted to do?"

"Vaguely. What about it?"

Pam shifted in her seat. "This is the thing, Krissi. Right now, everyone's nervous. You haven't toured in a while. There's been a death in the family. Then there was the…incident at the hotel. Not to mention rehab."

Kristina still couldn't tell where this was going but she was even more sure she wasn't gonna like it. "Yeah…"

"TMZ, the entertainment blogs, the so-called press—they're all waiting to see what's going to happen next. Whether you'll be able to deliver on the first stop of the tour. There's already been some speculation and promoters are worried that all the rumors will affect ticket sales."

Kristina nodded. This was something she'd expected. Everyone had. Of course, people were curious to know what would happen next. Her life had become a primetime drama straight out of Shondaland.

"So, they had this idea for you to have a—I don't know—call it a pre-tour warm-up. Smaller than what you're doing on the tour itself. A more intimate venue, packed with only hard-core fans. Kinda like what they do in the theater world with the review night. They're hoping it'll give you a chance to perform post-rehab, but under less pressure. And they're hoping those hard-core fans will spread the word via social media and let everyone know that you're still doing your thing, rehab or not."

Knowing that such an in-depth explanation was Pam's way of stalling, Kristina waited for the hammer to drop.

"And…"

"And, it's actually a really great idea for several reasons. All proceeds after costs are being donated to that charity you worked with last year. The official name of the promotion is *Show Some Love*. And what they did is, well, whichever city showed you the most love in the online contest would win the performance. It's actually kind of clever. They show you love, you show them love, you all show the charity love—"

Kristina rolled her head back in exasperation. "Pam! Just spit it out already!"

Pam dropped her head to her shoulder and exhaled. She took out her phone and tapped the screen. "The city that won was the one you haven't performed in since your first tour."

She slid the phone across the table. Kristina looked down at the screen and saw the header of her record label's website. Under it was her smiling face and a banner that read:

Congratulations, Dallas, Texas! You showed Kristina the most love and Orion Records is thanking you with an exclusive one night only performance before the official tour kicks off!

"Are you serious right now?"

All traces of the morning's previous peace and calm evaporated.

Yes, old things had passed away, but that didn't mean

Kristina's feelings about her hometown had gone with them. There was a reason she avoided the Metroplex at all costs. When she'd been there a few months ago, it was only because her mother had died and she had no choice but to attend the funeral.

"Before you get started, I've already tried to change it. But there's no way around it. Dallas won. You're doing a show there, like it or not."

"But what—"

Before Kristina could finish her sentence, Tamia swooped in to the kitchen, a tablet in hand.

Pam sat up. "When did you get here?"

Instead of answering, Tamia folded back the tablet case into a stand and set it on the table. She turned it in Kristina and Pam's direction. The two sisters were greeted by a very uncomfortable looking Xavier on the screen.

Tamia leaned over the tablet so the top of her face was visible to the camera. "Just do it."

"Do what?" Pam asked.

Kristina looked from Xavier to Tamia and back to Xavier again. "What happened? What's wrong?"

Xavier gave them a weak smile and waved. "Hey, Aunt Pam. Hi, Krissi." He hesitated. "Nothing's wrong…"

Tamia snatched up the tablet and turned it to face her. "Xavier, no one's going to bite your head off. Just ask." She turned the tablet so Xavier and her sisters were again facing each other.

Pam leaned her crossed arms onto the table. "Xavier, if there's something you need, you know you can always come to us. About anything."

He nodded in acknowledgment but didn't take his eyes off Kristina. But because she'd just realized what the video call was about, Kristina didn't take her eyes off her cup of tea.

Xavier took a deep breath and exhaled. "I'd like to meet my biological father."

Pam looked at Kristina, who was still staring at her mug. Then Pam shot a look at Tamia.

"Okay," Pam said slowly. "We have no idea where he is, but we could give you his name. Or I could hire someone to locate him."

Xavier bit his lip and gave a slight nod.

"Better yet," she said, reaching across the table and touching Kristina's hand. "We could call Robin. If his family still goes to New Life Tabernacle, she could put you in touch with them."

Kristina nodded. "I can call Robin."

"Yeah. Tamia and I talked about that."

Both sisters glanced at Tamia, but their faces remained passive, aware that Xavier could see their every move.

"But here's the thing—you guys didn't even know about me. So what are the chances that he does? I just keep thinking I'll be on the phone with this guy and he'll think it's a prank. So, Tamia and I were thinking maybe it would be better if you contacted him first, Kristina."

Again, Pam and Kristina shifted their gazes to Tamia.

Xavier continued. "It might make it easier for him to deal with, you know, if it came from you."

Kristina could see how nervous he was. She knew he'd wanted to ask her for a while now. And every time, she ducked the question or changed the subject. Not because she was worried about Omar's reaction. If the man was anything like the boy she knew all those years ago, he wouldn't hesitate to open his arms or his life to his son.

No, her reasons were far more selfish.

She hadn't wanted to talk about Omar because of the jumbled feelings she had about him. Despite the many relationships she'd been in and out of over the years, she'd only ever loved one man. But it was a foolish torch to carry and she knew it.

First, there was no way a guy like Omar would still be single. Second, even if he was, he wouldn't be interested in a wreck like her. She knew that seeing him in Xavier's life was going to break her heart and, ashamed as she was to admit it, that was something she wanted to avoid as long as possible.

But looking at Xavier, so nervous to ask for an answer every child had a right to know, seeing that sweet face she'd never hoped to see, there was no way she could deny him his request.

"Okay," she said. "We'll hire someone to find him and I'll talk to him myself."

Xavier dropped back against his headboard, his face awash with relief. "Thank you, Krissi! Thank you so much!"

Tamia flipped the screen around. "See. I told you. We'll call you the moment we have news."

Chapter 3

No sooner than Tamia signed off Skype, Pam dropped her mask of polite calm.

"What were you thinking?"

"About what?"

Pam stood and put her hand on her hip. "You know *exactly* what. Why in the world would you put Kristina on the spot like that?"

Kristina tugged on Pam's arm. "It's okay, Pam—"

"No! It's not!"

Tamia showed zero signs of guilt or regret. Pam may have been her older sister, but she wasn't about to back down. "He wants to meet his father. He has a right to know him."

"Then he should meet him. But there was no reason to bring Kristina into this."

"She's the best person to make contact with Omar!"

"But right now, Tamia? Really?"

"If not now, when?"

Pam threw her arms up. "Oh, I don't know... *After* she's been out of rehab for more than a minute. *After* she's through being followed around twenty-four-seven by a drama hungry camera crew. *After* she's finished all the preparations for the first full-scale tour she's done in years." Pam chopped one hand against the palm of the other. "How about when she's not already dealing with a dozen other complications!"

Tamia looked at Kristina. "He was your first love. He's the father of your son. How is that a complication?"

Pam's jaw dropped. "Tam, did you really just say that?" Pam turned to Kristina. "Seriously. Did she really just ask that question?"

Even amid the heated disagreement, Kristina had to work hard to suppress the smile she felt tug at her lips upon looking at Pam's disbelieving expression.

"Love and support is what she needs most right now. For the short time that Omar was in our lives, he was our backbone."

"You just hit the nail on the head, little sister. *For the short time.* Nearly two decades have passed, Tamia. We don't even know anything about him."

Tamia cocked her head to the side. "I know people change, but not *that* much. Omar was a good guy. A great guy. He's probably an even better man."

"And you think a man like that is still single and pining over some aging, crackhead popstar?"

Tamia and Pam stopped and looked at Kristina. Though she'd made the statement plainly and without an ounce of sadness or self-pity, Tamia and Pam looked on the verge of tears.

Tamia's eyebrows furrowed and she took a step toward Kristina, her chin quivering. "You're not—"

Kristina put her hand up. "In God's eyes, I'm not. In God's

eyes, old things have passed away and all things have been made new." She put her hand down on her Bible, smoothing out the pages. "But Omar is only human. Besides, he's probably married, with a house full of kids by now."

Tamia lowered her eyes. "I'm sorry, Krissi."

Kristina shook her head. "You want me to be happy. I get that. But it's not going to be with Omar, honey. We lost that chance a long time ago. I've accepted it and you need to do the same."

The sun had gone down, cloaking the whole house in darkness, by the time Omar put his key in the front door. That's how it always was. Unless he had Chloe for the evening, there was no reason for him to leave work before nightfall. What was the point? He was only coming home to an empty house anyway.

Once inside, he dropped his briefcase on the entryway table and without a thought, went about his evening routine. The same one he'd had since he and Marisa stopped trying to resuscitate their dead marriage and moved into separate homes.

Number 1: Call Chloe

"How was your day, baby?"

"Good! I watched Frozen."

Omar's heart warmed. The sound of her voice had a way of doing that to him, no matter how he was feeling at the time.

"You did?" He tried to sound surprised, but he knew her too well. "How many times?"

"Uh…" Omar heard her turn away from the phone and whisper. "Mommy, how many times did I watch Frozen?" In the background, he heard Marisa's voice, inaudible. Chloe returned to the phone. "Just enough times to drive her crazy, mommy said."

Naturally.

"How was *your* day?"

Omar leaned back and crossed one leg over the other. "Oh, you know… I spent it thinking about my Chloe."

She giggled. "You did not. You built houses."

"You don't think I can build houses and think about you at the same time? You must take me for a pretty silly daddy."

She overflowed with giggles again. "No, you're the *best* daddy! And that's why I'm so happy about my birthday present!"

Not that she had to tell him. Her squealing the words 'birthday present' instead of speaking them were enough to clue him in.

"Oh… I don't know, Miss Chloe. You sound too excited. You know what I think you're going to do when you see your birthday present?"

"What?"

"You're going to faint. Fall flat out on the floor. Just like daddy did when baby Chloe got her first shot."

Again, she erupted into giggles. "You did not! You did not faint!"

"How do you know?"

"Because I know! You're G.I. Joe, daddy!"

"Okay, okay. You're right. I didn't actually faint, but I wanted to."

Chloe became quiet and Omar knew what it meant. She was contemplating one of the great mysteries of her life. Omar waited, a smile on his face,

"Ummm, daddy? If I faint, then everyone else will get to play with my present and I'll just be on the floor."

Now it was his turn to laugh. He loved how she always thought things through.

"Okay, how about this. I'll show you some of your presents before everyone else arrives, so you'll have plenty of time to regain consciousness. Plus, I'll make sure I catch you so you won't have to be on the floor."

Chloe shrieked. "That's a great idea! Thanks, daddy!"

Number 2: Heat Takeout

One of their company's real estate agents, Sondra, was a flirt. She couldn't talk to Omar without touching his forearm or trying to rub his back. Her most frequent offer involved her coming over and making him a "lip-smacking, home-cooked meal."

"Don't you get bored eating takeout every day?" Her voice was always low and seductive, making even the most innocent question sound like a proposition. Sondra never spoke to Omar, she purred.

"Nope."

It was the answer he gave every time she asked. She, of course, thought he was playing hard to get. But he was being honest. His refrigerator door was proof of that. On it was a takeout menu from just about every restaurant within a ten mile radius. Not to mention the selection offered by dining delivery and all the fast food establishments between the office and his front door.

Did he get bored?

No.

Lonely?

That was another question…

Number 3: Check DVR

For being such a simple task, this was the one most fraught with emotion. And there were several involved. Anxiety, anticipation, dread. There was no guarantee that what he wanted to see on the DVR would be waiting.

It's not like he'd set it to record CSI or Law & Order. Like he could come home knowing what he'd find. It was always a toss-up. It could be good. It could be bad. There could be nothing at all. Why? Because the DVR was programmed to record any item that had the keywords "Kristina Langston" in the program info.

Sometimes he got a movie. Sometimes an award show. Sometimes a music video retrospective. Now and then, a news item. Those were the ones he always hoped for. Glimpses into her life. Proof that she was happy and doing well, despite the look in her eyes that sometimes said otherwise.

A few months ago, he came home, checked the DVR and saw video footage of her body being rolled out of a hotel on a gurney. Two paramedics rushed her to a waiting ambulance. Another frantically administered CPR while in motion. He'd watched the news footage five times in a row before he realized he was holding his breath, waiting to take one until she could, too.

After that, the hope went from just coming home and seeing her face, to coming home and seeing her alive. So even later, when he saw the stories about her and the new young guy, he was too relieved to be anything but grateful.

But with the hopeful expectation, there was a tinge of guilt and a hint of shame. It was the secret he kept even from Brock. And why wouldn't he? He couldn't help but feel this part of his late-night ritual was somewhat akin to stalking. Or at least, he was sure that's what others would think.

But if someone ever asked him why he'd do such a thing, he would have explained it like this: he'd only known true love once in his life.

And although he'd been blessed to have Chloe, his marriage to Marisa was based on something that didn't even come close to the real thing. After they separated, he tried to fill the hole with other relationships. But the only thing that ever succeeded in bringing him healing was his relationship with God and the gift that was his daughter.

So though it would be strange to some, his watching over the woman he had loved more than any other in his life was just his way of coping.

Omar turned on the flat screen and the DVR, wondering what he'd find. Would tonight be a good one or a bad one?

There was one new recording. An interview. And in it, Kristina came into the room, as usual, like a boss. Even without an entourage, she owned the place the second she took her seat. Omar had to smile. He hoped this interviewer had himself together, because if he didn't, he'd have a hard time keeping up.

But seconds into the conversation, Omar realized something was different.

First, after Kristina sat, she took off her sunglasses. She hadn't done that in years. Omar never knew why she kept them on, but whatever the reason, it always put interviewers slightly off balance, giving Kristina the upper hand.

The second thing he noticed was the look in her eyes. Something about her was changed. She laughed and talked with the interviewer openly and freely. Without any of the reluctance and guarded suspicion she'd become known for. Was this the result of being sober? Or was it something more?

Omar leaned forward in his seat. She was practically glowing. There was something about her, something he hadn't seen since they'd been together. Something that had been missing for a long time.

Joy?

She talked about the promotion that her record company was hosting in Dallas. She was going there to do a pre-show of which the proceeds would be donated to charity.

But try as she might to stay on topic, the interviewer had other ideas. After several attempts, the man was successful in bringing the conversation around to the question he'd been waiting to ask from the moment she'd arrived.

"You know what we're all dying to hear about. Are you going to give us any details?"

Kristina shrugged and feigned innocence.

"I've been giving you all the details I have, Scott. If you want to know more you have to go to the Show Some Love website."

"No! I'm talking about details on how Kristina got her groove back!"

Omar rolled his eyes. How many times was the press going to use that one?

The man laughed and Kristina played coy, shaking her head. "I keep telling y'all, he's my *protégé*. I know it's a fancy word, but just look it up."

Kristina laughed, but the interviewer wasn't buying it. Omar wasn't either. But he couldn't blame her for being tight-lipped. Better for her to keep her private life, private.

And despite the uncomfortable twinge he felt at every mention of her so-called *protégé*, Omar couldn't be happier. Kristina looked good. *Really* good. She appeared healthier than she had in years. Her skin was glowing and her face was fuller. When she laughed, it was loud and sincere. Not the hollow little chuckle she'd used for so long. And that meant everything to him.

As long as he had God, Chloe and the knowledge that Kristina was all right, he would be all right, too.

Even if it was far away from her, watching her thousand watt smile flicker across his TV screen as he sat in his favorite chair, eating that night's takeout.

Chapter 4

As her driver turned the jet black BMW 760 onto I-75, Kristina offered up a little prayer of thanks that she didn't have to do the driving herself. She was far too nervous.

Tamia called her that morning saying she had information on Omar. She wanted Kristina to come to her townhouse so they could talk without Pam or the camera crew hovering.

The anticipation had caused the day to move at a snail's pace. Kristina must've checked her watch a thousand times. She would have asked Tamia to give her the information right then over the phone, but she'd become paranoid by the constant presence of the producer and his watchdog, Amy.

She was more than relieved when they finally decided that they had their footage for the day and left. Not that the crew were bad people. Kristina got along well with the cameramen and the sound guy. But she couldn't say the same for the producer or his production assistant. More than once, she and Pam had caught the girl lurking in a corner while they were trying to have a private conversation.

Of course, it was to be expected. While the contract had specified exclusive behind-the-scenes access, she knew that it also implied exclusive behind-the-scenes dirt. She knew they were waiting for something, *anything*, to happen. No doubt, the producer went to bed each night praying she'd show up high the next morning. Or better yet, not show up at all. Because of that, she and her sisters had to be on their best behavior.

But she'd be lying if she said it wasn't exhausting. She felt as if she were constantly walking on eggshells. Careful not to do or say anything that could be misinterpreted or misconstrued. There was a lot riding on the upcoming tour and she didn't need any more doubt or speculation to hit the press as a result of this reality show.

Then there were her own secrets.

The last thing she wanted was for Amy to get a whiff of the Omar/Xavier situation. It wasn't that she was ashamed of Xavier. It was just that they'd both decided they wanted time to get to know each other before going public. And as far as Omar, any connection to Kristina might give him and his family unwanted attention. She had no desire to disrupt his life any more than necessary. Introducing him to his now eighteen-year-old son would be disruption enough.

But she hoped it would be more than that. She could see how much Xavier wanted this and she didn't want him to get hurt. Hopefully, Omar was still the person she remembered.

Tamia had called him her first love. But really, he was more than that. He was her best friend. Her lifeline. And at a time when she desperately needed both.

He did the most surprising things to show her how much he cared. Things that anyone else would call silly or even childish. Like the year he gave her a jar of pickles for Valentine's Day. Even now, she couldn't help but laugh at the thought of it. What made it such a perfect gift was what it represented.

Growing up, Kristina and her sisters never got presents. Not for birthdays or even Christmas. So when he told her he'd bought a gift for her, she knew she'd love it. When it turned out to be a jar of Vlasic pickles, she knew she loved him.

Kristina adored pickles, but her mother rarely bought them. And when she did, it was always the generic brands. When Omar found this out, he decided to get her the best pickles on the store shelf. Although it was a small thing, it meant the world to her.

As far as friends, all she and her sisters ever had were each other. At church, it was because Mahalia kept them so close to her. At school, it was because they were labeled "church girls." They were the ones that never wore pants and never went sleeveless. The ones that couldn't go to movies and never watched TV. They weren't allowed to go roller skating on Friday nights, much less, to a party. They were made fun of more than anything else, so it got to the point that they just stopped trying.

Omar, on the other hand, never judged them or made them feel like outsiders. At the same time, he never did what the other kids did, either. Like try to pressure them to do the things Mahalia had already told them not to. He would, however, now and then, break the rules if he thought it was something completely innocent.

Like when all the kids at school were talking about the new Eddie Murphy movie. When it came out on video, Omar sneaked Kristina into his house while his parents were at work and surprised her with the VHS rental. It became her favorite movie, so he bought the tape and whenever they could, they'd watch it while eating Moon Pies and drinking RC Cola.

In so many ways, Omar made her life worth living when she didn't think it was. A man like that was hard to forget.

In the Valentine's Days since, Kristina received everything a woman could dream of—diamonds, cars, vacations and even handbags that cost *more* than most vacations. But no gift, however expensive, ever came close to that one jar of pickles.

When Tamia answered the door, she nearly knocked Kristina over. "Krissi, he's here!"

Kristina backed away. "What!"

"No, no, no. Not here, in my house, here. Here, in Atlanta, here!"

She grabbed Kristina's hands and pulled her inside. Once Kristina was settled into one of Tamia's baby blue, overstuffed chairs, she continued.

"I don't know a lot. But I do know that he's a commercial real estate investor and developer and he's lived in Atlanta for years now. He runs some type of housing charity with his friend. A guy named… I don't remember. But anyway, they find homes in good neighborhoods, renovate them and *donate* them to needy families."

Tamia took a breath and looked to Kristina, eyebrows lifted, waiting for a response.

"That's…good."

Tamia rolled her eyes. "That's not just good. It proves my point! Years may have passed but Omar is the same guy that we knew back in the day."

Tamia swiped a card off her coffee table and handed it to Kristina, along with the cordless phone.

Kristina looked at the card her sister handed her. Seven digits. Seven digits were all that stood between her and the man she hadn't seen for eighteen years. She tried to take a deep breath but couldn't get her lungs to open fully. She put her hand on her chest.

Tamia noticed she was trembling and moved to sit next to her. She took the card and phone and dialed the number, before handing the phone back to Kristina.

With each ring, Kristina became more and more light-headed. Finally, the line clicked and she heard a voice. It took her a few moments to realize that it was a recording and not Omar himself. But it didn't matter, just the sound of him was enough to bring tears to her eyes. Immediately, she ended the call.

"I can't do this." Kristina choked the words out, doing what she could to keep from completely breaking down. "You can call him. Xavier can meet him. But I don't want any part of it."

Kristina got up to make a dash for the door but Tamia stopped her.

"It's just a phone call, Kristina."

Kristina spun around to face her sister. "No. It's not. It's—" With each passing moment, Kristina found it harder and harder not to cry. "I know he's moved on with his life. I've always known that. And I accepted it. But his family—his wife and kids—they were just some blurry figures in the background. If I talk to him, if I know more about his life, they'll come into focus. They'll have names and faces and they'll be real. And if they're real…" Kristina lost her battle to keep her composure. And Tamia finally understood.

"If they're real, you'll have to let go. For good."

Kristina covered her face with her hands, her body trembling with sobs. Tamia hugged her.

"I'm so sorry, Krissi."

Kristina shook her head. "No. It's what needs to happen. I've been stupid to hang on for this long. It's just a fantasy and I know that. And I *will* let it go, but I have to do it from a distance. I can't be the one to make that call."

Tamia rubbed her sister's arm. "You don't have to. I will. Okay?"

Tamia went back to the phone and dialed the number. She listened to the message, then said, "Hello. Omar? I don't know if you remember me, but my name is Tamia Langston…"

When Omar got home from church, Marisa's Infinti Q60 was parked smack in the middle of his driveway. He glanced at his dashboard clock. She wasn't supposed to be there for another half hour. He shook his head. They'd already had a rather heated discussion about her letting herself into his house, but he was determined not to get into it with her today.

Today was all about Miss Chloe.

At any moment, the vendors would be arriving. The event planner he hired was giving his sunroom, veranda and lawn a royal makeover. By the time she and her crew were done, it'd be a fantasy land fit for a princess and her court.

Omar grabbed the garment bag containing the custom made replica of Cinderella's dress from his backseat and went to the house. No sooner than he stepped through the front door, Marisa got in his face.

"Where have you been? I've been waiting here forever!"

Omar walked past her and carefully laid the garment bag down on the table in the entryway.

"First of all, keep your voice down. Where's Chloe?"

Marisa yelled up the staircase. "Chloe!"

The little girl came out of her room and peeked over the banister, before making her way slowly down the stairs.

"Put your shoes on. We're leaving."

Chloe stopped on the step she was on and looked at her dad. "But I thought—"

Omar felt his temper go from zero to sixty, but tried to keep his emotion out of his face or voice. He forced a smile. "Baby, go back upstairs. I've got to talk to mommy, then I'll be up with your first surprise!"

Chloe jumped up and down. "Yay!" She bounced back up the stairs and into her room. Once Omar heard the door close, he turned to Marisa.

"What's wrong with you?"

He was used to her acting a fool. She did it on a regular basis. But this was just crazy, even for her.

"What's wrong with *me*? I've been waiting all damn day! That's what's wrong with me! You're not the only one with plans. My family is taking her out to eat."

"Not today, they're not. She's supposed to be here overnight and you know it. We've talked about this at least three times and you're not taking her anywhere. I don't know what's going on with you but I suggest you calm down. Right now. Don't play games with me, Marisa. My daughter is not a pawn."

"Overnight?" She folded her arms. "I don't know what you're talking about."

"Don't give me that. Me and Brock have been planning this party for months."

"You and *Brock*?" She snorted. "No wonder people

think you're a couple. Running around, planning little girls' parties…"

"What people, Marisa?"

Now he *knew* there was something going on with her. The three of them had known each other for years and the last thing anybody would ever accuse Brock of was being gay.

"I don't want him hanging around here when it's your turn to have Chloe. I don't trust him."

"Since when? He's her godfather!"

"Why do you always take his side?"

Out of the corner of his eye, Omar noticed movement outside the window. A couple of white trucks and a van pulled up to the curb.

"Marisa, I don't know whether you're having some kind of mental break or just a really bad day. Honestly, I don't care. Today is my daughter's birthday and no one, including you, is going to ruin it. If you think you can get it together, you're welcome to stay and enjoy it with her. If not, you need to leave and come back in the morning."

"I'm not staying unless Brock gets uninvited."

Omar picked up her handbag from the table and tossed it to her. "Then I'll see you in the morning." He walked to the door and opened it.

Marisa's anger was so palpable, he half expected her to pick up the glass vase at the center of the table and aim it at his head. Instead, slowly and calmly, she walked up next to him and leaned in close.

"You were always choosing someone over me." Her eyes were bright with fury and wet with tears. "Always wanting someone else other than *me*. Well, you're going to regret it. I promise you. You're going to come to regret it."

Looking her in the eye, he knew she meant it. Whatever it was she had planned, she had every intention of hurting him.

He opened his mouth to speak, but right as he did, the event planner reached the front door with several people behind her, their arms full of imported Winchester Cathedral roses and English garden style chandeliers.

"A beautiful day for a princess party, isn't it?" The event planner seemed absolutely unaware of the tension between Omar and Marisa as she walked in and past them, followed by her entourage.

Not taking her eyes off Omar, Marisa responded, her voice bright and cheery. "It certainly is." She walked out the door. Omar followed her, but was stopped.

"Daddy? Where are you?"

Whatever was going on with Marisa, he was going to have to deal with it later. He went back into the house and picked up the garment bag. Chloe was standing on the staircase, her entire body abuzz with excitement. He tried his best to give her his biggest smile.

"So, baby girl, are you ready for your first surprise?"

Chapter 5

Chloe was so in love with the dress Omar had made for her, she hardly knew what to do with herself. And when he brought out the Swarovski crystal studded shoes, his prediction of her fainting out of sheer glee nearly became a reality. Once he placed the sparkling tiara on her head, she was a genuine, head-to-toe princess.

So much so, she decided it was necessary to have a royal tea party. He was glad, as it gave the event planner and various vendors time to transform the party space without her suspecting what was going on.

It was all as magical as he'd hoped. The table set aside for party favors looked like it belonged in a royal treasury. Jewel encrusted tiaras were laid out for the girls and shining, silver crowns awaited the boys.

Sheer, silver fabrics draped the tables and served as a backdrop for the cake—a scaled down reproduction of the plain pumpkin, turned diamond inlaid carriage.

But the highlight of the event would be the playhouse that he'd hired a specialty building company to design and construct. The castle-like structure had been brought over by the construction crew and reassembled in the backyard the night before. After Atlanta's premiere interior designer furnished it to look like something straight out of a little girl's fantasy, the event planner had workers arranging its turrets with thousands of tiny, twinkling white lights.

Sterling and crystal lanterns were strategically strung along the pathway from the lanai to the castle, making it a truly magical sight. Walt Disney couldn't have done a better job himself. Omar should've been thrilled. The party was turning out to be even more than he'd hoped. Chloe was sure to be walking on air when she saw it all.

And yet...

He couldn't stop thinking about Marisa and how she'd acted. Obviously, something had happened. After their separation, there was always a thin layer of hostility involved in their interactions, especially on her part. But this was different. She was in attack mode from the moment he walked through the door. And the threat? Whatever had gone on between them, she'd never said anything like that.

She knew good and well the only weak spot he had was Chloe. And that's what concerned him. Would she sue him for full custody? Or worse, would she just up and disappear, taking his daughter with her?

Though it was a Sunday and he knew the offices were already closed, he decided to call his family lawyer. He needed to do something. Even if it was just leaving an urgent message, requesting a call back first thing in the morning.

Omar picked up the handheld phone on the side table in the living room. The path between the front door all the way to the sunroom was abuzz with activity, florists going out, photographers coming in. Definitely not a place to have a private call. He cut across the living room and past the catering staff moving about like worker bees in the kitchen. He went into his office and closed the door behind him.

He was about to dial when he noticed something. The last received call on the ID screen. A local number. But it was the name that got his attention.

T. Langston

He read the name over and over again to make sure he'd seen correctly. He'd only ever known one T. Langston in his life. Tamia, Kristina's baby sister. His mouth suddenly became dry and his heart beat a little faster.

Could it be?

He used the button to scroll back through the numbers. Whomever it was, they'd called twice. The first call, about seven minutes before the second.

Immediately, he dialed his home number and waited for the prompts to lead him to his voice mailbox. He held his breath as he skipped through previous missed calls.

Finally, he got to the time around which a voice mail would have been left. But instead of what he hoped to hear, all he got was: "End of new messages. Dial one to hear saved—"

Omar let out the air he was holding in his lungs and sat on the edge of his desk, surprised at the depth of his disappointment. He rubbed his hands over his face. It probably wasn't her anyway. What were the chances? None of the Langston sisters had any reason to contact him, especially Tamia. She was so young the last time he saw her. He doubted any of them even remembered his name.

He stared at the number again. He could always call. Just

to be sure. His thumb hovered over the keypad as he listened to the activity in the kitchen just outside his office door.

He finally dialed, but when he did, it was not the mysterious Langston number. It was that of his lawyer.

Recording Kristina's appearances just so he could see her smile was the only connection he had to her. The truth was, a romantic reunion with her was little more than a foolish fantasy. What they had was long gone. It was amazing, but it was in the past. And what he had left, a few recorded interviews he couldn't bear to erase from his DVR, were just fuel for a dream that wasn't ever coming true.

None of it was real.

Chloe, on the other hand, *was* real. He needed to focus on that one true thing. He needed to focus on keeping his daughter in his life.

Chloe's birthday party looked like a scene right out of a fairytale fantasy.

All the children were dressed up in their Sunday best, wearing white, light gray and baby blue, as requested in the parchment scroll party invitations.

Chloe was the perfect little hostess. The crystals sewn into the tulle skirt of her dress shimmered furiously under the glow of the sterling lanterns as she played with the other children. And between her tiara and her scepter, she looked every bit the part of Daddy's Little Princess.

But Omar was happy and proud to see she didn't act like one. She flitted like a sparkling hummingbird from child to child, making sure all her friends were having enough fun and cake.

The castle playhouse was unveiled at dusk and even

the adults became speechless when the structure lit up. "It looks like it's been dipped in sugar," one mother exclaimed to another.

Chloe must have felt the same. She was so happy at the sight of it, she burst into tears. She clung to Omar and cried, "It's so pretty, daddy! Thank you thank you thank you thank you."

Later, he leaned against one of the pillars on the outdoor patio and watched her with one of her friend's little brothers. The boy couldn't have been more than three, but Chloe treated him like he was her baby. She took him inside the castle and pointed out all the special touches, just as her father had done for her less than a half hour before.

"Mr. Williams, you've outdone yourself. And that's saying a lot!"

Omar turned to find a woman next to him and he recognized her as one of the mothers from Chloe's school.

"I thought the Little Mermaid theme you did last year was the most magnificent thing I'd ever seen. But this?" She gestured over the whole of the magical looking lawn. "This is every little girl's fantasy." She grimaced. "What am I saying? This is *my* fantasy."

They were laughing and enjoying the view when Brock snuck up behind Omar.

"She's right. You really went all out." Brock turned his attention to the woman. "He even arranged for there to be an evil queen. Although I have yet to actually see her..." He looked around at the other guests. "Speaking of Marisa, shouldn't she be at her own daughter's party?"

The woman gave a weak smile and quickly excused herself to get more punch.

"Nice. Make the guests uncomfortable."

Brock leaned on the opposite side of the pillar and

crossed his arms. "Hey, I was gonna call her something else but I thought evil queen sounded more elegant."

Omar shook his head. "I'm not in the mood to talk about her right now."

Brock put his punch on the standing cocktail table beside them. "What happened?"

Omar exhaled. "I think she may try to get full custody of Chloe."

Brock straightened up. "What?"

Omar recognized the look on his face. It was the expression he got when they were younger and on leave, at some bar getting drunk and Brock was primed for a fight.

"I don't know for sure, but something's going on. And Chloe is really the only leverage she has, so…"

"I don't know how you even put up with that woman! She can't do this. She's not even fit to be a mother, so why in the world would she take away the one decent parent Chloe has?"

Omar shrugged.

"What are you gonna do?"

"The only thing I can do at this point. Pray and prepare. I can't imagine my life without my daughter."

"Anything you need—whatever it is—I'm with you." Brock shook his head and snorted. "I'm not surprised though. She's a vampire. She sucks people dry. I told you that a long time ago."

"I know, I know. And if it'd been *any* other time, any *other* weekend… Me and Marisa never would've happened."

"That's exactly what I mean. She knew you weren't interested. You had made that abundantly clear. She saw you were in a low place after that concert and the fangs came out. She took advantage of you then and she's trying to do it now. It's not gonna happen. Not this time." Brock exhaled. "I still regret that I wasn't on base that weekend. But like I said, I'm here now. I know you're a Christian and all, but I'm not. I fight dirty, just like she does."

Omar appreciated Brock having his back, but the last thing he wanted to talk about was that weekend. Low place? That was an understatement. He was devastated. It was the closest he'd come to seeing Kristina face to face since his father had shipped him off. After years of wondering and hoping and waiting, he finally got his opportunity. He thought it was a sign. That they were meant to be and had been given a second chance to get it right. It turned out to be anything but.

The conversation reminded him about what he'd seen earlier.

"So get this, after my run-in with Marisa, I decided to call my lawyer. Guess what was on my caller ID?"

Brock shrugged.

"A local number. T. Langston."

"As in, *Kristina Langston*?"

"I don't know. That's what I thought, at first. But…"

"But what?"

Omar shook his head. "It was probably someone unrelated."

"Probably? You didn't call the number to find out?"

Omar watched Chloe giggle and run circles with her friends around the front of the castle.

"Naw, man. Whoever it was, they didn't even leave a message. So it couldn't have been that important, right? Besides, I have bigger things to worry about."

Chapter 6

"So, what do you guys think about that one?"

Kristina, her background singers and her band had been rehearsing for most of the day. Usually, they would just be running through the set, tightening the vocals and blocking the movement on stage. Instead, they were tearing the whole show apart and putting it together again. Since recommitting her life to God, Kristina had decided to remove certain songs from the set list. Now they were all trying to decide on which to add back in and where to put them.

Although they'd been there for hours, she hadn't been able to grab a moment alone with Tamia. During the two breaks they'd had, she was interviewed by the producer or pulled to the side by Pam, needing her to sign off on something. The rest of the time, Amy was watching her like a hawk.

At one point during rehearsals, Tamia approached Kristina, eager to talk. But as much as she wanted to hear what Tamia had to say, she sent her away with a quick shake of her head.

Usually, the production crew was covering her with a boom mic. The advantage of that was she could sneak out of its range when she wanted some privacy. But because she was rehearsing on stage and the sound guy didn't want to miss anything, the producer decided to also mic her up.

Absolutely *everything* she said was recorded.

"I don't know," Adrian, her music director said. "What if we tried putting *Love Story* after *Be Mine*, then go right into *Secret Lives*?"

The other musicians and singers nodded in agreement.

"Yeah, okay. That would work. We'll run it through in that order, but before we do, let's take a short break, okay?"

Adrian nodded and called out to the group to take five. Kristina motioned at her assistant in the front row of the auditorium. When she came over, Kristina got her phone from her and went to her text app.

Any news?

Kristina watched Tamia talking to the other background singers as they drank water and checked their phones. She knew Tamia got the text when she got a quick glance from her. She texted back a sad face.

Kristina could fill a lump rising in her throat, but swallowed hard. No matter what she was feeling, she couldn't react. Not with cameras on her and an entire crew watching and waiting for some meltdown, blowup or repeat of her hotel bathroom incident.

She texted back.

Been 2 weeks. He's not interested.

Tamia looked over at her and made a face as her fingers flew over her phone's keyboard.

> *You don't know that.*
> 2 weeks, Tam. 2 weeks.
> *I'll call him again.*
> No. Just leave it. Please.

They went back to rehearsing and quickly knocked out a few more songs, finally locking in the new set list. Kristina told Adrian she wanted to take a lunch break and told the producer she wanted her mic off. What she didn't tell them was that she needed to be alone. She needed the chance to feel what she was feeling without witnesses.

The moment she was free, she went past the green room and through the stage door to the trailers set up outside in the parking lot. They were using them as temporary dressing rooms and her trailer was the only place the TV crew had yet to invade.

Just as she was opening the trailer door, Tamia called out behind her. Without pausing, Kristina said over her shoulder, "I've made my decision, Tam. Let it go." Then she went inside her trailer and closed the door.

No sooner than she was inside, her phone's email notification sounded. After taking a glance at it, she smiled and shook her head.

Xavier and his daily devotionals…

With the forwarded devotion was a message: "I love you and hope you're having a blessed day. This is one of my favorites!"

Truth be told, Kristina didn't want to read the devotion. She didn't want to be spiritual at the moment and she didn't want to walk by faith. She didn't want to do anything but feel what she was feeling and curl up on the tiny couch in her trailer and cry like a baby. But despite her temptation, she decided to go ahead and give it a look.

> Isaiah 41:10
> *Don't be afraid, for I AM with you.*
> *Don't be anxious, I AM your God.*
> *I strengthen you. Be sure, I help you.*
> *I hold you up with my victorious right hand.*

It doesn't matter how dark your situation is right now. HE is with you. HE is your God.

Is your heart broken? He's taken on the task of mending it. Not sure what to do? He's become your wisdom. Are you on the verge of giving up? He's pledged to carry you.

When God is with you, you have all you need. Remember that. Remember HIM. Look neither to the left or the right.

Look up!

He's on your side!

Kristina remembered what Robin told her a few months ago about God loving her and always listening.

While blubbering in the fetal position might make her feel a little better, going to God with the situation would be a lot more productive. So that's what she decided to do.

"Father, help my heart to only want what's meant for it and not what it can't have. And help Xavier. He wants to know his father. Right now, it doesn't look like that's gonna happen. If it doesn't, show me what to do, how to tell him. I don't want to break his heart."

Although there was more she wanted to say, she

couldn't get the words out. She remembered the song by Karen Sheard about not being able to say a word. So she raised her hands and did the only thing she knew to do. She began to worship.

And like an answer to her prayer, the words from the devotional rose up in her spirit. A peace came over her and an assurance that God was, indeed, her Father. And not just any Father, but a Father Who loved her enough to number the hairs on her head.

"Thank You." She whispered. "Thank You for being in control of this. Help me remember that, no matter what, You love me and You love Xavier. And even if things don't work out the way we'd hoped, we don't have to be afraid because You always have something good in store."

Omar leaned over the table and studied the changes the contractor was proposing. He held the phone between his ear and shoulder as he compared the sets of blueprints.

"Okay, I think this will work," he told the contractor awaiting his decision. "Just remember, no matter what, we want quality above all else. I never want you to make a difference between the properties we flip and the houses we donate."

"I hear ya', man. I'm on it. By the way, I sent Rob over with work orders to be signed. And I'll email the new estimates when we hang up."

As he spoke, the doorbell rang.

"Sounds like Rob's here now. I'll call to check in later."

Omar disconnected the call and slipped the phone into his pocket as he opened the door. But it wasn't Rob he saw standing on his porch steps.

It was the last person he ever expected to see.

༄

"You didn't return my message, so I decided to drop by."

Omar was having too much trouble believing Tamia Langston was at his front door to even comprehend what she was saying.

After a few moments of him staring at her, mouth gaped, she said, "Do you know who I am?"

He wondered whether he was having some sort of waking dream. "How? I mean— What?"

She raised her eyebrows. "I called and left a message. Two weeks ago."

Omar shook his head, as if to clear the cobwebs. Then it dawned on him. The day of the party. The caller ID.

"Someone named Langston called, but I never got a message…"

Was Marisa there when Tamia called? Did she listen to the message, then erase it? He didn't have any proof, but it would explain a lot. Specifically, her aggressive behavior when she saw him.

As he stood there trying to make sense of it, Tamia cocked her head to the side. "You gonna let me in?"

He blinked and nodded. He stepped back and opened the door wide. "Of course. I'm sorry. Come in."

Tamia walked in and looked around the impressive entry. "You've done well for yourself."

He shoved his hands in his pockets and nodded. "Yeah, we've all come a long way from the old neighborhood, haven't we?"

"You got that right."

He led Tamia toward the living room, but she stopped

when she saw the framed photographs on the large, round marble table in the entryway. She picked one up.

"Oh my goodness. She's beautiful."

Omar came up next to Tamia and looked over her shoulder. "That's my Chloe. She's a sweetheart."

"How many do you have?"

"Just one."

Tamia arched an eyebrow and set the photograph back on the table.

"Yeah…about that. Can we talk?"

As they went to the living room, Omar's mind was still reeling. "It's been a long time. I have to admit, I never expected to see you again."

Tamia sat on the leather sectional and nodded. "You know, we live here in Atlanta. All three of us. Me, Pam, *Kristina*."

He sat across from her. "I know."

Tamia's eyes widened. "You know? Why didn't you ever contact us?"

Omar shrugged. "I couldn't imagine a reason any of you would want to see me. Come on, you ladies run in different circles. The rich and famous. I'm just a regular guy. Besides," he said, lowering his head. "I always felt a bit guilty. To be honest, I didn't know if I could even face you."

Tamia leaned forward. "Why?"

"For leaving you. It wasn't by choice. But still, I could have fought harder."

"You were underage, Omar. Your parents sent you away. You were just as helpless as we were. What could you have done?"

He shrugged. "Nothing, I guess. But knowing that didn't make it any easier. I was supposed to be your protector. In the end, I was useless."

"Omar..."

He shook his head and rubbed his eyes. "You girls got out. That's all that matters."

Tamia chewed her bottom lip. "Did anyone ever tell you what happened? After you left, I mean?"

"Yeah. My father."

Tamia sat up. "What did he say?"

"Not much. Only two words. 'She miscarried'. We were having some argument about my life and how it had turned out. He wanted me to go into the military. I told him I wanted to be with my family." Omar rubbed his forehead. "That's when he said it: she miscarried."

Omar paused. Tamia could see how tightly his hands gripped one another by the way the skin stretched over his knuckles.

"I wanted to come back. He said it was better to let things be. 'You done that girl enough damage,' he said. I asked my sister to check on you all. But she said Pam and Kris stopped coming to school and your mother wouldn't allow any outside contact."

Tamia pressed her lips together. It was not something she or her sisters liked to talk about, but he needed to know.

"Yeah. After our mother discovered Kristina was pregnant, everything changed. She pulled us out of school and homeschooled us until they took their GED's. And as far as church, what little social life we had there was taken away."

Omar shook his head. "I'm so sorry."

"It wasn't your fault."

They sat in silence for a few moments before Omar spoke again.

"Not too long after that, my sister told me she'd heard a rumor that you'd all left Texas. Once she confirmed it, I saw no reason to go back there. But...I never stopped thinking about the three of you. About Kristina." He bounced his heel with nervous energy and asked the question that had been on his mind since he'd opened the door. "How's she doing?"

"She's good. Really good. For a while there, it was like she was someone else. But that was the drugs and alcohol more than anything. Since she turned her life back over to God and checked into rehab, she's like her old self again."

Omar grinned from ear to ear. "And Pam?"

"She's good, too. Although, she'd have a fit if she knew I was here."

Omar raised his eyebrows. "Here? As in, with me? Why?"

Tamia scooted forward to the edge of the couch and took a deep breath.

"This is probably the equivalent of dropping a ton of bricks on your head without warning, but here it is: That baby Kristina miscarried? He lived. His name is Xavier and he'd like to meet his father."

Chapter 7

Despite the blank look on Omar's face, Tamia laid it all out for him.

She told him about how it'd all started as problems with her mother's will and how that led them to Xavier. She told him about how the baby must have cried or moved and how their mother dropped it off at the Morris house. She explained how Mahalia became something of a fairy godmother to Xavier and watched him grow up.

She got it out as fast as she could, then waited.

From the look of him, she wondered whether she should call 911. He opened his mouth to say something, but instead of speaking, put his hand over his chest and leaned back in his chair.

"And she never even hinted at this? To *any* of you? Over all these *years*?"

"Not a word."

His eyes grew wide. "Do you think my parents knew?"

"I doubt it. I doubt *anyone* knew except my mother. You know how she was. Always had to control everything. I think she knew the only way to do that was to make sure no one else was involved."

"What's he like? Where does he live? Is he here? In Atlanta?"

Tamia took her phone out of her handbag and navigated to the selfies she'd taken with Xavier in Dallas. "Well, to answer your first question…" She handed him the phone.

Omar looked at the picture and covered his mouth with his hand. He laughed out loud.

"It's the boy toy!"

Tamia narrowed her eyes. "The what?"

"The younger man. The reason Kristina supposedly got her groove back. All this time, I thought he was her new boyfriend."

He shook his head. He knew Kristina was hiding something in the interview, but he had no idea this was it.

Tamia rolled her eyes. "Yeah, we have the geniuses over at TMZ to thank for that. They reported it first. Next thing we know, it'd spread like wildfire. Mind you, no one's ever seen them so much as touch in public, but there you go."

"Maybe it's for the best. If everyone already thinks they know the story, they won't go digging for the real one."

She nodded in agreement. "They decided to keep their relationship under wraps from the beginning, just to give themselves time to adjust. Unfortunately, that's led to a lot of rumor and speculation."

Omar nodded without taking his eyes off the picture. He didn't know whether to laugh or cry. He had a son. "When do I get to meet him?"

" I guess that's up to you. Whenever you'd like."

Omar looked up at her, his face beaming. "How about this minute?"

Tamia laughed. "I knew this would be your reaction. Kristina was worried about disrupting your family."

"Oh, no. She shouldn't have been. Chloe will be thrilled."

"What about your wife?"

He shook his head and handed the phone back to Tamia. "My *ex*-wife. I'm sure she'll find a reason to be upset. But since we aren't together anymore, it's not my problem."

"Huh. Sorry to hear that."

Omar waved his hand through the air. "Don't be. It was a mistake from the beginning."

Tamia offered her phone back to Omar. "How about you give me your phone number. You know, so I can set up a meeting…"

❦

Omar was reeling.

The moment he closed the door behind Tamia, he took out his iPad and did an Internet search for *Kristina Langston protégé*. He watched every video clip and studied every photo he could find. He could see a bit of his mother in Xavier's features. But even with that, he could hardly wrap his head around it.

He had a son.

With *Kristina*.

His heart was so full of joy, he thought he'd start levitating at any moment. But the joy was mixed with sadness, as well. He'd missed eighteen years. Eighteen years of father-son talks, birthdays, Sunday dinners, fishing trips, driving lessons.

Maybe if he wasn't already a father, it would have been

easier to take. He could've imagined what he'd missed out on without knowing the actual pain of it. But having changed Chloe's diapers as a baby and taken care of her when she was sick, having kissed her goodnight and comforted her when she woke from nightmares, he knew *exactly* what he'd missed. The fun stuff *and* the hard stuff. Chloe was only five and he couldn't bear to miss a day.

So how was he supposed to deal with missing eighteen years?

༄

Kristina sat in the corner of the rehearsal room, out of view of the dancers moving in rhythmic unison at the far end. The show's choreographer, Felix, had asked her to come and sit in on that day's dance rehearsals. Usually, she would've waited until the final ones, just to work out blocking. But he'd reworked the choreography to make it less suggestive and wanted her opinion on the changes.

As usual, the camera crew was there, recording her every reaction.

So far, she liked what she saw. The two new girls were at the top of their game and seemed to be jelling well with her regular dancers.

The music was loud and thumping and her eyes were focused on the girls, so she didn't see Tamia come in. Her sister grabbed her arm with such intensity, Kristina jumped.

"Xavier—"

Kristina gripped Tamia's hand and leaned over, crossing her legs in an exaggerated fashion as she tilted her head toward the camera crew a few feet away. Tamia got the hint and took notice of the microphone pack at Kristina's waist. Tamia nodded slightly and sat, keeping her mouth shut.

The moment Felix announced he was giving the girls a break, Kristina took off her mic and went to the producer.

"Kristina, we need to—"

She handed the mic pack to Paul and put her finger up. "I'll be right back. I promise. I just need to run to the restroom."

She grabbed Tamia's hand and they took off.

Once they got to the bathroom, Kristina peeked out the door to make sure no one had followed them.

"We need to be careful. Paul still has Amy snooping around and he puts me on a mic every chance he gets."

Although they were alone, Kristina still kept her voice low, so Tamia responded in kind. "Xavier will be here in a few days!"

"What? Why? Is everything okay?"

"He's fine! He's great! And he's coming here!"

Kristina could tell by her sister's giddy demeanor that there was more to it. "Why?" She asked the question but wasn't entirely sure she wanted to know the answer.

Tamia grinned, took her sister's hand and led her out of the bathroom, to the back door and out into the parking lot.

And there, as Kristina stood on the loading dock, completely unprepared, she saw him.

Chapter 8

Although Omar had seen Kristina on television and in magazines over the years, none of those images came close to how beautiful she was in person. She had no makeup on and wore a t-shirt and jeans. Instead of the superstar he'd come home to find on his DVR so many times, she was just Krissi, the girl he thought he would get to spend the rest of his life with.

It was his dream come true, but from the way her face went slack the moment she laid eyes on him, he realized she didn't feel the same. For a moment, he was sure she was going to turn and run back inside. So he smiled, hoping to reassure her. Kristina remained planted where she stood, but didn't smile back. Tamia, however, did and waved him over.

Omar approached them and Tamia said she'd have Felix carry on with rehearsals and that she'd stall the producer so they could have a few moments of privacy. She turned to walk away, but Kristina wouldn't let go of her hand.

When Omar saw the panic in Kristina's eyes and realized his presence was the cause, it broke his heart.

Maybe his coming hadn't been such a great idea, after all.

Tamia whispered something in her sister's ear and after a few moments, Kristina released her hand and Tamia left.

❧

Kristina couldn't stop staring at his face. She'd tried, innumerable times over the years, to imagine what he'd grown to look like. But all she could ever see was that seventeen-year-old kid. At first glance, he looked so different. Like a stranger. But when she looked into his eyes, she recognized the boy that was her best friend. And that's when something inside her clicked.

All at once she became painfully aware of her appearance. She didn't have on a stitch of makeup. Not even some mascara or a touch of lipgloss. Just cherry Chapstick. She didn't want to reach up to fix her hair and draw attention to it, but she knew it was sticking up on her head.

He smiled at her and it brought up a mix of memories. Good and bad. She had to look past his face and over his shoulder so she wouldn't cry.

He came up to her, so close that she had no choice but to look directly into his eyes. And when she did, she saw that they were damp and filled with emotion.

He put his arms around her, drew her to him and whispered in her ear. "I'm sorry. I never should have left you alone. I'm *so* sorry."

Kristina's breath caught in her throat. In his arms, she was sixteen again. But instead of being alone and afraid, her heart was full to bursting. She let her head rest on his shoulder as the tears fell from her eyes.

When she looked up at him, he wiped the wetness from her cheekbones and smiled again. But the moment was interrupted when the stage door abruptly opened and Kristina jerked to turn away from it. The intruder turned out to be some kid with earphones and music so loud, he didn't even notice them.

In that moment, Omar realized what it was like for her to have millions of strangers interested in every little detail of her life.

"Let's talk somewhere more private."

He took her by the hand and led her to his Range Rover. He opened the passenger side door and after she was in, got into the driver's side. The windows were tinted and he hoped it was enough to make her feel less exposed.

For a while they sat in silence.

Finally, he said, "Xavier."

And for the first time, she smiled. It was a genuine smile. Not the polite grin she flashed the interviewers or paparazzi.

"Xavier," she said.

The sound of her voice was like music to him.

"I'm still trying to wrap my head around it."

"Me, too. I have an eighteen-year-old son." She shook her head in disbelief.

"Tamia said y'all just found out."

"Not even a full year now. Mama was full of surprises." He could hear the small, but noticeable trace of bitterness in her tone.

"At least, this is a happy one."

Kristina leaned her head back against the headrest and smiled again. "You're right. It is."

Omar leaned his head back, too.

It was just as he'd hoped. The first few moments may have been bumpy, but now, they were settling in to familiar territory. He could see the tension had gone from her shoulders and she no longer looked as if she'd take the first opportunity to escape.

He opened his mouth to ask her a question, but was cut off by the growling of her stomach.

Kristina sat straight up, her eyes wide. He couldn't help it, he laughed.

"Now look, if you want to have lunch with me that bad, all you have to do is say so."

She covered her face. "I'm so embarrassed."

He laughed and started the car. "Seat belt."

She looked back at the door of the rehearsal studio. He held his breath, waiting.

"We'll come right back?"

He nodded.

She buckled up, a grin on her face. "You're buying."

Kristina had to make a concentrated effort not to stare at Omar as he placed their order at the drive through. Which was difficult, being that it was all she wanted to do. That, and pinch herself. Because how in the world could it be so easy? Like no time had passed at all?

"And an extra side of pickles, please," he said, winking at her.

As they ate, Kristina wondered how it was possible. How could you go that long without seeing someone and then just pick up where you left off? But that's what it felt like. Like the world had turned and changed, but they remained the same.

He caught her looking at him out of the corner of her eye. Instantly, she felt her cheeks go hot. He laughed again.

"Yeah, I see you over there looking at me. What? You trying to figure out why I kept aging while you stayed the same?"

"No!" She said, her voice much louder than she'd intended. "Not at all. I was wondering… We haven't seen each other in eighteen years, but it feels more like eighteen days."

He shrugged. "Not quite eighteen years."

"Well, yeah, you've seen me on TV and everything but—"

"I'm not talking about any of that." He set his tray on the dashboard and used a napkin to wipe his mouth. He turned slightly in his seat to better face her. "Remember the concert you did for the soldiers in Norfolk?"

"Of course," Kristina said, taking another bite.

"I was there."

Kristina stopped chewing, covered her mouth and swallowed. "You were there? At *that* concert?"

He nodded. "That's where I was stationed at the time."

"But why didn't you come to me?"

"I almost did. I had it all worked out with one of my buddies. He was part of your on-base security detail and arranged for me to see you after the concert."

"Wait a minute…" Understanding dawned on her face. "That was you? He never mentioned the name." Her eyes narrowed and she shook her head. "But we waited. He even called, but no one ever showed. What happened? Why didn't you come?"

Omar balled up his paper napkin. "Because I was at a bar getting drunk with another soldier."

Kristina raised her brows and her mouth formed a little *oh*.

"Yeah." He drew the word out, long and slow, debating

whether he should stop there or tell the whole story. He decided on the latter.

"I had flowers and everything. It was all planned out. I was going to profess my undying love." He chuckled. "I don't know. I'd been living with this fantasy of the two of us somehow meeting up again. Even after you hit it big, I thought it would happen. So when I heard you were doing a concert there at the base," he shrugged a shoulder. "I just knew. I *knew* it was the moment I'd been hoping for. Praying for. What I hadn't anticipated was you announcing your marriage and bringing your new husband onstage."

Kristina shut her eyes and stifled a groan.

His name was T-Dogg Payne. He'd been one of the rappers featured on her new album and they were married within a week of meeting. It lasted three long and tumultuous years.

"I'm sorry."

It seemed insufficient. But she didn't know what else she could say. She put her unfinished food in the bag, suddenly not able to take another bite.

"What happened after that?"

Omar looked up at the ceiling of his car and exhaled deeply. "You know that soldier I was getting drunk with?"

She nodded.

He squinted. "I married her the next day."

"Wow."

"Yeah. Not one of my shining moments." He rubbed the back of his head. "Actually, I could say that about the next few years. I quickly realized it was a mistake and took any deployment they would let me go on. That went on for a while. Then our daughter was born and I stayed home more often. It didn't take long for us to realize it was even harder being married when we were actually living in the same house. Chloe wasn't even a year old when we separated."

"Chloe." Kristina smiled. "I always loved that name. Please tell me you have pictures."

"That's all my phone is. A storehouse of Chloe memorabilia." Omar navigated to his photo gallery and handed her his phone.

"Look at that little face! She's an angel!"

"She really is. Probably the one and only thing I did right in my life."

Kristina swallowed hard. "Yeah. I know that feeling…" Her voice trailed off and her expression grew solemn.

He wondered if it was due to the same kind of regret he felt on a regular basis. The regret that nearly suffocated him when he thought about the choices he'd made and the moments he'd missed.

But he hadn't wanted to make her sad. In fact, it was the exact opposite of what he'd intended. With only a short time to spend with her, he wanted to make her smile for every second of it, if possible. And he knew just how to do it.

Still somber, she opened her mouth to speak, but he covered her lips with his finger. He grabbed the food bags and got out of the car to toss them in the trash. Once back inside, he started the car and said, "I hope you still have room for dessert."

Omar came out of the grocery store with a bag and put it in the backseat so Kristina couldn't see what was inside. Then he restarted the car and parked at the empty end of the lot.

"What are you doing?"

Omar grabbed his iPad from the backseat. He grinned and arched an eyebrow. "Patience."

He set the iPad up on the dashboard and retrieved the grocery bag from the backseat. When he revealed its contents, Kristina folded over in laughter.

"I haven't had this in… Oh my goodness, since I was sixteen!"

He handed her a Moon Pie and a can of RC Cola. "But wait, there's more!" he said, in his best TV infomercial voice.

He tapped the screen of the iPad and a movie started playing. She put her hand on her chest and looked at him.

"How many times did we watch this?"

"However many times it took to wear the tape out."

Mahalia Langston was like a warden when it came to Kristina and her sisters, so she and Omar devised an imaginative plan to spend time together. They told her mother they'd joined the school choir, so they had a cover for the afternoons when Omar's parents were still at work.

The "rehearsals" were actually the two of them sitting in his basement, watching movies and eating sweets her mother never allowed her to have.

Then, like now, she'd watch the movie while he watched her. He loved the way she'd throw her head back and laugh. The way she'd hide her face each time Eddie's character made a fool of himself. The way she always fell asleep before the movie ended.

Back then, she'd tell him, "Don't let me fall asleep". But of course, he always did. Just so she would sleep with her head on his shoulder. Then he could lean his head over on hers and breathe in the scent of her hair.

Now she was across from him, her head leaned back on the seat, fast asleep.

As he watched her, he thought about the night that

changed everything. The one time they were together. He wondered if their lives could've been different. If he was never sent to military school, could they have toughed it out and raised their son together?

His chest ached at the thought. But he knew there was more to it than that. If they'd stayed together, there'd be no Chloe. That thought was just as heartbreaking as the knowledge of everything he'd lost.

As the end credits played, Omar turned on the overhead light. Kristina's lashes fluttered and she opened her eyes. She looked at him, a content and sleepy smile on her face. But then the serenity turned to panic. She sat up and looked out the windows. The sun had gone down and the parking lot lights had turned on.

"Oh, no. What time is it? Pam is going to kill me."

Chapter 9

Despite the fact Kristina was walking through the front door of her own house, she couldn't help but feel like a teenager that had stayed out too late. On the drive over, she imagined a dozen different ways Pam was going to let her have it. And she couldn't even blame her.

Pam took the brunt of everything for Kristina. She was the buffer between her and the label, the production company, the press, and everything else out there. When things went wrong, Pam was the one that had to deal with it.

Paul, the TV show producer, was forever trying to make sure none of them were hiding anything from him. Though he took it a bit too far, the truth was, Kristina had promised unprecedented access to her private life. Ducking out in the middle of rehearsals after saying she just needed a few minutes in the bathroom must have made him livid. No doubt Pam had spent the entire afternoon trying to smooth things over.

Kristina hadn't meant any harm, but she'd messed up and she knew it. She wasn't looking forward to the onslaught her sister was sure to throw at her, but deep down, she knew she had it coming.

Once they arrived, Kristina went straight to the office that Pam kept at her house. She put her hand on the knob, took a deep breath and opened the door. Pam was pacing back and forth in front of her desk and stopped the moment she saw Kristina.

She came to Kristina, took her face in her hands and examined her eyes.

Kristina had expected Pam to yell at her until the light fixtures shook. But this reaction was worse. Pam was trying to figure out if she was high.

Once she realized she wasn't, Pam took her hands away and stepped back, the expression on her face unreadable.

"Pam—"

Pam put up her hand to stop Kristina and grabbed her phone off the desk. She navigated a few screens and came to Kristina, holding the phone out in front of her.

"You see that? Thirty-two calls. And that's just the ones I refused to answer. What did I tell you the day you got back from rehab?"

"That they weren't coming to film behind-the scenes tour footage."

"Exactly. They're not coming to film behind-the-scenes. They're here hoping they'll get a whole lot more." Pam tossed the phone onto her desk.

"You weren't gone fifteen minutes before Paul started calling me. Thirty minutes after that, he was calling the head of the production company and then *she* started calling me. Next thing I know, TMZ is calling your publicist and *he's* calling me because he needs a statement to address the rumors that you've fallen off the wagon. And I don't have to tell you how quickly a rumor can turn into a news item, do I?"

Kristina shook her head.

Pam sat against her desk and crossed her ankles. "I need to know now. Are you in or are you out? Because I'm not doing this again, Kristina. I mean, dealing with all of them out there? *That* I can handle. But having to do that when you're intentionally sabotaging the situation?" Pam shook her head. "I won't do it."

"Sabotage? But—"

"What else do you call it when you up and disappear like that? The production company was on my back because of a crew that's being paid to just sit around and wait. Since you left, Felix couldn't run the last three songs for your approval, so we have to squeeze that in elsewhere. You have fittings that had to be rescheduled and a dozen other things that I needed to talk to you about, but I couldn't get a hold of you."

Suddenly, Kristina understood. "Oh, no! My phone!"

"Yeah."

"No! I mean, I wasn't ignoring your calls. Carmela has my phone. I'd put it on silent because of dance rehearsals. She probably doesn't even realize she still has it. Pam, I am so sorry. I didn't realize I'd left it behind."

Pam threw her hands up in exasperation. "And what in the world were you doing for all those hours that you didn't even realize you'd left your phone?"

"She was with me."

Pam stood and looked past Kristina to the man standing in her office door. Her eyes narrowed and she stepped forward. "Omar? *Omar Williams?*"

Pam looked from Kristina to Omar and back to Kristina again.

Omar came into the room. "I'm sorry Pam. I really am. The time got away from us."

Pam put her hands up and shook her head. "Wait a minute. Time got away from you? What are you—when did you two even—"

"Tamia contacted me. She told me about Xavier and that he wanted to meet me. I thought maybe Kristina and I could reconnect before he got here."

Pam stared at them in stunned silence. "Is that so?"

She said it softly, but Kristina knew Pam well enough to know she was seething. But as usual, Pam remained polite.

"I appreciate you bringing Kristina home. But there are a lot of things we need to catch up on due to her being absent today, so…" She motioned toward the door.

Omar got the message and touched Kristina's elbow. "Tamia has my number. Feel free to call."

Kristina nodded and he left.

Pam folded her arms and stared at Kristina, saying nothing.

"I know. I know."

"Stay out of stressful situations. Avoid any emotional triggers. Take on only what's necessary. Isn't that what you were told?"

Kristina remained silent.

"The tour, the reality show and a son you didn't even know existed wasn't enough? You have to add Omar Williams on top of that?"

"He's his father—"

"Yes! *His* father. I'm not denying the boy should know him, but that has nothing to do with you. The Omar we knew was from nearly twenty years ago. *Twenty years,* Kristina. You have no idea what kind of baggage he's carrying now. And you already have plenty of your own. Why in the world do you want to take on more?"

Kristina wanted to argue with her sister. To explain the way it felt to be around him again. But she couldn't deny that Pam had a point. Kristina had always gone after what felt good at the moment, be it drugs, alcohol or men. And it never worked out well. As good as she felt being around Omar, maybe feeling good wasn't enough.

"Please." Pam put her hands together as if she were praying. "If Xavier wants to get to know Omar, let him. But you focus on what's in front of you: the tour, fulfilling your contract with the production company and most importantly, your sobriety. Omar can wait."

Chapter 10

ey, doesn't the Princess come home today?"

Brock and Omar had just returned to the house after their workout and, as usual, Brock was eating his way through Omar's pantry as Omar made a protein shake.

"Actually, Chloe and Marisa got back into town yesterday. She's bringing her over today and that's why I called you here."

Brock tossed a couple of honey roasted peanuts in his mouth. "Me and Marisa in the same room? Not one of your best ideas, my brotha."

"Normally? No." Omar said as he sliced a banana. "But I need you to be on your best behavior. I'm starting to think there needs to be a witness whenever she's here."

Brock's eyebrows shot up. "Whoa. I know we haven't had time to catch up this past week, but that sounds like something big went down."

"Well, you know how she showed out just before Chloe's party?"

Brock nodded.

"I think I know why. Like I told you before, that was the same day I got the mysterious Langston call."

Brock nodded again. "Yeah, yeah."

"Turns out it wasn't a wrong number. It was Tamia."

"As in, Kristina Langston's sister, Tamia?"

"Yep."

Brock put his fist over his mouth. "You got to be kidding me! Why? How do you know? Did she call back?"

"She came over. But get this, she *did* leave a message. But it somehow disappeared from my voice mailbox."

Brock narrowed his eyes. "Just when Marisa happened to be alone in your house?" He shook his head. "What did she say when you confronted her?"

"I haven't."

"Why not?"

"She'd just deny it. Besides, I've got too many other things to deal with right now. As much as I missed my baby, it worked out that she and Marisa were gone this week. It's taken me that long just to wrap my head around this whole situation. That call? It was to tell me I had a son."

Brock's eyes grew wide and he nearly choked on his peanut.

"Kristina had a baby, man. I have a son that just turned eighteen."

Besides being a ladies man, there was something else Brock was known for—his mouth. But for the first time in all the years Omar had known him, he was speechless.

After a few moments of dumbfounded silence, he recovered and asked, "What's he like?"

"I haven't met him yet. We talked on the phone for a few

hours but I won't see him until he gets to town on Friday. We're all having dinner together. Me, Chloe and Xavier. Maybe Kristina, too."

"Whoa. You're having dinner with Kristina Langston? Now see, I woulda thought you'd be swinging from the chandeliers about now. You've been pining after that woman for as long as I've known you. So why you looking so worried?"

Omar shrugged and shook his head. "Maybe it's nothing. But I spent some time with Krissi and—"

Brock straightened up from where he'd been leaning on the counter. "Wait. Rewind. Are you telling me you met up with your Number One?" He was grinning from ear to ear. He reached out and smacked Omar on the shoulder. "And you didn't lead with that, man? Tell me! What happened? How did it go?"

"It was better than I ever could have imagined. But…"

"But what?"

"I don't know. I just thought she would've called by now. I'm trying not to overthink it. It's just, I thought we'd reconnected. But now…"

"Isn't she supposed to be touring soon? I can't listen to the radio for more than thirty minutes without hearing the announcement featuring her Atlanta dates. Maybe she's just busy. And she knows she's going to see you for dinner, so—" Before Brock could finish his sentence, the doorbell rang.

The moment Omar opened the door, Chloe tackled him with love. He swooped her up in his arms and kissed her all over her face. "I've been waiting for this all day!"

Chloe kissed him back. "You missed me?"

Omar made a face at her. "Are you really asking me that? Of course, I missed you!"

Chloe put her finger up. "Okay, daddy. I promise I'll spend time with you. But first I need to go check on my castle, okay?"

Omar laughed. "No problem."

He put her down and she ran toward the back of the house, stopping only to give Brock a high-five as she went.

Marisa sauntered in, walking past Omar without so much as a hello. When she saw Brock, she turned to Omar and said, "I thought I told you I didn't want that man around my child."

"*Our* child. And I thought I told you he's her godfather and nothing's changing."

Brock followed Omar and Marisa into the living room, a grin on his face. "Long time, no see, Marisa. By the way, your daughter's birthday party was beautiful. Too bad you had to miss it."

"Go to hell, Brock."

"Hey!" Omar looked toward the back patio, checking for his daughter. "Both of you need to act civil. Chloe's just outside."

"Whatever." Marisa dropped down on the couch, crossing her legs.

"How's your family? Did you two have a good time?"

"Of course, we did. Chloe always has a good time when she's around her family. I heard you had a pretty eventful time yourself."

Omar and Brock exchanged glances.

"I don't even know what that's supposed to mean. What did you hear and who did you hear it from?"

"Oh!" Marisa covered her mouth and feigned surprise. "We're gonna play that game? Okay. Cool. Forget I said anything." She took a stick of gum from her purse and put it in her mouth. "So what did you call me here for that you couldn't just say over the phone?"

Brock snorted. "Wow."

She cut her eyes at him. "You got something to say?"

Brock ducked his head and sat in one of the chairs. "Naw. I was just trying to figure out why you always got such a bad attitude." He shrugged. "Doesn't matter, I guess. But just in case you're wondering, it's probably the reason you can't keep a man."

Omar could've sworn he felt the temperature drop as Marisa glared at Brock.

"Look!" Brock motioned at Omar. "She's not even gonna deny it. Self-awareness is a beautiful thing, isn't it?"

Inwardly, Omar groaned. He wasn't in the mood to play referee today. "Come on, now. Settle down, man."

"You just don't know when to quit, do you?" Marisa leaned forward, her elbows on her lap. Her voice was low and even. "One day, you gonna push me too far, Brock."

He leaned forward and matched her deadly tone. "And then what?"

"And then," she said, leaning back and stretching her arms over the top of the couch, "Omar might finally get to see what a lowlife he has for a best friend."

The cocky grin Omar wore only moments before, faded. He sat back in his seat, gutted.

Marisa kept her eyes on him, savoring the sudden shift in his mood. "That's it. Down, boy."

"Marisa!"

But neither she, nor Brock, looked at Omar. Their gazes remained fixed, one on the other, like predator and prey. Omar just wasn't sure which was which.

Brock chuckled. "Naw, man. Don't sweat it. You know how she is."

The way they stared each other down made Omar uneasy. They'd never gotten along. That was old news. But something had changed.

"What is this? What's going on with the two of you?"

Marisa shrugged and put her hand up to check her manicure. "Revulsion. Disgust. The usual. Now, are you gonna tell me what I was summoned for or not?"

Omar looked at Brock, but Brock avoided eye contact. Whatever was going on, they obviously didn't want to elaborate. That was fine with Omar. He already had enough drama in his life.

"This week I want Chloe to spend Friday night with me. It shouldn't be a problem since—"

"Why?" Marisa popped her gum and gave him a sidelong glance.

Omar immediately pushed down the annoyance he felt come up at her question. He never once asked her to explain herself when she wanted to change up the schedule. But while he didn't appreciate her aggressive tone, he didn't need to start a fight with her either. So for the sake of keeping the peace, he decided to ignore his aggravation and answer as simply as possible.

But before he could, Brock said, "To meet his son."

Marisa stopped swinging her crossed leg and narrowed her eyes at Omar. "*Son?*" She stood and folded her arms. "What *son?*"

Omar wanted to punch Brock in the face and gave him a look that said as much. He would deal with him later.

"This is not how I wanted to tell you, Marisa, but last weekend I learned I have a son from a relationship I was in as a teenager."

Marisa's face crumpled and her shoulders dropped. "From when you were a teenager?"

He nodded, unsure of what to make of Marisa's reaction. He knew she'd be upset, but hurt? He didn't even know her back then.

She smiled, though her chin quivered and tears sprung to her eyes. "Wow. Okay. Now I get it."

"Get what?"

Marisa marched toward the doors to the back patio. "Chloe!"

Omar got up and followed her. "Marisa—"

She turned on him and jabbed her finger in his face. "You're not taking my child around some stranger I've never even met."

"Stranger? He's my son, Marisa. *Her* brother. And he's a good kid. He has a right to meet his *sister*."

Brock came to where they stood. "Yeah, Marisa. He has a right to meet his sister."

Omar didn't understand what happened next. All he knew was that only a split second passed before Marisa charged Brock and hit him in the face.

Before Omar even had time to react, Brock grabbed Marisa's wrist, yanked her toward him, twirled her around and put her up against the wall. Marisa scratched at Brock's hand as he held her up by her throat.

"Brock! Stop!" Omar grabbed him from behind and pulled at him, but Brock didn't budge.

Omar saw the terror in Marisa's eyes as she struggled to breathe. No matter how hard he pulled, he couldn't get Brock to let go. He was like a man possessed and Omar had no doubt that if he didn't do something, Brock was going to kill her right then and there.

Omar let go, came around and punched his friend in the side and face, causing Brock to release his grip.

Marisa stumbled to the side for a few steps, using the wall

to hold herself up. Brock was leaned over, his hand holding his busted lip.

"Are you okay?" Omar asked Marisa.

"Yes," she whispered, her voice hoarse.

Omar turned her chin to the side to get a better look at her neck. But as he did, he noticed her eyes grow wide. He turned to look over his shoulder and saw Chloe standing there, still as a statue, frozen with fear.

He rushed to Chloe and picked her up. She felt like a little bird, trembling in his arms. He pushed her head down on his shoulder and rubbed her back, rocking her gently. "It's okay, baby. It's okay."

He turned around to see Brock coming toward him, his hands up in surrender and his eyes full of desperation. "I'm sorry. I don't—"

"You need to leave."

"But I—"

"I said *leave.*"

Brock took a couple of unsteady steps backward and nodded his head. He turned around to leave, but slowed as he neared Marisa.

His voice was barely above a whisper and Omar was sure he'd intended for no one but Marisa to hear him. But it didn't matter, Omar did.

"I swear to God, if you cross the line, I will, too. And you know exactly what I mean."

Instead of some kind of reaction that made sense, Marisa looked at Brock as if to challenge him to make good on his threat. Omar couldn't believe what he was seeing. Minutes ago, Marisa appeared as sure as Omar that Brock was going to kill her. Now, her eyes didn't hold an ounce of fear.

After Brock left, Marisa silently gathered her keys, handbag and phone.

"What was he talking about?"

"Chloe, kiss your daddy. We gotta go."

"Marisa."

She motioned for Chloe to come to her, as she picked up the girl's My Little Pony backpack.

"Marisa!"

She aimed her finger at him. "Don't raise your voice to me in front of my child!" She came to where he stood and snatched Chloe away, dragging the girl with her as she walked to the door.

"I'm so sick of this. All of this. You're going to have to meet your bastard by yourself, because you're not taking my daughter with you!"

Chapter 11

Although Tamia visited Xavier in Dallas every chance she got, she still felt like a giddy little girl when she finally spotted him amid the sea of travelers arriving at Hartsfield–Jackson.

She used to say her two favorite people on the planet were her sisters. But both had been unceremoniously bumped down to second and third position since she'd been reunited with her nephew. Xavier was her best friend and, occasionally, her partner-in-crime.

"I can't believe you're here!" Tamia said, her arm hooked in his, as they made their way to her MINI Coupe.

"I know, right!" Xavier was smiling even harder than she was. "And now you can finally give me all the details on this Omar and Kristina situation."

Tamia opened her car trunk and Xavier dumped his duffle bag inside. She went to toss his carry-on, as well, when he stopped her.

"Not that. I'm keeping it with me. There's something in there for y'all."

Tamia unlocked the doors.

"What is it?"

Xavier got in and reached for his seatbelt, shrugging. "I have no idea."

"How you gonna tell someone you brought them something and then say you don't know what it is?"

Xavier grinned. "I'll explain later. First, tell me what's up with these wayward bio parents of mine."

Once they were out of the parking garage, Tamia launched into the story thus far.

"Okay, so first of all, there's definitely some sparks there. I saw them myself. But don't mention none of this in front of Pam. She's been in a mood ever since she found out."

"Because they might get together? Why would that put her in a bad mood?"

"I guess she's worried if it doesn't work out, Kristina will relapse."

"Oh."

"But I don't think she would. She's so different now. You'll see. Even better than when you saw her in New York. She's more stable than I can ever remember her being."

"Man, you don't know how good it feels to hear that. I just want her to be okay."

"Me and you, both."

"So…"

Tamia stole a glance at her nephew. "So, what?"

"Are *you* dating anyone?"

"And how in the world did we get on this subject?"

Xavier chuckled. "I don't know why you're acting so surprised. I ask you every single time I see you. And every single time I ask, you find a new way *not* to answer."

"And see, one would think you'd get the hint and stop asking."

"The sooner you answer, the sooner I will."

Tamia groaned. "Okay. Fine. But first, tell me this: why do you want to know so bad?"

"There might be someone who's interested."

Although he thought he was being coy, Tamia already knew who Xavier was talking about. And while the man in question was a great guy, Tamia decided long ago that relationships weren't for her. Why invest your heart and soul in something that won't last?

She loved her nephew and the way he lived life with a heart full of hope, but their childhoods had been as different as night and day. While he grew up always believing for the best, she grew up always finding the worst. How could she explain that to him so he'd get where she was coming from?

"It's like this. I think only certain people find true love. True love being, someone that will love you through it all. The good stuff. The bad stuff. The boring, regular ol' in-between stuff. Pam and Reiland found it. And though they were just kids, I think your parents had it. But it doesn't happen for everyone."

"That doesn't mean it can't happen for you."

"Look around, Xavier. Ninety-five percent of people out there just settled for the best they thought they could get. It may start out fine, but eventually they end up resenting each other and getting divorced. Or they just stay married and miserable. I don't need to be with someone to be unhappy. I can do that on my own."

Xavier remained silent, staring out at the cars that passed on the freeway. She hated to burst his bubble. But if being blunt with him was the only way to stop the relationship questions, she had no choice.

"So…are you telling me I can't set you up?"

Tamia moaned. "You must be the most single-minded individual I've ever met outside of your mother."

"Is that a yes or a no?"

Tamia shook her head, beside herself. "The minute we get to Kristina's, I'm kicking you out of my car."

Kristina smiled as she cleaned up the excess flour and bits of dough from the granite countertop. The aroma of the buttery, sweet peach cobbler baking in the oven, filled her with a greater sense of satisfaction than making a pie probably should. It'd been years since she'd baked anything and she'd forgotten how much joy it gave her.

For all the hurt and pain their mother caused them, the one thing Mahalia did give her daughters was some mad cooking skills. And each of them had a specialty. Pam was the soul food expert. Greens, sweet potatoes, fried chicken, melt-in-your-mouth brisket—she could do it all. Tamia, on the other hand, was the family's Casserole Queen. It didn't matter what the ingredients were or whether they made sense, give them to Tamia and she could whip up a casserole that would make your mouth water.

Kristina's domain was desserts. Cakes, trifles, cookies—you name it, she could make it. But pies were her specialty. Cobblers, in particular.

The three of them used to cook all the time. Especially after Pam turned eighteen and Kristina, seventeen. That was when they left Mahalia's house, taking Tamia with them.

There was a big fight, of course. Their mother tried to threaten them like she usually did. But at that point, Pam was no longer afraid. She knew she was over age and could go to the police without fear of being put into foster care, or worse, returned to her mother. But there was no way she was leaving her sisters to fend for themselves.

Mahalia told Pam she had no right to take them and threatened to call the police and report the girls kidnapped. But Pam countered with a threat of her own.

Pictures.

Dozens of them.

After their mother had beat Kristina into giving birth too soon, Pam and Kristina began making an escape plan. They knew the only way they'd be able to leave was to have leverage. So that's what they got. With the Polaroid camera Pam kept hidden under her bed, she documented every bruise, scratch and laceration. Their careful planning paid off and the day they walked out of her house became their very own Independence Day.

But the joy was short lived. Being on their own was even harder than they'd anticipated. For a long time, all they could afford for food were bags of uncooked rice. They would have it with sugar and a splash of milk in the morning and salt, pepper and a pat of butter at night. Some days, they didn't eat at all. But none of them ever regretted leaving. Going to bed hungry was better than going to bed afraid, any day.

And later, once they had steady money coming in, they were able to flex their culinary muscles. They were always learning new recipes and trying to outdo one another whenever it was their turn to make dinner.

But once Kristina's career took off, all that changed. She knew she had an opportunity most people would kill for, so she spent every second working for it. Her sisters joined her, first as background singers. Then later, Pam became her manager.

If they weren't on a tour bus, they were in a hotel room.

Even after Kristina bought the sprawling eight bedroom mansion in Atlanta's Tuxedo Park, she was rarely there. And when she was there, during breaks or the holiday season, she was usually high and hold up in her bedroom.

But since she'd gotten her life back together and come out of rehab, she'd rediscovered things she didn't even realize she missed. Reading her Bible, listening to gospel music and now, baking.

Kristina used the side of one hand to wipe the last of the excess flour on the counter off the edge and into the palm of her other hand. She stepped on the lever to open the trash can lid and swiped her hands together to remove the flour.

"I knew I smelled peach cobbler!"

Pam came through the archway from the back of the house where her office was located and headed straight to the oven. She opened the door and bent over, taking in a deep breath.

"Girl, you still got it. That smells amazing."

Kristina broke out into a grin. "Don't compliment me yet. We still need to taste it."

Pam opened the drawer opposite the kitchen island and pulled out a serving spoon. "Don't worry. The second it cools, I'll make sure it's safe for general consumption."

Kristina laughed and wiped her hands with a kitchen towel. "I bet you will."

"We're home!"

Tamia and Xavier came into the kitchen, luggage in tow. "Xavier!"

Kristina opened her arms wide and waved her fingers for him to come to her. He dropped his duffel bag on the floor and wrapped his arms around her, squeezing her tight.

"Are you reading those devotionals every day?"

Pam laughed. "He's been in here, what? Two minutes?"

Kristina pulled away from him so she could see his face. "Yes, Pastor Xavier. Between you, Robin and Jesus, I may end up a good Christian woman yet!"

Tamia walked around the kitchen island and, like Pam, opened the oven door to look inside.

"Kristina René Langston! Is this *your* cobbler?"

"Yes, ma'am."

Tamia clapped her hands. "Oooh, Xavier! You are in for a treat! Nobody, and I mean *nobody*, out-bakes my sister. She can put a hurting on a cobbler."

"Like I already told Pam, this is the first one I've made in a *long* time. So don't get your hopes up." She grabbed Xavier's hand. "Now, come on. Let me take you to your room. Are these all your bags?"

"Yep. This is everything. But I didn't know how I was supposed to dress for the dinner. If I need something more formal, I'll have to go to a store. What are you wearing?"

Tamia grimaced at Xavier and shook her head. She called herself being discreet, but Pam picked up on it.

"What dinner?"

Kristina and Tamia exchanged looks.

Pam put her hand on her hip. "What dinner?"

"Okay, Pam, before you get all wound up, it's *one* dinner." Tamia put up her finger to emphasize her point. "One. Dinner."

Pam swung around to face Kristina. "Dinner? With Omar?"

Kristina put her hands up. "Pam—"

"I thought we talked about this? Does anybody ever listen to anything I say? Seriously!"

"After all she's been through, she deserves this. Why are you making it so hard? You keep seeming to forget, Omar was a good part of her life. Probably the best part."

"Yes, Tamia. Eighteen years ago. And it wasn't all hearts and roses, either. It was traumatic." Pam motioned toward Xavier. "Thank God, it wasn't as bad as we thought. But that doesn't mean it wasn't hard on her. I don't expect you to understand this, because you've never had an addiction problem, but sobriety is fragile. Especially this early on. She's already got too much to deal with."

As her sisters argued, Kristina looked at Xavier. He offered her a weak smile and squeezed her hand.

"If you two would stop talking about me like I'm not here, I'd like to ask Xavier a question."

Tamia and Pam became silent. All eyes were on Kristina. She, however, was focused on Xavier.

"I've heard what Tamia has to say. And I've heard what Pam has to say. I know what I think about the whole thing, but what I want to know right now is what you think."

Xavier took a deep breath and stuffed his hands in his jean pockets. "I never even thought I'd meet my parents. I mean, I always wondered where I came from, but after being anonymously abandoned on a doorstep, I figured there was no way to know." He paused and looked down as he blinked back tears.

"I'm so grateful. I already have more than I ever thought I would. First, finding you three. And now, I know who my biological father is and he wants me in his life. I'm blessed. Beyond blessed and I know it. That said," he looked at Pam apologetically. "I'd give anything to be in a room with both my biological parents at the same time. Just once. Even if only for a couple of hours. It would be a dream come true."

He looked back at Kristina. "I'm only telling you this because you asked. But the truth is, I can wait. I've waited this long just to meet the two of you. So if this will, in any way, jeopardize your sobriety, please understand, you don't have to do it."

Kristina's heart was full to bursting with love for him. Though anyone else would look at him and see a grown man, she couldn't help but think of him as her baby. And that he was willing to put off having something he wanted more than anything, just for her, overwhelmed her with warmth and affection.

She knew Pam was worried about getting into a relationship with Omar, but this dinner was about more than that. There was so much she had never been able to give Xavier. Not a kiss, not a hug, not even a bottle when he was a baby. She thought she'd missed all her chances, but here was one thing that he really needed. And she was the only person that could give it to him.

"Pam…"

Pam nodded. "I know. I know."

"I'm not asking permission. I'm just asking you not to give me a hard time about it."

Pam sighed. "Girl, I could tell you'd made up your mind halfway through his first sentence." She put up her hands. "I promise. I'll stop giving you a hard time. But please, if any of this becomes too much for you, emotionally—"

"I know. I'll come to you. I'll make sure I get help." She held her sister by her arms and kissed her cheek. Then she nudged Xavier.

"Now, follow me, kiddo. Your room is upstairs."

Chapter 12

Although she'd felt confident about her decision when she made it, by the next day Kristina was a bundle of nerves. And the upcoming dinner wasn't the only reason.

Production Assistant Amy was even more sticky than usual. Kristina couldn't take a step or look at her phone without turning to find the girl inches away from her. It reminded Kristina of a documentary she'd seen about sharks and how they reacted when they smelled blood in the water.

Did Amy somehow know about Xavier? He'd only come to town the day before, but it might explain the girl's behavior. Kristina didn't even want to imagine what life would be like for Xavier if the true nature of their relationship was leaked to the press. But as worrisome as that thought was, it wasn't the only thing that had Kristina's nerves frayed.

As much as Amy tried to mirror Kristina's every step, the

girl had a shadow of her own. A scruffy looking man with a camera.

Kristina didn't recognize him as part of the regular camera crew, but he did look familiar. After wracking her brain for about an hour, she realized when and where she'd seen him before. It was the day Omar came to see her during rehearsals.

And once she became aware of the camera guy, she couldn't help but notice he kept watching her. To say that the strange man made her uncomfortable was an understatement.

The moment there was a break in the rehearsals, Kristina made a beeline for Pam. "Who's that guy?" She said, nodding in the man's direction. "What's he doing here?"

Pam, finalizing a checklist with the road manager, lowered her chin to look over her glasses. "Who?"

Kristina pointed, not caring whether he knew they were talking about him. He saw her giving him her attention and immediately turned away, heading to the other side of the stage.

"Oh," Amy said, suddenly right behind them. "He's the set photographer."

Pam cut her eyes and turned to the girl. "I know you've got something better to do than listen in on a private conversation."

"I, uh—"

"Go."

Amy blinked a few times before scurrying off. Once she was out of earshot, Kristina continued.

"If he's with the crew, where has he been this whole time?"

Pam shrugged. "I don't know. Why?"

"He creeps me out. I feel like he's watching *me* more than anything else."

Pam took off her glasses and looked in the direction the man had disappeared. "Do you want me to get rid of him?"

Kristina nodded. "Please."

"Okay. I'll take care of it. You sure it isn't just nerves about something else?" Pam raised her eyebrows.

"I already told you. There's nothing to be nervous about. It's just a dinner. I'm doing it for Xavier more than anything else."

"Sure you are." Pam slipped her glasses back on, a smile pulling at her lips. "Don't worry about the creeper. I'll have him gone by the end of the day."

Kristina stood in the middle of her walk-in closet, frozen. It was one of the largest rooms in the house and had enough couture to stock a block of 5th Avenue boutiques.

Normally, she loved being there, but at the moment, it made her feel like the world's biggest cliché. She was surrounded by fashion's finest designers and all she could think was: *I have nothing to wear.*

She'd told the truth when she spoke to Pam earlier. This dinner really was for Xavier. At the same time, the thought of seeing Omar again made her heart flutter in her chest.

Get a grip. This is not a date.

"I've seen houses smaller than this closet."

Kristina turned to find Xavier standing behind her and staring at his surroundings, his mouth hanging open. If it weren't for the goofy look on his face, she would have called him red carpet ready. He was in a smoke gray vintage style suit, sporting a black satin skinny tie. His hair was freshly cut and he looked like he'd just stepped out of a photo spread inspired by the old-school style of Motown.

"Look at you!"

He smiled and tugged at his jacket lapels before taking a spin. "I've never been to a fancy restaurant. I hope this is okay."

She walked up to him and put her hands on his shoulders, running them down his jacket sleeves. "You look perfect. Now if only I could come close." She turned back around, surveying her closet. "And I know, I said it a million times. It's not a date. But still, I want to look… I don't know. Pretty."

"That's why you're looking so worried? I can solve that dilemma."

He pulled a tan dress off the rack and offered it to her. "You could wear this. Or…" he said, choosing a black cocktail dress. "This." He pointed to a magenta shift dress. "Or that." He shrugged. "Anything, really. Because if being pretty is what you're going for, it's basically impossible for you to be anything else. You wake up beautiful."

Kristina tilted her head to the side. "That's so sweet."

"It's true. And that's why I'm keeping an eye on this Omar fella. Baby daddy or not, he's gonna have to pass my test before he can get to you."

Kristina laughed. "He really is a good man." She felt heat rise to her cheeks and put her hands up to cover them.

Xavier lowered his head to get a better look at her down-turned face. "Are you blushing?" His voice was playful and teasing as he reached out, grabbed her by the shoulders and gently shook her.

Kristina groaned. "I'm so embarrassed." She laughed again. "For years I told myself it was just puppy love and that I needed to move on. But then I saw him again." She took a deep breath and exhaled. "He came to the rehearsal studio and it was like… It was a feeling I've never had with anyone else."

She dropped down in one of the upholstered chairs set up by the mirrors along one wall. Xavier followed and joined her.

"Can I ask you something?"

She nodded.

"Is it just your sobriety that's holding you back?"

She narrowed her eyes at him. More than once he'd proven to be insightful beyond his years. It was hard to hide anything from him, so she decided not to try.

"It's a lot of things. But I guess the main one is…" Kristina's voice faded and she bit her bottom lip. What she felt was hard to admit, especially to Xavier. "I know I'm not good enough for him."

Xavier leaned back and made a face. "Not good enough? Are you serious? You're good enough for *anybody*. And if anyone ever tells you any different, I'll sock 'em in the mouth."

Kristina's eyes widened. "Sounds like you need to be reading those devotionals as much as I do!"

"I'm serious." Xavier leaned forward, his elbows on his knees. "Look, I'm not just saying this because I'm your son or because you're beautiful or talented or one of the most amazing people I've ever met in my life. Even if you weren't any of those things, you're still a daughter of the King. That makes you a princess. It's not a question of whether you're good enough for somebody. The question is, is he good enough for *you*?"

Omar stared at the red light, willing it to turn green. He took yet another glance at the dashboard clock. He'd been looking forward to the reunion for so long, the idea he might be late put him on edge. But then again, it had been that kind of day.

From the moment he arrived at work that morning, it was one thing after another. First, the walk-through for the Centre Street property was pushed back. Then, he ended up being on the phone for over an hour and a half with the city zoning committee, trying to get them to push through on a project that they previously approved but were now disapproving.

And if that weren't enough, Brock never showed up to the negotiations they were scheduled to have with a prospective buyer.

Not that Omar was surprised. Brock hadn't shown up to work for days. He tried calling him several times. First, to find out what caused the blowup at the house. Then later, because he'd become worried. Brock's voice mailbox eventually became full and the two times Omar drove to his house, he wasn't there. To say Omar was concerned would be an understatement.

With Brock's history of alcoholism, Omar's mind immediately went to the worst-case scenario. He had to keep reminding himself that Brock had been sober for close to six years. Still, Omar couldn't help but wonder whether what happened with Marisa was enough to cause a relapse.

Omar exhaled.

More than anything, the Brock and Marisa incident had him stumped. They'd never been fans of one another, but a physical altercation? Even years of their shared animosity hadn't prepared him for that. And as much as Marisa hated Brock, Omar couldn't understand why she hadn't filed charges. She'd never been one to pass up an opportunity for retribution. Especially when, for once, she was in the right.

He'd spent more than one sleepless night trying to figure it out.

Finally, he decided to just give it to God. As much as he

loved Brock like a brother, he had more pressing things to attend to. He had not one, but two children to parent now. And nothing, including Brock and Marisa's inexplicable drama, was getting in the way of that.

Once traffic began flowing, Omar looked at the clock again and took a deep breath. He'd have to get home and change his clothes like his name was Clark Kent, but there was still time to make it.

Despite the problems at work, all he could think about the entire day was meeting Xavier. They'd talked on the phone a few times, but seeing him face to face was something else altogether. Omar wanted to touch him and see him laugh. He wanted to know every detail of his life. His likes and dislikes, hopes and dreams. He wanted to do and say and know so much, he had to keep reminding himself not to overwhelm the boy at their first meeting.

Then there was Kristina.

He couldn't help but hope she'd be there, too. His heart skipped at the thought of it. But he understood she had a lot on her plate. And he'd already decided that if she wasn't ready to start anything with him, he would back away.

Not *go* away, but back away.

He made the mistake of giving up on his feelings for her once and ended up in a marriage doomed from the start. He wasn't going to make that mistake again. Since he was seventeen, he'd only ever loved one woman. Then, he'd waited two decades before he even spoke to her again. Now, if he needed to, he'd wait another six just to convince her she was the love of his life.

Omar pulled up to his house with that very thought on his mind, when he saw something completely unexpected.

Brock's car in his driveway.

Chapter 13

No sooner than Omar got out of his Rover, Brock opened his car door and did the same.

As Omar walked up to him, his heart sank.

Brock was disheveled and his eyes had the glassy, unfocused look they always got when he'd gone on a bender.

"We need to talk." Brock stumbled as he tried to approach Omar. If it weren't for the bumper of his own vehicle, he would've been facedown on the in-laid brick of the driveway.

"Oh, *now* we need to talk? Because I've been calling you for days with no answer. Not to mention you not showing up to the office. Not cool, man."

"I know, I know. I'm sorry. But—"

Omar waved his hand and continued on to his front door. "We're definitely going to hash this out." He unlocked the door and stepped inside. Brock followed close behind. "You and Marisa don't get to come into my house and act like that and not explain yourselves. But now is not the time. I have somewhere to be."

"This can't wait, Omar. Marisa's done mess you don't know nothing about."

Omar exhaled and loosened his tie. "Not my problem, man. Not anymore. That's why it's called divorce." He continued to the downstairs bathroom where he'd left his change of clothes that morning. "Whatever's going on between the two of you is just that—between the two of you."

"It's Chloe."

Omar stopped and stood stone still at Brock's words. He had an idea of what Brock was going to say, but he didn't want to hear it. More than once, he'd had doubts about his daughter's paternity, but by then, he'd already fallen for his little girl.

Omar chewed at his bottom lip. He wasn't stupid. And he wasn't blind. But when he'd held that newborn in his arms, he promised he'd be a father that never left. And it was a promise that even DNA wouldn't break. Besides, he never knew for sure one way or the other. He didn't *want* to.

"Trust me, Brock. I know my ex-wife. Whatever you have to say about her, I've already figured out. More than once."

Omar took off his tie and unbuttoned his shirt. Brock stood in the doorway, only upright because he was supported by the door frame. There was no way Omar could let him drive home in his condition.

"Look, man. You can stay here and sleep it off until I get back. And then we're going to talk about this. All of it. Including you not showing up to a negotiation that meant millions to our company."

Brock came in, dropped down on the edge of the tub and buried his face in his hands. Omar couldn't help but feel bad for him. He'd be there for him like he always was, but right now, it was more important that he was there for his son.

"It's so messed up, man."

"Just take it easy. It's gonna be okay. You're going to get through this."

Brock looked up at him, his eyes red and watery. "But, Chloe… She'll use it to take her away from you."

Omar stopped and looked at Brock's distraught expression in the mirror's reflection. Now it all made sense. The confrontation with Marisa and the repercussions it would have on Chloe and Omar was what put Brock over the edge.

Omar buttoned up his shirt and put on his jacket. "Don't worry about Chloe. She's my daughter and I'll take care of her. Marisa will never be able to stop me from doing that."

Omar turned and started for the door.

Brock struggled to stand and follow Omar. "But that's the thing. Chloe's not your daughter. She's mine."

❧

When Xavier stole another glance at his watch, he tried to be subtle so Kristina wouldn't notice. He didn't succeed.

"You don't think there was an accident or something, do you?"

It had been like this for the past hour. About every ten minutes, she'd come up with another reason for Omar not being there.

First, it was that he was probably running late at work. Then it was traffic. Then she wondered if he'd had car trouble. Next, she thought maybe he'd forgotten. After that she wondered if any roads had been closed. And now it was an accident.

Anything but the one option she didn't want to consider: that Omar had second thoughts and changed his mind.

Xavier took out his phone and dialed Omar's number

for the eighth time that evening. And for the eighth time, Kristina watched him expectantly. But when he put his phone down, a grim expression on his face, she knew what it meant. He'd gotten Omar's voice mail. Again.

"Are you sure you wouldn't like to enjoy an appetizer while you wait?"

It was the same server that had introduced himself when they were seated. She could tell the guy was trying to pretend he didn't notice they'd been stood up.

Kristina gave him a weak smile and shook her head no. He nodded and refilled her glass of ice water. A few moments later, he brought another saucer of freshly cut lemons.

"Maybe we should tell her to call the local hospitals. You know, see if he's been brought in."

The "she" Kristina referred to was Tamia, who'd been calling Omar's office and house phone while Xavier called his cell.

Kristina attempted to keep her voice steady and without emotion. When a tear escaped her eye, she grabbed her napkin from the table and turned to the side to dab at her cheek, not wanting Xavier to see.

She was so angry at herself. How many times had she told Xavier and Pam and anyone else who would listen that this was more about Xavier than it was about her? And yet, here she was about to fall apart over being stood up. And at a dinner she wasn't even supposed to be at, no less.

The last thing she wanted was for Xavier to see her break down. From the moment she realized that he existed, she felt like she'd been a disappointment to him. Yes, she had platinum records and Grammys and film awards, but all she could see when she looked in the mirror was the cocaine and the alcohol and the promiscuous behavior. She'd spent most of her life being a wreck, but the only people that knew how bad it was were her sisters. She wanted to keep it that way.

She'd done her best over the past few months to turn her life around, naturally and spiritually, and she felt like she was making some headway.

But now, instead of being the alcoholic crackhead, she was the desperate and pathetic woman, brokenhearted over a lost love. And she could tell by the way Xavier was looking at her that he felt sorry for her. That wasn't how it was supposed to be. She was supposed to take care of him, not the other way around.

Xavier cleared his throat. "Maybe we should just go."

It wasn't the first time he'd made the suggestion. But Kristina couldn't stop watching the door.

"Just ten more minutes…"

Chapter 14

Omar felt like his mind had shut down.

He tried concentrating on what Brock was saying, but he might as well have been speaking a foreign language. The words didn't make sense, no matter how hard Omar tried to understand them. The phone on the side table, ringing and ringing and ringing, didn't make it any better.

"It wasn't like I had intentionally gone behind your back. I mean, you know how it's always been with me and Marisa. We can't stand each other. But Janae had just left me. I was so messed up, I ended up in a bar. That one we used to go to just off-base. Marisa was there. And that night…" Brock clenched his jaw and rubbed his hands over his head.

Omar's head was swimming. He tried to steady it by leaning over and putting his face in his hands. The phone started ringing again.

"She was a mess. She said she knew you were going to

finally leave her once you got back from Turkey. That you had all but said it. She was crying and we were drinking. And I don't know… It just happened."

Brock paced back and forth in front of Omar. When the phone finally stopped ringing, Omar took a breath. He felt like he was going crazy.

"I hated myself. And I planned telling you the minute you returned. But on your way back, during that stopover in New York, you called and said you two were going to split. You said you were telling her that night, when you got home. So I…" Brock shrugged. "I thought maybe I wouldn't have to tell you. I know it was wrong. I should've said something. But I couldn't. And then you guys ended up staying together."

Omar *had* intended on leaving her. That was the plan. But when he got home, Marisa was like he'd never seen her. She was begging him for one last try and told him about how she'd loved him from the moment they'd met but felt like he never really loved her back. She asked him how he could end their marriage when he'd never even given it a chance. She asked, no, pleaded for just one thing. A six-month trial. One in which he'd actually try to be a husband to her and love her as much as she loved him.

Maybe it wasn't a good idea. But he couldn't deny that she was telling the truth. If he'd ever had one major regret in his life other than Kristina, it was that he'd married Marisa when he knew good and well he wasn't in love with her. And she was right about him not trying. He had to take responsibility for that much. Instead of trying to make the marriage work, he went on deployment every chance he got. Because of that, he decided he'd give it his all for six months. In an effort to renew their commitment, they slept together that night. It was something that hadn't happened for the entire year prior.

So when she told him she was pregnant a few weeks later, he had no reason to think the baby wasn't his.

But even later, when he began having his suspicions, he never guessed it was Brock.

Never.

"...and when I brought it up, she laid into me. She kept saying things like, 'You were a crap son, a crap husband, and a crap best friend. Three guesses what kind of father you'd make'. She said you were the best thing that could've happened to Chloe and did I really want to take that away from her? She was right. I would be ruining both your lives. I knew that. And that's the only reason I kept quiet."

"I need you to leave right now."

Brock stopped pacing and looked at Omar. "Look, I can imagine how you're feeling. You hate me. I don't blame you. I hate myself. But I'm telling you the truth. I wasn't out to betray you. I know you're the best thing that happened to Chloe because you're the best thing that happened to me. And maybe I should've kept my mouth shut, but when Marisa told you that you couldn't take Chloe with you, I just snapped."

Omar looked up at Brock, his eyes narrow and dark. "I asked you to leave."

"But I—"

The phone started ringing again and it was the last straw. Omar reached over and yanked it so hard, the cord ripped out of the wall. He threw the phone in Brock's direction with a force powered by the rage he could feel rising from the pit of his stomach.

"Get out!"

Brock opened his mouth to speak, but thought better of it. He backed away and then left.

Omar rubbed the back of his head with his hands. Christian or not, he wanted to break every bone in Brock's body. But that wasn't what mattered. The only thing that mattered was Chloe.

He couldn't stop thinking about her. The way she poked out her little lips to give him a kiss every time she saw him. The way her long eyelashes shadowed her cheeks when she slept. The way she still snuggled in his arms to watch cartoons.

How could she not be his daughter?

But that was only one of the questions on his mind. Could Brock being her biological father affect his rights? He remembered the threats Marisa made. He glanced at his watch. He needed to call his lawyer. At the very least, leave him a message to let him know he would be waiting in his parking lot first thing in the morning.

He reached for the phone and in a split second realized what a bad idea yanking it out of the wall had been. He got up and ran to the entryway table, where he'd left his cell phone and keys.

He picked up his phone and when the screen lit up, he paused. Nine missed calls.

Nine missed calls? What in the world could have—

The dinner.

Omar resisted the urge to send his phone flying across the room. It'd been on silent since the last meeting for negotiations. He hadn't thought to turn the volume back on. He tried calling Kristina but got no answer. He thought about leaving a message but it didn't seem right.

Within minutes, he was out the front door and in his car. But by the time he arrived at the restaurant, Kristina and Xavier were long gone.

Pam went into the kitchen the next morning, ready to

go over the day's itinerary with Kristina. But instead of her sister, she found her nephew at the breakfast nook, reading his devotional and eating cereal.

"Well, good morning!"

Xavier looked up from his Bible. He smiled, but she couldn't help but notice how distracted he looked.

"I didn't mean to interrupt your devotion time. I'll be quick and quiet. I promise." She reached in the cabinet and pulled out a coffee mug.

"Oh, no. It's okay."

Pam put her mug in the pod coffee maker, inserted the pod and added water. As it began to percolate, she leaned over on the granite countertop of the kitchen island. "So, how did last night go?"

Xavier's eyebrows furrowed. He opened his mouth to respond but stopped when Kristina came in. She walked over to Xavier and kissed him on the forehead. Then she turned to Pam.

"What time is the crew arriving?"

Pam glanced at the kitchen clock. "In about an hour and a half."

Kristina nodded and headed to the counter toward the coffee machine, just as it finished Pam's cup.

"You can take that one if you want. I can make another."

"Thanks." Kristina took the coffee, adding nothing, and went back upstairs.

Pam repeated the process and once the coffee machine started working, she went to the breakfast nook and sat across from Xavier.

"What happened?" Pam kept her voice low in case Kristina returned.

"He didn't show."

Pam's face fell and she slid down in her seat.

"To be fair, he had a good reason. But still…" Xavier pushed his spoon around in his cereal. "I can understand now why you were reluctant. You should've seen her last night. She was trying so hard not to cry. The only reason we waited as long as we did was because she didn't want to leave."

"What do you mean, he had a good reason?"

"He finally called late last night. I don't know all the details, but some pretty intense stuff went down having to do with his daughter and his ex-wife. It's bad enough he thinks he's gonna have to fight her for custody."

Pam raised her eyebrows. "Wow. I didn't even know he had a daughter. Or an ex-wife, for that matter."

"Yeah, it's pretty complicated. Complicated enough that I told him I think we should wait on this whole reunion thing."

"Really? It's that bad?"

Xavier shrugged. "I just keep thinking about what you said about sobriety and it being a fragile thing." He glanced at the staircase up to the second floor. "I don't think he'd ever intentionally hurt Kristina, but with this custody thing, I don't know if it's the best time for any of us to be around each other. His ex doesn't even want his daughter to meet me."

Pam folded her arms and considered what she'd just heard. "But what does Kristina think about it?"

"What? The whole issue with his ex-wife? She doesn't know yet. By the time he called me, she'd already gone to her room. Should I tell her?"

Pam tapped the table with her acrylics and thought for a moment. "I think you should. She needs to know he didn't blow you off."

And maybe, Pam thought, *she'll finally decide to put the brakes on this thing.*

Chapter 15

Omar shifted in his seat. The oversized and richly upholstered chair in which he sat was more than comfortable, as were his surroundings. The elegant dark wood paneled walls, fresh cut flowers and sound of classical music in the background should've put him at ease. But he imagined it was hard for almost anyone to be too comfortable while sitting in the waiting room of a family law office.

How did his life turn out like this?

His parents were married for over forty years. Up until his father passed away, they never spent a night apart. They raised four kids together, went to church every time the doors opened, and always kissed each other good night. Omar assumed his life would be the same.

Instead, he was divorced and getting ready to fight for custody of his wife's child with his best friend. He felt like the main character in a Tyler Perry movie. Entertaining on the big screen, not so much in real life.

Besides him, there were two other men waiting to be seen. One across the room and one in the chair next to him. The guy closest to him looked about as bad as he felt. The man's foot hadn't stopped its frantic bouncing since he'd sat down. He flipped through the pages of a magazine so swiftly, Omar knew there was no way he was actually reading it. Like him, the man was doing what he could to pass the time.

The phone rang at the front desk and the secretary picked it up. After mumbling a few sentences, she stood and approached the man on the other side of the room, notifying him it was time for his appointment.

After the man left, the one sitting next to Omar flipped his magazine shut and tossed it on the table in front of them with a loud slap. The sound made Omar look up.

"Sorry. I didn't mean to make so much noise."

Omar shook his head. "No problem."

The man leaned over and ran his fingers through his hair, exhaling roughly.

"I hate these places. Law offices. Lately it seems like I see these people more than I actually see my kids."

"That's rough, man." Omar suddenly felt a kinship with the stranger. Sharing custody with Marisa, he didn't get to see Chloe as much as he would've liked. But the thought of hardly seeing her at all? He didn't even want to imagine it.

"So, did you just get divorced?"

Omar shook his head. "No, it's been a while. But..." He couldn't bring himself to say it. He couldn't bring himself to repeat the words Brock had used to blow his life apart. "Some things have changed."

The man nodded and leaned back in his chair. "And not for the better, I'm guessing." He exhaled. "Well, believe me, it's gonna get a whole lot worse. I wish my ex-wife and I could have gotten along well enough to just talk this out. Come to some sort of agreement on our own, you know? All this family court stuff has been tearing the kids up."

They sat in silence until the man went in for his appointment. But even after he'd left, Omar couldn't get his words out of his head. He didn't want him and Marisa to treat Chloe like a wishbone, each tugging on a part until they tore her in half.

Maybe there was still a way for them to resolve this on their own. It would take everything he had, but he could be civil with her, even now, knowing what he knew, if it meant making things easier for Chloe.

Omar got up and told the secretary he needed to step outside for a moment to make a call. Once out there, he dialed Marisa.

"Hello?"

He'd expected to leave a message. Like Brock, she'd been avoiding his phone calls for the previous week.

"Hey. Listen—" Omar took a deep breath.

Watch your tone. Don't antagonize her. Think about Chloe.

"Brock came over to my house last night. Drunk."

After a long moment of silence, Marisa said, "Okay…"

"I don't want to point fingers. I don't want to wage war. I just want to take care of Chloe."

Again, Marisa was silent for a while before she responded. "What exactly did Brock say?"

Omar still couldn't bring himself to repeat the words out loud. "Come on, Marisa. You know what he said. What you've been afraid he'd say since the night it happened."

He waited, but this time there was no response, so he continued. "It doesn't even matter anymore. Like I said, I don't want this to affect Chloe. So I say instead of going to lawyers or doing anything crazy, we just meet so we can work through it."

"Yeah, okay. Fine." Her tone was clipped and monotone. "When and where?"

Omar almost didn't know what to say. The last thing he expected was for her to be agreeable. He thought for sure he'd have to jump through hoops just to get her to talk. Maybe now that the secret was finally out, she knew she didn't have anything to fear.

"As soon as possible. Today even."

"Text me the details and I'll be there."

Relief settled over Omar and for the first time since talking to Brock, he felt like everything would be okay.

Omar chose a picnic table under a huge maple. Around him, the air was filled with the squeals and giggles of children. Nearby, a large family had music playing and meat on the grill. A grandmother danced alongside teenagers, all of them wearing purple, family reunion tee-shirts. A little ways off, another family tried to make their kites take flight.

Omar couldn't help but notice the irony of him and Marisa meeting to discuss the custody of their daughter in a park filled with loving, happy families.

But he was glad she'd agreed to meet in a public place. Hopefully, being on full view would keep Marisa from going into complete drama mode. The less histrionics, the better chance they had to actually work something out. Not that he even knew what that would be.

If he were honest, what he really wanted was full custody of Chloe. But he knew that was never going to happen. And maybe it was for the best. He knew his daughter needed a mother and despite her many flaws, that's what Marisa was.

And however much Omar loved Chloe, he could never fill the void not having a mother would make.

But that didn't mean he had to like it. Now that he was a grown man, he finally understood all the advice his father gave him and his sisters when they were kids. He always told them to be careful who they chose as a life partner because they weren't just choosing for themselves. They were choosing for their future sons and daughters as well.

If he'd actually followed his father's advice all those years ago, he wouldn't be sitting where he was now.

Omar scanned the parking lot for Marisa's car. Nothing. He'd already decided that if she didn't show, he'd go to her house. Either way, they were going to address this. Today.

A group of screaming kids from the family reunion rushed past him in a game of tag. It was after they'd gone by, he noticed the woman.

She looked out of place at the park. While everyone else wore t-shirts, tank tops, shorts and jeans, she dressed in a powder blue, button-down shirt, a navy blue jacket and tan slacks. If that wasn't enough to get Omar's attention, her marching like a soldier in his direction certainly did.

Omar sat up straight and looked behind him. No, there was no one else she could be looking at. It had to be him. He waited till she got closer before he stood; ready to ask what she wanted. The moment she got within a foot of him, she snatched something out of the inside pocket of her blazer and thrust it in his hand.

"Mr. Williams, you've been served."

Chapter 16

amia came out of her closet with another suitcase and dropped it on her bed next to Xavier. He was lying on his back with his head hanging over the edge, looking like his dog had died. It was the only look he'd had since the failed family reunion. Tamia must've cracked a dozen jokes since then, trying to pull him out of his funk, but nothing worked. If she didn't do something soon, she knew she'd end up walking around just as depressed as he was.

Tamia scooted the luggage over and got on the bed. She stretched out next to Xavier and hung her head over the edge so they were in the same position.

"What are you doing?"

"Trying to understand how blood rushing to your skull makes you feel better."

"It doesn't."

"I agree. How long are you going to stay like this?"

"I'm sorry. I know I'm bumming you out."

"No, I understand. You were really looking forward to meeting your dad."

"Yeah, but it's not just that. It's everybody. This was the only chance I had to be around my birth family. I start college in the fall. I mean, I know we'll get to see each other now and then, but it's not the same."

Tamia knew that Xavier was starting school in the fall, but she hadn't thought about the impact it would have on their time together.

"Don't get me wrong. I'm really glad Kristina's going back on tour. I just wish it wasn't so soon. I thought we'd have more time."

Just as Tamia opened her mouth to agree, an idea struck and she bolted upright.

"That's it! The tour! Why don't you come with us?"

Xavier sat up, too. "I can do that?"

"Of course, you can. Everyone already thinks you're her *protégé*, so it won't seem unusual. I bet Pam could have you hired as an intern or something. You could hang out with us *and* get paid for it!"

A grin slowly spread across Xavier's face. "You, Tamia Langston, are a genius."

Tamia cocked an eyebrow. "Duh."

Xavier put his hands on his belly, threw his head back and laughed. To Tamia, it was one of the most beautiful things she'd seen and heard in days.

Omar sat at the long, mahogany wood table with his lawyer beside him. Despite the court summons, his attorney convinced Marisa and her lawyer to meet and try arbitration first. And while he was grateful for the opportunity, he suspected he wasn't going to get very far. He knew Marisa well enough to know her tendencies, and her avoiding his phone calls the way she had since he'd been served was her way of digging her heels in.

He also suspected she was doing this only to hurt him. But why? And why *now*? The only thing he'd ever been to Chloe was a good father. And he knew, despite her sometimes questionable behavior, Marisa loved her daughter. So why in the world would she try to separate him and Chloe now that the truth was out? If anyone had a right to drag someone into court, it was Omar.

She had knowingly deceived him about Chloe's paternity even long after they'd split. And now, after all that time and child support, she pulled this move. It didn't make sense.

The only reason he could think of was the call from Tamia. He still hadn't asked Marisa whether she'd heard the message, but he was convinced she had. Was that what set her off? Though she hadn't met her, Marisa never liked Kristina. That was no secret. She, like Brock, knew Omar had been in love with her for years. So if she saw the Langston name on the caller ID and then listened to the message, maybe it was enough for her to put two and two together. If Marisa thought Omar and Kristina were back in each other's lives, that would definitely explain her recent behavior.

When Marisa and her lawyer finally arrived, he could tell he was in for a fight. She swung the door open so hard, it slammed against the wall. Then she yanked out one of the chairs and threw her purse on the table. He tried to make eye contact with her, but she refused.

His lawyer began. "It is Mr. Williams' belief that resolving the custody situation outside of family court would be the best course of action. Especially for his daughter."

Marisa scoffed and rolled her eyes.

"What is that about?"

She cut her eyes it Omar. "Like you don't know. You can come in here and play the perfect father in front of these two, but I know better."

Omar could hardly believe what he was hearing. "When have I ever been anything but a good father to Chloe?"

"Look, I didn't come here to get into an argument with you. You said you wanted to discuss it, to keep it out of family court. Fine. That's what I'm trying to do. So how about we just let the lawyers handle it? I don't even really want to do this, but you forced my hand. I'm only here for the safety of my child."

Omar tried to control himself, but nearly jumped out of his seat. His lawyer put his hand on his arm and squeezed. "Mr. Williams…"

Omar put his hand up to his lawyer. "When has she never been safe with me?"

"It's not you I'm worried about." Marisa took out a manila envelope and slapped a stack of photos on the table. Dozens of them. They slid and fanned out across the high gloss finish of the wood.

"I'm not trying to have some drug addict, alcoholic ho around my child."

Omar and his lawyer picked up the pictures, looking them over. It took him a second, but then Omar recognized what they were. Pictures of him. Of Kristina. Of the day they'd spent together.

"Wait a minute. You had me followed?"

But upon further inspection, he realized it wasn't just pictures of him and Kristina. There were pictures of Kristina and her dancers, Kristina and Pam, Kristina and Tamia.

How in the world did Marisa get them? While the pictures of he and Kristina looked like they were taken from a distance and possibly a covert location, the others didn't. Whoever took the photographs had up close and personal access.

"How did you even get these? What? You're a stalker now?"

"I'm only trying to look after my child. I really don't want to cut you out of Chloe's life, but someone has to be the *responsible party*."

Omar swept all the pictures back across the table in Marisa's direction. "I've always known you had problems, but this is just spiteful, even for you. With our history, there's no way any judge in their right mind would call you the responsible party."

Marisa smirked and looked over at her lawyer. The lawyer took out a tablet and, after navigating a few screens, turned it around so Omar could see it.

It was amateur video. Probably from a phone camera. At first, it was hard to make the scene out. It was chaos. Individuals yelling and running about. The picture wasn't steady and people kept getting in the frame. But quickly he realized what the camera owner was attempting to film. It was paramedics on the floor of a bathroom stall, feverishly working to save a woman's life.

Kristina's life.

"I don't have a problem with you, Omar. I really don't. But your little girlfriend? That's a whole other story. You may look good on paper, but Kristina Langston ain't so lily white, is she?"

Omar looked to his lawyer and the expression on the man's face told him all he needed to know. Marisa had him right where she wanted him.

"It's an easy decision, Boo. If you want to stay in my daughter's life, stay *away* from Kristina Langston."

Omar stood in the parking lot, leaned against his car, arms folded. His lawyer stood in front of him, briefcase in hand.

"Going into this, I was all for taking it to court. You know that. With everything that's gone on between you two, you are obviously the better choice. While most judges seem to prefer the mothers, I felt I had enough to turn things in your favor. Now, however…"

"But I've been her father from the moment I learned Marisa was pregnant. It's my name on the birth certificate."

His lawyer put his hand up. "I know. I know. But this Kristina Langston thing… It doesn't look good. I would avoid going before a judge at this point. I think it's best for all parties. We have no way of knowing who we're going to get. There's judges that harbor an inexplicable ambivalence toward the entertainment industry and like to use cases like these as examples. If we got someone like that, we'd be dead in the water. Then again, we could get someone that has a real issue with women lying about paternity. The problem is, there's just no way of telling."

Omar ran his hand over his head and exhaled. "I can't lose my daughter."

His lawyer nodded and patted him on his shoulder. "Listen, I'll schedule another meeting. Hopefully, she will have cooled off by then. Maybe she'll be more reasonable. But if I were you, I'd cut this Langston woman loose."

When Omar opened the door of the church and walked into the sanctuary, he heard a familiar sound.

It was noonday prayer. And while everyone was welcome, the group usually consisted of the mothers of the church.

He sat on one of the back pews and closed his eyes. He listened as the various shouts and cries of the older women filled the empty sanctuary.

Hallelujah.

Help us, Jesus.

We're leaning on You, Lord.

Take us through, Father.

His own spirit echoed every one of the sentiments being cried out. His heart was breaking and his mind was too clouded to think straight.

He thought he had it all figured out. He was sure Kristina coming back into his life was a miracle God Himself had set into motion. And then to learn he had a son with her? It was all he'd ever hoped for and more. So why did it seem that everything was set against it?

When he'd seen Pam's reaction to him showing up at the house, he could understand that. It didn't make him happy, but he could see where she was coming from. He figured he would just have to prove his intentions and she would eventually accept him and Kristina together. But this issue with Marisa was on a whole other level. How in the world did it come to having to choose between Kristina and Chloe?

As much as his heart longed for Kristina, his daughter was first place. That was the commitment he'd made the day she was born. That was his responsibility to her as a father. To love her, keep her and protect her when she couldn't do it herself. There was no question in his mind that that's what he'd do. But why did it have to hurt so bad?

Just the *thought* of saying goodbye to Kristina made his chest ache. How was he going to actually do it? He knew she wasn't the kind of woman that would want him to choose her over his daughter, but that didn't mean it wouldn't hurt her when he did. It seemed that's all he did lately. Hurt her.

He'd spoken with Xavier after missing their dinner engagement and his son made it very clear how upset she'd been. And though Xavier said he understood, Omar couldn't help but sense some resentment. Not that he could blame him. He'd be angry with any man that made his mother cry, too. What impact would this new turn of events have on his already fragile relationship with his son?

It seemed no sooner than he got everything he'd ever hoped for, the world came crashing down around him.

Omar leaned over and put his head in his hands.

"Father, I don't understand what's going on here. I know You said You never leave us and never forsake us, but I'm feeling pretty alone right now. Still, I trust You. I have to. What else can I do? Everything is so messed up. I wanna keep my family safe, but I don't know how. Please…help me.

"I know You see the end from the beginning and You know what's best. Keep Your hand on my daughter. You love her more than I ever could and I love her with my life. No matter what I want or what I *think* I want, please work this out so Chloe and Kristina and Xavier don't get hurt. In Jesus name, I pr—"

The high pitched ring of his cell phone sounded, echoing in the darkened church. Omar jumped up and raced out of the sanctuary, hoping he hadn't disturbed the praying women. The moment he got through the church doors, he looked at his phone screen. Immediately, he felt both joy and dread.

It was Kristina.

Chapter 17

When she asked if they could meet, Omar didn't hesitate to agree. Less than twenty minutes later, he was back where they'd reconnected only a short while ago. But this time, when Kristina came out of the rehearsal studio's back door, she wasn't wearing an expression of self-doubt or apprehension. She was smiling and shining like the sun.

Seeing her so happy tore Omar up inside. *Please help me do this*, was all he could pray.

"That's a pretty serious face you've got." Her voice was light and playful.

"I'm sorry about the other night."

She shook her head. "No, no. Don't be. Xavier filled me in. No details. Just that there's a problem with your ex and custody. Has anything changed? Have you met with her? Where are you with that right now?"

Omar clenched his jaw. He didn't want to lie to her, but at the same time, he didn't want to tell her the whole truth, either.

"We just had a meeting with our attorneys. I'm hoping we can settle this outside of court."

Kristina nodded, her eyebrows knit with concern." Of course. It would be so much easier on your daughter."

He nodded.

"Is there anything I can do?"

"Not really. Marisa can be pretty stubborn, so I'm gonna have to take it one day at a time. Just remember me in your prayers."

"Of course, I will. But you know, I could probably do a little more than that." She smiled at him, a mischievous twinkle in her eye. "It's been a few years since I cooked a full meal, but I made a pretty amazing peach cobbler the other day. Why don't you come to the house for dinner? You and Xavier could spend some time together and maybe you could forget about all this for a couple of hours."

She smiled at him and looked like a shy teenage girl asking her crush out on a first date. It broke his heart.

"Yeah, I don't know…"

She shrugged. "No rush. I know you have a lot on your plate right now. It doesn't have to be today. Whenever you want is fine." She chuckled. "Well, whenever you want as long as it's before next week. Xavier is heading out with the rest of the band for the Show Some Love date in Dallas."

Dread settled like poison in his stomach and he exhaled, leaning against the car. Kristina's smile faded and she looked at the ground, her hands in her pockets.

"Xavier said you wouldn't have a lot of time on your hands. I get that. But why do I have a feeling there's something more? Something you're not telling me?"

Omar rubbed the back of his neck. "Because you're not stupid and I'm not very good at keeping secrets."

She took a step toward him and reached out to grab the corner of his jacket, tugging at it. "I'm a big girl, Omar. Whatever it is, just say it."

He took her hand that held on to his jacket and enclosed it in his own. "Marisa threatened to use my relationship with you against me to gain custody."

Kristina's eyes narrowed. "*Relationship* might be a strong word. I mean, we just started talking again and it's not like—" Her face went slack and she stepped back. "Oh."

Understanding dawned on her face, only to be quickly replaced by humiliation. He wished there was a rock big enough for him to crawl under.

"Let me guess. Rehab. The incident at the hotel." She bit her lip. "And that's *before* they do a little digging."

"Kristina—"

"No. I understand. Believe me, I do." She swallowed hard. "I'm just sorry my past put you in this position. You don't deserve this."

She didn't deserve this. Marisa didn't even know her and yet she was ready to expose all her dirty laundry just to get back at him. It wasn't fair. Especially after all the hard work Kristina had put into getting her life together.

"And please, get that guilty look off your face." She smiled. "You're making me feel worse than I already do."

"I'm sorry."

"Don't be. We waited eighteen years. What's twelve more?"

He looked at her, hardly able to believe what he'd just heard. Was she really saying she was willing to wait for him until Chloe was eighteen?

"I can't ask you to do that."

"You didn't."

He took her by her shoulders and pulled her in, putting his arms around her. The feel of her face cradled in the curve of his neck was like an answer to a prayer. Twelve years seemed an eternity after coming so close to being with her again, but what choice did he have? There was no one else for him but her.

"Okay," she said, pulling away and taking a few steps back. "So it's a date? Me and you. In a decade. Give or take a couple years?"

She laughed but he could see the sadness in her eyes. She blew him a kiss, then turned and ran to the studio door. She wiped her cheeks with the edges of her sleeves as she went.

It should have been easier than this.

He'd already said goodbye to her once before. Why was watching her walk away today a thousand times harder?

∽

"Hello?"

Kristina hadn't planned on crying the moment her friend, Robin Jones, answered the phone. She hadn't even planned on giving her an update on the whole Omar situation. Kristina didn't want to think about it, much less, talk about it. All she wanted to do was what they always did during their weekly phone call: laugh, talk and pray together.

God knows she was in desperate need of all three. Not that she couldn't do the same with her sisters, but since her overdose in Dallas, Kristina and Robin had become especially close. Not just as friends, but as spiritual sisters.

"Kristina? Sweetie, what's wrong?"

Kristina tried to respond more than once, but failed each

time. Robin, as usual, knew just what to do and waited until her friend could speak without choking back tears.

"I'm sorry."

"Girl, please. You know you don't have to say that to me."

Kristina sighed. "I don't even wanna tell you why I'm over here sobbing like some big ol' baby."

Robin laughed. "I'm sure you don't. But since we both know you're gonna, you might as well just get it over with."

Now Kristina was the one laughing. It was true. However dark, shameful or embarrassing, her secrets never remained secrets for long when Robin was around. What she still couldn't get over was that Robin never judged her or made her feel bad about any of it. She just listened and then suggested one thing: Let's take it to God.

"Well, like I told you before, it looked like Omar and I—" Kristina stopped, not wanting to cry again. "I don't know. It just seems a lot of things are rushing in on me at once. Things I thought I'd gotten past."

"Like what?"

"When I found out about Xavier, all I could think about was what mama had taken from me. Then I thought, you know what? Just forget it. You have him *now*. Be grateful for that. But since Omar came back into the picture, I keep thinking about what our lives could have been like. I can't stop wondering what it'd be like to be a wife and mother. To wake up with my family in the morning and go to bed with them at night. For a moment, I thought it might happen. Today I realized it's not.

"One day Omar and I might end up together, but even if we do, my chance to hold a baby or read a little one a bedtime story will be gone. I never let myself admit to wanting those things because it hurt too much. But being so close to having that dream come true …" Again, Kristina stopped until she was sure she could continue without crying. "I'm being greedy. I know that. I should just be grateful that Xavier is here at all. There's so many women who lost their babies and would give anything for my second chance."

Robin remained silent for so long, Kristina thought maybe the call had dropped.

"Robin?"

There was a muffled sound, something like a sob on the other end of the line.

"Just a minute."

Robin's end was muted, but only for a few moments.

"Robin? Are you okay?"

Robin cleared her throat. "Yeah. It's just… I can relate to what you're saying."

Kristina's heart went out to Robin. In the short time they'd known each other, their relationship had consisted of Robin helping, holding and praying Kristina through. It'd never occurred to her that Robin had her own struggles to deal with.

"Robin—"

"It's okay, Kristina. It's something I made peace with a long time ago. Just every now and then…" Robin exhaled. "Don't worry about me. And listen, don't give up, either. Before this whole thing even started, God knew how it would end. Remember how hopeless everything seemed just a few months ago? You were ready to die. But look at what God did! I don't know what He has in store this time, but if I know Him at all, I have to believe it's something good."

Chapter 18

When Brock showed up for work at their office, Omar did his steady best to avoid him. They crossed paths a couple of times—in the break room, at the front desk—but Omar made sure he left the room before Brock had a chance to speak to him. The others in the office noticed, of course, but wisely kept their questions and suspicions to themselves.

Then, just as Omar was getting ready to leave for the day, Brock came into his office, closing the door behind him.

"I can't deal with you today, man."

"I understand—"

"No. You don't."

Brock swallowed and ducked his head. "Wrong choice of words. I just meant I know you don't want to see me right now. And if it'll make it easier, I'll take a leave of absence for a while. The only reason I even came in today was because of Gina."

Omar stopped packing his attaché case and looked up. No, he didn't want to talk to Brock right now, but they were still co-owners of a company. And Gina, as Brock's administrative assistant, was one of their employees. If something was going on with her, he needed to put his issues with Brock aside long enough to deal with it.

"Is something wrong?"

"She's worried about you. Everybody is. That's why she called me. The office gossip is that Marisa's trying to—"

"Don't worry about Marisa. Or Chloe."

"I can help."

Omar laughed. "Trust me, you've done more than enough, *my brotha*."

Brock looked as if Omar had just punched him in the gut. He hung his head. "I'm the last person you want help from. I get that. But believe it or not, you *are* like a brother to me. One I never deserved, but a brother all the same."

Omar stared down at his desk. As much as he wanted to be angry at Brock, Omar knew he wasn't a bad person. He also knew this secret had eaten at Brock like a cancer for years. And though he wasn't ready to admit it out loud, he'd given him a gift when he chose to let Omar be a father to Chloe in his place.

Brock took a step toward Omar and placed the manila envelope he'd been holding on the desk.

"What's this?"

"Paperwork regarding the negotiation you just completed on the commercial property. It's my portion of the sale. I've had everything drawn up by my lawyer, all you have to do is sign."

"You really think you can give me a few million dollars and everything's cool?"

"Of course not. I'm not trying to buy your forgiveness.

I'm giving it to you because it's the only way to resolve this problem with Marisa."

Omar snorted. "And that's a subject you know all about, isn't it?"

"Yeah, actually, I do. And it's part of the reason she and I never got along. Just stop hating me long enough to hear me out."

Omar shook his head, but came around to the front of his desk and sat against the edge. "Fine. Talk."

"Look, *you* wanted kids. You. Not Marisa. All she ever wanted was you. Everything she's ever done, including having Chloe, was about you. This custody thing? Still all about you. She couldn't care less what it's gonna do to Chloe. And now that Kristina's in the picture?" Brock shook his head and exhaled. "She's gonna be out for blood. And there's only one way to get to you."

Omar didn't need Brock to spell it out for him. He already knew the answer: Chloe.

"With Kristina back in your life, Marisa can't lie to herself anymore. There's zero hope for reconciliation. Chloe's the one that's gonna pay for that."

Omar stood and went back around his desk, dropping in his leather executive chair.

"Kristina's not back in my life. Marisa's already made sure of that."

Brock frowned. "What happened?"

"What difference does it make? She has the leverage she needs to make me look like the unstable parent. And if I don't stay away from Kris, she'll use it. Case closed."

Brock sat in one of the chairs on the other side of Omar's desk. He tapped the manila envelope on the desk's surface.

"And that's why you need this. Shared custody is not

enough. You need full custody. And I know how you can get it."

"There's no way Marisa would agree to my having full custody. That would mean giving me everything I could ever want. She'd die before she did that."

"Not if you gave her what *she* really wants first."

"Money? If it were that easy, I would have done it already."

"It's a little more than money. And in the grand scheme of things, it won't be all that hard, either. But trust me, you're not gonna like it."

Xavier brought his duffle bag and carry-on down the stairs. Upon seeing the luggage, Kristina feigned complete and utter devastation. Pam caught on and joined in. Tamia, at the kitchen island, bent over a bowl of cereal, rolled her eyes.

Kristina grabbed Xavier's shirt and shook him. "No! Don't go! What will we do without you?"

Pam flung herself over the counter and wailed. "Don't leave us, Xavier. Don't go!"

"Y'all need help." Tamia said, shoveling another spoon full of Cocoa Puffs in her mouth.

Xavier put his hands up. "Ladies, ladies. Please. Try to control yourselves. I break hearts. It's what I do."

Pam stopped wailing and busted out laughing. "Now, I don't know about all that. But I *am* gonna miss you."

Kristina hugged him and nodded. "Me too."

"First of all, you'll see him again in two days. Second, why don't nobody care that I'm gonna be on that bus, too?"

Pam went and draped herself over Tamia's shoulders. "Oh, is the baby feeling neglected? It's okay. We're gonna miss you, too."

Xavier reached into his carry-on and pulled out a cardboard box, setting it on the countertop.

"I'd planned on giving you this when I first got here, but I forgot. Anyway, I thought you might wanna open it in private, so I wanted to make sure you had it before we left for Dallas."

Kristina turned the box to better read the writing across the top of it. Pam and Tamia came to where she was to do the same.

"What is it?"

Xavier shrugged. "I have no idea. My mom and I were clearing out Mother Mahalia's house and we found it. It had your names on it so I didn't open it."

The sisters exchanged looks.

Pam cleared her throat. "Well, that's... Thank you, Xavier. We appreciate you doing that."

He grinned, obviously pleased to have helped. "No problem." He pointed at Tamia. "Are we still doing that Star Wars marathon before we go to your house?"

She nodded. "Yeah, I'll meet you in the media room."

All three women watched and waited for him to leave before returning their attention to the box.

"What do you think it is?"

"Who knows?"

"Who *cares*?"

"Tamia."

"What? When has a surprise from mama *ever* been good? Well, with the exception of Xavier."

Kristina leaned one arm on the counter and took another look at the box. "She has a point. Do we really want to know what's inside?"

Pam picked up the box and shook it. "So...what? We just toss it?"

Tamia and Kristina looked at each other and nodded.

"Okay. But let's wait until you two are already on your way to Dallas. He went through all the trouble to bring it here. I don't want him to know we have no intention of opening it."

❧

When Omar arrived at the meeting to finalize the shared custody agreement, his attorney was waiting for him in the parking lot.

"I don't know what's going on, but Marisa's lawyer says she's furious."

That was an understatement.

The moment Omar walked through the door of the conference room, Marisa threw a stack of pictures at him.

"*She means everything to me, I'd never do anything to endanger her, Chloe is number one in my life, I'd sacrifice everything for my daughter.*" Marisa was doing what Omar guessed was supposed to be an impression of him. "Right. Everything but drop that crackhead slut."

Omar picked up one of the pictures from the floor and saw that they were of his conversation with Kristina.

"I was saying goodbye to her."

"Liar! You thought you could sneak around and I wouldn't know about it. Well, guess what? All bets are off. You're gonna wish you never crossed me. By the time I'm done, Chloe won't even remember what you look like."

"It doesn't even matter what the truth is, does it? All you want is revenge. You don't care who it hurts. How did you become so heartless?"

Marisa whooped and smacked the top of the table. "Oh, now that's rich! The Tin Man is calling *me* heartless! I guess I learned from the best, huh, Boo?"

Omar's lawyer tried to interject, but Omar put his hand up to stop him. As much venom as Marisa was spewing, Omar noticed something in her eyes when she said that last sentence.

Pain.

And in that moment, he realized that Brock was right about the only way to end the battling over Chloe, once and for all.

Omar looked at both the attorneys. "I need you to give us a moment alone."

His attorney nodded and stood up, almost eager to leave, but Marisa's didn't budge.

"You, too."

She arched an eyebrow. "I'm not going anywhere. Anything you have to say to her, you can say in front of me."

Omar looked at Marisa. He could tell she was curious to know what he had to say.

She nodded at her attorney. "It's okay. I can handle him."

The woman took her briefcase by the handle but looked at Omar over her glasses. "If you so much as lay one hand on my client…"

It took everything Omar had in him to stay calm. He could only imagine what lies Marisa had told the woman. He never laid a finger on her in all the years they'd known each other. Though at the moment, he was feeling some great temptation.

Through gritted teeth, he managed to say, "Not even a hair on her head."

Satisfied, the woman got up and left the room. The moment she was gone, Marisa jutted one hip to the side and folded her arms. "So, you have your private time. What do you have to say?"

He took an envelope out of his sports coat and placed it

on the table. "I opened an offshore account in your name. All the verification you need is right there."

Marisa threw her head back and laughed. "Are you really trying to buy my child? I coulda sworn that's illegal or something."

"Never. There's not enough money in the world to do that."

Marisa narrowed her eyes, glanced at the envelope and then back at Omar.

"Go ahead," he said. "Open it."

Marisa snatched the envelope off the table and ripped it open. She scanned the document inside and blinked twice. She opened her mouth and then closed it again. She read the words twice more before speaking.

"Is this some kind of trick?"

"No trick."

"I don't understand."

"Think of it as a do-over. The money and freedom to have the life you dreamed of instead of the one I gave you. A chance to experience all the things you hoped for. Painting in Paris. Riding a Vespa through Rome. Finding true love in London." He took a deep breath before saying the next part. "Without any baggage."

He cringed at referring to Chloe as baggage, but according to Brock, that's what Marisa thought of her. Omar watched his ex-wife's every movement and every breath. He watched for absolutely any sign that would prove Brock wrong. Because while he'd never nominate Marisa for Mother of the Year, he didn't want to believe she saw that perfect little girl as little more than a pawn.

Marisa took a seat, still staring at the paper she held in her hand. "I told you about all that stuff the night we got drunk in that bar." Her voice was soft and low. He'd almost

forgotten what it sounded like before it'd become permanent-
ly sharpened with anger.

He sat down as well. "I know."

She turned away and wiped at her eyes. "I can't believe
you even remember…" And then, after a few moments passed,
she said, "You only got part of it right, though. I didn't want to
find true love in London. I wanted to visit London with my
true love." She shook her head. "There was no reason to look
for something I thought I'd already found."

They sat in silence for several minutes, neither of them
moving. Then, staring at the paper again, Marisa exhaled. "So
basically, you're saying if I let you have full custody, you'll give
me a brand-new life? No strings attached?"

"No strings attached."

He couldn't read her expression. As dumb as it sounded,
part of him hoped she would refuse his offer. Because if she
took it, how in the world would he explain to his daughter
that her mother walked away from her for eight figures?

Marisa tossed the envelope back onto the table and headed for the door. Omar closed his eyes as relief and gratitude
washed over him. He was glad Brock was wrong. He knew
fighting her for custody was going to be the battle of his life,
but he couldn't help but feel it would be easier than what he'd
just proposed.

Marisa opened the door and called the lawyers back in.

She looked to her attorney and nodded toward Omar.
"We've come to an agreement. But I want both of you in here
as witnesses to make sure he doesn't back out of it."

Chapter 19

'm about to looked busted! No eyelashes, no Spanx, no nothing! Girl, I'm so happy those folks are gone, I might have to have a praise break right here!"

Without getting up from her chair, Kristina balled up her fists, threw her arms out and proceeded to shout it out. Pam burst out laughing. Both women were in Kristina's bedroom, unwinding from the busy day and celebrating the last-minute announcement that the crew was taking the following day off.

Pam was stretched across Kristina's bed, watching her remove the day's makeup at the vanity. "Who you telling? Now we don't have to hide Xavier from that nosy little girl when the bus leaves in the morning."

Kristina jerked around in her seat to face her sister. "Oooh! I hadn't even thought about that! Well, thank the Lord for Jesus!"

"Right."

"And you already called about the flight schedule? I want

to get there early enough to have a good look at the venue and—"

Pam sat up. "Excuse me, ma'am. I know how to do my job, thank you very much. That's why you haven't fired me yet."

Kristina looked at Pam through the mirror's reflection, a twinkle in her eye. "Actually, I've fired you more than once. It's just that I was usually high when I did it, so you thought it didn't count." She let out a high-pitched cackle that prompted Pam do the same.

"I know you got it handled. I'm just so excited to have Xavier on the road with me. Add to that the usual nerves before a tour and a day off for the film crew and I don't even know what to do with myself."

"Well," Pam said, getting up and going to her sister. "I have an idea. You have those final fittings tomorrow, so why don't we feast tonight? You'll have to watch your diet for your voice over the next few months, so let's go all out while we still can."

"Yasss!" Kristina did another chair shout and Pam shouted her way to the door, laughing.

Alone, Kristina looked at herself in the mirror. She couldn't remember the last time she'd done it without flinching. She'd spent so long hating herself, she knew it'd take her a while to get used to it. She sat back in her chair, closed her eyes and said a silent prayer of thanks. Despite her relationship with Omar not moving forward, she had an inner peace about her life and that situation, in particular. After her talk with Robin, she decided to stop dwelling on what she'd lost or would never have. Instead, she'd live one day at a time and be grateful for each moment as it came, trusting God to handle the rest.

Kristina jumped up and ran to her closet. If she was going

to truly pig out, she needed to dress for the occasion. She retrieved the one set of old and ratty pajamas she owned from the bottom drawer of her dresser.

After changing, a thought occurred to her and she ran downstairs, hoping to catch Pam before she left to pick up the food.

"Pam! Pam! Make sure you get an extra helping of—"

Halfway down the staircase, Kristina came to a full stop when she saw Pam and Omar standing in the entryway. He had a bouquet of Gerber daisies in his hand and a smile on his face.

Kristina trudged down the stairs wearing, not a smile, but a scowl. "Why can't you ever show up when I'm looking presentable?"

"You look beautiful."

Pam chuckled and headed toward the garage. "I'll leave you two alone." Then, as she saw Kristina open her mouth, "And yes, I'll make sure to get an extra helping of macaroni and cheese and a side of pickles."

"Just so you know," Kristina said, after Pam had gone, "I don't care that you're my baby daddy. I'm not sharing the mac and cheese."

Omar laughed and put his hand up. "I wouldn't even ask." He offered the flowers to Kristina.

"Thank you. They're beautiful." She admired the petals. "But, as happy as I am to see you, weren't we supposed to avoid one another for a decade?"

"That's why I'm here. I'll give you all the details later, but I had to drop by because the second the papers were finalized, there was only one person I wanted to tell. I now have full custody of Chloe. Marisa's no longer going to stand in our way."

Kristina's mouth dropped. "But how?"

"Like I said, I'll explain it all later. But what it boils down to is this, we have our second chance. Only, things are different now. While Chloe and I have always been a package deal, it's no longer weekends and some holidays. It's full-time. So, do you still want to sign up for this?"

The conversation with Robin flashed through her mind and Kristina's heart pounded against her ribcage with excitement. She knew parenthood wasn't a walk in the park. She knew Chloe might not even like her at first. But she couldn't help but feel somehow, someway, this was the family she'd spent so many years yearning for.

Did she still want to sign up for that?

"Absolutely."

"I wish I could be here tonight to meet Chloe," Xavier said as Kristina kissed him goodbye. They stood amid a flurry of activity as the long and rumbling tour bus beside them was loaded with passengers and luggage.

"Me, too!" Tamia came up behind her sister, wrapped her arms around her waist and laid her head on her shoulder.

"Don't worry. Omar is coming to the show and he's bringing her with him."

"I still can't believe this is happening. I never thought I'd know where I came from. Now I have a whole family, baby sister included!"

Kristina put her arms over her sister's and swayed back and forth. "Well, if that's what you really wanted, I have one I'd be willing to sell you."

"Ugh!" Tamia pretended to be thoroughly offended and stomp off, but Kristina grabbed her by the arm and pulled her back. She hugged her and kissed her all over her face.

"You know I'd never get rid of you!"

"Thanks for that, at least."

"Not for a million dollars. Now, if somebody offered me two million…"

"You're a brat." Tamia was still trying to act mad, but had trouble hiding the smile that tugged at her lips.

After seeing Xavier, Tamia and everyone else off on the tour bus, Kristina did her best to get through the next eight hours of final dress fittings, a hair color touch up, and a last-minute visit to her chiropractor. Along the way, she tried to be polite and seem unhurried, but on the inside she was begging each person to cut the small talk and demanding every driver on the road to speed up.

All she really wanted was to get home and get ready. Her life was about to change and whether that change would be smooth or bumpy, she had no idea. What she did know was that she couldn't be more excited to find out.

Omar stood in the bedroom doorway and watched Marisa fold the last few items of Chloe's and put them in a suitcase. She was at a playdate and he and Marisa thought it would be better for him to pick up her stuff then.

He knew it was all for the best, but the sight of a mother packing her child's things to send her away still brought him down.

"Please get that look off your face."

"What look?"

"Like you're getting the last glimpse before they close the casket." She picked up another small shirt and folded it. "I'm a big girl. You don't have to hide your relief for my sake."

"I don't feel relieved. I feel…"

What did he feel? A lot of things. Almost too many to make sense of. Almost.

"Forgive me."

The words that came out of Omar's mouth seemed to shock Marisa almost as much as they surprised him. She sat on the bed, speechless.

"I never admitted it, not to you or even myself, but I used you to mend a broken heart. I didn't realize that's what I was doing at the time, but that's what it was. It wasn't fair. You deserved better than that."

Marisa blinked. After a few moments, she threw her hands up and shook her head. "See? This. *This* is why I fell in love with you. Because, in spite of everything, you're a real man. A good man." She laughed. "If only I could have made you love me..." She said it flippantly, but the regret in her voice was hard to miss.

Omar came in and sat on the bed. "I just keep thinking about all the mistakes we've made. And I can't help but wonder if we're making another one. I tried explaining this to Chloe, but I'm not sure she understands. Just because we signed that agreement doesn't mean you have to completely disappear from her life. I think it'd be better if you didn't. No matter what's gone on between us, you're her mother and she loves you."

Marisa folded her arms and chuckled, but he could see the tears forming at the corners of her eyes. "Wow. You really do try to see the best in people, don't you? Even people like me and Brock."

"I think anybody can change for the better. I did."

Marisa stared out the window for a moment before speaking. "You wanna know the God's honest truth?" She looked at him.

"Sure."

"If you and I hadn't slept together the night you got back from deployment, I would've had an abortion. The only reason I even went to term was because you thought the baby was yours." She wiped away tears before they had the chance to roll down her cheeks. "*Your* baby I could have loved. But Brock's?" She shook her head. "We were nothing but two desperate and lonely people that hated each other the next morning even more than we had the night before. *That's* what Chloe came from. Maybe it makes me a bad person to admit it, but there it is."

"It doesn't have to be that way though. You don't have to see all of your regrets and mistakes whenever you look at her. You could learn to love her for who she is."

"I tried to make you love me. Didn't work, did it? Omar, you can't make your heart feel something that's not there. You taught me that. Do you really wanna put her through the same thing? I think in the long run, that would hurt her more than me leaving. Besides," Marisa said, standing and picking up another shirt. "Chloe understands a lot more than you think she does."

Omar felt a lump rise in his throat. Was Marisa right? Would having a parent abandon you be better than having them stay, but not be able to love you?

Marisa shrugged. "If it makes me a terrible person, so be it. But at least she'll know I chose not to lie to her. And if she wants to get to know me later or just cuss me out for being the world's worst mother, all she has to do is look me up."

"If this is how you felt, why fight for custody? Especially after I told you I didn't care that she wasn't my biological daughter?"

Marisa stopped folding and looked at him in disbelief. Then she laughed. "Wow. You still don't get it. Omar, that's why I sued you for custody in the first place."

"That doesn't make any sense."

Marisa tossed the shirt back in the laundry basket and put her hand on her hip. "Well then, let me break it down for you. I used to daydream about the day you'd discover what Brock and I did. In my daydreams, your reaction would be different each time. Sometimes you'd be angry, sometimes you'd be hurt. But whatever your reaction, it was always big. And I lived for that moment. That moment when I'd be able to look in your eyes and see all the pain I'd caused you. Because then, even if it were for just a moment, I'd know I made you feel something. *Finally.* You have no idea what it's like being with someone that's so indifferent. You never loved me. You never hated me. You never felt *anything* for me. It was like I didn't exist."

She laughed, but it sounded hollow. "So imagine my surprise when the moment I'd dreamed about for so long finally came and you did what you always do. Nothing. *'It doesn't even matter anymore.'* Like, what man even says that? *'You slept with my best friend and passed his daughter off as mine, but you know what? That's okay. We're cool.'*"

"That's not what I was saying."

"Wasn't it?"

Omar opened his mouth, but Marisa stopped him. "Don't. Please. What I want, you can't give me. You never could. At least, now I have a chance to start over. And that's what I need. No baggage. That's what you promised."

Omar nodded. "You're right. That's what I said."

"The deal was I get to walk away and that's what I'm doing. For good."

Chapter 20

"How do I look?"

Pam peered up from the contracts on her desk to see Kristina spinning around, her arms out.

"You look great."

Kristina wrinkled her nose. "Your lips say great, but your face says something else."

"No. I mean it. You look wonderful. I don't think I've ever seen you so happy." Pam closed her laptop and put her hand on her chin. "I'm trying not to let it scare me."

Kristina sat in the chair opposite her sister. "Why would my being happy scare you?"

"Because…" Pam exhaled. "What if it doesn't work out? This wouldn't be just any breakup, Krissi. It'd be a breakup with your first love and the father of your only son. And now he has full custody of his daughter. I know you always wanted a family. Now you'll have an instant one. But if it goes sideways, you lose him *and* her."

"Maybe. Maybe not. You can't always go worst-case scenario, Pam."

"That's my job, remember? Look, I'm not trying to rain on your parade, but I don't want you to get hurt either. This is a big deal. And it could go wrong in a big way. I've seen you spiral out once before. We came so close to losing you in Dallas." Pam rubbed her hands over her face. "All of us, being like this? So…happy? It feels fragile. It scares me."

Although Pam was definitely the 'prepare for the worst' type, Kristina couldn't say she hadn't felt a tinge of anxiety herself. For years, the only thing she'd ever experienced that came close to happiness was being high. But even that was empty and short-lived. The hope and joy she experienced now was brand new. Almost too good to be true. Did that mean it was?

"Let's put it in God's hands. In my heart, I feel this is right, but let's trust God that if Omar and I aren't meant to be together, He'll take care of me. He'll take care of all of us."

Pam bit her lip. "You're starting to sound like Robin. Next thing I know, you'll tell me I'm operating out of fear, not faith."

"I sound very wise."

Pam chuckled. "For years I've tried to keep us from falling apart. It's been my full-time occupation. Putting things in God's hands and trusting Him to take care of it is going to take some practice."

"Well, I'll keep you in my prayers."

"Shut up," Pam said, grinning. She stood and stretched. "All right then, I'll be in the media room if you need me. Bring Chloe in. I'd like to meet her. Omar, too. I promise I won't bite."

"Just bark, huh?"

"I'm serious. I'll be good. Chloe and I can hang out

together in there. Tamia and Xavier just bought and watched every Star Wars series, cartoon and movie in existence. We can do that just in case you two want to feed each other shrimp or something silly like that."

Kristina wrinkled her nose again and Pam laughed.

"Hey, enjoy it while you can. From what I hear, privacy is something you don't get much of with a five-year-old running around."

Kristina put on her earrings just as the doorbell rang and rushed down the stairs to open the door. Waiting on the other side was an awestruck Omar and the most beautiful little girl she'd ever laid eyes on. She stepped back to let them in, glad to see that Omar couldn't stop staring at her.

"I thought I'd, you know, put makeup on, run a comb through my hair. Make myself presentable. Stuff like that."

"It's working for you." He looked down at his equally awestruck daughter. "What do you think, Chloe?"

"You look like a supermodel."

"Believe it or not," he said in a stage whisper. "She's been one. And she sings, too."

Chloe's eyes grew wide as saucers. "You do?"

"I do."

"I think somebody's got a new crush," Omar whispered as Chloe gazed at Kristina.

Kristina held her hand out to the little girl. "Wanna come with me? There's someone I'd like you to meet."

Chloe, suddenly shy and blushing, took Kristina's hand. She looked back at her dad and cheesed so hard, he started laughing. As they walked toward the media room, Chloe continued to gaze at Kristina.

"Is it Xavier?"

"No, honey, not Xavier. He's in Dallas right now. But you'll get to see him soon. He can't wait to meet you."

That news made Chloe so happy, instead of walking next to Kristina, she began to skip.

"Now I know it's not as exciting as meeting your brother, but how about meeting one of my sisters? Her name is Pam."

"How many sisters do you have?"

"Two."

Chloe held up two fingers. "Two? Do they look like you?"

"Pretty much."

"Wow…"

Omar shook his head and laughed along with Kristina as she opened the door to the media room. "Pam, this is—"

Pam put her hand up to signal Kristina to stop talking. She stood in the middle of the room, glued to the news report on the enormous TV screen. Kristina let go of Chloe's hand and moved to the screen, trying to make sense of the images flashing before her.

It was a car accident on a freeway near several overpasses. The camera footage was aerial, from a news helicopter, so it took her a moment to comprehend what she was looking at.

There looked to be several vehicles involved, but it was difficult to tell how many. At the center of it all was a bus, her name partially visible along the side of it that wasn't caved in.

Once the images started making sense, Kristina found herself struggling to remain upright. She didn't know if she was awake or dreaming and the voice of the news reporter sounded muffled and far away.

"…have just confirmed that despite previous reports, Kristina Langston was, in fact, *not* on the tour bus at the time of the fatal accident. According to sources, she is in Atlanta due to a prior engagement and was scheduled to meet with the bus in Dallas on tomorrow evening. No official statement has been made from Langston or her camp, but this is what we know so far:

"Authorities cannot confirm whether there are any survivors of the horrific accident. Of the seven people removed thus far, all were deceased.

"According to sources, the usual passengers of the singer's tour bus would include Langston's band, her backup singers, dancers and on rare occasions, Langston herself. Among those, is the pop star's youngest sister, Tamia Langston.

"As always, stay tuned as we continue to bring you up-to-the-minute coverage on this unfolding tragedy. Once more, current reports are that Kristina Langston was not on the tour bus involved in the deadly freeway collision earlier this evening."

MY Soul is Satisfied

The Langston Family Saga: Book 3

Chapter 1

Kristina Langston wasn't sure how much longer she'd last without knowing whether her son was dead.

"Why isn't anybody picking up? "

Kristina disconnected the call and fought the urge to throw the phone at the vehicle dashboard. She couldn't believe she'd been put on hold with the hospital.

Again.

She'd called on the way to the airport, while waiting for the plane to takeoff, at the car rental counter, then again, when they got the car. Now, she, Omar and Chloe were on their way to the hospital and still had no information.

Omar stole a quick glance at her from the driver's side before returning his attention to the road. "There was something like eight cars included in the accident. Not to mention the bus. And how many people were on there?"

Kristina leaned her head against the passenger side window and shut her eyes. "Twelve. Thirteen, with the driver."

She hadn't yet met the driver. But the others? Those twelve were everything to her. Her family and loved ones. Her closest friends. Dancers, musicians and singers she'd known for years. Her baby sister. Her son.

"They're probably swamped, Kris."

She knew he was right. It's what made the most sense. But it didn't keep her mind from racing with all the terrible possibilities. The news reporter had speculated that there were many more fatalities than originally reported, but that's all it was, speculation.

Supposedly, bodies were seen removed from the scene, but whether those moved were being taken to the hospital or the morgue, she had no idea. And maybe those reported dead weren't even her own. Like Omar said, there were eight other cars involved in the accident. Maybe, by some miracle, the bus looked worse off than it actually was and everyone on it walked away with no more than a few scratches or broken bones.

What she needed to do was take a breath and remain positive. They'd be at the hospital in a few moments and would know all they needed to soon enough.

Kristina looked at Omar. His back was straight as a board and he stared ahead at the road with the intensity of a man on a mission. He'd been holding on to the steering wheel with an iron grip from the moment they'd gotten in the car.

Ordinarily, Pam would've arranged for a driver to take Kristina wherever she needed to go, but Omar insisted on driving. He said he had to do something other than sit in a backseat and twiddle his thumbs. But other than that, he'd barely spoken a word since leaving Atlanta and she knew he was probably doing the same thing she was—trying to get the horrific images he'd seen on TV out of his head. She didn't know about him, but she sure wasn't having much success.

Every few moments, her inner eye was assaulted by visions of the twisted and smoking metal alongside the busted bits of tire and shattered glass littering the freeway. But that wasn't all.

What they'd seen was live aerial shots from a news helicopter camera, panning over the scene. For a moment, the cameraman zoomed in on the pileup and Kristina saw someone that'd been thrown from the wreckage. Like a rag doll that had been tossed on the floor by a careless child, the person's legs and arms were sprawled about in an unnatural way. The cameraman finally noticed it too, because seconds later, the camera was quickly jerked away.

Part of her was relieved for that. But as much as she didn't want to see it, another part of her wished he'd zoomed in closer so she could know whether she was looking at one of her loved ones.

The phone rang and Kristina jumped to answer it.

"It's Pam," she said, putting it to her ear. "Hello?"

"Has she heard anything? Does she know—"

Kristina put her hand up to quiet Omar.

"Pam, I didn't catch that. Start again."

"I said I keep getting put on hold with the hospital, but I've had the news on in the background. They've confirmed nine fatalities so far, but they're not giving any names or more information, so I don't know how many of those are from the bus. The only thing I do know is that they're still removing people from the wreckage. I just got a call from Amber, though. The other two buses were twenty minutes ahead of the main one. All of them are okay."

Kristina took a breath. "Thank God for that."

"Have you heard anything?"

"No, it's been the same here. I keep getting put on hold. I've been calling Tamia's phone, but there's no answer.

But we're almost to the hospital. I'll call you when I know something."

"Okay."

"Pam?"

"Yeah?"

"I know how it looks, but… God's brought us through too much for this to be how it turns out. We've got to trust that."

A few moments of silence passed. Then Pam said, "Call me the minute you know anything. Our flight leaves in just over an hour."

Kristina knew her sister well enough to understand what her response meant. Pam liked to call herself a realist. She was never one to look for the silver lining or get her hopes up. She did the complete opposite. "Expect the worst and you won't be disappointed" were words she lived by.

Not that Kristina judged her for it. If she were honest, she was part of the reason Pam found it hard to be hopeful. Her sister had spent the past fifteen years trying to hold her, her career, *and* their family together. Kristina didn't even know some of what Pam had seen or dealt with because Kristina spent so much of that time in a drug-induced stupor. So even if she didn't agree, she understood why Pam wouldn't allow herself to hope for the best.

But Kristina didn't mind. She had enough hope for both of them. There was a time in her life when she thought she'd never be free of addiction. There were nights she would get high, hoping it was finally the night she'd overdose. But God did the impossible and set her free. If He could do that for her then, she sure wasn't about to lose heart now.

After a quick goodbye, Kristina checked the backseat to see if Chloe was still sleeping, and then told Omar, "Nine confirmed dead. People are still being pulled out—"

Before she could finish, sirens blared from behind them and lights flashed through the interior of the car. They looked in the rearview mirror to find an ambulance speeding in their direction and another rounding the corner to do the same.

Omar pulled over to let the two vehicles scream past them. But even after the street was clear, Omar didn't move a muscle. Kristina didn't have to ask why. The tight expression on his face was explanation enough.

No parent wanted to see their child rushed away in an ambulance. But in this case, they hoped that's exactly what happened.

Because the alternative meant their son, the son they hardly knew, was one of the nine.

Chapter 2

"Oh, no," Kristina groaned as they turned in to the parking lot and saw the front of the hospital.

Along the edge and in front of the doors, a large crowd had gathered. Some wore huge backpacks and had long lens cameras pointed toward the hospital entrance. Others stood next to tripods, eyeing the passengers of every car that drove by. Still others held up signs and pictures of Kristina and some of Tamia, with hearts drawn on them.

"Who are all these people?" Omar leaned forward to look out the windshield, his brows furrowed.

"Mostly paparazzi." Kristina squinted. "Looks like some fans, too."

"Maybe we should try to find a back entrance."

"We usually need escorts for this type of thing, but we left in such a hurry, I didn't even think about that. I have no idea how long it would take for someone to get here. We've already waited so long to know what's going on, I'd rather just brave it."

Kristina peered in the backseat and saw that Chloe was still sleeping.

"Drop me off as close as you can, then go find a place to park and wait. I'll call you once I find out about another entrance."

"No way. I'm not letting you push through that alone."

"But what about Chloe?"

Omar stared at his daughter in the backseat, a frown on his face. "I'll hold her. Keep her eyes and ears covered. That way we stay together."

It was a plan easier said than done. Even with sunglasses and a hoodie over her head, Kristina was made the moment she came within five feet of the crowd. What had been a low hum of activity turned into an earsplitting cacophony of shouts, accompanied by hundreds of blinding flashes of light.

"Kristina! Kristina! What are you feeling?"

"Kristina! How many are dead?"

"Kristina! Why weren't you on the bus? Do you feel guilty?"

Kristina kept her head low and held the back of Omar's jacket. She looked up for a moment to see how close they were to the entrance and caught a glimpse of Chloe's face. Although her father held her close and kept her head on his shoulder, the child looked terrified. Kristina relaxed her hold on his jacket and reached up to touch her, but when she did, the shuffling of the crowd separated them. Seeing the opening, the photographers encircled her like a pack of hungry wolves.

"Have you spoken to their family members?"

"Do they blame you for the deaths of their loved ones?"

"We understand that some of your musicians and singers are dead. What are you feeling right now?"

Kristina tried to move through them, but they pressed in on her, making it almost impossible to take a step forward. But even with all the chaos, she heard Omar shouting for her over the crowd. Searching in the direction of the shouts, she saw him trying to hold onto Chloe and push paparazzi out of the way at the same time.

She raised her arm and yelled back. "Get her inside! Go!"

Another man bumped right into her and shoved his phone in her face, the camera light on.

"Is it true your sister was decapitated? Can you confirm that?"

Kristina froze.

Decapitated? Why would he even say that? Her many years in the entertainment industry had shown her what depths people would go to for a story and her experience with the paparazzi had shown her what they were willing to do for a reaction. But she'd also learned there was usually a kernel of truth to their rumors. However small, it was always there.

"What?" Her voice sounded breathless in her ears as she rocked unsteadily, feeling as if the wind had been knocked out of her.

He nodded his head enthusiastically, pleased to have gotten a TMZ worthy sound bite out of her.

"We have a source on the inside, Kristina. Apparently she was—"

Omar came out of nowhere, shoving the guy in the chest.

"Shut your mouth, man! Show some respect!"

The anger that flashed in Omar's eyes made Kristina worry the young man would go home with fewer teeth than he came with. To make matters worse, Chloe was whimpering and trying to cover her face with her tiny hands. Kristina grabbed Omar's arm and turned his face to her.

"It's all right. He was just trying to get a reaction. He probably doesn't even know anything. Let's just get inside."

Omar wrapped his free arm around her and they tried tunneling their way through the crowd again. Kristina kept her eyes down and her ears covered, so she didn't know why their task suddenly became easier until she looked up.

Robin Jones, Pastor Thomas and a familiar looking young man in scrubs were in front of them and pushing people away to get them through.

Once inside, Robin hugged Kristina and looked her over.

"Are you okay? If we'd known when you were coming, we would've been out there waiting."

"It's okay. I'm fine. But what's happening? Do you know anything? Who have they brought in?"

Robin put her hands on Kristina and Omar's backs and, along with Pastor Thomas and the man in scrubs, led them through the corridor.

"I couldn't get much information because I'm not family. But I know your son is here. Esther is in with the doctor. She should be out soon. She'll be able to tell you more. Where's Pam?"

"We came the minute we saw the news report. She stayed behind to pack and make hotel arrangements for everyone, but she'll be here in a few hours."

"Okay, well, I have to go out of town tomorrow, but you're all welcome to stay at my house if you'd like. It may be more comfortable than a hotel." She looked over Kristina's shoulder in the direction they'd come from. Hospital security was trying to manage the crowd and prevent people from taking pictures through the sliding glass doors. "It might be more private, too."

"Really?"

"Of course. I'll talk to Pam when she gets here and work out all the details."

Robin rubbed Chloe's back. "And who's this beautiful little lady?"

Kristina was immediately reminded of the calming effect Robin's presence had on others. Chloe, who'd looked terrified only moments before, was now giving a shy smile.

"I'm Chloe."

"Chloe? What a beautiful name. It fits you!"

"Thank you."

When the group reached the waiting room, it was overflowing with people. Most were too grief stricken and worried to pay them any mind. But a few recognized Kristina and whispered while watching her.

No sooner than they found a free corner to stand in, Esther Morris, Xavier's adoptive mother, came out of the double doors with her husband, Deacon, close behind. After a few introductions, Esther told them what she knew.

"He's in surgery right now. He suffered multiple contusions to the head and face. There are some internal injuries and broken bones, but what they're most concerned about right now is the apparent swelling on the brain."

"Oh, Lord…" Omar whispered

Robin put her hand on his shoulder. "Why don't you let me take Chloe for a walk? It's a little crowded in here anyway, isn't it?" Chloe nodded, obviously uncomfortable being in a room with so many upset people, but still hesitant to leave her father.

"It's all right, princess. I'll be with you just as soon as I finish up here."

Satisfied with his promise, Chloe took Robin's hand and followed her down another hall. Once they were out of ear-shot, Esther continued.

"I wasn't here when they brought him in, but—"

"I was." Deacon, towering over all of them at six foot four, looked as if he were barely managing to stay upright. "He looked…" Deacon shut his eyes and rubbed his face with his hands. "There was blood everywhere. He looked like he was drowning in it."

Esther pressed her lips together. "We just need to wait and not jump out ahead of ourselves. The night he came to us? It didn't look good then either, but he made it through, didn't he?" Esther grabbed Kristina's hand and squeezed it.

Kristina nodded; overwhelmed with gratitude that Esther was there. She'd never met her face to face. They'd talked on the phone only once, but then, like now, she'd felt nothing but love and warmth from the woman that mothered her son when she couldn't.

"And what about Tamia? Were you able to find out anything about her?"

"I didn't even ask. I'm not family so I know they won't tell me anything. But now that you're here, I can take you back."

Omar nodded at Kristina and she followed Esther through the swinging, double doors. While the waiting room was heavy with grief, worry and anticipation, behind the doors was a flurry of frantic activity. Kristina was thankful when she and Esther reached the nurse's station and some relative calm.

"Excuse me? My name is Kristina Langston. I'm checking

to see if my sister, Tamia Langston, has been brought in yet. She was one of the passengers on the bus involved in the accident."

No sooner than she'd spoken, Kristina realized several of the nurses recognized her. Usually, that recognition caused people to approach her, or, at the very least, smile in acknowledgement. None of that happened. Instead, the nurses exchanged glances and two actually backed away. She didn't know what to make of the expressions on their faces. Reluctance? Fear? Pity?

The young nurse closest to her was the only one who attempted to speak. "Um…"

But then, just as quickly, she lost her nerve and looked at the nurse next to her, who quickly turned his attention to the computer screen in front of him. Finding no help there, the young nurse turned back to Esther and Kristina.

"Could you, uh, give me just a moment?"

Without waiting for an answer, she made a beeline to an older nurse on the other side of the station, checking a patient's chart.

"What's that all about?" Kristina whispered to Esther.

The older woman watched both the nurses across from them through narrowed eyes. "Good question."

Esther raised her voice and waved at the nurses. "Excuse me, ma'am? Is there a problem?"

The older nurse came to the desk, a somber look on her face.

"I'm sorry for the confusion. I'm not sure how to explain this but…" She took a deep breath and exhaled. "Three young women were brought in from the bus. We've not yet been able to locate proper identification. Authorities at the scene are trying to recover any identifying items as we speak. All three women are of a similar height, hair color and skin tone." She looked at Kristina. "Do you know what you sister was wear-ing, by any chance?"

Kristina tried her best to recall the moment she said goodbye to Tamia and Xavier, but for some reason, every-thing but their faces was a blur.

"I don't."

The woman's shoulders dropped and she gave Esther a meaningful look.

"What?" Kristina looked at both women.

Esther put her hand on Kristina's back. "What she's say-ing is, they don't know who's who."

"Having no way of identifying which woman is your sis-ter, well, it complicates things."

"I know every single person on that bus. You don't have to wait for police. I can clear this up now."

The nurse cleared her throat and exchanged looks with Esther again. "Miss Langston…" Kristina couldn't help but notice the nurse doing her level best not to make eye contact.

"Just take me to them. I can—"

"How many survived?" Kristina's head snapped in Esther's direction.

Before she could wonder why she'd ask such a thing, the nurse answered.

"One died at the scene. The other, shortly after arrival."

Chapter 3

Kristina felt her whole body go numb. She knew there'd been casualties, but she kept telling herself they were passengers from the other cars. She gripped the edge of the counter to steady herself. Esther came closer and drew her arm around Kristina's waist, as she addressed the nurse.

"And the third young woman?"

"In surgery."

Esther tapped on the counter with her index finger, then turned to Kristina. "You could wait for her to get out of surgery—"

"What if she's already in the morgue?" Kristina's voice broke.

Esther gripped her shoulders. "What if she's not?"

Kristina knew there was only a one in three chance her sister was still breathing. She'd already spent the last two and a half hours waiting and hoping and praying her loved ones had survived. Now she knew at least two of them hadn't. She wasn't sure she could wait another minute to learn which two they were.

"How long? How long until she's out of surgery?"

The nurse shrugged. "The damage was extensive. Another three hours, at least."

Kristina closed her eyes and shook her head. "I can't wait that long." She looked at Esther and tried to keep the panic out of her voice. "I can't. I can't."

"That would mean having to identify the other bodies, Kristina. Are you sure you want to do that?"

What choice did she have?

"I do."

The nurse moved to come from behind the desk, but Esther put her hand up to stop her. She led Kristina a few steps away from the station and lowered her voice to a whisper.

"I've seen accident victims, Kristina." She raised Kristina's chin so she could look her in the eye. "The images stick with you. Even when they're strangers. But we're talking about people you love and work with. Maybe even your own sister. This is the kind of thing that could jeopardize your recovery. The situation is stressful enough. There's no reason to add to it. Maybe Pam—"

"Pam won't be here for another four hours."

Esther turned back to the nurse. "Do you know whether any family members have arrived?"

"I don't."

"I'm not sure how many even know," Kristina said, the reality dawning on her just as she said it. "And even if they did, they wouldn't be here yet. Most of the dancers and musicians were from LA or New York. Their families don't have access to a private plane like I did. They'd have to get tickets and wait for the flight."

A thought occurred to Kristina and she addressed the nurse. "You can't even notify families until they're identified, can you?"

"No," the nurse said. "We can't."

Kristina imagined that most of the families had heard about the accident, but what if there were some that hadn't? And the ones that *did* know were probably trying to get answers as frantically as she had. She looked at the nurse.

"I'll need a few minutes. But then, I want you to take me to them."

As Kristina made her way down the hall and toward the doors labeled MORGUE, she thanked God for the two women walking beside her. Esther held her arm on one side and Robin gripped her waist from the other. Omar had offered to come, but after a short prayer session with the women, she knew they were the spiritual warriors she needed by her side.

I can do all things through Christ which strengthens me...

Kristina rolled the words over and over in her mind. Even as she was brought into the viewing room, even as a covered gurney was rolled to a stop in front of the glass, even as she felt like her knees were about to give away.

I can do all things through Christ which strengthens me...

"Whenever you're ready," the nurse said.

Kristina tried to say she was, but her mouth was so dry, her tongue wouldn't separate from her palate. So instead, she nodded. She held her breath and felt the two women beside her come closer.

The nurse gave a signal to the scrub-clad man that

brought the gurney out. As he reached for the sheet that covered the body, Kristina felt herself sway. Heat flashed in waves throughout her frame and she felt the tips of her fingers, and then hands, tingle.

There would be no relief, whoever was under the sheet. Her blood sister or not, it would still be family.

When the attendant pulled back the sheet, Kristina clenched her jaw so hard, her teeth hurt. It was all she could do not to scream. Even with the gashes and swelling, Kristina instantly recognized the face. It was one of her dancers, Peanut.

She'd gotten the nickname because of how tiny she was when she joined the group. She was the one who called Kristina every Tuesday like clockwork when she was in rehab. She'd become engaged to her longtime boyfriend over the Christmas holidays. She was only twenty-eight.

Kristina could feel everyone watching her. Waiting.

"Kerry Palmer. Inglewood, California."

Her voice was barely a whisper as she gave the contact information, but somehow the nurse heard and scribbled the details on her pad. When she was finished, she held up two fingers to the attendant. He nodded, covered Kerry and rolled her body out of the room.

Despite the sound of blood rushing in her ears, Kristina heard Esther praying quietly. Robin gave her a squeeze.

"You don't have to do it again. We can wait for Pam."

Wait for Pam. It's what Kristina had always done. It was always Pam who had to see the tragedy, keep the secrets, clean up the mess.

Kristina knew she could leave it to Pam and Pam would identify every body pulled from the bus, without hesitation. Because that's what she always did. She handled it. And Pam handled it because she could. That's what Kristina always thought. It wasn't until recently she learned that Pam *couldn't* handle it. At least, not all the time and not all on her own. And that was when she turned to alcohol.

Pam was already struggling with the situation. That much was clear when she spoke to her on the phone earlier. No. For once, Kristina was going to take the hard part. She'd do it for Pam and for Tamia and for the family of musicians and singers and dancers that had always had her back. More than once, they'd each taken care of her. Now she'd do the same for them.

Kristina squared her shoulders and cleared her throat. "I'm ready."

At least, that's what she thought.

༄

The attendant brought out a second gurney. But instead of uncovering it, he watched the nurse. She came to Kristina.

"Now, we're going to only uncover her face partially, okay?"

"Why?"

The nurse hesitated. "This was an incredibly violent accident. In such cases, the body can sustain great injury. Things happen that you wouldn't want to see."

"Like what?"

Esther tugged at Kristina's arm. "Kristina."

"I want to know. Just tell me what happened to her."

The nurse looked down at her notepad, as if to buy herself a few moments before having to answer.

"According to rescue workers, her body was recovered from the part of the bus that sustained the initial impact. She wasn't wearing any restraints and you have to understand that when something like this happens…"

As she spoke, the nurse absentmindedly put her hand to her throat and ran her fingers across it. It was a reflex. Something she probably wasn't even aware she was doing. But it immediately brought to mind what the paparazzi had said outside the hospital.

"One of the men—" Kristina shuddered at the memory of the look of glee on the man's face. He seemed excited to be the first to give her the news and record her reaction. "One of the men outside said that my sister was…" Again, Kristina felt herself sway. She steadied herself. "He was trying to get confirmation that my sister was…" Kristina closed her eyes. "He said she was decapitated."

The nurse took a step back and her arms dropped to her sides.

"Lord Jesus, help us." Robin whispered.

"Wait. Somebody told you that? But how? We haven't released any information!"

"He said there was a source on the inside."

The nurse looked down and then back at Kristina, Esther and Robin.

"I am so, so sorry. I had no idea. The moment we leave here, I'll take care of this. We'll have all patients associated with the accident moved to a different area. I'll personally select the staff and we can make arrangements for your additional security."

"So it's true?"

Decapitated. The thought of her baby sister dying was horrific enough, but like that? It was almost more than she could take.

"Show me. Please. Now."

The nurse took a deep breath and exhaled. On her nod, the attendant pulled the sheet down to the young woman's chin.

Kristina felt the room turn sideways.
Two seconds later, everything went black.

Chapter 4

When Kristina opened her eyes, she was being held up by Esther and Robin.

"Over here," she heard the nurse say. Esther, Robin and the nurse supported Kristina and eased her into one of the chairs lined up against the wall. Robin got on her knees in front of Kristina and put her hands on either side of her face.

"It's not Tamia. It's not Tamia, Kristina."

Kristina nodded. She knew that the moment she saw her. But it didn't make it any easier. Though it wasn't her sister that died so violently, it was still a beautiful young woman, full of life and promise. She was Tamia's best friend and Kristina's only other female backup singer.

"Michelle Singleton." She said. "Queens, New York." Kristina doubled over and buried her face in her hands. "How am I going to tell Tamia? How am I going to tell her this?"

Esther rubbed Kristina's back. "Don't worry about that now. When was the last time you slept?"

Kristina didn't know. But it didn't matter. What difference would it make?

"You should probably lie down. Even if it's for just a few minutes."

"There's an empty bed she can use," the nurse said.

"I want to wait until Tamia gets out of surgery."

"That may be what you want, but that's not what's gonna happen. You still have hours before that and before Pam gets here. You need to take a rest. Robin will stay with you. I'll come give updates, if there are any."

Robin took her hand into hers. "Esther is right. Come on."

Kristina stood, but took one last look as the attendant rolled Michelle's body away.

Sleep? Kristina knew that wasn't what she needed. What she needed was to wake up. Wake up from the nightmare that had become her life.

❦

"Krissi?"

For the first few seconds after Kristina opened her eyes, she was still in Atlanta and nothing bad had happened. But then she saw the stark white walls, the harsh lighting above her and remembered that she was lying in a hospital bed. She wanted more than anything to go back to the blissful unconsciousness where nothing had changed, but she sat up on her elbow to face Pam, standing next to the bed.

"I'm sorry to wake you, but I thought you'd want to know. Tamia just came out of surgery. She's in her room but hasn't woken up yet. The nurse said the doctor will be ready to give us details on her condition in just a few minutes. Do you want to come?"

"Of course. Is she okay?" Kristina said, getting out of the bed.

"According to the nurse, the surgery went well."

Kristina let herself exhale. Maybe there'd be some good news today after all.

When they got to Tamia's room, the doctor hadn't arrived yet. But the young man in scrubs, the same one who helped Kristina get past the paparazzi, was there. He had a Walkman clipped to his pants and earphones hooked around his neck. He kept pacing in front of Tamia's door and looking in, as if trying to decide whether to enter. When he turned and saw the sisters approaching, Pam tilted her head and pointed at him.

"I know you. We met you at our mother's funeral, right?"

"Yes, ma'am." There was a kindness about his eyes and warmth to his voice.

Pam turned to Kristina. "This is one of Xavier's brothers. They came to our table, remember?"

Kristina smiled and nodded in acknowledgement. "Do you work here?"

"Yes, ma'am. I'm a physical therapist. I actually," he turned and glanced into Tamia's room before continuing. "I'm off right now. But I thought I'd just hang around. You know, check in on her while we wait to hear about my brother."

"I didn't realize you knew Tamia," Pam said.

He nodded and Kristina noticed a tinge of pink blush his cheeks.

"Yeah. She's been back and forth to Texas a few times to visit my brother and we kinda got to know each other."

Pam shot a glance over at Kristina. Kristina tried to hide her smile.

"Well, thank you for checking in on her."

"No problem. I'm Russell, by the way. Anything y'all need, let me know. I've been working here a while and have a lot of friends on staff. I may not be a doctor but, my friends are your friends."

He looked in one last time on Tamia and waved goodbye before heading down the hall.

Pam arched an eyebrow. "Looks like baby sister has an admirer. And one with a flat top, no less."

Kristina chuckled as she watched him turn the corner. "Stop. He seems sweet."

"Are you Tamia Langston's family?"

The sisters turned to see an older gentleman in scrubs standing behind them.

"Yes," Pam said. "Are you Dr. Ackerman?"

"I am." He held his hand out toward some chairs along the wall. "If you'd like to sit, I can explain where we're at with your sister and discuss options."

They did, exchanging looks as they went.

"Options? We were under the impression the surgery went well."

Dr. Ackerman sat next to them. "Oh, it did. Better than expected, in fact. But that surgery was only the beginning."

"Wait," Pam said. "Are you saying Tamia's not out of the woods, yet?"

"Well, there are always risks involved in surgery, especially a major one, such as your sister's. We'll be keeping an eye out for infection and such, but I think it's safe to say she's out of immediate danger."

Pam leaned back, one hand on her chest and the other on Kristina's arm. "Thank God. You had me worried for a minute there."

"Don't misunderstand. Yes, she made it out of the

accident alive and that's good news. Unfortunately, it's not the only news."

⁕

Kristina stared straight ahead and Pam sat, hunched over, her head in her hands.

"First Michelle, now this." Kristina shook her head. "How is she going to come back from all of it?"

Pam sat up and leaned her head back against the wall. "She's tough. If she could survive growing up under Mahalia Langston, she can survive this."

Pam's face was set hard as stone. Kristina knew that look. Pam was gearing up for a fight. She was preparing herself to get Tamia through this ordeal, come hell or high water.

"It's gonna be hard."

"Speaking of hard," Pam rolled her head to face her sister. "Before Robin left, she told me what you had to do. Identifying Michelle and Kerry. Kristina, I am so sorry. I wish I'd been here. You shouldn't have had to do that on your own."

"Don't be. I wasn't on my own. I—"

Before Kristina could finish her sentence, Esther came rushing down the hall toward them.

"He's out of surgery. The doctor wants to talk to us."

Kristina stood. "Good news or bad news?"

"I don't know. We wanted to wait until everyone was there. But I didn't like the look I saw on his face when he came out."

⁕

"Mr. and Mrs. Morris…"

The group was gathered in the private waiting room the

hospital had made available to them. Besides Kristina and her family, there were the Morrises and Omar, along with his sisters. Not one of them made a sound as they waited for the young doctor to speak. His drawn face and grim demeanor made the tension in the room unbearable.

"I'm sorry to inform you—"

Before he could complete the sentence, Deacon wailed and dropped to his knees. His boys gathered around him, but he was inconsolable. Esther remained still. Kristina imagined that, like her, she was too stunned to do much else.

Kristina had carried Xavier, not even for a full nine months, but she loved him with her life. Esther, on the other hand, had fed him, diapered him, and raised him to be the outstanding young man he'd become. If Kristina felt as numb and hollowed out as she did, she couldn't even imagine what his adoptive mother was experiencing.

The doctor went on to explain the damage done, but Kristina hardly understood what he was saying. It was as if her capacity to comprehend had shut down. Bits and pieces came through. *Swelling. Brain damage. Unresponsive.*

"But people wake up from comas all the time."

Kristina wasn't sure who'd made the statement, but the doctor shot down any hope it raised by assuring them that it was next to impossible in Xavier's case. A few questions were asked, but the answers all amounted to the same thing: no hope.

When the questions died down, the doctor cleared his throat. "At this point, the only decision left to make is when to remove life support. Once again, I'm incredibly sorry for your loss."

He turned to leave, but stopped when Esther called out. "Wait!"

All eyes turned on her. Until that moment, neither she nor Kristina had spoken a word.

"Nothing will be done without our consent, correct?"

"Of course, not. But Mrs. Morris, there's really no reason to prolong it. I assure you, there's no coming back from this. You should say your goodbyes and begin funeral preparations."

Chapter 5

After the doctor left, the room filled with the sounds of hearts breaking. Deacon remained on the floor, one of Xavier's brothers holding him in his arms. Russell sat in one of the waiting room chairs, his face buried in his hands. Omar openly wept in one of his sisters' arms. The other picked up Chloe and took her out of the room.

Kristina turned to locate Pam and found her standing only a few feet behind her, shaking. When her husband, Reiland, tried to reach for her, she jerked away and stormed down the hall toward the elevators.

He looked at Kristina and reached out to touch her elbow. "I'm so sorry."

Kristina nodded and glanced in the direction her sister had gone.

"You should probably follow her."

He nodded and left.

Kristina felt she should do something, but she wasn't sure

what. Cry? Scream? Curl up in a ball and…what? It was then that Esther put her hand on Kristina's shoulder. When she spoke, her voice was low.

"Take a walk with me."

Kristina nodded and they started down the hallway. Once they were at the end of the hall, just beyond the nurses station, Esther stopped.

"Listen, you and I? We're his mothers. That puts us in a different position than everyone else. I'm not saying that we have more of a right to him. Or that what we think matters above all else. But I've always believed there's something about a mother's prayer…" Esther interlaced her fingers and put her hands on her chin. "This is the thing… The night he was left at our doorstep? We took him to the hospital and the doctors told us he wouldn't last through the night. The next morning? They told us he wouldn't see twenty-four hours. After that? They said he wouldn't make it a week."

At Esther's words, Kristina felt something stir in her chest.

"I can't accept God seeing him through all that, only to let him go out like this. I just can't."

"Look at them." Esther motioned down the hall to the waiting room where the rest of the family mourned. "They've already got him dressed up in his suit and laid out in the casket. And I'm not judging them for that. But I just…" She curled her hands into fists and shook her head.

"I'm not letting him go. Not yet. But when I think back to those days and nights with him in the hospital, all those times when the doctors told us he would be brain-damaged, or his organs wouldn't develop properly, I had my husband standing by me. Firm. But the moment the doctor gave us that news, I felt him break. I'm not blaming him. I'm not judging him. It's just what happened.

"What I'm saying is, I don't know if I can do this on my

own. Sometimes you doubt. Sometimes you look at that person in the hospital bed and it seems like change is the most impossible thing in the world. And in those moments you need someone that can stand with you. And regardless of our backgrounds or what we've been through, we have one thing in common: this boy.

"No matter how much they all love him," she said, pointing toward the waiting room. "*We* are his mothers. And if anyone can stand and see this through, it's us. I know what I'm asking you to do is not easy. Some may even call it ignorant. But I'm telling you right here and right now, if you've got my back, I've got yours."

The stirring that Kristina had felt was now a fluttering, like the fragile but strong wings of a butterfly. Was it faith? Hope? She wasn't sure. But it was the first good thing she'd felt since the doctor opened his mouth. Whatever it was, no matter how faint, she was going to hold onto it with her life.

"I'm in. What do we do?"

"Pray. Every day, come two o'clock, we'll meet in his room and pray. And no matter what happens, no matter how bad it looks, we'll keep praying and believing until we no longer have reason to."

Pam and Kristina sat outside of Tamia's room, waiting for her to wake. Kristina stole a glance at her sister. She was sitting next to her, staring straight ahead, her face like stone. Her hands were in her lap, clenched into fists.

They hadn't spoken since the doctor gave news on Xavier's condition an hour earlier. But Kristina didn't need words to know what was going on with her sister. It was clear.

Pam had shut down.

It was what she did when crisis hit. Tamia and Kristina always called it her Robot Mode. They weren't making fun, just stating a fact. That so-called Robot Mode got them through some of the worst times. Like a soldier, Pam would grit her teeth and do whatever needed to be done.

That was one of the things that'd moved Kristina the most during the weekend in the hotel with Robin. Until then, she'd rarely seen Pam cry. She might've shed a tear, here and there, but that was it. There was no lamenting, no shaking her fist at God, no asking *why*. Pam just took it as it came and moved forward. From the looks of it, that was exactly what she was doing now.

"I can't imagine what Esther is going through." Pam said, her voice even, without emotion. "You either."

She turned and looked at Kristina. "I'm not gonna ask you how you're feeling. I'm sure I couldn't even fathom the depth of it. And I'm not gonna tell you that God must've wanted another flower for His garden or any of the other pointless things people say when someone dies. But I have to know…are you okay? I mean, are you feeling like you might, well, wanna use?"

Kristina shook her head no and it was the truth. But she didn't want to tell Pam it was because, as far as she and Esther were concerned, there was no reason to begin grieving.

Not yet.

Pam resumed staring at the wall opposite them. "Well, thank God for that. I'm not gonna lie. I could really use a drink right now."

Kristina reached over and took Pam's hand, giving it a squeeze.

Pam looked down the hall and in the direction that led to the waiting room.

"I wonder how this is going to play out. Is Esther and her family handling all of the arrangements?"

Kristina shrugged.

"I'd understand if they did. They've been his family his entire life. But it would be nice if they'd let us participate. I thought about asking, but I don't want to cause any drama. Maybe we should just wait. Follow their lead."

"Yeah," was all Kristina said.

"Just in case, you should think about what you'd like. Any particular songs you'd want to hear or poems you'd like to have read—"

Kristina stood abruptly. The action stopped Pam mid-sentence.

"Maybe we should go wait inside Tamia's room. You know, so she sees us the moment she wakes up. I'm sure she's going to have a lot of questions."

"Oh, yeah." Pam stood. "Good idea."

Kristina followed Pam into the room, grateful not to be talking about burying her son. But she knew she'd eventually have to tell Pam the truth. And one thing was sure, she was *not* looking forward to that conversation.

Tamia didn't so much as stir for another hour. When she did, her eyelids flew open and she tried to sit up.

"No no no no." Pam jumped up and held the sides of Tamia's face while Kristina swept out of the room to get a nurse.

"Don't move, sweetie."

Tamia's eyes searched down and around at the constraint that held her neck and head.

"Why am I like this?" Her voice was gravelly, a result of the damage done to her vocal cords. "Take it off."

"Tamia. Stop. Look at me. Look at me."

Tamia did as Pam instructed. Once her breathing had steadied, Pam continued.

"I know you're scared and I'm going to explain everything, but I need you to promise me you'll be still, okay? There was some damage to your spine and that's why you're strapped in this."

Tamia blinked. "My spine?"

Pam nodded. "You just came out of surgery. You were in an accident."

Tamia's eyes went wide and the panic returned. "The bus. The bus!"

"Okay, okay, okay. Remember what I said, sweetie."

Tamia took a deep breath as tears sprung to her eyes. Pam caressed the side of her face.

"You had us scared for a minute there. It was touch-and-go."

Kristina returned and the nurse she brought with her asked Tamia how she was feeling as she checked her vitals.

Tamia squinted, as if having to concentrate on the meaning of the question. "Some places feel numb. Some are…" She searched for the word she wanted. "Tingling. And my neck," she started to lift her hand, but instead of it touching her neck as she'd intended, her arm swung out to the side.

Tamia's breath caught and she looked at Pam, her eyes wide with fear again. The nurse took her hand and guided her arm back to her side, but remained silent. Pam had already made it perfectly clear to her and the doctor that the sisters would break the news to Tamia.

After the nurse left, Tamia searched her sisters' faces for explanation.

"Say something. Tell me what happened. What's wrong with me?"

Chapter 6

*K*ristina, would you give her some water, please?"

Kristina quickly poured a cup, then held up the straw so Tamia could sip. Tamia took a drink, but kept her eyes on Pam as she brought her chair close to Tamia's bed and sat down.

"There was some internal damage. Your organs. Fortunately, the surgeon said he sees no reason you can't make a full recovery in that respect. But your vocal cords..." Pam clenched her jaw and swallowed. "Tam, the doctors say you may not be able to sing again."

Tamia didn't make a move or a sound, but Kristina knew the news had gutted her. With the exception of Xavier, Tamia loved singing more than anything else. It was all she'd ever known. Whether on stage before thousands, or alone in her shower, it was one of the few things that brought Tamia joy.

Pam exhaled. "But the biggest concern has been your back. Several vertebrae were fractured and the part that protects your spinal cord was crushed. These bits of bone have made their way to the spinal cord—"

"I'm paralyzed?" Tamia's voice was so small, she sounded like a child.

"Not paralyzed." Pam hesitated. "Not yet. But the neurologist said it's a likely outcome. Your spine wouldn't be able to withstand the weight of your body unless you had surgery."

Tamia watched Pam and waited. There was more and she knew it.

"The thing is, the surgery would mean putting rods in your back. In that case, you'd probably be able to walk again." Pam clamped her hands together and stared at them. "However, there would be chronic pain. And chances are, you'd also be disabled."

Tamia stared straight ahead, completely still, completely silent. Her sisters exchanged glances, unsure of what her silence meant. She'd just been told she might never walk again and instead of crying or shouting or railing against God, she didn't make a sound.

Pam got up and took a step forward. "Tamia? Do you understand what—"

"It's my body that's messed up, Pam. Not my brain."

Pam stepped back and looked at Kristina again. There was a venom in Tamia's voice they'd never heard before. Not even for their mother, probably the one person who deserved her disdain more than any other.

Out of all they'd been through in their lives, all the pain and abuse, Tamia experienced the worst of it. But through it all, she somehow remained tenderhearted. Hopeful, even.

She didn't hesitate when she discovered Xavier was alive. She couldn't wait to wrap her arms around him and tell him how much he'd been missed and loved. And when she saw that Kristina still loved Omar, it was she who went out of her way to bring them together, despite Pam's disapproval. And while she'd fight if it meant defending her family, it wasn't who she was. Even when she was putting on a tough act, everyone knew Tamia was the gentlest of the Langston sisters.

But now it was clear something had changed. It appeared that life, finally, had broken her.

"What about everybody else? What about Michelle? Xavier? We were sitting at the dinette, playing dominoes. But after the accident—" Tamia closed her eyes and took a deep breath. When she spoke again, her voice was raw with emotion. "After the accident, I opened my eyes but I couldn't see either of them. I called out, but no one answered. Where are they? Did they need surgery, too?"

"Tamia..."

Pam cut Kristina off. "We can talk about all that later. For now, rest."

"I just woke up, Pam. Trust me, I'm rested. Where's everyone else?"

"I think we should talk about this after—"

Tamia began to struggle against her restraints. Kristina and Pam moved to stop her and she shouted. "Don't touch me!"

Pam pressed her lips together and Tamia glared at her. Neither of them was about to give in.

"If you're not gonna tell me what I want to know, then get out."

Kristina saw a crack in Pam's cool calm. Tamia's words had hurt her. But they didn't change her mind.

Pam picked up her purse. "Like I said, you need rest. We'll talk about this later."

Pam signaled for Kristina to join her as she made for the door and reached for the handle. But before she could touch it, the door swung open and Russell peeked in.

"You're awake!" His eyes were puffy and pink, but his face lit up with a smile upon seeing Tamia looking back at him.

"Where's your brother?"

Russell, coming in the room, stopped in his tracks at Tamia's question. He looked at Kristina, then Pam, then back at Tamia. No one moved, each waiting for someone to say something, none wanting to be the one to do it.

"Uh…". He looked down and away, his eyelids blinking rapidly.

"What? What happened?" When no one answered, Tamia grew desperate, nearly choking on her tears. "Please! Just say it! Where is he?"

Pam exhaled and reluctantly returned to Tamia's bed. "Jamail and Dede barely have a scratch on them. Joseph and Michael…" Pam cleared her throat before going on. "The accident was so bad, Tamia—"

"I know. I was there. That's not what I asked you."

"Not everybody made it out…"

Tears filled Tamia's eyes and she balled her hands into fists. "Pam, I'm not going to ask you again. Where is he?"

Pam choked back a sob. "They did everything they could."

"No!"

"The only thing left to do is take him off life support."

Tamia let out a cry that nearly brought Russell to his knees. Pam backed away and turned to the wall. Kristina wanted to do something, anything, to relieve her sister's pain. And though she knew she'd pay for it later, she did the only thing she could think of.

"That's what the *doctors* say."

Pam, Tamia and Russell looked at her.

Tamia blinked. "What? What do you mean, that's what the *doctors* say?" She looked at Pam, then back at Kristina. "What aren't you telling me?"

"I'd like to know the same thing," Pam said.

"What I mean is," Kristina said, wiping her suddenly sweaty palms down the front of her pant legs. "The doctors aren't always the final say."

Pam took a step back, a frown on her face. "What are you talking about? Were you not standing in the same room as the rest of us? There's nothing that can be done, Kristina. No other hospital, no specialist, no expert in their field can save him now. I know you want to have hope, but—"

"I wasn't talking about any of them."

Pam raised her eyebrows. "Well then, just what are you talking about?"

Kristina hesitated. She'd been a Christian for, what? Two minutes? And though she'd been raised in church, she spent a good part of her life chasing her next high, not Jesus. No one would call her a saint. And she certainly couldn't be compared to the great women of the Bible, and yet…

"Remember that Old Testament story? We heard it in Sunday School. The one about the woman who prayed and asked God for a son? And then he died and she went to the prophet and God raised him back to life?"

Pam stared at the ceiling and shook her head. "You've got to be kidding me." She turned and dropped down in one of the chairs in the corner of the room. "Kristina, please, don't do this."

"What? Believe God?"

Pam sighed and scrubbed her face with her hands. "This is not the Old Testament. It's not even the New Testament. Jesus is not walking the earth. I'm not saying people can't get healed or miracles don't happen, but I think we're past that point."

"But isn't that what a miracle is?"

All three sisters looked at Russell. They'd forgotten he was there.

"That thing that happens when you're past all hope?" He looked at Kristina. "If you ask me, this is exactly the kind of situation you believe in miracles for."

Pam stared at him, astounded, and shook her head. "I can't. I just can't. Not right now." She got up and started for the door.

"But Pam, that's what Xavier's whole life has been." Kristina motioned at his brother. "You were there. You saw the condition he was in when he was born. Your mom just told me today, no one expected him to live."

"They didn't. Not once, not twice, but three times. Three different times they told us he would die. And three different times, he made it through. And that's not even counting all the surgeries. They also said he'd have learning disabilities. That he'd never be able to keep up with kids his age. He graduated at the top of his class."

"And what about us?" Kristina asked Pam. "We thought he was dead. And after all those years, we got him back."

"But he *wasn't* dead, was he?"

"That's not the point, Pam. The point is, miracles *do* happen. And if they do, why can't we have one more?"

"I don't want you to get your hopes up and end up having a relapse when it doesn't work out."

Kristina came to where Pam stood at the door. "Listen to yourself. Listen to what you just said. *Relapse.* We've never even talked about a relapse before because there was never a time when I was clean. But you put your faith on the line. You and Robin and Tamia believed God would give me a breakthrough and that's exactly what He did. I should've died in that bathroom and you know it. But you didn't give up on me and neither did God. I'm not giving up on Xavier."

Pam only stood there, a stunned look on her face. She slowly shook her head and rubbed her eyes. "You know what? It's been a long day. We're all exhausted. Let's just talk about this later, all right?"

"Pam."

Pam went through the door, not looking back. "Later."

Kristina turned to Tamia. "I don't want you worrying about this. The only thing I want you focusing on is getting better."

Kristina smiled, but Tamia didn't respond in kind. Instead, she looked away and said, "I'm tired. I'd like to be alone."

Chapter 7

The rest of that day and the morning of the next passed without change. Having spent the night in the hospital chapel, Kristina tried to snatch a few minutes sleep while sitting outside Tamia's suite. No sooner than she closed her eyes, she heard footsteps. Pam sat next to her, offering a steaming cup of coffee. Kristina groaned.

"I appreciate the thought, but I don't think I could drink one more ounce of that stuff."

Pam stared at the two cups in her hand. "You know, neither can I. I don't even know why I got them." She sat both cups on the table next to them and leaned back in her seat.

"Have you talked to Esther today?"

Kristina rested her head against the wall. She didn't want to have this conversation with Pam. Not again.

"Not since this morning."

"So you two haven't decided when you're going to do it?"

"We're praying about it."

"But—"

"Don't, Pam."

Kristina had hoped to stop the discussion before it started. Unfortunately, her sister had other thoughts.

"Prolonging it isn't going to—"

Before Pam could launch into her advice, a commotion at the end of the hallway caught their attention. Kristina got up and walked down the hall a bit before Pam grabbed her by the arm.

"Don't. Let security take care of it. That's what we hired them for."

It was hard to make out what was happening on the other side of the doors, but from the sound of it, someone other than family or authorized staff was trying to get through. The disorder only lasted a few moments before all became quiet again. Soon after that, the double doors opened and Pam's husband, Reiland came through.

"What was going on out there?"

Reiland just looked at them, his expression tight. An older man and woman came behind him, neither of which looked like hospital staff. Kristina shot her brother-in-law a look, trying to figure out why in the world he wasn't doing anything to stop them.

"It was me," the man said. "I was trying to come in but the guards wouldn't let me through." He walked with a slight limp and looked somewhat disheveled. The woman, fair-skinned and small, was also rumpled. She seemed so exhausted, Kristina felt bad for what she was about to do, but with all the tricks the media had resorted to over the last two days, she wasn't taking any chances.

She approached the couple, her arm extended. "And for good reason. This area has been blocked off. If you're looking for a patient, I guarantee you they're not in this area. I can show you to the nurses' station—"

"No. The patient I'm looking for is here."

Kristina turned to Reiland again. "Can I get some help here? Or should I go get security myself?"

"Kristina, before you do that, you might wanna hear what he has to say."

"And why would I do that?"

"Because, according to him, he's your father."

Kristina stopped, her mouth open. She turned and looked at her sister. Pam glared at the man and retreated to the row of chairs she and Kristina had just left.

"Please. My wife and I drove straight through. All the way from Seattle. We left as soon as we saw it on the news."

Kristina waved her hands and took a step back. "I'm sorry. But can we rewind to the part where you claim to be my father?" Kristina whirled around and looked at Pam again. "Did you hear this?"

Pam remained silent, picking up one of the abandoned coffee cups and taking a drink.

"I know I probably don't even have a right to be here, but I had to try. When I heard about Tamia—" His voice faltered and he took off his glasses to wipe his eyes with the back of his hand. The woman put her arm around him and looked up at Kristina, her eyes pleading.

"When we left, there was no news on who made it out. Did she? Make it out?"

The woman's desperation to know and her genuine concern took Kristina by surprise and she nodded before she could stop herself. The man clasped his hands together and looked heavenward.

"Thank you, Father!"

The woman buried her face in the man's shoulder, crying. "See, honey? Prayer works!"

The man took a step toward Kristina, his face bright with joy and tears. "Where is she? Can you take me to her?"

"Whoa." Kristina put her hand up again. "Take you to her? I don't even have any proof you are who you say you are. If you think I'm about to let you—"

"Oh, he's who he says he is, all right."

Kristina turned to see Pam getting up from her chair and walking toward them. She stopped in front of the man, glaring at him.

"This is most definitely the sorry excuse of a man that left us alone with mama." She scoffed. "Just as useless now as he was then. I guess some things never change."

The man tilted his head to the side, as if he hadn't understood the words Pam said. She looked him up and down, then sucked her teeth before looking at Kristina and her husband.

"I need some air. He had better be gone when I get back. If one of you two don't take care of it, I'll bring in somebody who will."

As she stole a glance at the couple sitting at the cafeteria table with her, Kristina felt like she was having some sort of waking dream.

First, the baby she thought was stillborn turned out to be alive. Then, she was reunited with his father after nearly two decades. Only to face losing that same child less than a year after meeting him. Not to mention her sister, who was now looking at life in a wheelchair. And to top it all off, the father that left when she was too young to even remember him was sitting next to her, along with his new wife. When did her life turn into a soap opera?

"This must be overwhelming for you." Justina, her father's wife, put her hand on Kristina's arm. "We never wanted to disrupt your lives, but after hearing Tamia was on that bus, we knew it might be our last chance to see her."

The woman's eyes became wet as she spoke. Kristina didn't know what to make of it. She'd always imagined their father as some deadbeat player, taking up with a different woman every night and keeping the children he left behind, a secret. But from what she was seeing, he and Justina had been together for quite some time. Not only that, Justina talked about them as if they were her own.

"I'm just trying to take it all in."

Her father, Gerald, nodded. "I understand. It's a lot. Especially on top of all you've been going through. That news report we saw? The reporter said your mother just recently passed. I'm sorry. I didn't know."

Kristina wasn't sure how to respond to that. Didn't he know what their mother was like? He'd lived with her for a few years, hadn't he? Was she so different back then that he thought her passing was actually a loss for them and not a relief?

He shook his head, grinning. "My little Krissi, all grown up. I never thought I'd see you again. Not face to face like this."

Justina chuckled and nodded. "God is good!" She stood and patted her husband on the back. "I'm gonna give you two some time alone." He kissed her hand, and then Justina came around to Kristina and enfolded her in her arms. "It sure is good to finally see you, baby."

Neither Gerald nor Kristina spoke for a few moments after Justina left. Kristina didn't know where to begin. What do you say to the stranger who fathered you?

"I don't remember you. I don't even know your first name."

"Well," he said, reaching into the inside pocket of his sport coat. "I know it's not the same as a memory, but it's what I've held onto for the past thirty-odd years."

He handed her a stack of photos, some Polaroids, some printed. Mostly, they were of her and Pam as toddlers. She was shocked. She'd seen very few pictures of them as children. But even more surprising was that, in every single picture, they were smiling. Actually smiling.

Other than her school pictures, publicity shots and red carpet snaps, Kristina had never seen a picture of herself smiling. If she hadn't been holding the proof in her hands, she never would've believed it.

Gerald put his glasses on and pointed at one of the pictures.

"That's you. Three years old. It was your birthday and you'd asked for a pony." He laughed. "Can you believe that? There we were, living in the sticks and you had the nerve to ask for a pony!"

He slapped his knee and laughed louder. It was warm and deep. And though Kristina never would've been able to pick her father out of a crowd, even with a gun to her head, something about that laugh was familiar.

"I tried to explain to you more than once that I didn't have the money to do that, but you were completely convinced I could. So I went and bought a toy saddle, got one of the guys at work to switch hours with me so I could get home before your bedtime and, well, as you can see…"

"You made yourself into a pony."

Kristina felt a lump rise in her throat. She flipped through the pictures and saw more of the same. Piggyback rides, ice cream cones, Popsicle stick houses. But none of it made sense. Sure, it was her face in the pictures. Pam's, too. But this wasn't their childhood. Not even close.

And how in the world did a man crawling around on his hands and knees to fulfill his daughter's outrageous birthday wish turn into the deadbeat that left them at the mercy of an abuser?

"I don't understand this. *Any* of this," Kristina said, holding up the pictures. "If this is who you were, if this is who *we* were, why did you leave? And better yet, why did you come back? Now? After all this time?"

"Leave? Is that what she told you?" Gerald shook his head and tightened his jaw.

"Well," he said, rubbing his hands down the front of his legs. "I'm not gonna call your mother a liar. I understood her better than most. Probably better than she did herself. And whatever story she told you girls, I'm sure she'd convinced herself it was true. But if you want to hear my side, if you're willing to give me that chance, I'd like to tell you what *really* happened."

Chapter 8

Upon entering the smoky and darkened pub, it took Reiland less than a minute to locate what he'd come in for.

"You have any idea how long I've been looking for you?"

Pam, on a stool and hunched over the bar, threw him a quick glance over her shoulder.

"Probably for as long as I've been staring at this glass of bourbon."

Reiland pulled out the stool next to her and sat down. She felt him looking at her but couldn't bring herself to look back.

"Have you had any of it?"

Pam wiped away the tear that rolled down her cheek and shook her head. "No. But not because I don't want it. I want it so bad, it hurts."

Reiland dropped his head and exhaled. He put his hand on her shoulder and gave it a squeeze.

"It's not too late then, is it? I know it's tough. It seems

like we just keep getting shoveled under it. But you can get through this without a drink, Pam. I *know* you can."

"Well, that makes one of us."

Reiland took the glass in front of Pam and slid it down the counter and out of her reach. Pam buried her face in her hands and shook her head.

"I don't know how much more of this I can take. I really don't."

"I hear you, babe. And now, with your father showing up? It's no wonder you're having a hard time. Seeing him must've brought up a lot of bad memories."

Pam looked up and took a deep breath.

"See, that's the thing. It's just the opposite."

"But how? You've never even talked about your father. At least, not to me. That's the only reason I never asked. I figured it was too painful."

"It was. *Is.* But only because I remember what it was like when he was there. Not a lot, but more than my sisters. I remember what it was like to laugh and play. I remember what it was like to be happy."

"That's crazy. All this time I imagined your dad to be the bad guy. Or some coward that couldn't stand up to your mother."

"Bad guy? No. Coward?" Pam shrugged. "If I took mama's word on it, then, yeah. But…" She stared at the wall behind the bar for a few moments before continuing.

"I just remember waking up one morning in the car. My sisters and I were still in our pajamas and all our belongings were stuffed in the front seat and the floor of the backseat. Mama was driving and I asked her where we were going. I asked her where daddy was. She said he'd left us and we had to find a new place to live."

"Did you believe her?"

"At the time? No. I knew there is no way he'd go anywhere without me. Without any of us. But each day passed and he never showed up. And then as I got older, I thought maybe it was true. Maybe he couldn't take how she was and had to get out. I certainly couldn't blame him if he had. After Kristina became famous, I just knew he'd show up one day, you know? I knew we'd walk out of some appearance or award show, and he'd be there, waiting with all the other fans. He'd show us his folder full of newspaper and magazine clippings. He'd tell us how he'd followed her career that whole time and waited for the moment we would be reunited."

"But that never happened."

"Nope. It didn't. So I thought he was dead. For a while there, I thought maybe he wasn't even real. Thought he was some fantasy I'd made up to get through life with mama." She shrugged. "One day I stopped thinking about him at all."

"And then today?"

"And then today he walked in and I saw his face and every single memory I ever had of him came flooding back. I realized he *was* real. Alive. And he *never* came for us. What in the world am I supposed to make of that?"

Reiland moved in closer and put his arm around her.

"I wish there was something I could do to make it better."

Pam leaned over and pointed at the glass of bourbon. "You could slide that back over here."

Reiland pressed his lips together. Pam laughed.

"It was a joke, baby."

"You need to brush up on your comedic skills."

"Yeah, I know. But I'm not really at the top of my game nowadays, am I?" Pam cocked her head to the side. "And can you explain something to me, please? When did Kristina become the pillar of strength in this family?" She laughed. "Seriously. I spent the last fifteen years being the only thing standing between her face and the floor, but now… Now it's like no matter what comes, can't nothing knock her down. Meanwhile, I'm falling apart at the seams, trying to mess up five years worth of sobriety."

Reiland stared at her, his eyes narrowed. She knew that look.

"What? Just spit it out."

"You're not gonna like it."

"I never do. But that hasn't stopped you before."

Reiland snickered. "True, true. Well," he said, rubbing his hands together. "You know that Bible toting nephew of ours? That boy is forever sending me sermons and devotionals."

Pam smiled, but it was tinged with sadness..

"Yeah," she said quietly. "No one is safe."

"I was reading this devotion he sent me about the grace of God. It's like that song, when I am weak, He is strong. Krissi already knows how much she needs Him, so instead of depending on herself, she leans on Him. But you? Since day one, you've been trying to do it all on your own. Kristina is resting in Him and letting Him do the work. You're wrapped up in doing the work, instead of just resting. She's Mary and you're Martha. Like Jesus said, only one thing is needful. I think Kristina found that one thing. "

Pam leaned back and stared at him.

"Should I start calling you Rev. Ray now?"

Reiland laughed out loud. "Please don't. I might lose all my street cred."

Chapter 9

See, the first thing you have to understand about your mother is where she came from." Gerald told Kristina. "First off, things were different back then. Nowadays, anything goes. But when we were coming up, the world operated on a higher set of morals, even outside the church. Now , add to that her father being a traveling preacher. And strict!" Gerald shook his head. "You wouldn't believe the punishments he came up with, the stories she told me."

Actually, I can. It's probably where she got most her ideas.

"In spite of all that, she adored him. And I guess, in his way, he loved her too. He called her his Little Sparrow. They traveled from place to place, living off the offerings he got from preaching. She'd get up and sing before every one of his sermons." Gerald looked down at his hands. "She was a good girl. A *real* good girl. Until she met me." He smiled, but Kristina noticed it didn't quite reach his eyes.

"And talk about pretty! Oooh wee! Your mama was the

prettiest girl I'd ever seen. And when we met, it was like a lightning strike. For both of us. One thing led to another and…" Gerald sighed. "Truth is, I have to take responsibility. She didn't really want to go that far. She kept talking about how we'd go to hell, but I didn't let up and eventually, she gave in. But afterward? She felt so guilty, she wouldn't let me near her with a ten-foot pole. At that point, it really didn't matter. Pamela was already on the way."

Kristina put her hand up. "Wait a minute. You're telling me mama was pregnant *before* she got married?"

Gerald nodded. "And when her daddy found out? He liked to beat her to death." Gerald shook his head and rubbed his forehead. "I can still see what she looked like that night. I worked a factory job at the time and I'd just gotten home. My parents always went to bed long before my shift ended, so when I pulled up to the house, I was surprised to see someone sitting on the porch. At first, I thought it was my father, but when I got close enough, I saw it was Rev. Simmons. I just knew he was there to shoot me. But no, it was worse than that. He'd lain her in front of the screen door. Had beaten her to a bloodied pulp. 'She ain't no good now. You done made sure of that,' he told me. 'You ruined her, you keep her.' Then he spit on her and left. We never saw or heard from him again."

Kristina was speechless. She didn't know anything about her mother's past or family. They never had conversations about those kinds of things. About much of, really. Most of their interaction consisted of punishment, endless Bible studies or singing rehearsals. Now she was starting to understand why.

"My parents welcomed her in. Didn't hesitate to make her part of the family when we married. But I don't know… She was never the same after that night he left her on the porch. She was always religious, but it was like a switch had been flipped. She went from religious to downright fanatical. And as you girls came along, she seemed to get worse. It was like she believed what her father said about her being ruined and she was determined the same wasn't going to happen to you. That's what started most of our problems, that fanaticism. I had never been one to go to church. Until I married Justina, I never even shadowed the front door. But Mahalia wasn't having that. Oh, no. That's what our fights were about. At least, in the beginning."

"And after that?"

"You girls. She was so hard on you. Now, the way I was raised, we didn't hesitate to use the belt if it was needed. A few good swats weren't thought of as bad parenting like they are today. But she went beyond that. I'd come home, go to the room to say goodnight to you girls and when I'd try to hug you, you'd flinch. Then one day I found big ol' bruises on your arms and legs and I threatened to take you girls and go to my mother's house. I wanted to scare some sense into her. But then I got home after that next twelve-hour shift and you were gone."

"Just like that?"

"Just like that. I tried looking for you. But you gotta understand, this was before Facebook and Google. I had no idea she'd gone to Texas. After years of getting nowhere, I eventually gave up. I'm not making excuses and I'm not saying it was right. But it was what it was. And then one day, me and Justina were looking at one of those night talk shows and there you were, looking so much like your mother, I had to do a double take."

"The Late Show? David Letterman?"

Gerald nodded.

"But that was over fifteen years ago. Why didn't you contact us?"

"I almost did. It was at the beginning, before you became the big name you are now. You were doing a show at the Apollo. I'd been following news about where you were going to be playing at, so I bought a ticket and flew all the way there. After the show, I hung around outside. There was a car waiting for you and I had this idea I could catch you before you got in. It was like a mob out there. All these screaming boys and girls waiting to get your picture, your autograph. That's when I realized you were already more famous than I knew. And I thought to myself, what am I doing here? What right do I have? I hadn't seen you girls since you were tiny."

Gerald narrowed his eyes and pointed at Kristina. "Tell the truth. What in the world would you have thought of me, showing up at that point?"

"That you wanted money."

"Exactly. So I turned around, walked back to my hotel and flew home the next morning." Gerald took off his glasses and rubbed his face. "And from what I could tell of Pamela's reaction, she thinks I should do the same thing now."

Kristina patted him on the arm. "Don't worry about Pam. Besides, it's Tamia's decision to make, whether she sees you or not. At the very least, she should get to hear what you've told me."

Gerald gave her a tired smile and she wondered how she could feel such a rush of affection for someone she'd only just met.

"Whatever happens, good or bad, I just wanted you girls to know I loved you. Me *and* Justina. You've been loved your whole life."

Chapter 10

*O*n her dream, Tamia is still trapped in the bus. She can smell ignited gasoline mixed with the stink of burning flesh.

Someone's crying.

Someone else is calling for help.

But not the one person she can see. The drummer, Michael, father of four. She's known him since Kristina's first tour.

He's not making a sound.

His eyes are open and staring at her and even though she keeps calling out to him, she knows he won't answer.

She knows he's dead.

But she keeps screaming his name.

❧

When Tamia slammed back into consciousness, she was still lying in a hospital bed and her head and neck were still constricted by the halo brace. Though she hadn't moved a muscle, she was gasping for breath like she'd been running for her life.

Suddenly, Russell appeared over her, his face etched with concern.

"Tamia? Tamia! What is it? Are you in pain? Do you want me to get a nurse?"

He looked like he'd just woken up and she realized he'd probably been in the room the whole time, sleeping. The chair that was usually against the wall was now at her bedside. But she didn't want Russell there. She didn't want *anyone* there. Were the words, 'I want to be alone' unclear?

From her times visiting Xavier in Dallas, she knew Russell well enough to understand he was persistent. Like a dog with a bone, persistent. So she resolved to take away the bone. Instead of answering any of his questions, she decided to look away and pretend he wasn't there. Maybe he would get the hint and make it so.

After a few moments of watching her, Russell moved and she thought maybe she'd finally get what she wanted. But instead, he came around to the other side of the bed.

"Tamia?"

Tamia glared at him, then did the only thing she could to show her disdain for his presence. Cutting her eyes at him, she looked away again.

And again, he walked around the bed so he was in her sight line.

"Oh, I see how it is. You ain't got nothing to say, huh?"

Tamia could hardly believe the man. Didn't he have an ego? Any sense of pride? Fine. If he wasn't going to leave on his own, she would stare at him with such malice, he'd soon have no other choice.

Tamia narrowed her gaze on him, summoning her inner Pam and gave him her most withering scowl.

Only, he didn't wither. He howled with laughter.

"Whoa! If looks could kill…" He put his hands on his knees and leaned over to look her in the eye. "But you're gonna have to do better than that, baby girl. In fact, I *know* you can do better than that."

He straightened up, put his hands on his hips and raised his eyebrows. "What? No putdowns about my Walkman?" He patted the top of his flat top. "No jabs about my hairstyle?"

Tamia didn't even blink.

"Well, that's too bad. You always came up with the best ones." He chuckled. "Remember that time you told me I looked like I just walked off the set of *A Different World*? From then on, whenever you saw me, you'd yell, 'Chipmunk! Chipmunk!'" He shook his head. "Now see, you thought you were being funny, but that's when I decided you were my kind of girl."

His smile faded and his expression became serious. He looked away from Tamia and out the window. When he spoke, his voice was so quiet, she had to strain to make out the words.

"Working in a hospital, I see tragedy daily. And growing up, I used to hear my mom tell stories about her time as an ER nurse. You'd think if anybody knew life was short, it would be me. You'd think I'd take more chances. Go after my dreams."

He continued to stare out the window for a moment before turning and sitting in the chair next to her bed.

"No. I made the same mistake millions of people make every day. I kept putting things off until tomorrow. Next time, I told myself. There's always the next time…"

When he looked up and saw her watching him, his ears

flushed pink and he cleared his throat. She couldn't believe he actually had the nerve to be embarrassed. As if he'd just revealed something she didn't already know. Of course, she knew. And if he'd ever actually gotten up the courage to ask her out, she might've even been tempted to say yes.

But now...

"I'm sitting over here rambling on like an idiot." Russell dropped his head in his hands and rubbed over his head and the back of his neck.

"Would it be wrong of me to hope you're so doped up on painkillers, you won't remember this conversation tomorrow?"

He smiled, hoping for the same from her. She only stared at him. He sucked his teeth and shook his head.

"I didn't even come in here to say any of that. What I *wanted* to say, what I've been waiting to tell you is this: I can't even begin to imagine what you're going through right now. But I want you to know, for whatever it's worth, I'm here. Whenever, whatever. Anything. If you need me, in a heart-beat, I'm here."

His facial expression darkened and he swallowed hard. He stood again and came close to her bed.

"I also wanted to tell you not to give up, okay? No matter what the doctors say, no matter what it looks like, you can't give up."

He took Tamia's hand and gave it a squeeze.

"Just please...don't give up."

❦

"Not one word?" Pam asked.

She and Kristina stood with Russell just down the hall from Tamia's closed door.

"Nothing," he said. He shrugged and grinned. "But she didn't kick me out, either."

Kristina couldn't help but be amused at the young man's optimism. It was a quality they could use a whole lot more of at the moment. She put her hand on his elbow.

"Thanks, Russell."

He looked at his watch. "My lunch break is almost over, so I'm gonna grab something to eat real quick. Can I get anything for you, ladies?"

"We're good."

"I'll check in with y'all later, then."

After he was gone, Kristina nudged Pam's side. "Stop scowling. He's right. Her letting him stay in there, well, that's something." She chuckled. "I lasted less than sixty seconds. If she'd been able, I'm sure she would've sent a bed pan flying at my head."

Pam cut her eyes at her sister. "It's not funny."

Kristina sighed. "What's the alternative? More crying?"

She sat in one of the chairs clustered nearby and crossed her legs. "I don't know about you, but my tear ducts could use a break."

Pam dropped down beside her. "The decision she has to make? It's huge. Life-altering. She needs us right now. How can we help her if she won't even let us in the room?"

Pam leaned over, her head in her hands. Kristina rubbed her back.

"We pray. We wait. There's not much else we can do."

Pam groaned. "Praying, I can do. Waiting? That's not really my strong suit."

Kristina leaned back and gasped. "What? Are you kidding me? You're the most patient person I've ever met!"

Pam tried to roll her eyes, but ended up laughing.

"Keep it up, Kristina. Tamia won't be the only one aiming bed pans at your big head."

Chapter 11

"Kristina?"

Kristina, on her way to the cafeteria, turned to see who had called her name. Deandra, Omar's sister, gently transferred a sleeping Chloe from her arms to the padded bench she was sitting on.

"Can I talk to you for a few minutes?"

"Of course," Kristina said.

After checking to make sure Chloe was still sleeping, Deandra continued, her voice lowered to a hush.

"I know you already have a lot going on. I hate to add one more thing. But me and my sister, we don't know what else to do." She paused in an attempt to steady her wavering voice.

"It's Omar. He's taking this hard. I know everyone is. But I've never seen him like this. We've tried to get him to come home. Take a break. Eat. But he refuses. He won't even eat the food we bring him. I don't think he's even taken a nap since y'all got here."

With all the time Kristina had been taking up with Tamia and Gerald, she hadn't been focusing on how Omar was doing. Of course, she knew he was having a hard time. She knew that before they'd even arrived in Dallas. But they hadn't spoken about Xavier since the doctor gave the news. She got the impression he hadn't wanted to. Should she have pressed him anyway?

"I know that he's grieving. I get that. But Omar's a soldier. A rock. Always has been. Even when our dad died." Deandra quickly brushed away the tears that clung to her eyelashes.

"But right now? He's spiraling. He doesn't even look like himself. It's like he's hollowed out or something. I'm scared. We've tried everything. But I know how he feels about you. How he *always* felt about you. And if there's anyone that can make him come to himself, it's you. Please, can you talk to him?"

"He's in there now? Xavier's room?"

Deandra nodded. "We see him for a little while each day. Seems it's always around two o'clock, for some reason. But even then, he doesn't talk. He goes to the bathroom and walks the halls for about an hour. Then he's right back in there."

Kristina noticed he was always there when she and Esther came for prayer. He'd slip out when they arrived, mumbling a word or two. But she had no idea he returned the moment they left. What about Chloe? If he was always with Xavier, and as unresponsive as Deandra claimed when he *was* around, how was that affecting his little girl?

Kristina looked at Chloe, asleep on the bench, and Deandra, still on the verge of tears, and nodded her head.

"I'll see what I can do."

❦

When Kristina entered Xavier's room, Omar didn't even notice she'd come in. He sat at his son's bedside, holding Xavier's hand and stroking his shoulder. As Kristina came near, she understood Deandra's concern.

Omar's face was drawn and his eyes, bloodshot. Instead of its normal rich, pecan brown coloring, his skin had a sallow appearance. When she touched his shoulder, he started.

"I'm sorry. I didn't mean to startle you."

"I didn't realize what time it was." Omar's voice was hoarse with exhaustion.

"It's not two o'clock. I'm not here to spend time with Xavier. I wanted to see about you. Your sisters are worried."

"Let me guess. Deandra? She shouldn't have bothered you."

"I'm glad she did." Kristina pulled over a chair and sat down. "What's this I hear about you not eating?"

"She's exaggerating."

"Oh, really? When was the last time you ate?"

Omar remained silent and focused on Xavier's face.

"You can't do this. Wearing yourself out isn't going to help him or anybody else."

Omar just shook his head and rubbed his thumb across the top of Xavier's hand.

"I can't leave."

"No one's asking you to leave him. Just eat. Get some sleep."

"No."

Kristina dropped back in her chair.

"Omar—"

He turned to her and the sternness of his expression kept her from continuing. Then his face softened and he turned his attention back to Xavier.

"I can't."

Kristina remained quiet for a few moments. She considered leaving him alone like he wanted her to. But however good his intentions, he was hurting himself and, as a result, his family. Maybe not to the extent she had, but still, she couldn't help but make the comparison. If her sisters and Robin had left her alone like she wanted them to, where would she be?

"Talk to me."

Omar pressed his lips together and stared down at Xavier's hand.

"Tell me what's going on."

He didn't want to. That was clear. But she wasn't going anywhere until he did, and they both knew it.

"I know what the doctor said. I'm not stupid. But I just need a few moments. If he would only open his eyes for a few seconds…"

Kristina waited as Omar struggled with his emotions and the words he was trying to say.

"Then I could tell him…"

"That you love him?"

Omar nodded.

"He already knows."

Omar clenched his jaw and spoke through gritted teeth. "I need to *say* it to him. I need to be able to look in his eyes and say it to him. I need him to know how sorry I am for everything that happened."

Omar's voice broke and hearing it felt like a stab in the heart. Kristina looked away from him and used her sleeves to catch the tears before they dropped down her cheeks.

"Omar, you have nothing to apologize for. He knows that. I know that. You and I did the best we could. Xavier has always known that."

"I just need a few seconds." He said, keeping his eyes on Xavier.

"What you need is food. And a good night's sleep."

Omar cut his eyes at Kristina. She could see his patience was wearing thin, but she couldn't care less.

"You're no good to Xavier like this. I understand what you're feeling. But there's a better way. You can be here for him *and* take care of yourself."

"I'm fine."

"You're not. And even if you were, how long will it last, going at this rate?"

"I said I'm fine."

His voice was resolute, his face, hard. As far as he was concerned, the conversation was over. And if he'd been talking to anyone other than Kristina, it might have been.

Unfortunately for him, he wasn't.

She didn't even try to keep the irritation out of her voice when she spoke again.

"And what about Chloe?"

Omar looked at Kristina, blinking as if she'd just thrown a bucket of cold water at him.

"Have you glanced in the mirror lately? You look like something out of The Walking Dead. How do you think she feels, seeing you like this?"

Omar's shoulders dropped and he bowed his head. He put his elbows on his knees and pressed his fingers to his eyes.

"My Chloe…"

He stood and shoved his hands in his pockets.

"I tried sending her home with my sister. Deandra said she cried the whole time. But when she's here, she's so nervous she can hardly keep anything down. I actually caught her picking at the skin of her arm the other day. To the point of *bleeding*. She didn't even realize she was doing it."

Omar rubbed his hands over his head and the back of his neck. "I try talking to her, but she hardly talks back. I keep expecting for her to ask for her mom, but she doesn't. I don't think she understands she's not coming back."

Omar looked back at Xavier and shook his head.

"Everything is so messed up. All I ever wanted was to be a good father. I thought if I could be half the man my dad was, I'd be all right. I can't even be a decent father, much less, a good one."

Omar paced the floor at the end of Xavier's bed, and as he continued to speak, his volume and frustration escalated.

"I screwed up the one chance I had to look into my son's eyes. And Chloe? I don't even want to think about what kind of damage the last few weeks have done to her. And what's worse is, I have no idea how to fix it."

He raised his hands and tightened them into fists.

"It's like I don't know how to do *anything* anymore. I can't even pray. I try, but no words come out. My kids lives are being ruined and I can't even pray? I'm their father! I should at least be able to do that! I've never felt so helpless in my life!"

Kristina thought for a moment he would punch a hole in the wall. But he just stood there, shaking.

She went to him and put her arms around his waist and her head against his chest. At first, he didn't move. But then slowly, she felt the muscles in his body relax and he let his arms drape her shoulders. Finally, he took in a deep breath and exhaled.

"You're one of those guys who take care of business. You take care of your daughter. Your family. Your friends. When things are falling apart, you're the one who holds them together. In that way, you remind me of Pam."

She looked up at his face and he playfully grimaced, then smiled.

"I think God put me in your lives to remind the two of you that you don't have a cape or wear an 'S' on your chest."

Omar sighed, then looked at Xavier.

"I wish I did. I would turn back time."

His words were heavy with pain and regret. It broke Kristina's heart. She knew what it was like to live in that place. And it was pure torment.

"Nobody can do that. But maybe it doesn't matter."

She had decided to keep her and Esther's plan to herself. She knew how hopeless the situation appeared and she didn't need people telling her what a fool she was to think it could change. Pam was doing that enough for everyone.

But if it would help Omar...

"Chloe will make it through this. She has you. She has me. And we have Him," she said, pointing upward. "And as far as Xavier..." she looked at her son, battered and bruised. And, according to doctors, beyond all hope. "What if that wasn't your one chance? What if you could have more than a few seconds to tell him how you feel?"

Omar stepped back and searched her face, unsure of what she was saying.

"Okay. This may sound crazy to you. And if it does, that's fine. Just keep it to yourself, because nothing you say is going to change my mind anyway."

Omar blinked. "Okay..."

Kristina told him everything. What Esther had said about Xavier's close calls. About how the doctors expected him to have learning disabilities. She told him about their plan to meet in Xavier's room at the same time every day and to keep meeting until the situation changed.

When she was done, his only response was to stare at her. Finally, after what seemed to Kristina to be an eternity, he spoke.

"So that's what you two are doing when you come in here?"

She nodded.

Omar looked at Xavier, then walked past Kristina to the window and stared out of it.

Kristina didn't know what she'd expected his reaction to be, but it certainly wasn't silence. After a few moments, she followed him and put her hand on his back.

"Omar?"

When he turned to her, his face was streaked with tears.

"Thank you," he whispered.

She leaned her head on his arm and he held her hand.

"You just told me there's still a chance. That's the best news I've had since I found out he existed."

Kristina wiped his tears away. "So you'll go home with your sister? Maybe eat something? Sleep?"

"Yeah," he said, smiling for the first time that day. "Knowing what I know now, I'm gonna sleep like a baby."

Chapter 12

When Tamia heard the door open, she cringed. She didn't even have to open her eyes to see who it was. There was only one person who refused to leave her in peace and that one person was Russell.

"I'm sorry I didn't come by earlier. But I thought about how messed up the cafeteria food is, so I ran out and picked up something special."

Tamia didn't have to see him to know he was grinning.

She heard him set a bag down on the tray and roll it to her bed. The rich and heavenly aroma of chicken-fried steak and buttermilk biscuits filled the room, making her mouth water.

She wanted to kick him.

There was only one place Tamia *had* to visit whenever she was in the Metroplex and that was Babe's Chicken Dinner House. Russell must've thought he was being real slick, bringing all her favorites. But she wasn't giving in. She kept her eyes closed and her breathing steady.

"Ahh. So instead of ignoring me to my face today, you just gonna pretend you're asleep, huh?" He chuckled and she could hear the legs of a chair scrape the floor as he dragged it to her bed.

"All right, then. I guess I'll just have to enjoy all this good food by myself."

Russell hummed as Tamia listened to the rustle of the bag being opened and food being taken out.

"Between patients, I've been doing a lot of reading online about spinal injuries…"

Here we go again…

Tamia couldn't take it anymore, his upbeat attitude, his unrelenting hopefulness. It seemed as though every time he showed up, it was with new research or a testimony or some breakthrough. She was starting to hate him for it. The last thing she wanted to hear about was spinal cord injuries. Here she was trying to get through each day without imagining how to get her hands on a bottle of sleeping pills and there he was, constantly reminding her of the very thing she wanted to escape.

"Apparently, he was given no hope, right? But he said he just kept visualizing…"

The worst part was, there was nothing she could do about it. She'd already made it clear she didn't want visitors. When that didn't work, she'd tried to pretend he wasn't there. But no matter what she said or did, he kept coming back. And since she was in no position to physically remove him from the room, she was condemned to lie there and suffer through his nonsense until he left.

"And it made me think about how in the Bible, it says—"

"Why are you here?"

Tamia opened her eyes. Russell had his mouth open to

take a bite. He looked so shocked and happy, she wanted to punch him in the face.

"Hey there!"

"Why. Are. You. Here."

Tamia made sure there was no warmth in her voice. She left no room for him to think her finally acknowledging his presence was a good thing.

He swallowed and set his fork down. "Really?"

"I asked, didn't I?"

He gave a half smile and nodded. "Okay. Well, I thought it was clear, but since it isn't... I'm here because I care about you." Russell put his hands up, as if in surrender. "More than I ever thought possible."

He looked at her, expectation in his eyes, and waited.

"What's wrong with you?"

Her response was not what he'd anticipated and he was taken aback. But he recovered quickly, a smile on his face.

"Well, according to my brothers, a lot!"

He tried to laugh, but the stony expression on Tamia's face made it hard.

"I'm not playing. I'm not trying to be cute. I'm trying to figure out what kind of freak thinks girls in wheelchairs are hot."

Russell leaned back in his chair. "Wow..." He breathed the word out. His eyebrows were furrowed and Tamia felt a bit of hope rise inside her. Maybe she'd just insulted him enough to finally be rid of him.

"That day when we met you and your sisters at your mother's funeral? I remember looking at you and thinking, how can someone have eyes so beautiful, yet so sad at the same time? And then I wondered, what in the world had you gone through to put that sadness there? You were like a shooting star or something. Beautiful, but light-years out of my reach. Then you started coming to visit Xavier and it turned out you were as cool as you were stunning." He shook is head and laughed.

"I don't got a thing for girls in wheelchairs. I got a thing for you. On two legs or two wheels, you're everything I want." He raised his eyebrows. "That being said, you won't have to stay in a wheelchair for long. Not if you don't want to. Not if I can help it."

"You can't. No one can."

"Hey, I'm the best physical therapist in the state."

"Yeah well, you may be good at your job, but paralyzed is paralyzed. No matter how much physical therapy you throw at it."

"Now see, that's where you're wrong. You're looking at this like the die has already been cast."

"Hasn't it? Maybe you need to have a chat with my doctor because—"

"I'm fully aware of your diagnosis. But I take on every patient with one thing in mind."

Tamia rolled her eyes. "And what's that, Russell?"

"First Corinthians 2:5."

He reached around the back of his chair and unzipped the pocket of his knapsack. He took out a tiny New Testament and opened it.

"Read the highlighted part."

Tamia cut her eyes at him, but did what he'd asked. "That your faith rest not in the wisdom of man, but in the power of God."

"Doctors only know what they know. And that's not everything. If you had any idea how many patients I've worked with that were never supposed to walk or run or even stand up straight, but *did*—you wouldn't be so quick to give up. It's like your sister said, miracles *can* happen."

Tamia felt the heat of fury rise in her chest. She was so fed up with people talking about miracles. A miracle would have been all of them surviving the accident. A miracle would've been her nephew conscious and out of danger. A miracle would've been her closest girlfriend anywhere but down in the morgue. A miracle would've been not getting in the accident at all.

"Things can get better, Tamia. And they *will*."

Tamia scoffed. "Yeah, things will get better. That's what I told myself, too. For *years*. That's what I hung onto. Through the beatings, the anxiety, the fear. *It's going to get better.* Because it had to, right? It certainly couldn't get any worse. And just when I thought that's finally what happened, it all went sideways. Literally. Next thing I knew, the bus was flipping over itself and I was watching people I'd known and loved for years get thrown around like rag dolls. And I just kept thinking, *this is it*. After everything I've gone through, *this* is how I'm gonna die."

Tears burned Tamia's eyes and her head throbbed so painfully, it felt like it would explode, but she kept going. It was as if all the rage she'd swallowed since the moment she'd regained consciousness had been set aflame. She had to get it out, even if it tore her apart. And if it destroyed Russell in the process, so much the better.

"Only, I don't. No. I get to live. Better yet, I get to live with a choice: disabled and in chronic pain or paralyzed." Tamia laughed, but it was callous and devoid of joy. "I get to choose between those two prizes while my nephew—"

At the mention of Xavier, her face crumpled and her voice broke. "My beautiful, funny, talented nephew gets no choice but to die before he's even lived. So no. Things don't get better. They get worse. Way worse than you could even let yourself imagine. And it makes me mad! So mad I can hardly see straight. And instead of just leaving me alone to deal with it like I've asked you to, you keep showing up! When are you gonna get the message? When are you gonna get the hint? I don't want you! I don't want nothing to do with you! How many ways do I have to say it?"

Russell stared at the floor. Finally, he stood, unsteadily. "I'm sorry. Tamia... I never meant to upset you."

She said nothing, hoping the anger she felt rolling off her in waves was enough to do the communicating for her.

He picked up his knapsack, lingering for a moment. "I'm *really* sorry. I'll just... I'll just come back later."

"Don't. Don't come back at all."

Russell blinked. "Tam—"

"You heard what I said."

He gripped one of the straps from his knapsack and stared at the floor. "Ask me for anything and I'll do it. But please, don't ask me to do that."

"I'm not asking. I'm telling you. Leave. Me. Alone!"

He stood there for another moment, then attempted a smile. "Hey, if you're getting tired of looking at this ugly mug, I can understand that. So how about this: I won't come in. At least, not for a while. I'll just sit outside your door and when you're ready—"

"Do you even hear yourself? Do you have any idea how pathetic you sound?" She laughed, mocking him. "You're a joke and you don't even know it."

Russell chewed his lower lip, but remained silent.

"Sit outside the door. Sit out in the parking lot. I don't care. As long as I don't have to see you and your useless, pitiful face, you can do whatever the hell you want."

That's when she saw it. It lasted for only a split second, but the pain on his face assured her she'd accomplished what she'd set out to do.

She'd eviscerated him.

But instead of feeling the satisfaction she thought she would, she only wanted to disappear. He opened his mouth to speak, then closed it again. He looked so lost and confused, it made her eyes burn and her throat ache.

"Umm…" He clenched his jaw and furrowed his brows.

Tamia closed her eyes so she didn't have to witness his humiliation.

"Okay. I'll, uh…"

Leave. Please, just leave, she silently begged him.

"If, uh, that's what you want, then…I'll stay away."

Finally, she heard shuffling footsteps move toward the door. Then, just before he closed it, he mumbled, "I really am sorry."

Chapter 13

Pam closed her eyes and leaned her head back. She was so relieved to have the waiting room all to herself; she didn't even know what to do.

Correction. She knew exactly what to do. Sleep.

She couldn't remember the last time she'd been so tired. She turned sideways in her chair, propped her legs up and folded her arms. She snuggled in to the chair and exhaled, determined to grab a few minutes rest.

Her determination lasted all of three minutes.

As exhausted as she was, her worried mind wouldn't let her sleep. How could she? Between Kristina's misguided faith and Tamia's misdirected anger, Pam felt like her world was spinning out of control.

She'd dedicated her life to her sisters and their well-being, but now, when they needed her most, she didn't know how to help them. And if there was one thing that set Pam on edge, it was not knowing what to do. *Especially* when it came to her sisters.

She knew what Robin would tell her: Pray.

And while she knew it was probably what she should do, she didn't *want* to. What she really wanted was—

"Happy birthday!"

Pam jumped and her eyelids popped open. Standing over her was Justina, all smiles.

Pam sat up and smoothed her hair. "I'm sorry. What was that?"

"I said, Happy birthday!" Justina's twinkling eyes reflected the unrestrained merriment in her voice. In her hands was a small paper plate and on the plate, a cupcake.

If there'd ever been a sadder looking cupcake, Pam had never seen it. It looked like it came from a kitchen in the midst of a frosting famine and it had the world's skinniest candle sticking out of its uneven top.

Justina studied Pam's facial expression and frowned.

"I know. It's a homely little thing." She laughed and sat next to Pam, still looking at the cupcake. "But it's all they had in the cafeteria and I don't know my way around here well enough to find a bakery. I almost didn't get it, but I just couldn't let your birthday pass without at least a little something."

Her birthday…

Pam had completely forgotten it. Not that she ever made a big deal of it anyway. Not with the way she worked.

If it wasn't a record release date, it was a music video shoot. There were always appearances to book or, like now, tour preparations to make. And that was on a regular year. Now, with everything that had happened, her birthday was the farthest thing from her mind.

Besides, birthdays weren't really her thing, anyway. Especially her own.

So why did looking at that tired, little cupcake and the sweetness in Justina's expression put a lump in her throat?

Justina held it up."Go ahead. It's your favorite. Chocolate."

Pam took the plate. For some reason she didn't understand, she found herself unable to meet Justina's gaze. "But how—"

"Did I know? That you love chocolate cake or that it's your birthday?"

"Both."

"Baby, we celebrate your birthday *every* year. All three of you girls. I go all out. On Tamia's day, we go to a Thai restaurant and I make a six layer coconut cake. On Krissi's, it's my special Five Cheese Macaroni Bake and a pineapple upside-down cake. On your birthday," she said, patting Pam on the arm. "I make my white lasagna and my secret recipe devil's food cake."

Pam didn't know what to say. How in the world did this woman know these things? Yes, Kristina had done interviews. And there was an MTV special that followed her and the band during the holidays one year. But Pam steered clear of the public eye once she'd stopped singing backup for Kristina. Finding personal information about her sisters, especially on fan sites, was possible. But Pam? No way.

It must have been Gerald.

Pam stared at the cupcake. On one hand, she was uncomfortable. She'd never met this woman and wasn't even sure she wanted to like her. She already had one strike against her: being married to Gerald. On the other hand, she made something stir in Pam's heart. If there was anything Pam was unfamiliar with, it was warm and fuzzy. But that's exactly what she felt as she sat next to Justina and listened to her talk.

Not having grandmothers, aunts, godmothers—or anyone else like that in their lives—left a void. There was never anyone to bake a cake or remember a birthday. To go to for advice, encouragement or even a hug.

While Kristina and Tamia had expressed their wish for those types of relationships, Pam never did. Why should she? It wasn't like it was something that could ever happen. Especially after they'd grown up. The way Pam saw it, their opportunity to be mothered or shown affection as daughters or nieces or granddaughters had long since passed. There was no sense in yearning for something that would never be. At least, that's what she always told herself.

But now, as she sat next to Justina, she felt the emptiness she hadn't experienced since she was a little girl. That heartache she sensed whenever she saw mothers and daughters together at the grocery store or hugging each other in a restaurant.

Pam couldn't recall the last time someone called her *Baby*, like Justina just had. She wasn't prepared for the deep longing that gripped her heart as a result.

Pam cleared her throat. She couldn't go there. Too much was already happening. She needed to stay strong. For Kristina. For Tamia. She couldn't do that while wallowing in her own feelings. She needed to change the subject.

"This was kind of you. Thank you."

Justina chuckled. "You're so formal! Well, I guess that's to be expected. I keep forgetting you girls don't know me from Adam. I feel like I've known you your whole lives. Between the baby pictures and seeing Krissi—"

"Baby pictures?"

"You haven't seen them yet?"

"No. You mean you have some with you?"

"Do I have some with me?" Justina reached in to her purse and dug out a long wallet. "Always." She opened it and sure enough, there in the plastic picture sleeves were the Langston girls.

There was a hospital picture of Tamia, all new and wrinkly. The next was a snapshot of Kristina. Pam couldn't tell the age, but she couldn't have been more than six months. The next four pictures were all shots of Pam.

The edges were worn and the images had scratches and blemishes due to the passing of time.

"I can't tell you how many times I've stared at these pictures. Wondered where you were, what you were doing." Justina sighed. "You especially. I don't know why, but I always had such a soft spot for you. Well, look at those cheeks," Justina said, chuckling. "Who could resist those?"

Pam bit her lip. Could it be? Could a woman she'd never met *really* care about her enough to carry her baby pictures in her wallet for close to thirty years?

"I didn't even know pictures of me this young existed."

"And that's just the ones I stole from your daddy!" Justina laughed. Pam found herself growing more and more fond of the sound.

Justina got up and went to a chair a few feet away. Using the arm of another chair for support, she reached under the seat and pulled out an overnight bag. She brought it back to where Pam was and reached inside, taking out an old, worn envelope. She handed it to Pam and sat down again.

Pam balanced the cupcake plate on her knees and took the envelope. She gasped when she saw what was inside.

Dozens and dozens of Langston family pictures. There was one of her mother, younger than she'd ever seen her, holding a diapered Pam in her arms. In another picture, Pam was cradled by an older woman. Her grandmother? She had no idea. She'd never known or seen any of her grandparents.

"This one was always my favorite." Justina put on the readers she had hanging from her neck and pointed to the next picture in the stack. "Look at the two of you! Those faces!"

It was Pam and Kristina, dressed like twins and holding hands.

Pam shook her head and chuckled. "I can't believe this. We were so little. And cute!"

"You were precious, precious girls. I couldn't help but fall in love with you when I saw all these. Not to mention the stories your daddy told me about you three. Like this one here."

Justina shuffled through the pictures until she came across a much younger Gerald on his hands and knees and Kristina on his back. She had one arm up in the air and the other one holding on to the makeshift reigns he held in his mouth.

"Apparently, she wanted a pony for her birthday…"

Justina continued, but Pam didn't hear a word she said. She was too mesmerized by young Kristina's face.

From the moment Pam saw Xavier, she thought he looked like Omar. But now, as she stared at the picture of Kristina, only one thing came to mind. The baby picture she had seen of Xavier on the Morris mantle.

"Xavier looked just like her," Pam whispered.

Justina stopped telling her story and looked at Pam.

"Xavier? Who's that?"

"Her son," Pam said, without thinking.

"I have a grandson?"

The sound of Gerald's voice snatched Pam from her reverie. He stood a few feet away from her and Justine, a shocked expression on his face. She hadn't even heard him walk in.

He rushed toward her, his limp more pronounced as he hurried.

"Nobody told me. How old is he? Where is he?"

Upon seeing him, Pam felt her muscles tense and her temperature rise.

Talk about nerve. More than thirty years of silence from the man and he expected to show up and be taken to the bedside of the daughter he never knew. Now, he had the audacity to call Kristina's child his *grandson*?

Pam had never felt her temper rise so quickly. She stood abruptly, unintentionally causing the cupcake on her lap to fall to the floor and break into pieces. Immediately, Justina struggled to her knees to clean it up. Pam knew she should've helped. She *wanted* to help. But with Gerald there, all she could see was red.

She needed to get away and she needed to do it quickly. It was the only way she'd avoid making a scene.

She left Justina behind and tried to pass Gerald, but he grabbed her arm, pleading in his eyes.

"Please. If I have a grandson—"

Pam snatched her arm away and did her best to keep her voice even, but her hostility was too deep to cover.

"You don't. In order to have a grandson, you have to have a daughter. And you don't. I don't know what kind of excuses you've been feeding Kristina, but you can't try that stuff with me. There is no reason in the world you had to abandon us the way you did. And then show up now? In the middle of all this mess? For what? To offer your support? Newsflash: we don't need it. And we don't need you!"

Gerald took a couple of unsteady steps backward. "I know you're angry. You have every right to be. But we're still family. That means something."

"That don't mean jack! And in case you haven't noticed, we don't need no more family!" She threw the pictures she was still holding in his face. "And we don't need your happy family memories either. Ain't nothing but a bunch of lies anyway. Go back to Seattle. You never should've come in the first place!"

Pam went to turn, but caught a glimpse of Justina as she did. She was still on the floor, picking up the bits of cupcake strewn across the carpet. Pam saw the tears in her eyes, though Justina tried to hide them when their eyes met.

The hurt on her face made Pam's stomach twist. But instead of apologizing, she stormed out, running in to Kristina as she did.

Chapter 14

"That was rude, Pam."

Kristina followed her sister around the corner and to a bank of chairs until Pam stopped and put her hand up.

"Don't start with me, Kristina."

"There's no need to be so nasty to him."

"Please. I've already asked you. Just stop."

"I'll stop when you explain why you won't even hear his side of the story. He deserves that much. Here he is trying to offer his support and you acting like that. The least you could do is be polite. We need him right now."

Pam jerked back, and then made a big show of looking behind her and down the hall.

"*Need* him? Who? Not me. I haven't needed him since he left. And while we're on the subject, since when do you and Tamia need him? Didn't I take care of you two? Tell me one time I wasn't there when you needed me! But the minute this joker rolls into town, all of a sudden you *need* him? Please, somebody explain that to me."

Kristina put her hand on her hip. "Is that what this is about? You think somebody's trying to replace you? Oh, Pam. Nobody—not Gerald, not Omar—*nobody* could ever take your place. Not with me or Tamia. You were more of a mother to us than mama ever was. Don't think for a second we've forgotten that. But don't you ever get tired? Don't you ever wish you had someone *you* could lean on? It was just the three of us for so long, but look at what God's done. We're not on our own anymore. We have a family to draw strength from. Reiland, Gerald, Chloe, Omar, Xav—"

The silence hung between them, heavy with sorrow. Once Pam spoke again, her voice was quiet and all the anger had been deflated out of it.

"Yeah… Things just keep getting better and better, huh?"

Kristina sat down. Pam folded her arms and walked to the other side of the hallway before turning again to face Kristina.

"I see it coming." She closed her eyes and shook her head. "The train wreck that's about to hit us head-on and I'm the only one willing to admit it."

"It's not that I don't see what's happening, Pam. I just believe God is big enough to make it better."

Pam sniffed. "Make it better, huh?" She came back to where Kristina was and stood in front of her. "I'm all for living the Christian life. You know I am. And I respect that you want to have faith in God. But sometimes you have to be realistic. Some things don't get better."

"I can still have hope they will."

Pam shook her head and sat next to Kristina. "And that's the problem. Don't you see it? Even when we were little girls, you and Tamia were always hoping it would get better. I never did. You know why? Because dear old dad taught me otherwise. I didn't hope for things to get better because I knew it didn't make a difference. However good it gets, there's always another bad thing waiting around the corner. That's life. I got to where I finally understood that."

"You never gave up on me."

Kristina's words stopped Pam cold. She leaned back in the chair and rested her head against the wall.

"You're right. The one thing I could never accept was your nonstop efforts to put yourself six feet under. So yeah, I did everything I could to prevent that from happening. And by some miracle, it worked out. And I'll admit, for about a minute, I actually thought: Wow. Maybe life isn't just a series of tragedies. Maybe there's such a thing as being happy."

Pam laughed bitterly and rolled her head to the side so she was looking at Kristina. "Right up until I turned on the news about two people I love most in this world being in one of the deadliest crashes in Texas state history. Right up until I learned my nephew wasn't going open his eyes again and my baby sister would be disabled for life."

Pam sat up and turned to Kristina, putting her hand on her arm. "And then there's you."

She put her other hand on the side of Kristina's face, turning it so they were facing each other.

"I see you holding on for dear life. Hoping and praying God is going to swoop in and rescue us. But that's not how it works, Krissi. He never saved us from mama. He didn't save Tamia and Xavier from the accident. And He's not gonna save us from this."

"You don't know—"

"What? I don't know that's how it'll turn out? But I do, Krissi. I know it like I know my own name. And what terrifies me is the moment when you'll realize it for yourself. The moment you'll lose all hope. Because I'm afraid that when you do, that's the moment I'll lose *you*."

Kristina blinked back the tears and tried to swallow the doubt she felt rising like bile.

"Kristina, I'm scared. More afraid than I've ever been in my life. I'm terrified that if you don't accept reality, if you don't start dealing with what's about to happen, you're gonna end up where you were the night of mama's funeral. On a bathroom floor, alone and dying."

Pam's voice broke and her words came out in choked whispers. "I'm begging you. Please. Please. Accept this so we can move through it. I can get through anything else, but I can't lose you or Tamia. I can't."

Kristina put her arms around Pam.

"You won't. I promise."

She said the words, hoping she sounded more confident than she felt.

Kristina slipped in to Tamia's room and put her hand up before her little sister could say anything.

"I know, I know. You want to be left alone. Fine. I won't say a word, but I'm not leaving. I need to hide out from Pam for a minute and this is the only place I know she won't come."

Without waiting for a response, Kristina continued to the couch on the other side of the room. But on her way, she noticed the tears rolling down Tamia's cheeks and stopped.

"What is it? Are you hurting? I'll get a nurse."

"No."

Kristina stopped and turned back around.

"I'm not hurting. I mean, no more than usual."

She began to sob and Kristina rushed to her side. She took Kleenex from the nightstand and dabbed her tears.

"Oh, honey. Talk to me. What is it?"

"I'm so hateful," Tamia cried.

"Hateful? You? Why in the world would you say that? Tamia, you couldn't be hateful even if you tried. You're just going through some major stuff right now and we understand that."

"You weren't there," Tamia said, trying to catch her breath. "You didn't hear the things I said."

"To who? What are you talking about?"

"Russell. He kept quoting scripture and I got mad and basically told him he was stupid for thinking things could get better."

Kristina sighed and patted her sister's cheeks with a fresh Kleenex. "You, too? And here I was thinking I was jumping out of the frying pan…"

"Huh?"

"Nothing. It'll be okay, Tam. I'm sure it's nothing that can't be fixed."

"He probably hates me."

"I seriously doubt that, but if you really think you messed up, apologize. Tell him you were wrong."

Tamia furrowed her eyebrows.

"Oh, wait. Let me guess. You *don't* think you're wrong, do you?"

"It's not that. It's just—" Tamia's eyes welled up with tears again. "I want to believe what he believes, but how can I? With all the bad stuff that's happened to us? I'm tired. I don't want to keep hoping and believing. It's exhausting. I just wanna…"

"Close your eyes."

Tamia looked up at her sister and the tears started to fall

again. Kristina yanked another Kleenex from the box and dried her own cheeks.

"Trust me. I know the feeling. You know I do. Until you, Pam and Robin staged your little weekend intervention, all I wanted was to close my eyes and never open them again. There was no reason to, at least, that's what I thought. You three helped me see I was wrong."

Kristina swept the loose strands of hair from her sister's forehead and smiled.

"Remember when I was pregnant with Xavier? How I used to cry after everyone else was asleep?"

"I would get in bed with you."

Kristina nodded. "And you'd talk about what it'd be like when he was born. And then you'd sing to me."

Tamia laughed and sniffled. "God Put A Rainbow in the Sky."

"And I used to think, 'She's too young. She doesn't understand how bad this is. Over here singing about rainbows when our lives are about to blow up!'" Kristina chuckled. "Turns out, I was the one who didn't get it. But that's what He does. Waits until the darkness seems too deep to be overcome, and then, here comes the light. He's still the same God you sang about, baby sister."

"Yeah, well, I sure wish He'd put one up for me."

No sooner than Tamia got the words out, a realization hit Kristina. Her eyes grew wide and she started grinning so hard, her cheeks hurt.

"I think He already did!"

Tamia frowned. "What are you talking about?"

Kristina put her hands on her head. "I can't believe I hadn't thought of this before!"

"What?"

"You, Tamia! You! You and the only other person you

ever missed as much as you missed my baby." Kristina made a dash for the door. "I'll be back."

"Where are you going?"

"To prove you and Pam wrong. Things *do* get better. And guess what? God is still in the rainbow making business!"

Chapter 15

Tamia wished she had a mirror she could look in. After everything that'd happened over the past few days, she was sure she looked a mess. Kristina told her it didn't matter, not to worry about it. But how could she not?

Today was the day she would meet her father.

She couldn't remember the last time she'd been so nervous. She'd sung backup for Kristina in stadiums filled with thousands of people and not once had her heart ever beat so fast. She had to keep reminding herself to take a breath because every few minutes, she realized she was holding it. Questions were racing through her mind faster than she could process them. What did he look like? Did he ever think about her? Did he miss her as much as she'd missed him?

Kristina told her very little about him. But it was just enough to let her know that nearly everything they'd heard about him was a lie. But Tamia didn't care. Even if all of it were true, she still wouldn't have turned him away. She'd wanted, no, needed a father too much to ever do that.

Besides, whatever he was, he couldn't have been any worse than their mother. And even after everything she'd done, Tamia knew deep down, there was some part of her that still loved Mahalia.

Tamia glanced at the clock on the wall. It felt like it'd been at least an hour since she'd last looked, but it'd only been seven minutes. She closed her eyes and took a deep breath. She wished she knew what time he was coming. That might've made the time pass a little easier. But Kristina told her they would have to wait until Pam left for lunch or an errand. There was no way she was sneaking Gerald in as long as Pam was milling about in the hallway.

Gerald.

How many times had Tamia wondered what her father's name was? Growing up, it was her Holy Grail. She thought knowing would make him less of a mystery. That it would somehow transform him from the unreachable and shadowy figure he was, into something concrete and imaginable.

But now, she wouldn't have to imagine. Now, she'd actually—

Tamia heard the door open and she felt as if her heart stopped. She opened her eyes to see Kristina walk in and behind her, an older gentleman with coconut shell brown skin, followed.

He looked just like Tamia.

Since the moment she'd learned he was at the hospital, she'd spent every minute imagining their reunion. She'd wondered about the best way to greet him, what to say and how to say it. But now that the moment was here, all her plans left her nothing but speechless.

He walked to her bed, his eyes damp with tears and a warm smile on his face.

"My baby girl. You know, the last time I saw you, you fit in the crook of my arm."

Tamia was overcome with emotion. Even with all she wanted to say to him, all she could do was cry. Never in a million years did she think she'd meet her father, much less, hear him call her his baby girl.

He leaned over on her bed so his face was against hers, their tears intermingling.

"I'm so sorry. I'm so sorry." He whispered the words over and over. And over and over she told him, "It's okay. It's okay."

After a few moments, he straightened up and she was able to look into his face again. When she did, she laughed.

"I've always wondered who I looked like. Pam and Kristina look like mama. Despite what they said, I knew I didn't."

He arched an eyebrow and tugged at his lapels. "That's because you the only one fortunate enough to take after the old man."

Tamia couldn't help but smile. It was quite the compliment. Although he had the look of someone that had lived hard, it did nothing to diminish his handsomeness. With his red banded fedora cocked over one eye, he looked like the kind they sung about when they said, *Papa was a rolling stone...* Tamia decided that once she got over the shock of meeting him, she'd have to ask how in the world a man like him was able to convince a woman like Mahalia Langston to marry him.

"Mmm, mmm, mmm." He shook his head and brought a chair to her bedside. "I just can't get over this." He sat down and held one of her hands in his. "The whole time we were coming down from Seattle, I just kept saying, Lord, please keep her here and let me see her just one more time. Justina finally bopped me in the back of the head and told me to stop begging and get to praying!"

"Justina?"

"That's my wife. Talk about a praying woman. At one point, I thought I felt the car shaking! I'll admit, it scared me a bit, but I thought, hey, whatever works!"

"Thank her for me."

"You can thank her yourself. She's looking to see you just as much as me, but wanted to give us some time alone first. I know you girls had a mama and you're probably still hurting over your loss, but when you're ready, I hope you can find room in your heart to get to know Justina. She loves you like you're her own babies."

Tamia swallowed. Kristina hadn't told him what their childhood was like?

"Does that mean you're sticking around this time?"

Gerald leaned back. "Ouch."

Tamia hadn't meant her words to come out so sharp. She didn't even know why they did. It's not like she was angry with him, but for some reason, him bringing up her mother made her prickly. The last thing she wanted to do was end this reunion before it had a chance to begin.

"I'm sorry."

He waved his hand and took off his hat, setting it on the bedside table. "Little girl, you ain't got nothing to be sorry about. You yell, cry and kick, if you want to. God knows I deserve that and more."

"No! I mean, I don't care about any of that. It's all in the past. I just don't want you to leave. Not again."

He nodded his head and took her hand again. "I let you girls down once. I don't intend on doing it again."

She squeezed his hand. "I hear you have pictures."

"You bet I do. And stories to go with 'em!" He took out glasses from the inside of his jacket and an overstuffed and worn envelope from his pocket.

"You sure you're ready for this? Justina says I can talk a hind leg off a mule."

Tamia motioned at her halo. "Captive audience."

He laughed and Tamia felt her heart skip a beat.

"All right, baby girl," he said, eyeing her over the top of his glasses. "Just remember, you asked for it."

Chapter 16

The light coming through the hospital room window went from a stark midday brightness to a beautiful and flaming, sunset orange. Nurses came and nurses went. Tamia barely noticed any of it.

Turned out she and her father had a lot in common. All the little things that perplexed her sisters over the years, like her all-consuming love of Thai food and her passionate obsession with Star Wars, were courtesy of Gerald LeVar Langston.

The hours seemed to pass like minutes as they shared their lives and memories. Her father's stories, not only of her sisters as girls, but of his own life after them, had her sometimes laughing and sometimes crying. But she wasn't the only one. As Gerald told her about him and his brother growing up in Alabama, he was doing both at the same time.

"Wait. Did you just say he ran you over with a car?"

His high pitched peals of laughter filled the room. "Baby, not just any car. A boat! A big ol' avocado green Cadillac."

"Were you hurt?"

"Nah. But he didn't know that, so I played dead! And I didn't move a muscle until he was wallowing in the dirt and crying like a newborn baby 'cuz he knew my mama was about to end his life! He was drooling and flopping all over the ground for a good ten minutes before I jumped him."

"What did he do?"

"Wet his pants right then and there." Gerald laughed so hard, Tamia was sure he was going to fall off the chair.

"You wrong for that."

Gerald wiped the tears from his eyes, still wheezing with laughter. "I know it. But it served him right for trying to run me over."

Just then, the door opened and two flower arrangements and a bunch of balloons walked in. Hiding behind them was Pam.

"Before you start yelling, I'm just bringing—"

The balloons floated up to the ceiling and Pam's mouth dropped open. She looked from Tamia to Gerald and back to Tamia.

"So I guess you lifted the ban on all visitors, huh? Or does he just get special privileges?"

"Pamela—"

"I wasn't talking to you."

Pam slammed one of the flower arrangements down on a table to emphasize her point. She brought the other one to Tamia's bedside table.

"Don't worry. I'm not staying. Just making your deliveries."

"Pam, don't be mad."

Pam turned back toward the door, her hands up. "Mad? I'm past that. I'm done."

She opened the door with one hand and pointed at Gerald with the other.

"You and Kristina wanna cozy up with the man that left y'all in the hands of the devil? Fine by me. I'm not wasting another breath on the matter."

With that, she walked out the door, slamming it behind her.

A few awkward moments of silence passed before Tamia spoke.

"Don't worry about her. She'll come around."

Gerald gave her a halfhearted smile. "I expected you girls to be angry, but I think Pamela outright hates me."

"No, she's just..." Tamia exhaled. "We went through a lot. She was the one who had to take care of everybody else. Mama was... well, like I said, we went through a lot."

"That's what she meant, about me leaving y'all in the hands of the devil?"

Tamia nodded.

"What all happened?" He asked, but there was reluctance in his voice, as if he wasn't sure he wanted an answer.

Whether he did or not, didn't matter. Tamia wasn't in the mood to give one.

"Maybe some other time."

Her day had been going well. For the first time since she'd woken up, she wasn't drowning in her own sorrow. There was no way that would last if she started talking about the misery that was her childhood.

"That look on your face is saying a lot. Please tell me the reality wasn't as bad as what I'm imagining."

Tamia didn't have a clue what her father was thinking, but she knew there was no way it beat out the horrors they'd experienced growing up. Suddenly, she understood why Kristina hadn't told him about it. It was too hard.

He interlaced his fingers and put them over his head and stared at the ceiling. His eyes became damp and he whispered, "Lord Jesus."

"It's okay," Tamia said, her voice breaking. "It's over now."

He put his face in his hands. "I should've taken you girls to my mother that night. I should've taken you that night." His shoulders shook as he wept and the sight of it pained Tamia more than the damage the accident had done.

"Daddy."

Gerald looked up, blinking back tears. Tamia opened her hand so he would take it and he did.

"Please, don't. I know you feel guilty and I know it hurts you. But let's not dwell on that right now. There's already too much bad happening for us to drag along what's been left behind. Let's just talk about something else, okay?"

He nodded his head and wiped his eyes. "You're right. What you want to talk about, baby girl?"

"Anything."

"Anything?"

"Yep."

"You sure?"

Tamia narrowed her eyes. The mischievous glint in her father's eye reminded her of the look Kristina got whenever she was about to prank someone on tour.

"I was. Now? Not so much."

Gerald grinned. "What's with the young man wasting away outside your door?"

Tamia groaned. When Russell said he'd sit outside her door, she didn't think he'd literally do it.

"And explain the Walkman. I'm almost seventy and I don't even use those things. And I'm pretty sure those kind of flat tops went out with the nineties."

"He's—" Tamia started to explain he was Xavier's brother,

but if Kristina hadn't told Gerald about their mother, maybe she hadn't told him about her son, either.

"He's a friend."

"A friend?" Gerald wasn't buying it.

Tamia exhaled. "We had kinda, well, I guess you could call it a 'flirtation' going on."

"Before all this?" Gerald frowned. "I haven't seen that boy in any real clothes since I got here. The only reason I know he changes is because his scrubs are a different color from day to day. And from what I understand, he hardly goes home. He comes by and asks Kristina about you on every break. He even eats his lunch right out there in the hallway. That sounds like more than a 'flirtation' to me."

"Maybe for him, it is."

"So this is one-sided, then? I guess that would explain why he's always outside the room and never in it."

"I told him he couldn't come in."

Gerald moaned and crossed his arms.

"Put the poor boy out of his misery. And trust me, he's in misery. If you don't like him, why not tell him so?"

Tamia remained silent and stared at the wall.

"Ahhh, I see." Gerald took a deep breath. "I understand I'm the newcomer in all this, but it seems to me right now you need your friends close. Why would you push him away at a time like this?"

Tamia blinked rapidly in the hopes of stopping the tears threatening to roll down her cheeks.

"He cares about me too much. It scares me."

"Why?"

"Because I don't want to weigh him down with this. I don't want him to think he wants me today, only to wake up five years from now and realize he tied himself to a millstone."

"But isn't that his decision to make?"

Tamia kept blinking, but it didn't help. The tears fell quicker than she could stop them. Gerald stood and snatched a few tissues out of the box on the bedside table. Then he gently dabbed the tears from her face.

"Say what you will, but I know lovestruck when I see it. And that boy's got it bad."

Tamia fiddled with the sheet under her blanket and sucked her teeth. "Well, he needs to get over that quick, if he knows what's best for him."

"And why is that? You already spoken for?"

"Yeah," she said bitterly. "There's already a big, handsome wheelchair with my name all over it."

Gerald sighed. "After all these years, I know I don't have any right to come in here offering fatherly advice, so just think of me as Yoda. A wise little man that's been around a long time. If he's a physical therapist, I think he probably already knows what he's getting into. Maybe even better than you do."

Tamia had to admit, she hadn't thought about that. And maybe if her disability was the only problem, she would've told Gerald he was right. But there was another reason she wanted Russell to stay away, a reason that would have kept them apart even if the accident had never happened.

"None of that matters. I can't be with him."

Gerald sat back down and leaned in, his elbows on her bed. "Would it be all right if I asked why?"

After a few moments, she said, "You know that stuff I didn't wanna talk about?"

Gerald nodded. "Your mama."

Tamia swallowed. "The things that happened... She messed me up. Bad. Some days, I feel like I'm walking in quicksand. I'm sad and I don't even know why. Or I'm anxious and I panic for no reason. He doesn't know about any of that. I'm afraid of what would happen when he found out. Being broken on the inside is one thing, being broken on the outside is another. But both?" She closed her eyes. "He's a good guy. He deserves better than that."

"You know what else he is? Grown. What he does or doesn't deserve is not anyone else's decision but his own. And you should let him make it."

"So…what? He can eventually see what a bad deal he got and end up leaving anyway? It's better if he goes now. It'll hurt less."

"Oh, baby girl," Gerald sighed. "It's my fault you don't know this, but there are men that stay. Through good times *and* bad. Through stuff worse than what you're facing. They *stay*. They know the meaning of unconditional love. Any man that's gonna sit outside your room every available minute, even after you've thrown your worst at him, well, he may be one of the ones worth keeping. I've only talked to him in passing, but he seems like an upstanding man."

"He is," Tamia whispered.

"Then give him a chance." Gerald wiped away her tears again, balled up the tissue and stuffed it in his pocket. "You're a lot easier to love than you think."

Tamia studied him for a few moments before a smile slowly stretched across her face.

"Right you are, father. Much wisdom, you have."

Gerald laughed and cleared his throat so he could do his best Yoda impression.

"And if smart you are, daughter. Listen, you will."

Tamia laughed. Deep and from her belly. Like she had before the accident, when she still felt there was hope to be had. Maybe Kristina was right. Maybe miracles did happen. Because, paralyzed or not, she was alive and looking into her father's eyes.

And that was something she couldn't have imagined in her wildest dreams.

Chapter 17

"I hate to even ask this but, how are you holding up?"

Kristina was on the first floor of the hospital, alone in the hallway, leaned against the wall and on the phone with Robin.

"Believe it or not, I'm okay. Maybe I shouldn't be. That's the impression I keep getting from Pam. And yeah, with the way things look, maybe I should be feeling something else. But the truth is, I'm holding up."

"I wish I could be there with you."

"Girl, you and me both. Especially right now," Kristina said, looking down the hall.

"Why? What's going on?"

"I've been meeting with the families of my tour members and the last family is coming in today. Michelle's family. Out of everyone, we've always been the closest to them. One year we even spent the holidays together. You'd think our being tight would make it easier. But for some reason, I'm dreading seeing Michelle's mother the most. I have no idea what to say. If you were here, you'd know what to do."

"And so will you. You have access to the same God and the same wisdom I do."

Just then, Pastor Thomas, who had been waiting farther down the hall, waved his hand to get Kristina's attention.

"Robin, it looks like they're here now," she said. "I'll call you later. But please, keep us in your prayers."

"Of course. But listen, keep your eyes on God. Trust that He'll show you the way. He always does."

Kristina followed Pastor Thomas to where Michelle's mother, older brother and younger sister were coming down the hall. Michelle's mother, Rhonda, wore a weary expression and red-rimmed eyes. But she still smiled the moment she saw Kristina and opened her arms to embrace her.

After hugging Michelle's siblings and exchanging a few words, Kristina motioned to the pastor.

"Rhonda, this is Pastor Thomas. He heads a wonderful church here in Dallas and has been helping all of us through this."

Rhonda shook Pastor Thomas' hand.

"I'm here for whatever you need," he told her. "Even for what you have to do now. If you prefer to go in privately, we'll wait. But if you'd like me to accompany you, I'm more than willing."

Rhonda nodded and took a deep breath. "I appreciate that. Thank you. I…" Her voice faltered. She looked at her son and daughter, almost apologetically.

Her daughter, Marie, hugged her. "Mama, it's okay. He can go in with us."

Marie looked at Kristina and the Pastor. "She's been back and forth about this since we left New York."

"It's a lot to put on you kids, that's all."

Her son, Ezra, put his hand on her back. "We've got this. Don't worry about it. You stay with Krissi and we'll be right back."

Rhonda nodded. She wiped at the tears streaming from her eyes. "You all go ahead then."

Pastor Thomas led Michelle's siblings down the hall as Kristina and Rhonda watched them go.

"I know they think they're prepared. And I love them for wanting to spare me, but…" Rhonda exhaled heavily.

"Come on," Kristina whispered. She took Rhonda by the hand and led her to a bench and they sat.

"I saw the footage. I saw how bad that wreck was. I just keep imagining her cut up and broken…" She shook her head. "God forgive me, but I just can't do it. I can't see my baby like that."

"Anyone could understand that."

"I wanted to thank you, Krissi. I was told you had to identify two of the girls. They said it would've been a lot longer until we knew who was who if you hadn't done that. And thank you for taking care of the arrangements. For getting Michelle home, too. With the medical bills I've had piling up these last two years, I don't know how we would've been able to afford it."

"Stop. You're family. Anything else you need, let me know. I mean that."

"I know you do. And I can't thank you enough."

Rhonda leaned back and exhaled. "I've been through some stuff, girl. God knows I have. But this? I just can't wrap my head around it. I've heard people say losing a child is the worst thing a parent can go through. But the pain…" She held her fist to her chest. "It's almost unbearable."

Kristina looked away from Rhonda. It was in moments like these her faith wavered. That she wondered if Pam was right, that she was hoping for something impossible. If Pam *was* right, then this pain Rhonda described was what awaited her. The thought of it made her dizzy with fear.

"I can't imagine," she whispered.

"And I hope you never have to, Krissi. 'Cause I don't know how—" Rhonda's voice caught in her throat and her words came out like gasps of air. "I can't see how I'm gonna survive it."

Kristina clenched her jaw and tightened her fists. Esther told her about the bouts of doubt. She'd mentioned how lonely it could be, believing for something that seemed impossible. But she hadn't said anything about the terror. The way it made one's stomach churn and legs weak.

Kristina bowed her head and shut her eyes.

God has not given me the spirit of fear. God has not given me the spirit of fear. God has not given me the spirit of fear, but of power, and of love, and of a sound mind.

A sound mind. That's what she needed. A mind kept on Christ and His finished work at the cross. A mind that remembered His promise to never leave her or forsake her. A mind—

"Marie!"

Kristina's thoughts were interrupted when she felt Rhonda move. She opened her eyes just in time to see Marie run past them, her hand over her mouth and her face streaked with tears.

Kristina followed Rhonda as she continued to call after her daughter, but to no avail. Rhonda turned to Ezra and Pastor Thomas as they approached.

"I never should have put this on you. It should have been me."

Ezra blinked, his face blank. "It wouldn't have made a difference."

Rhonda went to him. "What do you mean, son?"

He sat and buried his face in his hands. "We're gonna have to bury her like that." He broke down in sobs.

Confused, Rhonda reached for him. "What are you saying? Baby, I don't understand."

"She's in bad shape, mama."

Rhonda looked from her son to Pastor Thomas and then Kristina. "What does that mean? Bad shape?"

Kristina and Pastor Thomas looked at each other, neither wanting to answer.

"What's he talking about? Tell me!"

Kristina opened her mouth, but no words came out. It seemed such a simple thing to do. They were only words, after all. But how in the world do you tell a mother something like that? How do you tell someone their baby was cut in pieces?

Desperate for help, Kristina looked at Pastor Thomas. He swallowed hard and put his arm around Rhonda's shoulders.

"Let's have a seat. I'll explain it to you."

Kristina knew she should stay. She knew it was her responsibility to give the family support. But against her best intentions, she began to back away. With each word Pastor Thomas spoke, she found it harder and harder to stop. By the time he got to the end of it, by the time he explained to Rhonda what the accident had done to her young and beautiful daughter, Kristina wanted to run.

And when Rhonda screamed and slid off the chair onto the floor, that's exactly what Kristina did.

She didn't stop running until she got to Xavier's room. She *needed* it to be two o'clock. She needed to retreat to that Secret Place. Because though she was hanging on, her fingers were starting to slip.

There was only one Person Who could catch her before she fell, and His name was Jesus.

Chapter 18

Kristina and Esther's prayer time began like it always had, with praise and worship. But then, about fifteen minutes in, something happened.

Like a mighty, rushing wind, a power swept into the room with such force, Kristina found herself prostrate on the floor. She wasn't quite sure how she got there. She never even felt herself fall. All she knew was the air in the room became heavy and unlike anything she'd experienced before.

The *Presence* in the room, however, was very familiar. It was the same Presence she'd felt at New Life Tabernacle the night she saw her son for the first time after seventeen years of thinking him dead.

Now, like then, she couldn't move. And now, like then, she didn't want to. It was too healing, too revitalizing. After the terror of the accident, the strife with Pam and the surprise return of her father, her parched soul needed this refreshing from God the way the desert needed rain. If she could've, she would have lain there all night, soaking it in until she could take no more. But, as suddenly as it came, it was gone.

The encounter seemed to have lasted only moments, but when she looked at the clock on the wall, she was shocked to see over an hour had passed. Feeling shaky, she braced herself against the bed to stand. She looked over to find Esther doing the same.

The experience was beyond words and Kristina was left breathless. But she was left with something else, too. Something she couldn't quite make sense of.

After easing herself off the floor, Kristina sat on a chair, her hands gripping the edge of the seat. Could what she was feeling be right? How could it? It didn't make sense.

Confused, she opened her mouth to ask Esther what she thought, but stopped short when she saw the expression on the older woman's face. The expression that told Kristina all she needed to know.

The feeling Kristina had was the same one Esther was experiencing.

And that feeling was this: it was time to let him go.

When Kristina slipped inside her little sister's hospital room, she found everyone inside, sleeping. Tamia looked just like she did when she use to curl up in the bed with Kristina when she was a girl. Pam sat at the side of her bed, her chin on her chest.

On the opposite wall, on the couch under the window, was Russell. Last she'd known, he'd been exiled from Tamia's room, but she was glad to see something had changed. He and Tamia were going to need each other now.

They all would.

Kristina gently shook Russell's shoulder. When he opened his eyes and saw her, an expression of alarm seized his face. He started to jump up, but she stopped him.

"It's okay. Everything's okay. But your mother wants you to join her and your father in the waiting room. She needs to talk to you."

Kristina could tell by the look on his face he sensed something had happened. She could also see he wanted to ask what it was.

Please don't. I already told Omar and I still have to tell my sisters and I don't know how I'm going to do it.

As if he'd heard her thoughts, he simply nodded and quietly left the room.

By that time, Pam was awake. She watched Kristina sit on the couch and studied her face.

"I heard you tell Russell everything was okay, but I know you better than that. What's happened?"

Kristina sank into the couch. She wasn't ready to say the words again. Not yet.

"Let's wait for Tamia to—"

"I'm awake."

Both sisters looked at Tamia, her face etched with fearful anticipation. Ready or not, Kristina couldn't stall any longer.

Taking a deep and wearied breath, she stood and came to her sister's bedside. She didn't know how to explain it to them. She didn't know how to accurately convey what happened to her and Esther during their prayer session. So instead, she just told them what it meant.

"Esther and I have decided it's time to take him off the machines."

At first, the only sound in the room was the faint buzzing of the overhead light while Pam and Tamia stared at her in stunned silence. But after a few moments, Tamia began sobbing. Pam stood and put her arms around her as best she could.

"But I thought—" Tamia choked on the words. "What about our miracle? You said we would hold out for one. You said he'd come through so much. That we couldn't give up now."

Kristina tried to swallow the lump in her throat, but failed. She wished there was some way she could make her sisters feel what she'd felt less than an hour earlier. Maybe it would make it easier for them to understand. But then she realized it probably wouldn't. Because she *was* there. Esther, too. And even they were struggling with it.

"I know, sweetie. I know. But Esther and I are sure it's what we need to do."

Tamia sobbed even harder and Kristina returned to her seat on the couch. There was nothing she could say. Nothing she could do. She closed her eyes and tightened her fists in an effort to hold back the tears.

Please God, we need You. I don't know how we are going to do this.

She sat like that for the next twenty minutes, until Tamia stopped crying. Kristina knew it wasn't because her sister was hurting any less. If anything, she'd just run out of tears.

"When?"

Kristina opened her eyes to look at Pam.

"Tonight. Esther's two other sons have to get off work. And Omar has to make arrangements for someone to watch Chloe. Pastor Thomas is coming, too. We want to make sure Xavier's surrounded by family."

Pam nodded and wiped her eyes with the back of her hand.

"We have a little time then. There's something I want to do first. I'll be right back."

Pam left the room and returned a little while later with a sealed, brown cardboard box in her hands. She set it on Tamia's bed and motioned for Kristina to come closer.

"Is that...?" Tamia narrowed her eyes as she looked at the box.

Pam moved her hand over the top of it.

"Yeah. Kristina and Omar left Atlanta the moment we learned about the accident. I stayed to pack and make arrangements. I was on my way out when I saw this on the counter. I know we'd decided to throw it away, but I brought it. I don't even know why. Everything mama ever gave us ended up causing pain."

"Not everything," Tamia said, still staring at the box. "In a way, she gave us Xavier."

"And maybe that's the reason I kept it. It's been in the trunk of the rental car this whole time. I hadn't even thought about it until just now. But since we're going to—" Pam stopped and clenched her jaw. After a few moments, she continued. "This meant enough to him to bring it all the way to Atlanta. I don't want to wait till after he's gone. I want us to see what's in it together and while he's still here."

Tamia looked at Pam, but Pam looked at Kristina, waiting for her approval. When she gave it with a nod of her head, Pam broke the seal and opened the box.

Chapter 19

Upon looking inside, Tamia caught her breath. Pam pressed her lips together, unable to stop the tears rolling down her cheeks. Kristina just closed her eyes and shook her head.

"Oh, mama…" She whispered.

The box was a virtual time capsule.

In it were pictures, cassette tapes, grade school drawings and dozens of little, crayon written notes.

Kristina reached in and pulled out the small scrapbook tucked next to a stack of Polaroid pictures.

On each page, was a photo of Xavier and a notation of some kind. On the first page was a picture of him at thirteen months, alongside a picture of Kristina at the same age. The caption read, *Just as beautiful as she was at this age. And just as sweet, too.*

Kristina's heart felt like it would give out under the weight of all she was feeling. She'd never known her mother had pictures of her at that age. And that she'd thought she was beautiful? She wouldn't have believed it if she hadn't been looking at her mother's handwriting with her own eyes.

"Look at that." Tamia motioned at one of the Polaroids in the box.

Pam took it out and put it in her hand. In it, Xavier was grinning from ear to ear and holding up a magazine featuring Kristina and her third album release.

"She must've planned this from the beginning," Pam said, removing the contents of the box, shaking her head. "All this time, I thought she'd intentionally kept him away from us so she could have him all to herself. But this looks like she never meant for him to remain a secret. She wanted to make sure when you learned the truth, you'd still get to experience all these memories. She didn't make him her sole heir just because she loved him, she did it so we'd find out about him."

"But why not just tell us?" Tamia asked.

Pam shrugged. "I knew her better than anybody, but still, I never understood her." She exhaled. "Maybe she thought she was protecting him by keeping him in a family that loved God and kept him in church. Or maybe it *wasn't* her plan and she only decided to share it all after she got sick. I have no idea. But I never would've guessed she'd done this. Not in a million years."

Throughout her sisters' musings, Kristina remained silent. She flipped through the scrapbook, savoring every word and image of her son. The son she'd just met. The son she'd have to say goodbye to in just a few hours.

Tamia pointed to a cassette still at the bottom of the box. "What's that?"

Pam took it out and read the label.

"Xavier. Singing Lessons. Age five."

The words caught Kristina's attention and she looked up

from the scrapbook. Tamia patted Pam's arm and motioned toward the couch. Pam looked in that direction and wasted no time going to where Russell had left his knapsack and trusty Walkman. Returning to the bedside with the cassette player, Pam opened it, took out the cassette inside and replaced it with her mother's homemade one. Then, she offered it to Kristina.

Kristina backed away and shook her head. As much as she wanted to listen to the tape, she wasn't sure she could. Not if she was going to keep it together. It would only remind her of all she'd missed and all she was soon to lose.

"It's okay, Krissi. We're here with you." Tamia opened her hand and extended her arm to Kristina as best she could.

Kristina put her hand in Tamia's and made two small steps toward the bed. She took a deep breath and reached for the headphones. Once she put them on, she nodded at Pam, who then pressed PLAY.

> *Jesus loves the little children,*
> *All the children of the world.*
> *Red and yellow, black and white.*
> *They are precious in His sight.*
> *Jesus loves the little children of the world.*

It was nothing like the singing lessons Kristina and her sisters had grown up with. There were no perfect harmonies, no yelling, no threats, no swats. Just her mother's joyful voice and her son's slightly off-tune one.

It was a simple song. With a simple message. Being sung with love. Kristina would've given anything for just one moment like that with her mother. But whatever regret she felt was far outweighed by the joy it gave her to know it was a moment Xavier *did* experience.

And that was when the dam broke. All the sadness, the joy, the apprehension, the hope—it so overwhelmed her, she had to grab hold of the bed rails to remain standing.

Pam came from the other side of the bed and took Kristina in her arms. She rubbed her back and rocked her until she was once again able to stand on her own.

Kristina took off the earphones and dried her eyes. Her sisters stared at her with concern. "I'm okay." She reassured them. "I'm gonna be okay."

"I don't see how you can be." Tamia said.

"It's hard to explain. I mean, I'm sad. I'm *so* sad. But at the same time…" She shook her head, hardly understanding herself. "I'm grateful, too. I could've lived the rest of my life and never known him. Not that it would've been a very long one. I was hell-bent on checking out as soon as possible. But that didn't happen. I got clean. I reconnected with Omar. I have Chloe. It turns out we have a father! I mean, it hasn't been all bad, has it? And the truth is, I wouldn't trade the short time I had with Xavier for anything in the world. It might not have been much, but it was more than I'd ever hoped for."

Pam nodded and dabbed at her cheeks with the back of her hand.

"I want to be there. When they turn everything off. I *need* to be there."

Kristina half expected Pam to put up a fight with Tamia, but she didn't. Instead, she put her hand on Tamia's and said, "I'll talk to the nurses. One of them will know what we need to do to make that happen."

After Pam left, Kristina picked up one of the many pictures on Tamia's bed and stared at the face of her son.

"I guess there's nothing left to do now but say goodbye."

Chapter 20

Kristina walked the halls of the hospital floor that had become their home for the last few days, until she found a quiet bank of seats with no one else around. She took out her phone and stared at it.

Yes, everything she'd told her sisters was true. She *was* grateful. Having Xavier in her life, even for the short time they shared, was an impossible dream come true.

And yet…

Kristina wrapped her arms around her middle and folded herself over on her legs. The ache in her chest left her hollow. She wanted to crawl into bed and stay there until it was all over. Better yet, she wanted to wipe the last few days from her mind and pretend they'd never happened. But, of course, neither of those things were an option.

In less than two hours, she'd have to say goodbye to the son she barely knew. And that was just the beginning.

Afterward, there'd be funeral arrangements and burial

plans. There would be record label business and meetings about getting the tour back on schedule. She'd have to figure out how to mourn her now gone band members and dancers, while auditioning and hiring new ones.

And then there was Kristina, herself. How in the world would she be able to perform again? Even if she could find a way to get back on stage, she'd never be the same. Not after all the loss. Sure, the fans and the press and the label execs would give her a little understanding over the deaths of her band members, but their patience would run out. They'd eventually want her mourning period to end. They'd want her to be Kristina Langston, the songbird with the thousand-watt smile. How would she explain that that smile became impossible the day she lost the son they never even knew she had?

Kristina sat up straight and once again, stared at her phone. She navigated to the contacts and scrolled to the entry for David Bauer.

When she went into rehab, she'd erased all her drug contacts. She disconnected herself from anyone and everyone that had been a part of that life. Everyone *except* David. Of course, she had her reasons. David wasn't actually a dealer. He was one of the producers on her last three albums and a friend. A very discreet friend who just happened to be a casual user himself.

Kristina glanced up at the clock opposite her on the wall. If she called him now, he'd be able to get to the hospital just after they turned off the—

Kristina shuddered. Just the thought of what was coming made her feel as if she were going to pass out. She needed help to get through it. Just a little bit. How much damage could one hit do?

The moment she asked the question, she knew the answer. But how else was she going to make it? She needed something or someone to hang onto, but who could help her when everyone else was in as much pain as she was?

Kristina wanted to scream. She wanted to throw her phone against the wall and make it shatter into a million pieces, but instead, she let it slide onto the chair next to her and buried her face in her hands. She felt as if her whole world was disassembling itself and leaving her with no place to stand.

"Please. *Please* help me," she whispered. "Because if You don't, who can? Send a message, a sign, an angel—*anything*. I'm drowning. And I'm gonna be lost forever if You don't pull me out."

When Kristina felt the tap on her shoulder, she froze in place. She was almost too scared to uncover her face, but if God was going to answer her prayer that quick, she knew the least she could do was open her eyes.

And when she did, her heart melted.

Better than any celestial sign or heavenly being, the answer to her prayer came in the form of one little Miss Chloe.

"Can I sit with you?"

Kristina quickly dried her face with the edges of her sleeve and smiled.

"Baby, you can *always* sit with me."

Chloe climbed into the chair as she stole a few glances at Kristina. Kristina could only imagine what she must look like to the little girl. As hard as she had been crying only moments before, her eyes were sure to be bloodshot and swollen.

"I'm okay. I promise."

Chloe nodded, but didn't look convinced.

"Why are you all the way over here by yourself? Where's your daddy?"

Chloe's eyes filled with tears. She looked down the hallway and pointed. Unsure of what Chloe's reaction meant,

Kristina got up, held Chloe's hand and let the little girl lead her through a couple of turns and to the end of another hall.

Sure enough, Omar was there. And immediately, Kristina knew why Chloe had sought her out. As terrible as she must've looked, Omar was doing much worse. He'd struggled to be strong when Kristina told him about her and Esther's decision, but apparently, he'd finally been overcome with grief. He sat between Pam and Reiland, both trying to comfort him as he openly sobbed.

Kristina looked down at Chloe and when she saw the panic on her face, she knew what she needed to do. She took Chloe back to their quiet spot and sat her down. She wiped the tears from her face and looked her directly in her eyes.

"It's going to be okay, baby."

"But why is my daddy crying?"

"He sad. He's not hurt. Well, I guess he is hurting. On the inside. But he's going to be okay. It's just gonna take some time."

"Why is he hurting on the inside?"

"Because," Kristina paused, waiting until she could speak with a steady voice. "Because tonight we have to say goodbye to your big brother."

"Why? Where's he going?"

"To heaven. To be with Jesus."

"But I didn't get to see him yet."

"I know, baby. I'm sorry about that. And I know he is, too. He was really looking forward to spending time with you."

Chloe sat there, her tiny legs not even long enough to touch the floor, trying to comprehend matters that stumped adults.

Then, her voice a whisper, she said, "My mommy left, too. Daddy says one day I'll see her again, but I won't. She told me she's not coming back. But I didn't tell him 'cause I think it might make him sad."

Kristina didn't even know what to say to that. She wished she could gather Chloe up in her arms and rock all the bad things away. But as she wondered what in the world she could do to comfort the little girl, Chloe scooted near her and slipped her hand beneath hers. Kristina lifted her arm and hooked it around her, drawing her close. And when Chloe laid her head on Kristina's chest, the hollowness she'd felt before seemed to dissipate a little.

"Kristina?"

"Yes, baby?"

"Are you going away, too?"

She looked up at Kristina and the pleading in her eyes obliterated any need Kristina had for a hit.

"No, baby. I'm staying right here with you and your daddy."

Chloe nodded and a couple of tears escaped her big, brown eyes. Kristina wiped them away and caressed her cheek.

"Don't be afraid, little one. I know it's scary seeing all of us grown-ups be sad and cry like this. But no matter what, remember our God is a big God. Bigger than you. Bigger than me. Bigger than any bad thing that can happen, okay?"

Chloe nodded, then snuggled into Kristina's side.

Kristina closed her eyes and offered up a silent prayer of thanks. Not only was He bigger than the pain, He knew just what was needed to relieve it.

Leaning over, Kristina picked up her phone and navigated to the contacts again. And when she got to David Bauer, she pressed DELETE without a moment's hesitation.

Chapter 21

When Tamia noticed Russell hovering at her open door, she gave him a halfhearted smile.

"Hey."

He returned her smile with one of his own.

"Hey." He pointed to his knapsack. "I just need to grab my things."

She nodded and he came in and headed straight for the couch. They hadn't spoken since their fight. She was drifting off to sleep when she heard Pam tell Russell to come into the room earlier. Apparently, he'd nodded off while sitting in the hallway, so Pam told him to come in and take the couch. He tried to decline, but soon realized Pam didn't make requests, she gave orders. Amid her drowsiness, Tamia let herself hope them being in the same room would make it easier for her to finally apologize. But then Kristina came in with her news about Xavier and everything changed.

"I'm sorry."

Russell was on his way back out the door when Tamia blurted the words out. He stopped, but didn't turn around. Tamia expected he'd simply nod and keep walking. It was what she deserved and she knew it. Still, she couldn't help but hope and pray he'd give her more. So when he finally turned around and looked at her with the same warmth and tenderness he had a hundred times before, it was all she could do to keep from crying any more than she already had that day.

"I really am, Russell. I am so, so sorry."

Russell closed the door and came to the side of her bed.

"Don't be. It's not necessary."

"It is. Those things I said—"

"Were true." He pulled a chair closer and sat. "I didn't have any right to be here, especially after you'd asked me to leave. It's not like there was ever anything going on between us. But even if there was, I should have respected your space. You needed some time and I didn't give it to you."

His understanding made Tamia feel even worse. She wanted him to be angry at her. To give her as good as he got.

"I mean, what you're going through? Physical therapist or not, I can't know what that's like. Not really."

"But that's no excuse for the things I said and you know it. Why are you trying to be so nice about this? Just say what you feel. I can take it."

Russell sat back in his chair, his face grim. "I'm not sure you can."

Tamia wasn't either, truth be told. But she was willing. After the way she'd hurt him, she was *more* than willing to hear whatever he had to say.

"Try me."

She saw his jaw clench and braced herself for what was to come. But no amount of preparation could have readied her for what he said next.

"I'm in love with you."

Tamia's mind went blank. She asked him to go ahead and verbally punish her for the loads of abuse she'd heaped on him and his response was *I'm in love with you?* She stared at the ceiling, trying to make sense of it all.

Russell exhaled. "See, I was right. You can't take it."

"I—" Tamia tried to blink back the tears that welled up. "Why would you say something like that?"

"Why else? Because it's true."

"You're so stupid."

"Wow."

She looked at him again, not caring about the steady flow of hot tears, now running unchecked.

"You're stupid and blind. Look at me."

He smiled. "I am."

Tamia struggled to keep the anger building in her chest from affecting the tone of her voice.

"No, you're not. Because if you were, you wouldn't see girlfriend material. I may never walk again. And if I do, I'll be in constant pain. Have you ever been around someone like that? They're miserable, Russell. Not only that, I probably won't ever sing again. It's the only thing I've ever been any good at."

Tamia trembled and the effort it took to keep from screaming was making her head pound.

"And that's just after the accident. I was messed up way before that. There's things you don't know about me. Things you can't even imagine. So don't say you're looking at me, because if you were, you wouldn't even be sitting here right now."

Russell waited until she'd caught her breath, until she no longer had to grasp the bed rails to keep from shaking. When she was finally able to regain her composure, he leaned forward and took her hand in his.

"If you're done ranting and raving, I have something I want to say."

She exhaled and rolled her eyes, but instead of kicking him out of her room, she replied, "Okay."

"Despite your diagnosis of my problem, my vision is 20/20. I *am* looking at you, Tamia Langston. And what I see is all the things you can't. I see hope. And I see opportunity for miracles. I see a smart aleck who makes me laugh. I see a talented woman who is more than her vocal abilities. I see a heart that's tender and compassionate. And despite the anti-anxiety meds you have to take, I see that you're one of the strongest and bravest women I've ever met."

Tamia's eyes grew wide with surprise.

Russell nodded. "Yeah, you try to hide it, but I saw you taking them. It's nothing to be ashamed of. It doesn't make you weak and it doesn't mean you're broken. And it doesn't define you as a person, no more than singing does. There's so much to you, Tamia. So much you don't even see. But I do. And for all of those things, I love you. If that makes me stupid, well, I've been called worse."

"There's still a lot you don't know."

"I understand that. But has it ever occurred to you that all the things you think will make someone leave are the very things that would make someone love you more?"

"No."

"Exactly. You know why? Because you don't know everything. And sometimes you're wrong."

Tamia searched Russell's eyes and found nothing but sincerity there. If she wasn't already lying down, she would have needed to. Because for the first time in her life, she realized love was a possibility for her. The realization was like a thunderbolt that lit up the sky. Suddenly, everything changed. It seemed almost too good to be true.

"You love me?"

"With everything in me. From the toes of my Converse to the tip of my flat top."

Tamia laughed and looked up at the ceiling as the joy of this new revelation washed over her. From the moment she met Russell, she'd liked him. But because she'd sworn never to be in a relationship, she pushed her feelings aside. Even when she found herself thinking about him more and more. Even when she found herself looking forward to seeing him as much as Xavier. No matter what she felt or how much she felt it, she shoved it away. It looked like it was time to do something about that.

"Why didn't you ever ask me out?"

Her question caught him by surprise and a few moments passed before he attempted to answer. Once he did, it was her turn to be surprised.

"You're out of my league."

"Don't say that."

"Come on. It's true. I'm not rich or famous. And I'm not slick or good-looking like all the guys that probably come at you. I know that." He shrugged. "Like I said, out of my league."

She cut her eyes at him. "Well, I guess you don't see as much as you think you do, Mr. 20/20. 'Cause if you did, you'd know I've never been interested in slick or rich or famous."

"So what are you into?"

She raised her eyebrows and bit at her lip.

"Out of style haircuts and electronics old enough to be considered antiques."

He feigned shock. "That's crazy because I just happen to sport a high flat top and really old cassette player."

"What are the chances?" Tamia said, smiling.

He took her hand again and leaned on the edge of her

bed. "Seriously though. I don't have a lot to offer by way of big houses or fancy cars. But I'd follow you anywhere, through anything, for as long as I lived. No matter what. So if you think you could ever see yourself with a guy like me and decided to take that chance, I'd spend the rest of my days making sure you never regretted it."

Tamia narrowed her eyes. "Does this mean we're going steady?"

Russell laughed. "Going steady?"

"If I'm gonna be your girlfriend, I need to start using old-fashioned phrases and stuff, right? Maybe cut my hair in an asymmetrical?"

Russell covered his mouth with his fist and laughed out loud.

"Start dressing like Mary J. Blige and TLC back in the day. Or I could go old school for real and bust out a poodle skirt."

"Okay, okay," Russell said, still laughing. "You got jokes, but I don't even care 'cause I heard the word 'girlfriend' up in there."

He shook his head and grinned so wide, she thought his face would break.

She sucked her teeth. "Looking like you won the lottery…"

"Better! Wait until Xavier finds—"

That's when he remembered and every bit of joy was stripped from his face. Tamia could see him trying to fight it, the sadness that suddenly overtook him like a storm. He shifted in his seat and tried to smile again.

"He, uh… He was always saying, 'Go for it, man. You two would be good together.'"

Russell's eyebrows knit together and he cleared his throat.

"It's okay," Tamia whispered.

He shook his head. "No."

"You don't have to be strong for me."

Again, he shook his head, clenching his jaw. "No."

"He was your brother…"

He kept struggling against the grief, but then dropped his head on the edge of her bed. She put her hand on his neck and listened as he wept. She wanted to comfort him. She wanted to say something that would ease his pain. But she knew there was nothing left to say.

Chapter 22

When Pam entered the room where they would gather to say goodbye to Xavier, she wasn't prepared for how small and frail he looked in his hospital bed. To make space for all the family and to accommodate Tamia, he'd been moved to a much larger room and the size of it seemed to swallow him up.

Unable to move any further than a couple of feet into the space, Pam ran her hand along her chest and pressed down, hoping to relieve the tightness that seemed to constrict her breath.

"You all right, babe?"

Pam started when Reiland touched her elbow.

"I'm fine," she said, her words coming out with more of an edge than she'd intended.

Reiland knew her well enough not to believe her, but before he could say anything else, Pastor Thomas came through the door. Pam and her husband moved further in to let him pass, but he stopped next to them.

"Sister Pam, I want you to know that, right now, there's a group of women down at the church gathered for the sole purpose of praying for this family. They plan on being there all night. And I hope you know that whatever you need, you can come to us. I mean that. Anything—you need only ask. I'll be here for as little or as much as you and the rest of the family want me. All right?"

Pam nodded and watched as he made his way to the other side of the room, where Esther and Kristina waited beside Xavier's bed. How her sister was even functioning, Pam had no idea. Esther, either. But there they were, standing like two sentinels at either side of his bed.

Soon after the pastor arrived, Tamia was brought in. Immediately after that, Xavier's brothers and Omar's sisters arrived. As more and more people filled the room, Pam pressed farther and farther back, until she was tucked away in a corner near the door, as far from everyone else as she could get.

The air was so heavy with grief, she could hardly breathe it. And even with so many people in one place, the sound of the machines keeping her nephew alive were all she heard until Pastor Thomas cleared his throat, opened his Bible and read a passage. Which one, Pam wasn't sure. It was as if she were underwater and his words were too muffled to understand. Then he led the room in an old hymn Pam knew the words to, but couldn't bring herself to sing.

Around that time, the nurse came in and asked if they were ready. Esther said they wanted a few more moments to say their goodbyes. She nodded and stepped to the side as Xavier's brothers came forward first.

They were quiet and reserved, but it was clear to everyone

in the room, their hearts were breaking. As they leaned over and whispered in their brother's ear, Pam couldn't help but wonder what they'd been like when he was a baby. She imagined he must have been their little prince because, even now, they caressed his face and kissed his hands like he was just a child.

Then it was their father, Deacon's turn. The man approached the bed slowly, as if he were wearing shoes made of lead. As he looked down on his youngest boy, he swayed, causing his other sons to rush to his side. No sooner than they did, he broke down. What rose out of him must've been the most heart shattering sound Pam had ever heard. She had to close her eyes for a moment, just to be able to stand there.

After Deacon's sons helped him to a chair, Pam saw people in front of her turn toward her. As they parted, she realized it was because Kristina and Esther were looking for her.

It was her turn.

Though the other mourners watched and waited for her to come forward, Pam didn't move a muscle. She knew they expected her to go and kiss Xavier, tell him how much she loved him, say she'd see him on the other side. But she couldn't. It wasn't a choice she was making, it was something she knew. She physically would not be able to do it.

Reiland must've seen the panic in her eyes because he pushed past the people between them to be near her.

"Don't," she whispered, her finger held up as a warning.

But still, he continued toward her. "Pam—"

"No."

She tried to back up, but was already against the wall. When he was close enough, he reached for her hand.

"It's okay, baby. We'll do it together."

"Don't!" She hit him as hard as she could in the chest. "I said no!"

Pam shoved her way through the people to the side of her and bolted out the door. She knew she probably looked like a maniac, but she didn't care. Only one thing mattered, and that was getting out and as far away as possible.

Because when they turned off the machines and Xavier's heart beat its last, she couldn't be there to witness it.

Once out of the room, Pam trembled so violently she had to lean against the wall for support. But getting out of the room wasn't enough. She knew what she needed and no one, not even Reiland, was going to stop her this time. She headed straight to the elevator and pushed the DOWN button. Just as the doors opened, she felt someone grab her arm and yank her back.

She turned, ready to bring hellfire down on Reiland for daring to follow her. She was ready to fight, make a scene in full view of the nurse's station, if that's what it took to be left alone. But when she whirled around, it wasn't Reiland standing there, but her father, Gerald. His eyes were wet with tears and the expression on his face was one of overwhelming love and compassion.

It nearly broke her.

"Don't ask me to go back in there," she whispered.

"Oh, baby," he said, running his hand along the side of her face.

His touch felt like she remembered it. His voice sounded just like when her mother had been especially hard on her and she'd gone to bed wondering why she didn't love her. He'd come home from work and find her in her room, awake, crying into her pillow. He'd rub her back and kiss her forehead and say, *baby*. He'd put his hand on her cheek and she knew that even if no one else cared, her father did.

"I can't. I can't say goodbye to him."

"It's okay."

Pam shook her head. "It's not. It's not okay. I should be able to do this. I *need* to do this. I need to be strong. For Tamia. For..." She bowed her head. "For *Kristina*. He's her only son. I should be holding her up and I can't even be in the same room."

Gerald put his hands on her shoulders. "You can't always be strong, Pamela. You can't always be the caretaker Mahalia should've been. And you can't always be the rock I was supposed to be. It's not your job, baby. It's too much for one little girl to carry."

Him calling her a little girl made something around her heart break. Something very cold and heavy, that felt like thousand-pound chains. Something she'd put up as protection many years ago.

"I am sorry. So very, very sorry that your mother and I put you in that position. But I'm here right now and I'm telling you, you don't have to be strong and you don't have to be brave. The world won't fall apart just because you can't hold it together. Hear me, baby. Let it go."

The sob that rose from Pam sounded to her like it must've come from someone else. She tried to stop it. That's what she always did when she was at her breaking point. She had to because, if she fell apart, who'd help put her back together?

It's why she started drinking. To stop feeling. It was only when she realized no one else would be able to keep Kristina from drugging herself to death that she decided to get sober. But now, that wasn't working out for her so well. Now, she was facing more grief and sorrow and anger and regret than she could deal with.

Gerald drew her close. "Lay it down." He put his arms around her and though she tried to push him away, he wouldn't relax his hold on her.

"You let go and let someone else hold on for a change."

Afraid, Pam struggled, but still, Gerald held her. And when she stopped struggling, he rocked her.

"That's it. Lay it down, little girl. Just lay it all down."

So she did. Every fear, every hurt, every ache—she laid them all down. And for the first time in more than thirty years, she openly wept.

Chapter 23

As Omar and his sisters stood at Xavier's bed, Kristina kept glancing at the door.

"Don't worry about that now. Your father went after her. Just let God handle it. Be here. This is a holy moment."

Kristina nodded at Esther and took her hand. The woman was right. This *was* a holy moment. Kristina was there when Xavier's beautiful spirit came into the world and now, she'd be there when it returned home.

After Omar and his family said their goodbyes, the only ones left to do the same were Xavier's mothers. They approached his bed, hand in hand, their faces covered in tears.

"You are a good son," Esther whispered, her hand on his forehead. "The joy of our lives. I thank God for you. I believe we'll see you again, but heaven knows I'm gonna miss you till then."

Esther kissed his face and rested her forehead on his. After a few moments, she stepped aside for Kristina.

As she looked down on him, all Kristina could think of was that recording she heard of him singing with her mother. She realized then that, though he'd seen her perform on television and heard her voice on recordings, she'd never sung just for him. So she leaned down until her head was on his pillow and her lips were near his ear and slowly and softly, did just that.

> *Jesus loves the little children,*
> *All the children of the world.*
> *He sent me one that was a light,*
> *Such a joy, he shone so bright.*
> *Now with angels, he flies home*
> *From this old world.*

Kristina wiped the tears from her eyes and kissed his cheeks.

"Beauty for ashes. That was one of the lines in a passage I read in my Bible one day. And the first thing I thought of was you. You were my beauty for ashes."

She rubbed her thumb along his hairline. "I thought my life was burned to the ground and there was nothing worth living for, then God gave me you. But you don't have to worry about me. About any of us. He's going to get us through this."

She laid her head on the pillow next to his again.

"Thank you, my sweet boy. Thank you for loving me despite all my problems and imperfections. You'll never know how much it meant to me."

Kristina straightened up and took a step back so she was beside Esther. Again, they held hands as Esther nodded at the nurse, letting her know they were ready.

Kristina lowered her head so she wouldn't have to see the nurse remove Xavier from life support. She slowly took in one breath, then another, as she concentrated on the words she'd been leaning on since it had all begun.

I can do all things through Christ...
I can do all things through Christ...
I can do all things through Christ...
God, please strengthen me.

The room grew quiet, the machines no longer doing their work to keep her son alive. The only sound for the next few minutes was that of the heart monitor's faint *beep, beep, beep...* Kristina took a breath with each and prepared for the moment they'd stop altogether.

Then a sound came from Xavier, something like a gasp. When they heard it, everyone became still.

"It's okay," the nurse assured them. "It happens sometimes. Air that's in the lungs escapes and it sounds like a moan."

"Okay, but what does his lungs have to do with his eyelids?" Russell said.

The nurse and everyone else in the room turned to see what he was talking about. Sure enough, Xavier's eyes were open.

"Again," the nurse said, speaking patiently, as if to a young child. "It's a reflexive reaction. It doesn't mean he's conscious. It just means—"

As she was still speaking, Xavier blinked. Esther gasped audibly and stumbled back. The nurse, hearing this, turned from Russell and looked at Esther, and then Xavier.

They all waited for him to blink again. But he didn't.

"It can be somewhat disconcerting to witness, I know—"

The nurse stopped speaking and the family watched as her eyes grew wide. Slowly, she looked down at Xavier's bed, where she'd rested her hand. Tapping on her wrist was Xavier's index finger.

"Umm, what kind of reflex do you call that?"

The nurse watched Xavier and squeezed his hand. When he squeezed back, she yanked the remote with the call button and requested immediate assistance.

"I want to apologize."

Pam and Gerald sat in the empty hallway, several feet away from Xavier's room. Gerald waved his hand through the air, dismissing her words.

"No harm done. I knew you'd come around."

Pam leaned back, her eyes narrowed. "You did?"

"Of course, I did. You and me was like this from the minute you were born." He held up two crossed fingers. "Whether you can remember it or not, that's not a bond easily broken."

Pam took a deep breath. "I do remember. Some of it, anyway. I think that's why I was so angry." She rolled her eyes. "And now that I think about it, maybe that's why I've always had a hard time trusting God. I mean, I knew He was supposed to be good. But good didn't necessarily mean He'd be there when I needed Him, you know?"

Gerald exhaled and patted the top of her hand. "I'm sorry about that, Pamela. I truly—"

Gerald stopped talking when he noticed the sudden activity down at the nurses' station. Pam turned to see what he was looking at and saw three nurses rush from behind the desk, followed by some residents, rounding the corner.

"Something must have happened," Gerald said, under his breath. "Lord, intervene, whatever the matter is."

Before Pam could voice her agreement, the doctors and nurses barreled into Xavier's room. On reflex, she stood. And in a matter of seconds, a dozen different scenarios played out in her mind. Did Deacon have a heart attack? Did Esther collapse? Did Kristina—

Pam's heart seized with fear. Suddenly she was back in that hotel ballroom, watching the paramedics speed past the open double doors, not knowing the life they were running to save was her sister's.

Gerald gripped her arm and they rushed for the door. But before they got to it, it swung open and Justina ran out.

"I was just coming to find you! You need to get in here and see it for yourself!"

The once quiet and somber room was now filled with talking and laughing and praying and praising. Another group of nurses pressed through the crowd to have a look for themselves.

Xavier's bed was surrounded by medical professionals, all making checks and giving each other statistics. His main doctor, Dr. Cho, the one who had told them Xavier was beyond all hope, came to Kristina and Esther, shaking his head.

"I can't begin to explain what happened here. I don't know that I even want to try. It doesn't make sense."

"It's called a miracle," Esther said, laughing, in spite of her tears.

The doctor shrugged. "Whatever it is, I would be remiss not to advise you to manage your expectations. The trauma to his brain was extensive. He's not out of the woods. In fact, I can guarantee there will be brain damage. Only time will tell how severe. His speech may be affected. His thought processes, impaired. He won't be able to do all the things he did before. He has a very long and hard road ahead of him. He's alive, yes, but he won't be the young man you knew. It's important that you understand that."

Esther patted his arm. "Thank you, doctor."

The moment he turned away, Esther looked at Kristina. "That's *his* diagnosis."

Kristina nodded. "Like the song says, we've come this far by faith..."

"Amen."

"Look!"

Kristina and Esther turned to see one of Xavier's brothers pointing at him. "His lips are moving! Do you see his lips moving?"

Although most of the medical staff that'd come in the room were gone, two nurses remained. The one closest to Xavier's head leaned over and listened. Then she straightened, a puzzled look on her face.

"He's saying something about—" She hesitated. "He wants to know whether you have been keeping up with your Bible study."

The entire room erupted with laughter, hollering and shouts of praise. Esther dropped to her knees and cried out, while Kristina remained standing, her hands clasped and her head bowed. Despite their different reactions, both said the same thing:

Thank You, thank You, thank You, thank You.

Chapter 24

Two years later...

Ritz-Carlton Hotel
New York City

The Premiere Suite was 1,100 feet of pure luxury, overlooking the twinkling lights of Central Park and the bustling activity of Sixth Avenue. Its several rooms buzzed with activity as the groom, his groomsmen and the father of the bride prepared for the wedding scheduled to begin at dusk. It was wall-to-wall black tuxedos and platinum cufflinks. With one exception...

"Chloe," Xavier said, turning his chin side to side and looking in the mirror. "Did you ever dream you'd have a big brother this incredibly handsome?"

Chloe covered her mouth with her hands, but it did little to stifle her giggles.

Russell shook his head and groaned, as he adjusted his bow tie.

"Here we go again… Look, while you ask the mirror whose the fairest one of all, I'm gonna head to the photo setup."

Then turning and addressing the rest of the room, he said, "And y'all would be close behind, if you knew what was good for you. Monica's wound even tighter than she was at the rehearsal."

As most of the groomsmen filed out, Xavier held his hands up in mock dismay. "So…what? Nobody's gonna mention how good I look?"

Chloe's hand shot up. "I will! You look good!" Then she jumped up and down to display her enthusiasm. He turned around and gave her a high-five, before swooping her up in his arms.

"And you, my Chloe, look like the most beautiful girl in the world!"

Chloe pulled her shoulders up to her ears and giggled, her cheeks blushing.

"And you and Poppa are the most handsome men in the world," she whispered.

"Hey!"

Omar, already dressed and sitting in one of the gold brocade wingback chairs, feigned hurt. "Just X and Poppa? What about your good ol' dad?"

"You're handsome too, daddy!"

"Just not as handsome as me and Poppa," Xavier said to Chloe in a stage whisper.

Gerald, who was also occupied with his reflection, looked back at them and made a face.

"Well, if Poppa can't learn how to tie a bow tie in the next few minutes, he's gonna look like the biggest doofus in the world."

Chloe collapsed in giggles and her brother set her down on the footstool next to Omar, before going to Gerald.

"Here, let me help you." He began fixing Gerald's tie as his grandfather looked at him, his face aglow with pride.

Xavier noticed and gave a lopsided smile. "What?"

"I'm just standing here thinking about how far we've all come in the last two years. And I've only got one thing to say: God is *good*!"

"All the time!" Chloe shouted.

The four remaining men in the room laughed.

Deacon tapped Omar on the shoulder and said, "Looks like you're bringing that one up right."

"Don't you mean 'we'? With all the time she's spent with you and Esther and Gerald and Justina, everyone gets credit!"

There was a knock at the door and Chloe jumped up to answer it. Before she could, her brother picked her up from behind and dropped her back on the footstool.

"I don't think so, you little monkey."

Xavier opened the door and was quickly swept out of the way by the harried wedding planner rushing in the room and making a beeline for Gerald.

"Are you ready yet? Are you ready?"

"Yes, Monica. We're all ready. But you look like maybe you should stop and take a breath."

"Stop? Take a breath? I'll breathe *after* the ceremony." She twirled around and pointed at Xavier. "And *you*. You need to get out there, best man. It's almost time to start the ceremony and all the groomsmen are supposed to be taking pictures together *before* that happens. As in now! Right now! You were supposed to be out there five minutes ago."

Xavier raised his eyebrows and it was obvious to all but Monica that he was doing his best not to laugh.

"That goes for you two, as well," she said, pointing at Omar and Deacon.

"You heard the lady!" Xavier said, following her as she marched out the room.

"Well," Gerald said, offering his hand for Chloe to take. "I guess that means you and I should head to the bridal suite, my dear."

Chapter 25

"O kay, ladies. That was Monica on the walkie. The men are getting ready to start their photo shoot and she needs all the bridesmaids to make their way to the location."

With Erika, Monica's assistant, at the lead, the entire bridal party, except for Esther, Justina and the Langston sisters, was ushered out for pre-wedding pictures.

Watching as they left, Esther shook her head and dabbed at the corners of her eyes.

"Aren't they just beautiful? Those dresses! And my daughter-in-love is hands down, the most stunning bride ever."

Tamia smiled as the makeup artist began contouring her face. "Thank you, mommy."

Pam, sitting on a brocade loveseat with Justina, nodded her head in agreement.

"She is! Oh, you have no idea how happy I am about this wedding. A *real* venue. A *real* dress. A *real* wedding cake."

Kristina rolled her eyes at Pam and cocked her head at Esther.

"As you can see, Pam still hasn't forgiven me and Omar for our—what did you call it, Pam?"

Pam threw her arm over the back of the couch and crossed her legs. "Courthouse fiasco."

Justina covered her mouth, chuckling.

"Ahhh, yes. The courthouse fiasco. A.K.A. My wedding and the most important day of my life."

Tamia laughed. "Well, Pam, I'm glad Russell and I are making your dreams come true. Maybe now you'll do me a solid and let mom and dad come visit."

Kristina shot her hand in the air. "I know, right! It's like she's holding them hostage or something."

"Stop exaggerating," Pam said, rolling her eyes.

Justina went from chuckling to outright laughter.

Tamia's eyes widened. "Who's exaggerating? They were supposed to visit me twice last year and both times ended up canceling because something more pressing came up with you. The only reason I even got them there for my album release party was because *you* came with them!"

Pam turned to Justina. "Have I ever locked you in my house? Taken away your car keys? Hidden your shoes?"

Justina doubled over with laughter.

"Seriously, mom. Have I ever said you and daddy couldn't visit one of those other daughters you have? You know, the two you love slightly less than me?"

Justina wiped the tears from her eyes while she tried to catch her breath.

"You all need to stop."

"If you don't tell them, they won't believe me."

"Fine. Tamia. Kristina. Pam has never told your father and I not to visit the two of you."

"Exactly," Pam said. "They're grown. I couldn't tell them what to do if I wanted to."

"No," Kristina said. "Instead, she puts on her sad puppy dog eyes and says, 'But daddy, you'll be gone for Father's Day. Mom, you won't be here on my birthday. It's not the same without your chocolate cake.'"

"Spoiled," Tamia said.

"Rotten," Kristina added.

Instead of defending herself, Pam simply arched an eyebrow.

Esther pointed at Pam and laughed. "Look, she won't even deny it."

Kristina lifted herself slightly from the chair she was in and adjusted her positioning, cradling her bulging belly as she did.

"Well, since can't nobody seem to get mom and dad more than three feet out of Pam's reach, I decided to share my news with them while they're here."

Tamia grabbed the makeup artist's wrist and jerked it back so she could look at Kristina.

"News? What news? Baby news? Do you know what you're having?"

"I do," Kristina said, coyly.

"Tell us!" Pam shrieked.

"Not until dad gets here."

Pam jumped up from her seat and ran to the door. "Then I'm going to get him. Now!"

She swung the door open only to find Gerald on the other side of it, one hand holding Chloe's and the other poised to knock on the door. Without a word, Pam grabbed him by the arm and yanked him in the room.

Kristina laughed and shook her head while Tamia mumbled to her, "That is *your* sister."

"Look, little girl, you may be my baby, but that doesn't mean you can manhandle me."

Chloe bounced to where Kristina was, kissed her cheek and leaned over on her arm.

"Kristina has something to tell you," Pam said, pushing her dad to where Kristina sat.

Kristina reached into her purse, pulled out a white envelope and handed it to her father.

"What's this?"

Gerald flipped it back and forth, looking it over.

"Open it and see."

He raised his eyebrows and looked at Chloe. "Should we? Can we trust them?"

Chloe giggled. "You can trust mommy. I don't know about Auntie Pam or Auntie Tam."

All three sisters gasped and everyone else burst out laughing.

Gerald nodded as he opened the envelope. "Listen to my granddaughter. She knows what she's talking about." He drew out a powder blue card embossed with three words.

It's a boy

"A boy? A boy? You're having a boy?"

"Two, actually."

The room erupted with shouts and screams and laughter. The only one not joining in the festivities was Chloe. She sat with her arms folded, staring at Kristina as if she'd just betrayed her.

"Baby girl, why are you looking at me like that?"

"A boy? I didn't ask for a boy. I already have one. I asked for a girl. What am I supposed to do with two boys?"

Pam came over and knelt next to her. "This is a good

488

thing. In a house full of boys, you'll be the Princess. That doesn't happen when you have sisters. Trust me, I know."

Again, laughter filled the room.

"And," Kristina said, her voice raised to get everyone's attention. "We've even picked out the names. One will be Josiah, after your father, daddy. And the other," she said, looking at her stepmother, "will be named Justin."

Once Tamia's makeup was completed, the rest of the family waited in another room while her sisters helped her into her wedding dress. She walked to the full-length mirror and got her first glimpse of herself as a bride. Kristina stood on one side of her and Pam stood on the other.

"Look at us," Pam said. "Look at *God*. He really does do exceedingly, abundantly above all we could ask or think, doesn't He?"

Kristina started fanning her face in an effort to prevent the tears threatening to ruin her makeup.

"Amen, amen and amen!"

"And that's why..." Tamia closed her eyes and sang, "My soul loves Jesus..."

"Mmmm," Kristina sang, joining in. "My soul loves Jesus..."

Both sisters looked at Pam. She only stared back at them, eyebrow arched. Then, just when they thought they'd have to finish the verse without her, Pam hit the kind of high note usually reserved for Kristina.

"Oooh ooh ooh! My soul loves Jesus, bless His name!"

Tamia screamed and bounced up and down.

"She's still got it! She's still got it!"

"And don't you forget it," Pam said, hooking her arm around her sister's waist as they went to the door.

Kristina stayed back and watched them go. She was so full of joy, she was sure her face was shining.

What they'd sung wasn't just words to a hymn. It was the truth of their lives. But more important than their loving Him, was the knowledge that He loved *them*.

Kristina had started on this journey unsure of that love. With all her shortcomings, it seemed too good to be true. But she believed it anyway, because God said it was so. Even when she felt as if He were a million miles away, she held to it. And that was the day her life changed forever.

It didn't matter what happened or what tried to come against her. Her Father was the ocean-splitting, storm-calming, life-giving Creator of the universe and He loved *her*.

And because of that, she could truly say her soul was satisfied.

The New Life Tabernacle Series Begins With...

Book 1: **Nobody's Child**

Nineteen-year-old Makayla Dawson wants one thing: to find the mother who abandoned her as a baby. But she's not looking for a happy and tearful reunion.

After a life of pain, loneliness and neglect, Makayla wants revenge.

Her search leads her to Robin Jones, but she's nothing like the monster Makayla imagined.

While pursuing her mission to destroy Robin's life, Makayla comes to know, and even love her.

But by the time she realizes her mistake, her plan for payback has already been set in motion, leaving Makayla helpless to stop it.

With disaster looming, Makayla needs help. The kind only God can give. What she doesn't realize is, she's going to need Him for a lot more than that.

Robin's life isn't the only one about to be blown to pieces. There's a secret Makayla doesn't know. A secret worse than anything she experienced in her past. A secret that will change her life forever...

Turn the page for an excerpt...

Nobody's Child

It wasn't supposed to feel like this...

In just a few hours, Makayla would finally have everything she'd wanted for the past five years. She will have decimated a woman's life, publicly humiliated her before thousands and ruined her reputation forever.

It would be the culmination of years of hard work. Years of carefully planning every detail, devoting all her time and meager resources, anticipating every possible outcome.

And now her work was finished.

She must have imagined the moment a thousand times. It was her food and water. Sometimes the only thing that kept her going when all she wanted to do was die.

What she hadn't imagined, however, was that on the eve of her revenge being fulfilled, the woman whom she'd set out to destroy, the woman she thought she'd hate until the day she died—that very woman—would hand her a gift.

"Open it."

Robin slid the small rectangle box across the mahogany and leather coffee table. She was so full of excited anticipation, she could hardly sit still.

"What is it?"

Robin cocked her head to the side and grinned. "Do you really think I went through all the trouble of wrapping it, only to tell you what's inside? You better get to tearing that paper, girl!"

Makayla hesitated. If Robin knew what was coming... If she had any idea what awaited her in the morning...

Suddenly, Makayla's mouth felt so dry, she could hardly swallow. She took a long drink from her glass of lemonade.

"You've already done so much for me. Too much. I can't accept this."

For a moment, Robin's smile faded. Then, gently touching Makayla's hand with her own, she said, "But that's what today was all about." She held up the box. "This is what parents do. They give to their children. I could never do too much for you, baby. I thought you understood that."

That was another thing Makayla had never imagined: Robin being so...good.

It wasn't supposed to be like this...

Robin set the box down in front of Makayla again and watched her, her eyes sparkling with expectation.

Makayla made herself look at the box. The wrapping paper was an intricate foil stamp design that reflected all the light sources in the room. A beautiful satin ribbon was wrapped around the box and tied into an intricate bow. Makayla reached out and touched the ribbon with the tips of her fingers, but couldn't bring herself to do any more than that.

"Well?"

When Makayla didn't respond, Robin shook her head

and laughed. "I see the next thing we need to work on is your receiving."

She picked up the box and pulled at one of the bow's tails. Within seconds, she'd torn through the paper and opened the box it concealed. Robin took out the glittering platinum bracelet inside and put it on Makayla's wrist.

"There." She leaned in to admire it. "Perfect."

All Makayla could do was think about how much she wished there was a rock big enough for her to crawl under.

"Look," Robin said, turning the platinum and diamond studded heart over so Makayla could see the inscription on the back. "It's today's date. To commemorate the christening. When you look at it, I want you to know what this day means to me. What *you* mean to me."

A wave of nausea passed over Makayla and she clenched her jaw and held her breath. Seeing the pained look on her face, Robin pressed her lips together.

"Don't you like it?"

Makayla attempted a smile and nodded.

"Sure. Yeah. I love it. I just—could you give me a minute?"

Without waiting for a response, Makayla jumped up and rushed out of the room. Running down the hallway, she headed straight to the bathroom.

Shutting the door behind her, she took out her mobile phone and dialed the same number she'd been calling all evening.

"Please, please…"

If only someone would pick up, she'd be able to stop the wrecking ball set to level Robin's life.

As she waited, she did something she hadn't done in over five years—she prayed.

Are you ready for more?

Whew!

We made it through, y'all!

I hope you were blessed by the Langston Sisters' story of restoration. While the *Langston Family Saga* has come to its conclusion, it won't be the last you'll see of the sisters. They'll definitely have cameos in upcoming books.

And now begins the *New Life Tabernacle* series!

Unlike the Langston trilogy, these books will focus on various members' lives, instead of just one family.

In book 1, *Nobody's Child*, you'll learn Robin's story. Turns out the Langstons aren't the only ones with long buried secrets. And the one from Robin's past is about to make an appearance in her present.

In the book after that, *Restoration Song*, you'll get the story behind the regrets Pastor Avery Thomas mentioned to Pam. I don't want to give too much away, so I'll only say this: more than just a family will be affected by the outcome of this story. In fact, all of New Life Tabernacle will be rocked!

And that's just the first two books about the members of New Life Tabernacle. Omar's sister, Deandra, has a story coming out around the holidays and it's one I'm SO excited to write!

In the coming months, you'll be meeting all kinds of New Life members, new and old.

To make sure you don't miss any of them, there's several things you can do.

If you submit your email address to my list, I'll keep you updated. Plus, you'll be one of the few to learn about early-bird discounts and subscriber-only giveaways. You can do that by going to LashondaBowman.com and clicking STAY UPDATED.

If you'd rather chat on Facebook, you can find me at https://www.facebook.com/LashondaBowmanBooks

I'm not there every day, but I promise to check in often as I can.

Last, but not least, you can click the FOLLOW button on my author page at Amazon, and they'll email you when there's something new.

And if you'd just like to drop a quick note, my email address is lashondabowmanbooks@gmail.com

Before I go, I wanna give a huge thank you to all of you for your support and kind words. ESPECIALLY for those who are leaving reviews! When you are an indie author, reviews and word of mouth are *vital*. So again, thank you so much.

I hope you enjoyed these stories as much as I enjoyed writing them! May God bless & keep you.

Sincerely,
LaShonda

Q & A with LaShonda
The Making of the Langston Trilogy

Q: *Were the characters based on real people?*

A: For the most part, no. The one exception is Esther. In fact, I named her after the person I had in mind, just so she would know I'd created this character in her honor. (*If you're reading this Esther, I love you!*)

The part of the character I based on her was her loving and open personality, as well as her quickness to laugh and share joy. As a child, my aunt Esther was one of my favorite people because she just seemed so ready and willing to have fun. Those are the kind of adults children gravitate to. I thought it would be wonderful for Xavier to have been raised by someone who was the complete opposite of Mahalia.

Q: *Where did you get the idea?*

A: The initial idea came from an episode of a reality TV show. I watched an episode of *Iyanla, Fix My Life* featuring a gospel music family I'd grown up listening to. What struck me the most while I watched was how little we ever know about what's going on in someone else's household.

Someone may seem to have it all together, and maybe, to a certain extent, they do. But that doesn't mean they haven't endured great suffering or heartache. We tend to walk around so wrapped up in our own problems, we rarely stop to consider that others have gone through just as much, if not more, than we have.

I think it's so important to refrain from judging another based on their looks or possessions, accomplishments or success. That's what I wanted to convey in the writing of the first book in the trilogy.

Q: *There's lots of plot threads woven throughout the three books. Did you plan the entire series out before you started it?*

A: The entire series? No. I didn't even know it was going to be a series.

Most of the prose writing I've done has been short stories. I was a theater major and wrote plays and, later, short films. All of those are very lean mediums. So when I decided to take on writing a novel, I found myself overwhelmed.

Left to my own devices, everything I'd write would be a novella. I comfortably sit at 32k to 38k words for a story. So the idea of writing something at 80k-100k words just seemed impossible.

Thankfully, novellas have become more widely accepted with indie publishing. This trilogy wouldn't have been possible, if not for indie publishing. None of the major Christian publishers would've even looked at the Langston Family Saga based on length alone.

So since I tend to write short anyway, I thought I would write a novella after I'd seen the reality show I mentioned earlier. Once I'd finished, I gave it to one of my sisters. She read it and immediately said, "Okay, but what happened with Omar?"

As a result, I wrote the second book and then added the last scene in the first book as a lead-in to *Then Sings My Soul*. And since it didn't make sense for me to have only two books in a series, I decided to go for a third. By the time I finished book 2, I had no idea what the third would be about. Like the previous book, that last scene was added *after* I'd figured out what the next story was. That last book was written mostly out of order and without an outline (which I'll never do again).

If you looked at the notes I jotted down for book 3 as I was writing it, you'd see it went through several iterations. Most of which are nothing like the final product. Just about everything in that book was done on the fly. I didn't even know Gerald was coming until he showed up.

In fact, I was dictating the scene in which he arrived at the hospital when I got the idea about Mahalia's backstory. I just let him talk and it flowed. I am telling you the honest truth when I say, until that moment, I had never even thought about what Mahalia's backstory would've been.

Usually, I try to skip all backstory and let it come out here and there, through conversation. But it just felt right, at that moment, to finally explain who Mahalia was and how she came to be that way. I thank God for moments like that. Those moments when, you just give everything up to the grace of God, stop working so hard, and let Him do what He does best.

Q: *Do you think Marisa will ever come back in Omar, Kristina and Chloe's lives?*

A: That's not something I can answer definitively. I mean, I don't know. Do I think it's possible? Definitely. Marisa never said she didn't want to be a mother. She never said she didn't want children. The problem was, she didn't want *Brock's* child. If Omar had been the father, there's no way she would've let Chloe go. But because of her anger, desperation, and bitterness, she was never able to look past Chloe's DNA.

But people change. It's quite possible that time and distance will give her clarity. Maybe one day she'll finally be able to see Chloe for more than her genetic makeup. If and when that happens, will she return? Or will she stay away, feeling she has no right to? I think that's something I'd have to think about a little more before deciding. It might make for an interesting story at some future date.

Q: *Why did Mahalia leave the sisters the box of mementos? Did she really change in the end?*

A: Yes…to an extent.

I say that because, while she did change some before

she died, I don't think she ever felt she was completely in the wrong. What you have to remember is, although her methods were destructive, her motive was to make sure her girls weren't lost.

Because of what her father said about her that night on Gerald's porch, she was never quite sure where she stood with God. She thought the more good she did, the more she could get back on God's "good side." In her mind, making sure her daughters weren't "ruined" like she was, was the ultimate good deed.

Of course, it doesn't work that way. The blood of Jesus and the finished work of Christ is what makes us sons and daughters of God. Good deeds don't get you into heaven. The Bible talks about people who will cry out to the Lord about all their good works, but He'll tell them He never knew them.

But because she didn't understand that, because her motive, wanting her daughters to be godly women, was a good one, she used that to justify her actions to herself. Even later in life, when she began to doubt the ways she went about it.

But the changes that *did* occur, happened as a result of her relationship with Xavier, Esther and Deacon. Think about this: The only model she had for parenting was her father. He was extraordinarily strict and abusive. And he did it because he thought that was the way to "spare not the rod." Despite that, she still ended up pregnant. So in her mind, she needed to be even stricter than he was.

When her daughters left her, without a backward glance, she was completely bewildered, wondering where she'd went wrong. But then, she saw Esther and Deacon raising Xavier in absolute love. Sure, they disciplined him, but they never abused him. They never hurt him. They never did any of the things she or her father did. She saw him grow into a godly young man. He loved to sing. He loved to go to church. He loved to do all the things she'd wanted her own girls to do. He was all the things she had wanted her daughters to *be*.

But see, she didn't even know that was possible, not until she got to see Deacon and Esther's example as parents. The regret she felt as a result must have been overwhelming. I think she wanted to apologize to her daughters, but knew how inadequate that would be. In addition, there was still a sense of pride at having to admit how wrong she was. And even if she could have, they wanted nothing to do with her at that point. So the only way she could show her regret, sorrow and shame, was to somehow give them back what she'd taken in the first place. Xavier's childhood.

Q: *Do you have a favorite character from the trilogy?*

A: Uh, that's a hard one. Of course, I have to say Esther. And that's mainly because of the reasons I explained earlier. I would say I have a soft spot for Robin. Russell makes me laugh. Justina makes me smile. And Xavier... Well, I just love Xavier. Oh, man. Can I just say all of them? This is too hard a question to answer. Next please!

Q: *Will we get to see more of the Langstons in future books?*

A: Absolutely! In the New Life Tabernacle series, you'll see cameos of all the sisters and their extended families. You'll get to know Omar's two sisters, Deandra and Cassandra. They each have their own stories and they're stories I'm really excited to write. Beyond that, I'll do my best to fit the Langstons in elsewhere, whenever possible.

Q: *Will we get to see a story about Xavier as an adult?*

A: Man, that's a question I get a lot. Initially, I didn't think so. I thought, like the others, I would just have him come in for a cameo. But after getting so many requests and actually giving it some thought, I do have a story brewing in the back of my mind for him. I think it's going to end up being a novella trilogy, much like the Langston story.

But that's still further down the line. I already have my production schedule filled up with books for the New Life Tabernacle series, so at least until the end of this year, that's where my focus is.

Of course, that could change based on reader demand. If it did, I'd have to take a break from the NLT series to do it. We'll just have to see what happens!

Book Club Discussion Questions

The Complete Langston Family Saga

1. After keeping Xavier's existence a secret for so long, why do you think Mahalia made sure her daughters found out about him?

2. Baby Moses was put into a basket and sent away from his family for his safety, but God used that separation to eventually become the salvation of the children of Israel. How does Xavier's story mirror that of Moses?

3. Do you think Brock had good reason to keep his secret from Omar or do you think he was only acting out of self-preservation?

4. Should Omar and Brock repair their relationship or go their separate ways? Why?

5. The author created multiple instances in which Omar and Chloe's relationship mirrored that of God the Father and the Believer. Discuss those moments and their spiritual parallels.

Example: In preparing Chloe's birthday party, Omar made sure to do far over and above all she could have imagined. Much like Paul described God in Ephesians

3:20, being able to do exceeding abundantly above all that we ask or think.

6. Did reading Gerald's account of a young Mahalia alter your view of her? Did it help you better understand the kind of mother she became? Why or why not?

7. At the hospital, Omar expressed concern that Chloe didn't understand Marisa wasn't coming back. In truth, she understood all too well. Adults often underestimate what children know and comprehend. Have you ever seen or experienced this in your own life?

8. Why did Pam, the one sister who'd held the family together through years of trauma and heartache, find herself unraveling, while Kristina, persevered?

9. Which scene resonated the most with you? Either in a positive or negative way? Why?

10. Which scene in the book would you have written differently? What would your version be like?

11. Out of all the characters in the novel, which did you most relate to? Which did you find the most perplexing? Why?

12. In what ways, if any, has the story of the Langstons impacted your own faith walk?

Made in the USA
San Bernardino, CA
05 November 2016